D0595500

ALSO BY GITA TRELEASE

Everything That Burns

FLATIRON
BOOKS
NEW YORK

ALL THAT GLITTERS

GITA TRELEASE

ALL THAT GLITTERS. Copyright © 2019 by Gita Trelease. All rights reserved. Printed in the United States of America. For information, address Flatiron Books, 120 Broadway, New York, NY 10271.

Excerpt from *Everything That Burns* © 2021 by Gita Trelease

www.flatironbooks.com

The Library of Congress has cataloged the hardcover edition as follows:

Names: Trelease, Gita, author.
Title: Enchantée / Gita Trelease.
Description: First edition. | New York : Flatiron Books, 2019.
Identifiers: LCCN 2018036331 | ISBN 9781250295521 (hardcover) |
    ISBN 9781250295538 (ebook)
Subjects: | CYAC: Magic—Fiction. | Orphans—Fiction. | Courts and
    courtiers—Fiction. | Impersonation—Fiction. | Social classes—Fiction. |
    France—History—Louis XVI, 1774–1793—Fiction.
Classification: LCC PZ7.1.T742 Enc 2019 | DDC [Fic]—dc23
LC record available at https://lccn.loc.gov/2018036331

ISBN 978-1-250-29554-5 (trade paperback)

Our books may be purchased in bulk for promotional, educational, or business use. Please contact your local bookseller or the Macmillan Corporate and Premium Sales Department at 1-800-221-7945, extension 5442, or by email at MacmillanSpecialMarkets@macmillan.com.

Previously published as *Enchantée*

First Flatiron Books Paperback Edition: 2021

10 9 8 7 6 5 4 3 2 1

For Lukas and Tim,
who believed

And what costume shall the poor girl wear
To all tomorrow's parties. . . .

—The Velvet Underground

PARIS, 1789

1

Y ves Rencourt, the chandler's apprentice, had lost his wig.
        After the last customer left the shop, he searched
through baskets of curling wicks and blocks of beeswax and teetering stacks of bills. Rien. It was nowhere to be found. And he needed the wig for tonight: he alone was to deliver candles for the Comte d'Astignac's party, which would last until the sun came up. This was Yves's chance to be noticed. To rise. And he didn't want to show up wearing his own hair, looking ridiculous. He had to look promising. Like someone who could be Somebody.

At least his coat was good, he thought, as he lifted the dove-gray silk from its hook and shrugged it on. And voilà—there the damned wig was, its long white hair tied back with a black satin bow. He pulled the wig on and cocked an admiring eyebrow at his reflection in the window: he was no longer a tradesman's apprentice. He was absolument parfait.

Into a canvas satchel he tucked his most precious candles, the ones he'd tinted the hazy apricots and violets of dawn. All he needed now was money for the carriage. From under the counter he heaved up the strongbox and lifted its lid to reveal a shining pile of coins: rivulets of gold louis and livres and tiny sous. Candles were good business. No matter how little bread there was, how few people bought snuffboxes or plumed hats, they all needed light. In the back, Maître Orland kept the cheap tallow candles that reeked of hooves. They sold more of those every day. But in the front of the shop, nestled in boxes and dangling from their wicks, were Yves's own lovelies: wax candles, their colors like enchantments. A rose pink that made old women seem young, a watery gray that reminded him of the ocean. And one day soon—he hoped—he'd make candles for the queen.

For like himself, Marie Antoinette loved extraordinary things. Yves would make candles to suit her every fancy, candles she'd never even dreamed of. He'd be asked to make thousands, because in the endless rooms and halls of Versailles, candles were never lit twice.

From his coat pocket he pulled a leather purse and began to flick livres into the bag. Clink, clink, clink. But one coin made him pause. It was a louis d'or, seemingly no different from the others. Yet to someone who handled candles, always checking the soft wax for imperfections, it felt off. Holding it to the fading afternoon light, he saw nothing wrong. He put the gold coin between his teeth and bit it. It was as hard as any other. And yet. He found another louis and held one in each hand, weighing them. He closed his eyes. Yes—the one in his right hand was lighter. Still, who but a true craftsman such as himself would notice? He was about toss it back in the box when it twitched.

The louis d'or was moving.

Yves yelped and flung it onto the counter. The coin spun in a tight circle and dropped flat. As it lay there, its edges began to ripple, like beeswax in a flame.

"Mon Dieu," he muttered. What in God's name was happening?

The louis twisted upon itself and flipped over. The king's face with its curved nose had vanished, the familiar crown and shield, too. And as Yves stared, the coin lost its roundness, thinning and separating until it looked like a bent harness buckle. He reached out a tentative finger to touch it.

It *was* a bent harness buckle.

With a cry, he reached for the strongbox. Mixed in with the coins was an ugly tin button, dented on one side, and a crooked piece of type, a letter *Q*. Worthless scraps of metal.

He remembered her exactly. He'd even flirted with her. Red hair, freckles across her sharp cheekbones. Hungry. Not that that excused it. How she'd done it he had no idea—but what a fool he was to take a gold louis from a girl in a threadbare cloak. If he hadn't been dreaming of the figure he'd cut at the comte's house, he would have thought twice. Idiot! Maître Orland was going to kill him.

He wrenched open the door and yelled into the crowded street. "Help! Police! We've been robbed!"

2

But Camille had already slipped away through the arches of an arcade, across a tiny cobbled square, down a narrow lane perfumed by the scent of fresh bread, and into the bakery, where she now stood. She set her heavy basket, filled with candles and a rind of cheese, on the floor between her feet.

She inhaled deeply. *Heaven must be like this.* Like piles of raisin-studded rolls, braided brioches that flaked a rain of buttery gold when you bit into them, baguettes as long as your arm and still warm inside, sweet pastries that made your mouth water. The women ahead of her took their time, complaining about the cost of bread.

"Don't blame me," the baker's wife snapped. "Blame the weather!

Blame the queen! She'd rather fill her wardrobe than her people's bellies."

"It's true!" another woman grumbled. "Madame Déficit spends money like it's going out of style. And how does she pay for it all?" The woman grimaced. "With our money! They'll tax us even after we're dead and in the ground."

Camille's fingers twitched with impatience. People complained about the king and queen and they complained about the nobles, even when there was absolutely nothing that could be done to change things. Her father the printer had called the nobles bloodsuckers, but even he'd needed their business.

Hurry. Soon it would be evening, shadows gathering in the city's crooked places. Pickpockets would slink out, madams looking to trap young girls, men who didn't keep their hands to themselves.

"Oui, mademoiselle?"

Camille nodded at the day-old loaves. "I'll take one of those." She hesitated. "And a sweet pastry, s'il vous plaît."

Snugging her cloak around her shoulders, Camille stepped out into the lane. Over the rooftops of Paris, the sky hung like a lead curtain, and the air tasted of metal. This morning she'd found a skin of ice stretched over the water jug in the kitchen. But cold May or not, there was nothing for it; she had one last errand and the blurry sun was already sinking behind the towers of Notre-Dame. Leaving the lane for a busy street, Camille dodged piles of manure and pools of horse piss, not to mention whatever filth people tossed from their windows. To keep from gagging, she burrowed her nose into her worn cloak. It smelled faintly of her mother's perfume.

Her pocket felt too large and empty, only a few sous wedged against its lining. With her fingertips, she traced the coins' thin edges. Still round. She didn't dare to take them out and count them, not on the street. There'd be enough for Alain's wine.

As long as the coins didn't change.

At the wine merchant's, she chewed the edge of her fingernail, waiting for him to fill a wine bottle from a barrel. When she left, she kept her basket pressed close to her side. She avoided the quarter's crumbling passageways, their entrances as narrow as the doors of tombs. She could almost feel the hands that waited there. Somewhere above her in the tilting buildings, a child sobbed.

As Camille turned the corner, a girl as young as her sister came running down the street. Her white face was rouged with hectic circles, her hair aflame, her eyebrows darkened to seduce, and her corset pulled tight to give curves to her child's body. Under the dirty hem of her dress, bare feet flashed as she dodged shoppers and workmen.

"Stop, whore!" shouted a constable as he pushed through the crowd.

A prickling of fear made Camille pull her cloak up over her own red hair. But she couldn't take her eyes from the half-dressed girl, running like a spreading fire. She was living the life Camille feared—her nightmares made flesh.

"You there!" the constable shouted at Camille. "Stop her!"

Camille shrank back against the wall. As the running girl dashed closer, Camille glimpsed the whites of her eyes in the half-dark. The raw leanness of her face, the bruises on her arms—and the tiny roll of bread she clutched in her hand. How many days could she make that last while her stomach churned with hunger? And then what? Camille felt in her pocket for her last few real sous.

"Thief!" yelled the constable. His face was wild with anger as the girl slipped away through the crowds.

It was too risky. Camille clenched her empty hand as the sadness welled up inside her. It was wrong not to help—but it was too dangerous. With the constable coming, there was nothing she could do. The horror of living on the streets was too big, a wall of fear that blocked out everything.

As the girl fled past, her scared eyes flicked to Camille's.

Then both girls vanished into darkening Paris.

3

Camille lived at the top of an ancient building on the rue Charlot. The stone edifice had once stood proudly, but now it leaned against its neighbor, as if tired from standing straight all those years. Unlocking a heavy door, Camille let herself into the courtyard. In the close darkness, a dog yelped; a neighbor's hen flapped against her skirts. Up in their garret window, a light glowed: Alain had returned. She imagined her older brother hanging up his officer's cloak and kicking off his boots, sitting by the fire and roaring with laughter at some jest, tickling the cat. The way he used to be.

She started to climb the stairs, the heavy basket bumping against her legs. The once-grand staircase spiraled up seven treacherous flights, but she knew where the rotten spots were. As she passed the third-floor landing, a door swung open.

"Mademoiselle Durbonne? A word." Wearing a grease-flecked apron, Madame Lamotte raised her candlestick toward Camille. "The rent is two weeks overdue. This is not a charity home."

Camille blinked. She had nothing close to the full rent of two hundred livres—eight fat gold louis—and she couldn't risk giving magicked coins to Madame. When they reverted to scraps—and they would, because Camille couldn't get the metal to hold its shape—Madame would throw them out, bien sûr, no matter how much she'd liked their parents and felt sorry for the orphans. Then they would be tramps, living under a bridge. Prostitutes. Or dead.

Camille hated to beg. "A few days?"

Madame Lamotte nodded begrudgingly. Camille curtsied and began to climb the stairs again. "One more thing," the landlady called after her. "Your brother."

Camille stopped. Even Madame had noticed. "I'm sorry," she said, trying to keep the exasperation from her voice.

"I haven't said anything yet!"

"Go on, madame." If it had to do with Alain, it was bound to be bad news.

The landlady pitched her voice low. "Just be careful. Keep an eye on him."

"Of course, madame." It was impossible, a fairy-tale task. It'd take a thousand eyes to watch him.

When Camille reached the seventh floor, she paused, listening. Was that—music? She opened the door to their apartment. In the middle of the bare room, her little sister, Sophie, was dancing a sarabande while Alain piped on his army piccolo. In the candlelight, her hair shone pale gold, her wide-set blue eyes bright with amusement. She looked so much like their mother with her delicate features and slightly upturned nose, a princess in one of Perrault's fairy tales. Sophie had always been small: feet and hands dainty as cats' paws, an enviable waist that seemed even tinier as her skirts spun around her.

When Sophie saw Camille, she paused midstep. Her face was happy but flushed, the pulse racing in her neck.

"Join the revels, Camille!" Alain lounged in the best chair, boots on the table. The fire's light caught on the scruff of his unshaven cheek, while the cocked hat he wore slid the rest of his face into shadow. His hair, once golden like Sophie's, had darkened to amber and was tied with a black ribbon that threatened to come undone.

"I know you love to dance, darling," Camille said carefully as she watched Alain out of the corner of her eye, "but you've been so ill—"

"Alain asked me to." Sophie's narrow chest heaved. "He wanted to see if I was still a good dancer."

"And she is!" Alain's smile gleamed. "I'll find her a husband yet. See if I don't."

"Don't tease, Alain. No one will marry me now." Sophie bent her head so her hair hid the few smallpox scars on her forehead. "Isn't that so, Camille?"

Camille hesitated. There was no good answer to this question.

"Whatever Camille says, don't listen! At court the grand ladies wear beauty patches to cover their pocks." Alain raised his wineglass. "To Sophie! Keep up your dancing and your needlework, and we'll find you a husband, handsome as a prince."

"She's fifteen, Alain." Camille shot him a dark look. "Come sit by the fire, Sophie. Catch your breath while I put out the food. Boots down, Alain." She gave his feet a shove; it was a relief to set the heavy basket down. Brushing off the table, she placed the cheese and bread, along with a knife, on a scarred wooden board. The sweet pastry she handed to Sophie.

"Oh, it's too much," she said, but her face shone.

"Bien! Fatten her up, Camille. You've let her go to skin and bones."

Camille nearly snapped: I *let her? It was* my *fault?* but she pressed the words down.

"Something in the basket for me?" Alain demanded.

Camille set the flask of wine on the table.

"Nicely done," he said. "Pour yourself a little glass, too. We've plenty now."

"What do you mean, 'plenty'?" She saw a bottle by the fireplace and her heart sank. "Alain, where's the chicken?"

"What chicken?"

Camille sensed Sophie stiffen. The room suddenly felt very, very small.

"You know how Monsieur Dimnier always admired Maman?" Camille kept her voice even. "I asked you to pick up the chicken he'd set aside for us. One that hadn't gained weight, one he'd had to kill early."

Alain frowned. "You didn't tell me anything about a skinny chicken."

She had, but it didn't matter now. "I'll go fetch it; it's not far." Camille held out her hand. "I'll need the money back."

Alain laughed. "You'd better make some more, then, because I don't have it."

"What?"

"Just what I said." Alain took a swig of wine and wiped his mouth with his sleeve. "It's gone."

"You can't just squander our *real* money!" She reached into her pocket. Just as she'd thought, apart from a few real sous, the rest had lost their magic and were now what they'd been this morning: bent, useless nails she'd pried out of a broken door. "I can't pay Dimnier with this!" she stormed. "We have to give him real money, remember? If he stops selling to us, what then?" She threw the nails onto the table so hard they caromed to the floor.

Alain shrugged. "Just go farther away."

Camille stamped her foot. "There is nowhere else! You've no idea how far I had to go just for the bread. Dimnier's the last one in our quarter who trusts us. And you threw away our chicken for a bottle of wine."

"How was I to know you'd remember to buy some?"

Blood thrummed in Camille's head. It wasn't easy to make ends meet using la magie ordinaire—everyday magic—to transform bits of metal into coins. These days, her hands never stopped shaking, and she'd become nearly as thin as Sophie. Little by little, magic was erasing her. Sometimes she felt it might kill her.

She grabbed the bottle of wine.

"Don't." Alain swayed to his feet. "Give that to me."

"You don't deserve it!" Hoisting the bottle over her head, Camille hurled it into the washing tub. A grinding shatter—and the acrid scent of wine filled the room.

Alain grabbed the knife on the table and pointed it at her. "That was my wine."

"It was mine, idiot. I worked for it. I bought it."

"Hush, Camille!" Sophie said, desperate. "Please don't argue! Alain stands in our father's place now. You must listen to him."

Camille rounded on her sister. "Our father wasn't a nineteen-year-old wastrel!"

Alain lurched toward Camille, steadying himself on the table. Despite the cold, his face glistened with sweat. His eyes had a faraway look that raised the tiny hairs on her neck.

"Go sleep it off, Alain. I'll clean up—comme d'habitude," she added in an undertone. As always.

Before she could think, his knife was at her throat. She froze, sensing each throb of her pulse just under the skin.

"What are you doing, Alain? Put away the knife."

Alain's hand shook, and then—a bright line of pain. A trickle of blood curled into the hollow of her collarbone, hot and wet. All these weeks of threatening to hurt her, and now, drunk on who knows how many bottles of wine, he finally had. She wanted to rage and to weep at the injustice of it. But she did not flinch.

"You aren't my master, Camille Durbonne," Alain growled. "I'm a soldier, and I earn my keep."

"Then go earn it. Show up for duty for once. Pay the rent." She didn't move. Everything in her was shouting at her to run, but she would never let him see her fear. *Never.* "I can't keep on like this."

"Oh, I'll do my part. And in the meantime," he said, so close that Camille was forced to inhale the sour stink of his breath, "do the only thing you're good for. Go work la magie." Dropping the knife, he stumbled toward the door and flung it open.

Furious and heartsick, she listened as his stumbling footsteps echoed down the stairs. Working magic would be easy now, thanks to him. The petty magic of la magie ordinaire took all the skill she'd honed under her mother's supervision—and it took sorrow. Without sorrow, there was no transformation, no magic.

Tonight she would have plenty to spare.

4

That night, nightmares tore through Sophie's sleep. They'd begun when she was sick with the pox. Sometimes in her dreams, she'd told Camille, she went back in time, six months, a year, to when their parents were alive, kind and happy. Other times they only *seemed* alive, for when Sophie embraced them, they crumbled to ash in her arms. Or it was three months ago, when they were dying of smallpox, and Sophie had to retch up whatever scrap of food she'd managed to eat in order to feed them. It was an endless horror of fear, guilt, and anguish.

Perched on the edge of Sophie's bed, Camille watched as Sophie's eyes seesawed under their bluish lids and tensed each time Sophie drew a shuddering breath. When she was close to waking, she gasped for air, like someone drowning.

Then she woke, her eyes pinched tight. "Please," she begged. "My sleep medicine."

Camille held the brown bottle of laudanum up against the candle flame. It was nearly empty. She spooned the last few mouthfuls between Sophie's lips. It didn't take long before the drug worked its drowsy lull. Her eyelids fluttering, Sophie sank back into the pillow. "In my dream, Maman had no fingers," Sophie mumbled. "She had sold them all for food. Stay with me, Camille, so the dreams don't come back."

Holding Sophie's thin hand, Camille tucked her knees up under her chemise and rested against the wall. Sophie's coverlet rose and fell, rose and fell, as her breathing slowed, grew even. When the fire sank to embers, Camille pulled the blankets from Alain's empty bed and tucked Sophie under them all. Her black cat curled himself against her stomach, his low-pitched purr thrumming in the air. "Ah, Fantôme," Sophie breathed, letting go of Camille's hand to clutch at his fur.

"That's right. Sleep now, ma chèrie." Camille smoothed Sophie's sweat-dark hair off her forehead. Her hair would need washing in the morning. For that, they'd need more wood to heat the water. More wood, more money, more medicine, more magie.

She tentatively touched the place above her collarbone where Alain's knife had cut her. It had already stopped bleeding. It could have been worse, she told herself as she fingered the wound. Sometimes she hoped he'd never come back. It would make Sophie sad, of course. Camille knew she should pity Alain, or have sympathy for him, since he'd tried, at least in the beginning, to feed and clothe them. It wasn't his fault that he couldn't work magic; Dieu, he had wanted to. But all that came after? How he seemed to take refuge in the gambling and the drinking? That wasn't the brother she knew.

Perhaps her real brother was never coming back.

Alain had little money in his pockets but that wouldn't stop him: soon he'd be shouting out his bets at the gaming rooms at the Palais-

Royal, the grand Parisian palace belonging to the king's cousin and notorious gambler, the duc d'Orléans, who'd opened his house to the public. There Alain would stake whatever he had to win whatever he could, drinking on credit until he could no longer sign his name. She knew how the story went. In a week or two the collector would be standing on their threshold, Madame Lamotte peering in behind him, the man jabbing a grimy bill in Camille's face.

This was a certainty.

Leaving Sophie sleeping, Camille padded barefoot into the other room and paused at its far end, where a small door led to a room beneath the eaves. Slipping a key from its hiding place beneath a loose floorboard, she turned it in the lock. The little room was wallpapered with a faded pattern of cabbage roses. In the half-light, the flowers gawked at her like a crowd of faces. A few rolled-up old carpets, too worn to sell, lay in the gloom, and next to them, two wooden trunks. One of them looked as if it had been burned in a fire, its charred black surface greasy in the candlelight. Camille stepped past it, trying to pretend it wasn't there. Though of course that was impossible. Because just to think of it was to hear Maman's warning in her head—*Do not touch the burned box, for it is more dangerous than you could ever imagine*— and to feel a haunted breath along the back of her neck.

Maman had taught her that there were three kinds of magic. La magie ordinaire, for changing things. La glamoire, for changing oneself. And la magie bibelot, for imbuing objects with magic, making them sentient.

It was ridiculous to think the burned trunk was looking at her, but it felt that way. She pulled her shawl closer.

The other trunk was a strongbox, bolted to the floor.

From a secret pocket she'd sewn into the seam of her skirt, Camille took out a handful of coins: the change from the magicked louis she'd used at the chandler's shop. Twenty whole livres. Alain had drunk up the money she'd given him for the chicken. But he hadn't gotten any of this, the real money. She felt a twinge of regret as she dropped the coins into the box and locked it. Sophie certainly needed strengthening. But money for the rent was more important than meat, and she had only a few days to get another hundred and eighty livres.

Though her body swayed with fatigue, sleep felt like a distant country. There was so much to do. Closing the little door and locking it behind her, Camille stepped through the pale lozenges of moonlight that lay on the floor to kneel by the fireplace and warm her hands over the embers. From a stack nearby she took a handful of smudged proofs—*Rise Up, Citizens*, one of the pamphlets encouraged, *Our Day Is Come!*—left over from her father's print shop and tossed them on the coals. Flames stretched up through the paper, bright and hungry, illuminating the mantel. The costlier curios that had once stood there—a porcelain shepherdess, a Chinese lacquerware lion with a wavy mane—were sold when her parents died. Now only a few paper figures tilted against the wall. She picked up a tiny boat and blew at the sails so they billowed.

Bagatelles, Papa had called them—little nothings. Queens with towering wigs and milkmaids dangling pails from their hands, knights with lances and dragons breathing flame: all made from inky test sheets for the pamphlets Papa had written. Even now, his words marched across the schooner's sails: *It Is Time We Act*. The flames sparking from the dragon's mouth spelled out *Liberté!* though the *L* faced backward.

She prickled with embarrassment, remembering. It took skill and practice to set the type backward into the frame so that all the letters came out facing the right way, or so Camille had learned when she'd begged Papa to let her be his apprentice. He'd swept her up in his wiry arms and swung her in a circle when she asked, his face a blur of joy and pride. It was hard labor for a little girl. It wasn't just the hours standing on a stool while she set the type, but also rubbing the type with ink balls so it was black as black, hanging on the lever that brought the plate down so the inked letters kissed the paper. And inevitably she made mistakes: mixed-up letters, blots and streaks. She didn't want Papa to see, but he found the sheets where she'd hidden them. He knuckled away her tears and told her: *To try is to be brave. Be brave.*

So she wouldn't feel like her smeared test sheets were worthless, he folded them into ships, cut them into wigs, or made them into dancing bears. Most of the bagatelles had worn out long ago. The paper didn't hold. One icy night someone had burned most of them for fuel. But a few survived.

She kept them so she'd never forget.

She'd never forget the way Papa taught her his craft and art so that she might one day be the best printer in Paris, even though all the printers were men.

Nor the way his pride gleamed when her broadsheets hung drying on the line. She'd not forgotten the thrill when the paper went from blank to black, nor the excitement that came from knowing Papa thought her old enough and clever enough to think about the world they lived in. And by setting letters into a printing frame, to change it. A printing press took the thoughts from someone's mind and inked them onto a piece of paper anyone might read. It was a kind of magic. A magic to alter the world.

But that was all put away. Sometimes when she tucked into the bed next to Sophie, her feet aching from tramping and her soul bruised from working magic, she'd console herself that she'd get a chance at it again one day. Yet each day, that *someday* raced further and further away until she couldn't see it anymore. She tried to press the rising sadness down but it raked at her ribs, her throat. She could even feel it throb in her little finger: a pulsing ache.

She didn't want to do it—not now, she was so tired—but she had no choice. If she was awake, she might as well.

Setting down the paper boat, she fetched a heavy hatbox that rattled with metal bits. In it was broken type from the printing press. She ran her finger along the letters' curves: their metal edges remained unbent. They'd come from an experimental border she'd been working on before Papa had to close the printing shop and sell the press. How empty the workshop had been when everything—presses, paper, cases, type— was gone. All that was left were dust motes hanging in the light and the liquid scent of ink.

Empty, empty, empty.

As Camille remembered, sorrow rose in her and ran like wine or laudanum, dark and bitter and relentless. She didn't try to stop it. She
didn't tell herself that one day, things would be better.

Instead she worked the broken type between her fingers until it
warmed and began to lose its shape. She smoothed it, over and over,
while she held the memory of her parents' deaths in her mind. How the
first spots had pricked their skin like bites before they swelled. How the
angry marks were followed by weeping sores on her mother's arms and
chest, and how her father raved as his fever swallowed him up. How
lonely Camille felt when Maman told her *she* would have to work magic
now, that it was up to Camille to tap the source of her sorrow and use
it to keep the family alive.

She hated la magie, but it was all she had.

Sitting at the worn table, Camille went back, again and again, to the
shadowy, bottomless well, to the memory of their deaths and beyond
that, to her memories of their lives as they used to be. Then she reached
past even those for a deeper sorrow, one that glimmered darkly, like a
silvery fish deep in a black pond. Maman. Papa. Alain, too, the brother
who'd held her safe on a window ledge to show her a swallow's nestlings,
was gone into that fathomless water. Tears came but she kept working
the metal, until what once had been broken took on the hard, useful
shape of a coin.

5

In the morning, Sophie's cough was better. She'd been up before Camille, rekindling the fire in the stove, deftly toasting ragged ends of bread and heating old tea leaves for breakfast, which she brought in and set on the floor next to the chair in which Camille had fallen asleep.

"It smells like summer." There was a tiny, unexpected thrill in Sophie's voice.

Camille sat up and squinted. Sunlight poured in through the little window above the eaves. "What time is it?" She touched Sophie's hair where the sunlight warmed it to gold. "You've washed your hair."

"Clever of me, wasn't it?" Sophie fanned it across her shoulders. "And it's nearly dry."

"Alain carried the water up this morning?"

"Last night. Before you came home." Sophie's face clouded. "Do you think something's happened to him?"

Beyond drinking himself into a stupor? Wishing she had sugar for the tea, Camille swiveled the cup so the chip faced away and drank. "No."

"But imagine if he were pickpocketed at the Palais-Royal? It happens there all the time, he told me. Or—what if he's fallen into the Seine?"

"I'm certain he's somewhere safe, sleeping off his . . . mood." In her hand, the teacup shivered on its saucer.

"You're shaking."

"A little tired, that's all."

Sophie stretched her fingers toward Camille's throat, but she didn't touch the wound. "It's not right."

Camille raised an eyebrow. It wasn't like Sophie to see anything negative in her big brother. "He frightens me, sometimes. I don't know what's happened to him to make him like this."

"Not that it's an excuse," Sophie said, "but he gets so angry about our situation."

"Does he?" Camille bit back the rest of her words. Once, Alain had been a real older brother who'd cared for her. A brother she'd adored. But now he was a burden, one she seemed to bear the brunt of more and more.

"You needn't have turned coins last night. It takes too much from you. I know Alain will bring us his winnings." Sophie squeezed Camille's hand. "Écoute-moi. I have an idea—let's go out and have fun, just this once? I don't mind walking however far we need to. We both need new shoes."

Camille drank the last of her weak tea. "You *want* new shoes."

"I *need* them. How else can I look becoming? S'il te plaît?" She draped her arms around Camille's shoulders and whispered in her ear: "Please."

"Someday soon, ma chère," Camille said. "And until then, you do know you're becoming no matter what, don't you?" Camille slipped out of her sister's arms and stood up. Through the doorway she could see the table, and on it, the scratched green tin that served as their money box. Last night she'd used all the dented type in the hatbox, and even that wasn't enough; in the end, she'd resorted to prying nails out of the walls.

"But we've got so much now—"

"We don't!" The words burst out, meaner than she'd meant. "I'm sorry, darling. Madame Lamotte stopped me yesterday when I was coming up the stairs. The rent is past due. And Alain—"

"Fine." Sophie pushed her shoulders back stiff and tight, like a toy soldier's. "So where are we going to go?"

6

At the edges of Paris, the tall buildings shrank, and the cloud-dark sky reasserted itself. The houses, a few with thatched roofs, stood close to the road, sometimes separated from its dust and mud by stone walls. Peering over them, Camille spied the green relief of gardens: bright leaves of apple trees, a tangle of peas twined with pink blossoms.

Sophie tilted her head up and wrinkled her nose. "It was so nice earlier. Now it feels like it's going to rain."

"We're almost there." Attached to one of the larger houses was a farrier's shop, its back built into the wall that ran along the lane. Smoke drifted over the roof; from inside the workshop door sparks flew out to fizzle in the dirt yard where horses were shod.

"Here?" Sophie looked as if she were expecting handsome apprentices to hand them boxes full of metal scraps.

Camille laughed. There was no point in being frustrated with Sophie. Tucking her skirts behind her, Camille squatted in the dirt. Digging with a fingernail, she pried a bent nail out of the earth and held it up to Sophie. "See? No need for apprentices."

"I disagree," Sophie said petulantly, but after breaking off a couple of twigs from a branch that hung over the wall and giving one to Camille, she too sank to the ground and started digging.

Slowly, slowly a dingy pile of scraps grew between them. It wasn't hard work, but it was dirty, and it would be days before their fingernails were clean again. With each shard of metal, each nail she tossed onto the pile, Camille's resentment simmered toward boiling. Alain never helped dig. Nor did he wander the streets, eyes on the muck, ready to paw through it when metal glinted there. He didn't need to. He was full of puffed-up promises—when he rose through the ranks of the Guard, there would be plenty for them all! Camille pried a long nail out of the earth and flung it on the pile. Alain couldn't even keep his uniform clean. He seemed hardly to report for duty. How would he ever rise through the ranks? And his gambling debts only grew bigger and murkier, though he insisted they were nothing.

She continued to dig in the dirt, wrenching the metal bits free and hurling them at the bag, where they clinked dully together. Alain's promises were as worthless as the pieces of paper Papa's noble customers used to sign. They meant nothing. And it always fell to her to make something from that nothing.

"Any more and we won't be able to carry the bag home," Camille said, hoisting the flour sack they'd brought with them.

"Grâce à Dieu," Sophie muttered as she stood up. "We need gloves, Camille. There's so much dirt under my nails they hurt."

A horse cart rumbled toward them along the lane, kicking up clouds of dust. Before it'd even passed them, Sophie was bent over her knees, coughing.

"Shh, now." Camille hugged Sophie close. "Are you all right?"

"My lungs—not quite—better," she gasped.

Nearby a low wall ran toward an open field. On the other side of it, farmhands were cutting an early crop, their sickles flashing. A low wind billowed in their shirtsleeves. Behind the men, a band of trees crouched under a darkening sky. Camille dropped down onto the wall, pulling Sophie close beside her. Through the thin cloth of Sophie's dress, her shoulder blades jutted out; her breath hitched in her throat in a way that made Camille wish she could breathe for her and spare her the pain. With Sophie's fair head tucked against her neck, Camille closed her eyes and wished hard: somehow. Someday. Soon.

A moment later Sophie was kicking her heels dully against the stones.

"You'll ruin your shoes that way."

Sophie shrugged as if to say, *They're already ruined.* "I could take in more work from Madame Bénard. She's always saying I've got clever hands for trimming hats. I might even wait on customers in the shop."

It would certainly help. "Are you certain? With your health?"

With her dirty fingers, Sophie carefully straightened the pleats on Camille's sleeve. "Then you wouldn't have to work la magie—"

"That would be a lot of hats." Camille dropped her smile when she saw Sophie's eyes darkening.

"Not everyone can work magic."

It had been a vexed subject ever since the beginning, when Maman had begun teaching Sophie the simplest kind of magic, la magie ordinaire. Sophie insisted she couldn't do it. Camille knew she didn't want to. And unlike Camille, who could do it and who must, Sophie had walked away from working magic at all.

"Everyone's struggling these days," Camille said, pressing down her resentment. "We're not the only ones. Apart from the nobles, all the people of France are hungry." In the field, the farmhands worked their way through the green rows. "Perhaps this year's harvest will be better."

"One harvest won't make our lives better. Bread will cost a bit less, bien sûr. But we'll still be scraping through the mud for scraps of metal."

"We won't live off la magie forever. Something will change."

Sophie glanced sidelong at Camille. "Alain said he would take me to a dance at the Palais-Royal."

"And?" Camille said, uneasy.

"And," said Sophie, dragging her finger in curlicues along the top of the wall, "he said I might meet someone there. Plenty of noblemen come to the Palais-Royal for the duc d'Orléans' entertainments. He said he'd buy me a dress to wear and a friend of his would loan me some jewels."

"Oh?" If Sophie went, what would she find there, at the crowded gaming tables or on the polished parquet floor of the ballroom? An aristocrat looking for a wife? Hardly. A girl for an evening or maybe a week. Not the fairy-tale romance she was wishing for. "Who'll buy you a dress: Alain or the duc?"

"Alain, silly." Sophie gave Camille's shoulder a little push. "I can marry rich, I know it. Find someone who'd take care of us."

Camille wanted to scream. Or give up. Of all the things that Alain did—his drinking, his gambling, his utter disregard for money—encouraging Sophie to marry high was the worst. Even when their parents were alive, this had been ridiculous. And Maman had encouraged it with her stories. She told them she'd lived at Versailles when she was a little girl: she'd had a pretty dog on a red ribbon, a white pony, her own enameled box for her rings. But her stories had the dim, dappled feel of dreams—nothing to hold on to. And after Papa had to sell the press, after her parents *died*, a rich husband for Sophie was a very dangerous daydream. She caught Sophie looking at her: her blue eyes large in her face, her lips parted, waiting. Hoping.

She took Sophie's hand, the bones under the skin light as a bird's. "You're only fifteen, ma chère."

"The queen married at fourteen." Sophie sniffed.

Much good that did her, Camille thought. The French people despised Marie Antoinette. "Still, why not wait? You might—"

"Look!" Sophie slid off the wall. "There's something in the sky!"

Up, up against the slate-gray clouds, a large object shimmered.

Something that hadn't been there before. It was yellow and white, like a striped silk purse tossed high in the air.

"Dieu, it's a montgolfière!" Camille cried. "Remember?"

Sophie drifted into the lane, watching the flying machine. "How could I forget?"

Six years ago, Papa had taken them all the way out to the Palace of Versailles. Before they left, at home, he'd hoisted Camille up underneath the ceiling to feel how warm it was there compared to the cold morning floor. *Hot air rises*, he said. *Remember that.* She and Sophie were little then, and three bumpy hours from Paris to Versailles in a dray wagon had felt like a long way to go for a sack of hot air. Papa knew someone at the palace, a gardener who let them in through a narrow iron gate. There, in an enormous, crowded courtyard, it waited: a flying machine, its balloon made of paper and decorated like an embroidered pillow.

Her father held her and Sophie in his arms so they could watch as the animals—a sheep, a duck, and a rooster—were loaded into the basket. The stiff balloon tilted in the breeze. People clapped and cheered, chanting "Montauciel! Montauciel!" Camille shouted in her father's ear to ask who Montauciel was; her father laughed and tweaked her nose. Montauciel was the name of the sheep, "Rise-to-the-Sky." How the crowd roared when the assistants released the restraints and the flying machine rose into the sky.

It rose, but not like a bird. Like a saint in a church painting, straight up to heaven.

That balloon had been made of paper—the Montgolfiers were papermakers—but this one was made of a rippling fabric, silk perhaps. In its chariot-like basket, silhouettes moved back and forth.

"We'll get a better view by the field," Sophie said. "Hurry! I think people are in it!"

The balloon sailed toward them, higher than any church's tower. Higher than anything. *Like a dandelion seed*, Camille thought. *Like a wish.*

One of the two silhouettes bent over the brazier in the center. The other stood at the chariot's edge, a spyglass to his eye. The wind caught his dark hair. Behind him, banks of clouds darkened to storm as the pale undersides of the poplar trees flipped over. Rain was coming.

"It's like something from a fairy tale," Camille said, her voice low and reverent.

"There aren't balloons in fairy tales."

"In mine there are." Though Camille knew hot air kept the balloon afloat, it still *seemed* impossible. The balloon rushed down toward them, its gondola swooping over the treetops.

"It's going to land right here!" Sophie dragged Camille forward, toward a gate in the wall. "Come!"

As the balloon crested the trees, moving faster now, one of the figures heaved something large over the edge of the basket: an anchor. It plummeted to the ground, then scudded into the dirt. But the balloon continued to speed across the field, the anchor dragging uselessly below.

Thick smoke billowed from the brazier. The machine floated too low, neither landing nor going up.

"Something's wrong, isn't it?" Sophie bit her lip.

Over the field, the balloon's silk shuddered as it rushed along. One of the figures in the balloon shouted to the farmhands, "Help us, mes frères! Catch hold of the basket!"

Frozen by fear or wonder, the workers stared gape-mouthed, sickles dangling from their hands, as the balloon dropped. Inside the gondola, the two silhouettes braced themselves.

"They will die!" Sophie wailed, pressing her face into Camille's shoulder. "Why won't the farmers help them?"

Suddenly the balloon careened into the ground, spraying dirt and stones. The impact flung the gondola and the balloonists back into the air, like leaves tossed in a storm. Lost. Powerless. Almost gone.

In death, her parents' bodies had looked heavy, but empty. As Sophie wept, they were hoisted onto wooden boards and carried down seven dark flights of stairs. Camille followed them. Papa's arm had fallen loose of the winding sheet, his skin blackened with smallpox, the tips of his fingers gray with faded ink. All that light, snuffed out. She wanted to weep when she thought of the space Maman and Papa had left behind, like holes scissored from the sky.

"Stay here!" Camille shouted. Then she grabbed her skirts and ran.

7

ast the flowering chestnut trees near the fence, through the open gate, and into the soft soil of the field, Camille ran. She ignored the shouts of the farmhands and the violent jump of her pulse.

The balloon sped toward her, now only a few feet above the ground.

"Messieurs! Save us!" yelled the dark-haired balloonist. But the farmhands scattered, shielding their heads with their arms and careening toward the trees.

Camille lost her footing in the loose soil, caught herself, kept running. With each breath, her chest fought against her stays. Her lungs ached, sharp dust in her throat.

As she drew closer she saw the balloonists weren't men at all but boys, not much older than she. One of them—small, thin in his shirtsleeves—was pulling hard on a rope tied to the balloon's opening over the brazier. "The release valve is broken, Lazare!" he yelled.

"Whose fault is that?" the other one said. Behind him, his hair streamed out like a flag, his cravat a flash of white under his soot-streaked face.

"Yours!"

"If we'd had enough ballast, we wouldn't be in this predicament!" the dark-haired one shouted back. His face was tight with fear.

Far away, as if in a dream, Sophie called her name.

Camille was almost there. She saw how the gondola was fashioned only of woven willow branches, with simple leather straps holding its door closed; she saw how the taut ropes vibrated with strain. It was so fragile. In an instant, it could be smashed. Smoke poured from the brazier as the white-faced boy braced himself against the basket's edge.

Faster. Faster. She forced her legs to pump.

The chariot thudded hard against the ground. The basket did not break; the boys clung on.

Four lengths. Two lengths. Then she was an arm's-length away.

Crouched against the railing, the black-haired boy braved a smile, his eyes on Camille as she ran alongside them. "Save us, mademoiselle! Grab the edge!"

In his gaze, she saw herself as someone else. Someone who might do something.

She grabbed the gondola with both hands.

The balloon's momentum yanked her into the air. Under her feet, the field rushed sickeningly away. Scrambling over the objects in the gondola, the black-haired one grabbed her arms and pulled her higher. "Hold tight, mademoiselle, and watch your feet!" he shouted into the wind.

"Don't let go," she managed to say. His face was so near she saw the flecks of gold in his eyes, the determination in his face.

One agonizing breath.

Two. Three breaths.

And then it was over. With a sudden shudder, the balloon plunged to the ground, sending up a cloud of dust. The gondola rocked and then was still. Camille clung on, breathless, her mouth sandy with grit. Her legs were shaking so badly she wished she could sink to her knees, right there, in the dirt.

The boy was laughing.

Camille wiped the dirt from her mouth. "This is funny?"

"We're not dead!" The boy threw an arm around his friend, then reached out to Camille. "But you, mademoiselle! You saved us!"

A wild laugh burst out of her. She had. She, Camille Durbonne, whose only talent, according to Alain, was to briefly turn nails to coins, had saved them. And yet, here stood both boys, unbroken and solid.

"I was happy to do it," she said, and she meant it.

The other boy sighed. "We were never in any danger."

"Never in any danger?" Camille couldn't help herself. "What would you have done if I hadn't been here? Your balloon would have smashed to pieces!"

"Bah," the other one said. "It would have bounced."

But the dark-haired one, the one who had held her as they raced above the earth, didn't reply. Instead, he leaned on the basket's edge and looked at her.

Even beneath the soot and dirt, he was ridiculously handsome, with his warm, copper-brown skin and glossy ebony hair. High, finely cut cheekbones set off his deep-brown eyes, which were fringed with lashes a girl might envy. Black, expressive eyebrows curved above them; a scar skipped through the left one, slicing it in half. But what was most striking about him was that his whole face was animated with a kind of light that made him the most alive thing in the landscape. As if an artist, sketching out the scene, had used a gray pencil to draw everything except one figure, on which he'd lavished his richest paints.

"Incroyable," the boy said.

"What is?" Camille wondered.

"You have to ask?" he said, surprised. "You, of course. Our *rescuer*."

Leaping lightly over the basket's edge, he stood suddenly in front of her. "Lazare Mellais," he said, bowing very low, "your servant, for life."

She curtsied. "Camille Durbonne."

"Mademoiselle Durbonne, there aren't many people I can say this about, but after what you did today, I'd hazard that your disregard for your own life is probably equal to mine."

She wouldn't have *thought* that before today. The way he was looking at her made her feel braver. A bit reckless. "What else is there to do with a life than spend it?"

"Fetch the champagne, Armand," the boy said, his gaze not leaving her. "Let's celebrate."

"I'm not your servant," the pale boy snapped from inside the basket. "Besides, it's going to rain."

It was true. Behind the trees, anvil-shaped clouds loomed. Their bottoms were iron-gray with rain. Soon the storm would be upon them.

"I know it's going to rain," Lazare said. "Tell me, quickly—why did you do it?"

Camille shifted her weight, uncomfortable. How *could* she explain? After her parents died, her life had become so narrow, tight as a fetter. But sometimes surviving wasn't enough. A person needed more than a roof and food. She needed to hope, to believe she could do something.

"I thought I could," she said.

"We wouldn't have needed her help if we hadn't run out of fuel," the other boy said, coming forward. He was slight, narrow-shouldered, a streak of white running through his brown hair like a badger's. His fingers were stained blue with ink and black with soot; in his hand he held a pair of shell-rimmed glasses which he polished determinedly on his sleeve. "That was your job, Lazare."

"Mademoiselle, may I introduce our head engineer, Monsieur Armand?"

Camille curtsied, but the badger-haired boy merely nodded and went on talking. "You should have brought more straw for fuel!" He polished his glasses harder. "The air in the balloon got too cold."

"And extra fuel would have helped?"

"More straw equals more heat!" Armand said.

It isn't as simple as that, Camille thought. "When you burn your fuel, you also burn some of your ballast, don't you?"

The boy replaced his glasses and squinted at her. "And?"

"And then, if you need to rise, you've nothing to throw over to lighten the load."

A fierce blush crept up the boy's neck. "How could you possibly know that?"

She was about to explain but Armand looked away, crossing his arms. She'd been so desperate to join in the conversation that she'd offended him. And she didn't want to be shut out from this new world that had appeared in front of her. She tried again. "Do you know? Yours isn't the first balloon I've seen. My father took me to Versailles to see a mont-golfière."

"In eighty-three?" Lazare exclaimed. "I was there, too." Something faraway flickered in his eyes. "I kept wishing I were in the gondola with those animals."

"But instead, you got me," Armand muttered, as a cool wind rushed along the field, tugging at their clothes, the collapsed silk of the balloon.

"Don't be angry, mon ami. We need a better release valve to let out the hot air. Otherwise we're left hoping the hot air cools precisely as we're flying over a field. Or that Mademoiselle is here to help us."

Armand scowled. "Where's Rosier with the wagon? Any moment now the skies will empty on us."

"There's still time to toast our savior," Lazare said, bending his lanky form into the chariot and fishing out a wine bottle. "Lucky for us, I saved this one from being dashed on a farmer's head."

"Any moment those farmers will descend on us, ready to dismantle the basket for firewood," Armand snapped.

From somewhere else—his pockets?—Lazare produced a handful of glasses. "Let's pretend Armand's not here," he said in a stage whisper.

"Really, Lazare, this is too much," Armand complained. "Besides," he said with something like glee, "here comes Mademoiselle's sister."

Sophie arrived, out of breath, blond hair straggling down her back, skirts splattered with dirt. She threw her arms around Camille. "Grâce à Dieu," she said. "You frightened me!"

Camille burned with shame. She'd been so caught up in the moment that she'd forgotten Sophie. What if she had fallen from the balloon, been broken on the earth? What would happen to Sophie then? Sophie would be one more poor girl turned out on the dangerous streets of Paris.

Sophie's blue eyes snapped with fury. "What were you thinking, monsieur? You might have killed my sister!"

"My apologies, mademoiselle," Lazare said, true regret in his voice. "It was reckless of me to ask for her help. But admit it, your sister was magnificent!"

"She was," Sophie said, apparently unable to resist the handsome stranger. "Magnificent *and* mad."

She had been reckless, too. Thoughtless. She could see that now. And yet. For a moment, as she'd stumbled through the field, her lungs on fire, her heart a drum, she'd felt alive. Free.

Lazare held up the wine bottle. "Quick, a toast! To the mad dreamers, to all of us!"

The thunder growled again, closer now. But underneath the storm's low rumble, Camille heard something else. Hoofbeats.

Riding toward them at a pounding gallop was a boy on a rangy gray horse, his mousy hair frizzing out under his hat so that it seemed in danger of pushing his hat off altogether. Tucked under one arm was a notebook whose pages flapped in the wind. Behind him trundled the covered wagon, its horses keeping to the edge of the field.

"Très bien!" the boy on the horse shouted. "Stay just like that!"

Lazare laughed. "Let me apologize in advance, mesdemoiselles."

Before Camille could ask why, the curly haired boy was hauling his horse to a stop and leaping to the ground. He dropped his reins in the dirt and sprinted toward the balloon, pressing his cocked hat to his head as he ran. He waved the notebook at them. "I saw it all! Wrote it down! Death-defying! A Great Moment in History!"

What? Camille snuck a sidelong glance at Lazare. He raised a dark eyebrow, the one with the scar. When the boy reached them, he flung himself to his knees before Camille and clasped her hand.

"Mademoiselle! An angel!" His clever black eyes scrutinized her. "No—scratch that out. A Jeanne d'Arc of the air! A true heroine!"

"But I didn't—"

"Your name will be written in the annals of French history, mademoiselle!" he said, rising to his feet and removing his hat with a flourish. "Charles Rosier, your servant."

"A pleasure to meet you." Camille tried to keep a straight face. Who *were* these people? It was as if she had stumbled into Astley's circus or a play, something mad and wild and wonderful—completely apart from the rest of her life.

Rosier stood and bowed to Sophie, his hand on his heart. "Mademoiselle—thank you for coming to watch. We were lucky to have such a lovely audience."

Sophie said with a laugh, "It was quite something."

"It looked well, did it not?" Lazare threw an arm around Rosier's shoulders.

Rosier kissed the tips of his fingers. "Very impressive. Accidents become you, Lazare. You might plan them, in the future. Though next time we'll have a paying crowd for when you land."

Just as Camille was about to ask how one might plan an accident, the skies cracked open. Cold, fat drops of rain pummeled their clothes and darkened the dirt in the field. The farmers, who'd been cautiously approaching, ran back toward the gate and away. Closer now, thunder rolled around them; a fork of lightning whitened the tops of the trees.

It was ending, and Camille did not want it to end.

"Stop talking and help with the balloon!" Armand shouted. He dropped to his knees, roughly rolling up the silk. "One more minute and it'll be drenched!"

Lazare reached for Camille's hand. "Tell me, mademoiselle, do you live nearby?"

Camille had nearly given him her hand when she realized her mistake.

Her fingernails were packed with dirt from digging up the scraps: five filthy black moons. Mortified, she pressed her fingers deep into her skirts.

"I—" she began.

But the light had gone out of Lazare's face. For a moment he hesitated, as if he were going to say something else, then with a quick bow, joined Armand. Rosier helped maneuver the wagon into place. The wind snapping in the silk made the horses uneasy. The boys yelled encouragement and insults at each other as they struggled to get the balloon, the gondola, and all the equipment onto the wagon.

"If we don't go now, we'll be soaked to the skin." Sophie plucked at Camille's arm. "Come. The boys are busy."

In all the commotion, Camille tried to say adieu to Lazare, but his whole attention went to the balloon and getting it packed away on the wagon and out of the rain. It was as if she had never existed. She remembered how when the Montgolfiers' balloon rose into the sky, strangers in the crowd had embraced one another. In the excitement of the moment, people did strange things. But as she and Sophie trudged back across the field, she couldn't help looking back at him over her shoulder.

Lazare was steadying the lead cart horse, a reassuring hand flat on its curved neck. Slowly, as if he could feel her gaze, he turned his head. He waved, once, before his attention went back to the horse, the wagon, the balloon.

What had she expected? That when the world made a door for her to step through, the door would stay open no matter what she did?

"Camille," Sophie said. "Let's go."

Beneath Camille's shoes, the earth became mud, marbled with bright green weeds crushed into the muck. The sack of metal scraps thumped dismally against her skirts.

She determined not to think of them anymore. Out of sight, out of mind.

As they walked toward home, away from the fields at the city's edges, the streets of Paris grew more cramped. More shadowy. Police paced through crowds of tired people going home; boys shouted the day's scandals, broadsheets in hand, telling of smashed bakery windows and rising bread prices and taxmen burned in effigy. Horse carts and ox-carts churned in the filthy lanes, and over and through it all wove the church bells' solemn tolling and the cries of the market-sellers and the melancholy glitter of rain.

This was the Paris of the strivers, of those who dwelt low, not high. This was not the Paris of balloonists. It was her Paris, and it was the same as it had been this morning.

But she, perhaps, was not.

8

Back at their apartment, as the rain hushed in the half-light, Sophie began to plait a few silk roses into a hair ornament for Madame Bénard's shop. "He liked you, you know."

"Who? The one with the white stripe in his hair? Or the curly haired one who thinks I'm a Jeanne d'Arc of the Air? I think *he* liked *you*." Camille dried the last supper dish and put it away. In the bare cupboard, Alain's plate waited like an accusation. Once, Alain had tried to juggle plates, like the jongleurs at Astley's, and smashed two. How furious Papa had been until Camille called it an experiment, and they were spared.

Alain was the reason there had been so little to eat, but that would change tonight. On their way home, Sophie had stopped in the shop and told Madame Bénard that she would be happy to do more work. Thrilled, Madame had pressed a bundle of silk flowers and a small calico purse into Sophie's hands. They'd have enough for something good to eat. Camille's stomach tightened at the thought of it.

"Obviously not the striped one," Sophie replied, wrapping a ribbon around the flower stems. "The dark one, who was so handsome. Like a character in a novel."

"Lazare Mellais, you mean," Camille said, as nonchalantly as she could. In her mouth, his name felt like an incantation, a charm to bring him back. Before Sophie could see her flush, Camille picked up a rag and ran it over the table.

"I knew you liked him!" Sophie laughed. "That must have been the strangest way for any lovers to meet!"

Camille still felt the warm strength of his hands on her shoulders, how he seemed to be the only thing holding her up in a landscape that was tilting and spinning. "How does someone our age come to have a balloon?"

Sophie pretended to think. "Money? He's clearly quite rich."

But the Montgolfiers who'd launched their balloon at Versailles had been paper-makers, nothing more. "Didn't the curly-haired one, Rosier, say something about an audience? Perhaps they sell tickets?"

Sophie was about to reply when the sound of heavy footsteps echoed on the stairs.

"It's Madame Lamotte," Camille said in a hushed tone. "Tell her we have a plan for the money. She likes you best."

Sophie stood up, the fabric roses in her hands. "But I thought we still had four days?"

The footsteps paused. Someone pounded on the door so it shook in its frame.

"It's not Madame," Sophie said.

The door swung open so hard it crashed against the wall.

Alain stood in the center of the doorway. In the old days, before, Camille would have thrown her arms around his neck and kissed him.

Not now. Now there was an empty pit where once there had been that feeling.

"No smiles? No glad greeting?" He shook out his coat. Water streamed onto the floor. "I'd have guessed you would have been happier to see me, sisters."

"We are!" Sophie said, moving to greet him. "We were surprised, that's all."

"To see your own brother?" Alain sauntered into the room. His blond hair hung lank around his face, his cheeks unevenly shaven. He reeked of last night's wine and his shoes were caked in mud. "Well, I won't trouble you much longer. Just give me what money you have."

"Our rent is due, Alain," Camille said as calmly as she could. She'd not let him provoke her this time.

"That's fine." He shrugged. "Just give me whatever you have."

"We can't," Sophie said quietly. "We'll be thrown out if we can't pay Madame Lamotte."

"But you have it?"

Camille imagined the strongbox, the iron straps binding it to the floor, twenty real livres inside. That was all they had. The key was back under the floorboards, though knowing that didn't make it any easier to breathe. She wished hard that he would give up and leave. "We were hoping *you* might have some money, Alain. We're still short by a lot."

"If I had, why would I be here?" Alain stalked toward Camille. "Don't jest about that which you don't understand."

"I wasn't jesting."

"Help us understand, then," Sophie pleaded.

Alain clenched his hands. "I'm in debt to someone," he said in a strangled voice. Camille could not tell if he was angry or scared. "My debts to him are large. Larger than you can imagine. And he's tired of waiting."

As am I. As is Madame Lamotte. "We're all tired, Alain," Camille said.

Sophie stepped sideways, closer to Camille and the table where the calico purse lay.

"Still, he wants his money." Alain fumbled in his coat pocket and drew out a small bottle. He tipped his head back and drank, wiping his mouth on the cuff of his coat.

"It'd be easier to pay him if you stopped drinking," Camille said grimly. "And went back to soldiering."

Swaying a little, Alain let the bottle drop to the floor, where it rolled clinking toward the center of the room. "I will, I promise, but I must give him something now so he knows I'm keeping my word."

How could he ask such a thing of them? "Why not tell your creditor that you'll pay him piecemeal, when you have the money? Tell him how Sophie's getting better, but still needs medicine. Surely he can be reasonable."

"*Reasonable* is not the word I'd use," he said.

"Look around this apartment," Camille said, bewildered. "We don't have anything, brother. Not even a chicken bone."

"You think this is a joke?" Alain snarled. "He is not a kind man. I've seen what he's done to others. I could tell him where you live and he would come here and steal you away as payment for my debt. He'd eat your flesh and crunch up your bones." Alain wiped spit from his mouth. "Or make you his harlots. How would you like that, Camille?"

The girl in the street, her crimson lips, her filthy feet—a girl on fire. Camille would not let that happen to Sophie or herself.

"You are incroyable," she said, furious. "You drink away the money I give you and return only to demand more. Then you threaten to sell me as a whore to your creditor?" She took a step closer, eyes burning, chin up, defiant. "Whoring is something I will never do. And if you think I'd do it to save your pathetic skin, you are terribly mistaken."

His demeanor changed, then. She had only time for one thought— *this is the real Alain*—before he slammed his fist into her face.

Lightning exploded. The room collapsed.

Someone was wailing.

She didn't know if it was Sophie, or herself.

Camille pulled herself to her elbows. Firelight flickered. Something was in her eye: a kind of red curtain. With the back of her hand, she rubbed at it. Blood caught on her eyelashes, trickled hot into her ear.

By the fireplace, two figures struggled. *Alain*, she realized dimly. And Sophie. His broad back was to Camille, one fist wrapped in Sophie's hair. The other he shook at her white face. Something dangled from it. The calico purse.

"Is this all you have?" he shouted.

Camille tried to get up. The room spun and she lurched onto her side. Everything blurred. He had gone too far. Her true brother was never coming back. She'd get the candlestick from the table and crack this one's head open.

Camille grabbed at the floorboards with her fingernails, dragging herself forward.

"This is your last chance, ma soeur," Alain slurred. "I know you and your lying sister have more hidden away somewhere." He raked at Sophie's hair and she whimpered. "If our parents were alive, they would never say no to me."

Yes, they would. You're no longer their son. You've become someone else.

Camille slid a little closer to the table.

In that moment, Sophie's eyes met Camille's. They were enormous in her face, their pupils black. Behind Alain's back, Sophie motioned urgently toward the floor. She wanted Camille to lie down.

The floor tilted. Camille met it with a thud.

All she could see were his boots, filthy from the street. Straw crushed into the mud on their heels. Under his rumpled coat, the thready gleam of his watch chain—the watch itself pawned long ago—was strangely bare. It was missing its last remaining fob: a miniature portrait of Sophie and Camille.

Sophie pointed wildly. "See what you've done to our sister! You've killed her!"

Ah. Camille closed her eyes, held her breath. *My sister the actress.*

"Don't be a fool. She's not dead," he faltered.

Sophie dropped to the floor next to Camille. "Open the window and call the constable!"

Alain stooped to peer at her. "She's not moving."

Sophie pressed gently on Camille's throat. "Her heart's still beating."

"God in heaven!" he exclaimed. "Let her live! I never intended it. Never." He picked up her hand, held it to his cheek. "You must believe me."

"*This time*, she's breathing. But Alain, think! What were you doing?"

Alain flinched. "You don't understand. He's not like other people." He started to cry, abjectly. "If he doesn't get the money, he'll kill me. Or worse."

"But you hurt your sister!"

"To protect her!" He wept. "To protect all of us!"

Sophie pried his hands loose from Camille's; Camille saw a flash of silver as Sophie pressed some livres—how many, oh, how many?—into their brother's hand. "Take this and go before I call for the police. You can never come back if you're drunk."

At the door Alain hung on Sophie like a too-large child. He had always been the biggest, the oldest, the most daring—the one who carried both girls on his shoulders. Now he avoided Camille where she lay on the floor. "I promise. I will change. I will get rid of my tormentor and then, you'll see, we'll be free," he said.

She didn't believe in his promises. She wished he would go away forever.

He was still moaning as Sophie pushed him into the hallway and closed the door behind him.

Sophie waited, still as a watched mouse, as his footsteps faded. Then she wrenched the key over in the lock and dragged the table, its candlesticks wobbling and legs screeching, against the door. Her chest was heaving when she crouched down next to Camille.

"Does it hurt?"

Oh no, not at all. Camille's ears were ringing, her thoughts banging around in her head like a door in the wind. He had hurt her. Badly. What about her made him so angry? Her mind reeled back: the snap of her neck when he hit her. The slow drop to the floor. Alain's wet, crying mouth.

"Can you get up?" Sophie wriggled her arm under Camille's shoulder and helped her sit.

The ceiling loomed too close. "Everything's wobbly. Lean me against the wall. Is it bad?"

"Awful," Sophie said quietly. "His ring cut you above the eyebrow. That's why there's so much blood."

"Merde." Camille reached up to touch her brow. The raw pain made her wince.

With water warmed on the stove and a soft rag in her hand, Sophie worked away at the blood. She wiped it out of Camille's ears, off her neck where it had dried and cracked, soaked it out of her clotted hairline. When she was finished, Sophie looked grimly pleased. "It's just a small cut. I won't have to sew it."

Camille's stomach lurched when she thought of Sophie's tiny, even stitches in her skin. "Alain took it all, didn't he?"

Nothing stayed. No matter what Camille did. She gathered scraps of metal and dredged up sorrow to make them into coins, but they didn't stay. Maman and Papa, the printing press, her dreams, her family the way they'd once been. Though she'd tried so hard to hold it all, in the end it ran away like water through her fingers.

Nothing stayed.

"What do you mean, 'all'?" Sophie wrung out the bloody cloth and dropped it in the basin of pink water.

"Didn't he get into the strongbox?"

"Oh, no. He took only what was in my purse."

"But that was your wages!"

"Not all of it." Sophie smiled. "In fact, not very much of it at all."

"What did you do with the rest?" Camille asked, wonder in her voice.

"I threw it into the ashes when he had me by the hair."

Camille laughed, though it made her ribs ache. "Well done, my courageous sister."

"Bah, it's still not much. A few livres." Sophie's lower lip trembled. "I'm frightened, Camille."

Camille smiled wanly, as if she weren't at all afraid. "We'll get away, ma chèrie. I promise."

La magie was the only trick she knew. It could get them some of the way there, but not all. Because it wouldn't take long before working too much magic made her weak, liable to fall ill. Maman's death had taught her that. And she could not leave Sophie alone.

She needed a better way.

9

Camille woke too early the next morning. Her neck ached, her ribs, too, and under her heavy hair, at the back of her skull, she could feel a hard bump. Next her fingers went to her eye. The flesh around it was puffed up and soft, like a rotten apple. She could only imagine the color.

Rubbing her forehead, she wandered out into the main room. The basin of water still sat on the floor, its bottom rusty red with her blood. Just to be certain, she knelt by the door to the eaves and checked under the floorboard. The key was there, safe. As she replaced the board, she thought she heard a whispering coming from the little room behind the door. The tiny hairs on her arms stood up. There were no words, just a hush like wind across a silk skirt; the feeling it gave her was like the one she had whenever she went near the burned box. As if someone were there.

"What a nervous fool you are," Camille told herself as she stood up. She needed some air.

From their attic apartment, a narrow window opened onto the slant of the building's roof. Camille often scrambled out there in her bare feet to sit next to one of the mansard's dormers. A metal railing ran along the edge; if it hadn't been there, she would never have gone out.

Sometimes she had the feeling that if she went too close to the edge, she wouldn't be able to control her body and that it would fling itself out and over, into the air—and smash on the street below. Being this high up made her stomach churn, the muscles in her neck contract.

But she was drawn to what the roof gave her, a moment of solitude and a way to see beyond what she normally could—away to the Seine and beyond. So she stayed away from the drop. If she tucked her feet in close, she could settle back against the corner where the roof met the stone wall. Pigeons were her companions up there, and black-clad chimney sweeps. When they spotted her, they doffed their cloth caps and made extravagant bows, their teeth flashing white against their sooty faces. They never seemed surprised to see her.

Beneath her perch ran the rue Charlot, and out from it, other streets, like arteries in the huge body of Paris. Near to the Durbonnes' neighborhood sprawled the grand hôtels built by noblemen in the last century, each iron-gated mansion so large it occupied an entire block. Between where she sat and the watery curve of the Seine glowed a patch of emerald grass, embroidered with paths—the still somewhat-fashionable Place des Vosges. Elegant phaetons and carriages circled the square. Not far off, on an island in the middle of the river, rose the gray towers of the cathédrale of Notre-Dame and the single iron spike of Sainte-Chapelle, and beyond them, the rest of Paris, a haze of places she'd never been.

What if she dared to go farther? Higher? She wondered what it would be like to venture beyond what she knew. What would she see?

Somewhere there had to be a place for herself and Sophie. In that maze of streets, there had to be an apartment where they would be safe. Was it too much to ask, when all the nobles had their elegant, well-guarded fortresses? It was not. There would be a window—several windows, as long as she was dreaming—tall and full of golden light, rooms peacefully papered in pale pinks and blues, fireplaces in all of them, soft sofas and featherbeds and warm rugs on the polished floors, a maid to clean and scrub and carry water. It would be a secret place, a space without drunken brothers, fists, or knives.

Over the river, a flock of birds lifted and curved into the pale dawn sky. That balloonist—Lazare Mellais—he didn't think about things like this. He and his badger-looking friend were probably pondering release valves and fuel and ballast, not wondering if their brothers would hit them and take their money. Not wondering how they might be safe.

Her fingers ached with frustration and sorrow. She'd go make something of it, use her sadness to turn coins to buy ointment for her eye. Camille stood up, stretching her neck. A warm breeze playing in her hair, she stood—a fierce silhouette—on the roof for a moment longer, wishing.

After she'd turned the coins, Camille woke Sophie and they dressed to go out. Standing in front of the old mirror on the mantelpiece and settling her broad-brimmed straw hat on her hair, Camille tilted her face to the side and inspected her reflection. The crazed glass made the bruise around her eye even darker and angrier. "It looks like I've been beaten."

"I'm sorry, ma belle, but you *were* beaten." Sophie fiddled with the wide, yellow ribbons on her much prettier hat, a loan from Madame Bénard. She'd styled her hair so that it swooped across her forehead, hiding the pockmarks she didn't like. "The ointment will help your eye. And laudanum, for your headache. Plus the apothecary is right by the park. The queen believes fresh air solves a multitude of problems."

Camille frowned. She loved the fresh morning air as much as anyone, but she hated the way she looked. Broken. In the glass, shadows hung around her eyes, her cheekbones stood out, and her mouth felt too wide in her face. More than anything she resembled a hungry fox. Not exactly the right appearance for a stroll at the Place des Vosges. "Too bad I couldn't work one of Maman's glamoires, remember?"

"Maman did it once. She said it was too dangerous for you to do—*remember?*"

Camille did. She also remembered how radiant her mother had looked, more beautiful than ever, as she swept into the apartment in a silk gown Camille had never seen, diamonds at her throat and a glittering brooch on her shoulder, smiling as Papa spun her in a circle. Her face was her face, but not. It had been a dream face: Maman, perfected.

Which was exactly what she needed now, Camille thought, arranging her hat so it hid her eye.

Once at the Place des Vosges, Sophie forgot completely about Camille's bruise and their errand to the apothecary. In the park, the sun shone on the frilled, silk parasols of women who strolled the paths. It blinded as it reflected off the gilded ornaments of the carriages that spun, in a dance of sleek horses' legs, around the park's edges. The soft thump of hooves mingled with the jingle of harnesses and the lazy swat of the coachmen's whips. Ladies waved from gold-painted carriages or rode on glossy horses, the men next to them in tight suits and polished boots, all of them bowing and smiling, exclaiming and flirting and flicking their painted fans. Birds chirped in the clipped hedges. There was not a cloud in the sky, as if the nobles could buy even the sun and the rain and order the weather to their liking.

As a group of women in rose-sprigged gowns passed them, Camille tipped her head away, hiding her bruise the best she could.

"What pretty dresses—like darling shepherdesses." Sophie sighed. "Madame Bénard was right. Cotton's all the rage."

"Which means that the silk weavers of Lyon will starve, because of the queen's fancy to be a milkmaid."

"And see? Such wide sashes," Sophie went on, ignoring Camille's scowl. "C'est la mode. I wish we had dresses like that."

"This way," Camille said, guiding her sister into the sheltered arcade that ran around the park. In its cool shade, gilt letters announcing

Apothecaire Arnaud arched across one of the shop windows. Beneath the name gleamed row after row of glass bottles, some packed with powders and others full of syrupy tinctures. The bell jingled and a plump, tightly corseted woman stepped onto the street, clutching her package. She frowned when she saw Camille's bruise.

"You go," Sophie said. "I'll wait here."

"On the street?"

"Who are you with this sudden compulsion for etiquette? In any case, it's hardly a street. It's a *park*. Please—it's too dull to wait in there. And it always reminds me of Maman's illness."

Hopeless. Camille sighed and went in. The shop smelled of dried herbs, alcohol, and camphor. She inhaled and felt her head clear a little. The line ahead of her was long, as Sophie had suspected. Everyone relished the chance to tell the apothecary their symptoms before surrendering their money. Outside, Sophie stood alone on the grass, gazing at the carriages. A breeze played in the long ribbons in her hat. She swayed slightly, as if to music, as she watched the wheels spin. She looked very small, not much bigger than a child.

Sophie deserved better. They both did.

Camille was determined to change things. As long as Alain knew where they lived, a new lock for the door wasn't going to be enough. He would always be there, taking, taking, taking. She only wished there were another way besides magic.

When Papa lost the shop, all the children had to learn to work la magie. Alain had been first to volunteer, but he hadn't been able to turn even the simplest things, like a torn piece of paper into a whole one. He'd been resentful when Camille had done it, quickly—as if it had been easy. But it wasn't. Maman was exacting when it came to la magie, forcing Camille to practice again and again before she would accept the result. She didn't see how Camille hated it. But when the magic caught, when Camille changed something useless into something useful, Maman had praised her. She'd called Camille her magical daughter, and in that moment, she felt she was.

She should have worked harder at it, she saw that now.

"Oui, mademoiselle?" the apothecary said, wiping his hands on his apron. "What is your complaint?"

My complaints are many, monsieur. Carefully, Camille tilted her hat back to reveal the bruise.

The man pursed his lips. "You have hit yourself on a doorjamb."

Camille said nothing. The apothecary's eyes dropped to his ocher-stained fingers. "Une minute. I'll get what you need."

With the ointment jar and a laudanum bottle for Sophie wrapped in paper and tucked under her arm, Camille stepped out of the dusk of the shop and stood for a moment under the arcade, blinking at the bright sunlight, searching for the yellow of Sophie's dress.

There she was, at the far end, past the fountain. Camille was about to cross the street when someone called out to her: "Mademoiselle? Is it you?"

Her breath caught. Halfway down the arcade, coming toward her at a run, was the boy from the balloon. Lazare Mellais. He wore a plain brown suit, wrapped packages stuffed into its pockets. His cravat, as before, was carelessly tied and his hair was coming loose. As he reached her, Lazare swept off his hat and bowed.

"I can't say, mademoiselle, how I'd been hoping that I might pass you, just like this, on the street, so that I might tell you how much—"

He stopped speaking. His eyes fastened on her purple bruise with its sickly yellow edge.

Why, of all times, did she have to meet him now? Camille stared down at the cobbles, hoping her hat's brim would hide her face. She saw the toes of her shoes were dusty.

"Look at me." Lazare put his hand on her arm. "Mon Dieu, what happened?"

"Rien." Camille pulled her arm away. "It's nothing."

He stepped easily around her. "Whatever it is, it isn't nothing." His voice was soft, pleading. "Please, mademoiselle—what's wrong? I only wish to help."

Dropping her head, she tugged the brim of her hat as far down as she could. Humiliation burned hot in the tops of her ears. Any moment he'd realize what had happened to her and the awful greasy dirtiness of her life would be exposed. "If you wish to help, monsieur, just leave me alone."

"I can't do that, I'm afraid."

"Then please—please stop looking at me." Despite her intention to be brave, her voice shook.

Lazare stooped, his warm brown eyes meeting hers under the brim of her hat. "It wasn't a *what*, was it?"

She shook her head once.

"Then who did this to you?" he said, an edge in his voice. "The dishonorable—"

Camille shook her head again. Imagine if she told him. If this boy then somehow found Alain and—did what? Beat him? Threatened him? Had him thrown in jail?

Any good to come of that would never erase the humiliation of Lazare knowing about her drunken wastrel of a brother. And that she had allowed this, somehow, to happen. If she said anything about it, this beautiful boy with his balloon would know her life of pinching poverty, dirty nails, two decent dresses. Nothing could possibly persuade her to reveal that.

"Stop peering under my hat, monsieur. People are staring."

Lazare stood back. "Forgive me. I can't stand that someone would hurt you—"

"There's nothing to worry about."

He frowned, as if he didn't agree. He took a deep breath, exhaled. "Well, then. This is what I've been thinking since yesterday, hoping to see you again." He suddenly looked very young and awkward, all his easy grace gone. "Come visit our workshop, won't you? Where the balloon is kept? You could properly meet the others. Rosier has all these ideas."

"Me?"

He pretended to glance back over his shoulder, as if there might be someone there. "Who else? *You* saved the balloon and us, after all. You were so clever about the ballast, and, besides, I need all the help I can get to keep Armand in his place." That slow smile. "Don't say no."

Lazare was inviting her.

Her heart lifted. He hadn't thought her a fool. Her bruise hadn't repulsed him. He hadn't wanted to get away from her. It had just been the rain. He *had* been thinking about her. He wished for her to visit his workshop. He wished to see her again. He had been wishing it this entire time.

"Where—"

Camille's words were cut short by a scream.

10

Across the park, one of the gilded carriages shrieked to a halt. Its chestnut horses reared and whinnied as the coachman sawed on the reins. In front of the horses' legs, a young man—green suit, blond hair—bent and picked up a body from the street. Its head bobbed loosely on his shoulder, its yellow skirts catching around his legs.

Sophie.

The breath left Camille's lungs with a rush. Lazare said something—she could not heed it—she was already running. Her head spun. The park wasn't large, but full of people, walking slow as death, and she had to dodge them all. A group had gathered around the carriage but

Camille pushed her way through, using her elbows and feet to get them to move.

Please let her not be hurt. Please. Let her have fainted. Anything, anything, but not—

A dark-haired girl, white-faced and wearing an enormous plumed hat, rushed from the carriage, her mouth a pink O of worry. She was staggeringly pretty, with long dark lashes framing intelligent green eyes. Nearby, the boy knelt and laid Sophie in the grass. Her face was ashen, her lips bloodless.

Not dead, please, not dead, Camille begged, as she ran up to them. "What happened?"

"She's fainted," the girl murmured, without a glance at Camille. Careless of her extravagant dress, she dropped to her knees in the grass, unstoppered a bottle of sal volatile she'd pulled from her purse, and waved it under Sophie's nose. Camille threw herself down next to her sister's still body. She smoothed Sophie's fair hair from her forehead.

"Wake up, darling!" Her voice shook. "Wake up!"

Sophie's eyelids trembled, but she did not open them. Smiling a little, the girl gently slapped Sophie's checks.

"What are you doing?" Camille snapped.

The girl raised one elegant eyebrow, daggerlike against the alabaster whiteness of her skin. "Trust me, I've years of experience. Two sisters, both excessively sensitive. She took a fright, that's all. Poor petite!"

At that, Sophie opened her blue eyes. There was a smudge of dirt across her forehead. "Camille!" she said, wonderingly. "Who are these people?"

"Mademoiselle," the boy said to Camille, "do you know this girl?"

"She's my sister." Camille clasped Sophie's hand and kissed it. "How do you feel?"

"Well enough." Sophie blinked and tried to smile. "How pretty everyone is!" she said to the girl with the fan. "What a marvelous hat!"

The raven-haired girl laughed. "Fashion is the first thing you think of? It is lovely, isn't it? I bought it at Rose Bertin's."

Camille glared at the boy. "Tell me what happened."

"First, may I offer my deepest apologies," he said as his strange, golden eyes met hers. Like the girl, he looked about the same age as Camille. He was elegantly dressed, fair and handsome, though his mouth seemed as likely to curve into a sneer as a smile. "Just as your sister was stepping into the street, the horses shied at a flag. My coachman pulled them up immediately; rest assured, they did not touch her." He smiled faintly. "It was my friend the marquise's scream you heard, not your sister's."

"Ça alors," said the girl, her emerald eyes snapping. "What else was I to do, Vicomte? Allow your wild animals to run over this darling girl?" Her voice had a warning edge to it. "Never mind your reputation would be destroyed beyond mending if she'd been hurt."

Vicomte. Marquise. Of course it was a pair of aristocrats who'd nearly mown down her sister. They were as heedless as they were rich. Camille helped Sophie to sitting. "Come, ma chèrie, we've got to be going."

"So quickly?" There was a little color in Sophie's cheeks now, though she swayed a little.

"We'll take you in the carriage," the boy said. "It's no bother—in fact, I insist." He held out a ringed hand to Sophie.

But before Sophie could take it, Lazare appeared at the edge of the circle, breathing hard, his hand on the vicomte's shoulder, pushing him aside. "Your sister! What's happened?"

"She fainted, that's all," Camille said, relieved that Lazare was finally there. "Thanks to—the marquise—she's quite well now."

"All in a day's work," the marquise said, dropping her sal volatile into her purse.

Lazare bowed in her direction before his eyes went like arrows to the vicomte. "He was involved?"

"It was the horses!" the marquise said. "And a flag that ought to be torn to shreds, and a girl's sweet, sensitive nature. Nothing more." She smiled fondly at Sophie. "No harm done."

Lazare exhaled. "Are you well, mademoiselle?"

"How could I not be, when the kindest people in all of Paris are taking care of me?" Sophie said prettily. She took the vicomte's hand as he helped her to stand.

Taking in the little scene, Camille could practically see the wheels spinning in Sophie's head. Here she was, rescued by a nobleman with a fine nose and golden eyes! And a carriage painted Wedgwood blue and gold! She had stumbled into her very own fairy tale and she was in no rush to leave it. Camille bit her lip as the vicomte said something in Sophie's ear that made her laugh.

However well-intentioned this boy might be, she needed to get her sister home. "Thank you, messieurs, madame, for all your help." As both Lazare and the vicomte started forward, she held up her hand. "We won't need a carriage. A walk will be just the thing to revive us."

The vicomte bowed. "As you wish. Do accept my infinite apologies for having frightened you both. When we reach the stable, I shall whip my coachman and my horses to teach them a lesson."

"Hush!" The marquise slapped his arm with her fan. "They'll think you're serious."

"Of course, I'm only jesting," he said, but Camille wasn't certain he was. He passed a piece of paper to Sophie. "If there's anything," he said kindly, "anything at all, mademoiselle, please do not hesitate."

"He needn't go so far as that," Lazare said curtly.

"I only go as far as my morals compel me, monsieur," the vicomte tossed back.

Lazare ignored him, staring over the other boy's head as if he were suddenly fascinated by the treetops.

Sophie ducked her head. "Merci, Monsieur le Vicomte."

Good-byes and well wishes were traded and a moment later, the two aristocrats were stepping into the carriage, the breeze tousling their silken garments, the driver closing the gilded door behind them, and the horses stepping out briskly. Camille, Sophie, and Lazare watched as the carriage disappeared down the narrow streets.

Sophie sighed happily.

"Feeling well enough to go home?" Camille asked, as nicely as she could. She didn't blame Sophie—not exactly. But how could she have taken what must have been the vicomte's card? To acknowledge a relationship of sorts with a nobleman such as he?

"Perhaps Monsieur Mellais will accompany us?" Sophie tilted her head and smiled at him.

"We couldn't trouble you—" Camille began. The thought of him coming to their stooped building in the dingy rue Charlot made her cringe. It was like her bruised eye; she wished she were not ashamed of it, but she was.

Lazare's face fell. "I must be going, in any case. Good day to you, mesdemoiselles." He lifted his hat and turned away.

Camille watched him walk off with long strides, his coat billowing behind him. Each step he took pulled at her inside until she felt something would snap. But to call him back? To reveal herself that way felt too dangerous when she didn't know how he felt. She bit the edge of her fingernail, worrying at it.

He was nearly at the street when he stopped. "But you'll still come to our aeronauts' workshop, mademoiselle?" he called out.

Hadn't she wanted something more, the day of the balloon? A bigger life? Then why did saying yes to this boy feel like standing at the edge of a precipice and stepping into air? It should have felt easy, but it didn't.

"Say yes," Sophie nudged. "Remember, he likes you."

Lazare waited, fidgeting with the edge of his coat.

It was just him. It wasn't a precipice. It was only a tiny step.

"When?" she asked.

A smile spread slowly across his face. "Truly?" He told her where the workshop was and suggested they meet there on Wednesday. "I'll need the time to prepare Armand," he said.

"He dislikes me so much?"

He shook his head. "I'm teasing. Though, on second thought, perhaps not."

"Well, until then," Camille said, pointedly ignoring Sophie's look of triumph.

He hesitated. "One thing more, mademoiselle."

"Yes?"

"If there is any trouble from the person who blackened your eye, tell me. Because, pardieu, whoever he is, he will have to answer to me."

"He would have walked us home," Sophie said once they had left the grassy carpets and plush hedges of the Place des Vosges.

"He was being kind, that's all."

"He invited you to his workshop." Sophie rolled her eyes. "Truly, you are the most resistant to romance of any person I know."

She didn't want to respond to that. The less said about the confusing boy the better. There *was* something she wished to know, though. "What did the vicomte give you, Sophie? Was it his card?"

"Why should I tell you? You'll only be angry."

"Show me."

Sophie opened her hand. In it lay a square of the palest mint-green paper, barely as wide as her palm, with the boy's names and titles—Jean-Baptiste de Vaux, Vicomte de Séguin—engraved across it, very much like the expensive cards her father had resentfully printed to cover the costs of his pamphlets. It was soft from being clutched in her fist.

"À moi." Camille held out her hand for it.

Sophie slipped it into her purse. "It's *mine*."

Camille gritted her teeth to stop herself from saying something she'd regret. This was where Alain's tales about girls swept off their feet by princes led. "You don't know the ways of the world, ma chère."

"And you're an expert?"

"Just—don't trust as much. Be careful . . . of things."

"How specific you are." Sophie found a clump of grass on her skirt and flicked it off.

"You know what I mean," said Camille, exasperated.

"Do you mean runaway carriages?" Sophie said, knowingly. "Or is it handsome noblemen we're to be wary of? What about handsome balloon pilots?" Sophie poked Camille in the arm.

"That hurts," Camille said, pushing her sister's hand away. "And don't think you're being droll—you're absolutely not."

The look in Sophie's large blue eyes said she knew she was very droll indeed. "Alors," she said, tucking her hand under Camille's elbow and giving her arm a squeeze. "I will no longer be droll. But, sérieusement, Camille—how he looked at me! Don't you see that the attention of someone as important as the vicomte is a good thing? A way out?"

Camille fumed. Couldn't Sophie see that a rich nobleman was no real security, nothing assured at all? "But it's not the right way out, Sophie," she said, feeling she'd never convince her.

"Bah!" Sophie laughed. "In the end, who can say which way is right and which way is wrong, as long as one of them leads to happiness?"

11

On the way home they stopped at a patisserie so that, as Sophie insisted, they could recover from their fright. They paid with turned coins and walked away as quickly as possible. They were so hungry they ate the pastries the way stray dogs would, on the street outside their apartment, while people stared. Camille didn't care. The buttery flakes and the sweet marzipan tasted like sunbeams. After the pastry was gone, she licked her fingers, too. Her stomach filled, a sense of well-being came to her. They had the medicine they needed; Sophie had not been hurt. All of that was good. And underneath, a secret, almost painful joy: she'd seen Lazare again. She would visit his workshop in three days.

It was a far-off gleam, like a candle in a window. Waiting. Beckoning.

On the winding stairs to the apartment, Camille nearly tripped over Fantôme, who was lounging on the last step. "What's he doing here?"

"Chat méchant," Sophie scolded as she scooped him into her arms. "Naughty cats won't get anything for supper but nasty mice they have to catch all by themselves." The black cat snuggled against her shoulder and began to purr.

"Sophie." The door to their apartment stood open a hand's-width. "You didn't lock the door."

"I did." Sophie frowned. "Is it Alain? Maybe he's come to apologize." She pushed past Camille into the apartment.

The little salon was empty.

"Where is he, then?" The apartment was deathly quiet, as if the garret rooms were holding their breath. Even the light felt wrong. "Alain?"

On the table, crumbs lay scattered. Hadn't she cleaned up the night before? Ashes were heaped in the hearth, a dirty pot of washing water left to cool next to it. Surely she'd thrown theirs out. The air seemed to vibrate around her and from somewhere came that strange, insistent hissing. Perhaps she was losing her mind.

The cupboard yawned empty. "Did you eat the cheese this morning?"

"Of course not!" Sophie pressed shoulder-to-shoulder with Camille to peer at the bare shelves. "Not only the cheese, but the rest of the bread is gone, too."

The room tightened around her. "Alain came back."

"Alain might drink too much," Sophie said, "but he wouldn't have taken our last bit of food."

There was something worse he could have taken. Much worse.

Camille raced to the bedroom. There the wardrobe door sagged open. It was empty, their best dresses snatched off their pegs. The bed had been made when they left—now the bedclothes lay rumpled, straw loose on the floor. The mattress had a gash in it, like a terrible smile. On the floor in front of the little door that led to the eaves, the loose floorboard lay upturned. The key hung drunkenly in the lock.

Camille clasped her shaking hands. There was no need to fear. Not yet. Alain opening the door to the room under the eaves didn't mean anything. He still needed the key that opened the strongbox. "Bring a candle, Sophie!"

"Maman said we were never to go in there."

Camille nearly spit with frustration. "There are many things Maman told us not to do. But we've had to do them anyway. Going into this room won't be the drop of water that makes the vase overflow." Her hand trembled as she held it out. "The candlestick."

Once she had it, she stooped and went inside, holding the light up.

The lid of the strongbox was cracked open. Alain hadn't even bothered to find the key she'd hidden in a notch in the roof beams. She sank to her knees, laying her palm flat against the dusty floor to steady herself.

No money for rent.

No money for food.

Nothing, nothing, nothing.

"You're white as a ghost, Camille—tell me!"

"The money I'd been saving for the rent?" Her throat was so tight she could hardly speak. "It's all gone."

"How did he know where it was?"

Camille looked around the little room as if it might tell her. "He must have guessed, after he was here yesterday. Seen me glance in that direction—"

"Alain knew we weren't allowed!"

"That wasn't because of the strongbox. It was because of something she kept in there, to work la magie." *The burnt trunk.*

"But what will we—"

"Ne t'inquiète pas." She didn't want Sophie to worry. "I'll get the dresses back. They're worth too much to let him keep them."

Camille stood up, brushed the dust from her skirts. She couldn't bear to stay in the apartment any longer, where every empty space mocked her. She needed to go out. If she were lucky, she'd find Alain at the Palais-Royal.

If she were luckier, he'd have the money. He'd still have their best dresses, heaped on a chair next to him.

And if she were even luckier than that, she'd get it all back.

Tonight, she needed a gambler's luck.

12

Taking a deep breath, Camille joined the evening crowds
throurging the arcaded walk of the duc d'Orléans' home, the
Palais-Royal. She had no powder for her hair, nor her
pale green dress, so she made do with her second-best,
the chocolate-striped one that she could no longer fill out. Not that
anyone here would notice. This was a place where anything went. Like
his guests, the king's cousin loved a good entertainment. And like his
guests, he needed money—so he'd opened the arcades and invited everyone in. Here there was no etiquette nor police constables, only the duc's
own men and their own kind of laws.

It was a hectic carnival, a glittering city within a city. Everything
was for sale, but none of it was for her. She passed jewelers' shops

glimmering with diamonds and watches, wig shops and hat shops, a puppet theater, a troupe of ballet dancers, a lace maker whose fine work hung like webs in the window. It was said that anything could be bought or sold at the Palais-Royal: political pamphlets, pornography, pretty women. In the arcades and in the garden, aristocrats in costly silks mingled with women who wore the same clothes, only with false diamonds around their necks. In the crowd, no one could tell the difference. Gamblers and cheaters, drunks and magicians. Champagne or opium, girls or boys, cards or dice, dreams or nightmares: at the Palais-Royal, you picked your own delight—or poison.

Camille passed a darkened room where people sat transfixed for a magic lantern show. The heated lamp projected an image onto a screen: *Trappers of New France*. It showed a scene by a river. Two figures, their black hair in braids down their backs, stood solemnly on the grassy bank. The woman held a swaddling child, the man a quiver of arrows and a bow. In the placid water at their feet floated a strange boat, long and narrow, curved at bow and stern. It was piled high with furs. Enormous trees, taller than any Camille had ever seen, arched their branches protectively over the little family. They were going somewhere far away on that wide river, she was sure of it. Camille waited in the doorway for the next picture, until the barker snapped at her to pay her fee or move on. It didn't matter, she told herself. She had somewhere else to be.

Camille cut across the gardens, narrowly avoiding a man standing on a table. With his crushed right hand, he waved a political pamphlet above his head. The ink had run, it was barely dry. "Listen, my brothers, my sisters! See my maimed hand!" he shouted. "See how the masters broke it! While we die in the gutters like rats, what do the king, the queen, the nobles do? Nothing! Five hundred louis for a hat with a feather in it? Ten thousand trees planted at Versailles? And for us? Rien!" The clutch of men and women standing nearby roared and hissed. "Only when we are all dead will they care—because there will be no one left to farm their land, to clean up their shit, or to pay their taxes!"

Her father would have applauded. She could hear his ghost whisper in her ear: *See? When the taxes go up, when the harvest fails, the bread prices rise: see what happens. If we work together, things will change.*

But they hadn't, had they?

Camille knew she wasn't the only one struggling to survive. There were countless girls just like her. Girls who were caught, unfairly ensnared by husbands or fathers or brothers; girls who had no voice nor even a free moment to think what it was they might want to say or what to do. It was wrong, and unjust.

In her other ear, Maman whispered: *But you, mon trésor—you have your magic.*

What had Maman been thinking? No magic could change anything, not for long. And for the things that mattered—food in their stomachs, a place of safety—magic was as useless as a sieve to carry water.

At the far corner of the building's vaulted arcade, laughter and accordion music spilled out onto the walk. Two drunk men, their arms around each other's shoulders, stumbled down the stairs. Behind them came two of the duc's men, their hands on the pommels of their swords. They were escorting the men out. One of the drunkards was laughing so hard tears traced skin-colored rivulets down his powdered cheeks. Pushed along by the guards behind him, the other man stopped long enough to eye Camille as she tried to slip past. "Attendez, mademoiselle! Wait for us outside the gates!"

As long as she kept to herself and committed no crime, Camille had nothing to fear from them. Or so she told herself. Determined, she continued into a marbled entrance hall and ran up the staircase, her hand barely touching the banister.

If he was here, she knew where to find him.

She passed a room with blue walls where men played checkers and drank wine. Then a candlelit ballroom, where people danced: whether the girls were countesses or courtesans she couldn't tell. She wandered along a corridor full of landscape paintings hung floor to ceiling, a girl selling roses from a basket, a row of closed doors, one after another.

She heard the room before she reached it.

From it came shouts, groans, and the relentless clickety-clickety-clickety of the spinning roulette wheel. She went in, scanned the crowd for her brother's amber hair. A few people glanced idly at her, their fans flicking; none of them were Alain. A smaller room was lit by candelabras stuffed with wax candles, the floor soft with Turkish carpets. Here men in silk suits played faro, a card game so dangerously seductive it was banned by the king. It took no skill to play and each round promised a fresh chance to win. But one mistake and all could be lost. Applause erupted and someone exclaimed, *Bravo, bravo!* but Camille slipped by without looking too closely: the stakes here were too rich for Alain.

She found him in a dingy back room where tallow candles jammed into wine bottles cast a dim light over a few bare tables and wooden chairs, two of them lying toppled and broken on the floor. In the corners, uncomfortable shadows lingered along with the sickening scent of cheap wine. Her brother lay slumped across a table covered in a confetti of playing cards, as if he'd dropped dead in the middle of a game.

"Alain!" Camille shook his shoulder. "Wake up!" When he didn't stir, she shook him harder, so that his head wobbled on his arm. Damp hair stuck to his forehead, his eyes were shut tight; from his open mouth a line of spit ran to the sleeve of his coat.

"You are a pathetic excuse for a brother," she hissed at him. No response. As furious as it made her, if she couldn't wake him, she would have to go home empty-handed. As Camille prodded him again, a slight figure with ostrich plumes in her yellow hair and a sallow complexion stepped out of the far doorway. "Does he owe you, too, mademoiselle?" she taunted.

Who was this person? There was a hunger in her eyes that made Camille nervous. "What is it to you?"

"Oh, I'm no one important, bien sûr," she said, swaying closer. She wore two dresses, one on top of the other: a pale mint-green one underneath a rose-colored one. "Someone hit you?"

Camille stiffened. "Where did you get those dresses?"

The girl nodded at Alain. "He couldn't *wait* to wager them."

"They weren't his to wager! That's my sister's dress, the rose one. And mine is the mint green."

"I won them fairly." The girl gave a twirl, making the dresses dance. "He can play again to win them back, if he likes."

Alain snored on. This was a terrible place he had found himself in, and she was sorry he was a fool for drinking and gaming, especially when he had debts, but she was not going to leave empty-handed. Whatever Alain might have won by wagering the dresses was rightfully hers. Holding her breath, Camille stooped over him and slipped her hands into the nearest pocket of his coat. When her fingers touched metal, she scooped the coins out: ten livres, a few tiny sous. It was so *little*.

"Oh, that's too bad," the girl said, but she didn't sound at all sorry.

Ignoring her, Camille reached across Alain's back and into his other pocket. This one felt even emptier than the first. She shoved her fingertips into the lining, checking for any coins caught in the seams.

"Nothing there?" The girl strutted closer. "You're lucky to have found what you did."

Camille shook Alain again. She wanted to kick him.

"Dieu, he's too far gone to wake up. Besides, he's got nothing. Spent it all, foolish boy."

"If that were true—"

"Don't believe me? Ask around." As if she were a magician herself, the girl gestured in the air and a second girl, just as pale and insubstantial, slipped into the room. She wore a raspberry-pink wig, tall and frizzed. On her powdered face, one of the circles of rouge was smudged. "Tell her, Claudette."

Claudette smiled. Pockets of darkness showed where teeth once had been. "My friend Sandrine is right, mademoiselle," she lisped. "That one there's got a rich friend, and now, poor thing, he's in that man's debt. Whatever he makes—and it isn't much, for he's not the best at games, is he?—it goes to him. The *other* one."

Camille looked from one girl to the other. "Who is he? This other one?"

"You think I would tell you, even if I knew his name?" The ostrich plume in Sandrine's hair wobbled as she shook her head. "Not worth it to me. He's not kind."

"I'm not afraid of him. He's young, handsome," Claudette said, eagerly. "Wears a ring with a stone in it. Blue, maybe green? Filthy rich, of course."

"Where might I find him?" Perhaps if Camille told this rich man what Alain had done, he might help.

Claudette gave Sandrine a knowing nod. "Who knows? Perhaps he'll come by."

"And in the meantime," Claudette said, "I'll give you a chance to get your dresses back." Watching for Camille's reaction, Claudette swept up the scattered cards and deftly squared the deck.

"Those dresses don't belong to you. Why should I play to have them back?" The money clenched in Camille's fist wouldn't pay for one of the dresses, let alone two.

"That's a no, then?" Sandrine asked.

"I'll play, too, m'selle," said Claudette, pulling out a purse and shaking it so the coins clinked together. "Sweeten the pot a little." She flounced onto one of the chairs and propped her elbows on the table. "Come on! Now or never."

The coins Camille had would buy a little food. But they would not come close to paying the rent. And the rent was overdue. Alain had stolen their last good dresses and gambled them away as if they were nothing. He'd *hit* her. And whatever he'd gotten for them—he'd thrown that away, too. Worse, he was in debt to someone these girls were loath to tell her about.

Claudette emptied the contents of her purse onto the table. Four gold louis gleamed among the silver livres and sous. Sandrine flashed her pocked smile. "See?"

Camille wiped her sweaty palms on her skirt. She was certain that if she sat down at the table, she'd see the cards were marked. Foxed, or creased. A flame of anger sparked as Camille watched Sandrine shuffle the cards. As if she didn't know that someone with two good dresses doesn't wager them for a handful of coins unless they were going to cheat! She saw the knowing glances the girls cast between themselves, the smiles that crimped the edges of their mouths. They were relishing what an easy mark she would be: *That idiot's sister—coming in here and demanding the dresses, as if they were hers. As if she had a right to them. We'll take what she's got just for the fun of it.*

Camille couldn't wait to make them regret it.

13

Take off the dresses and lay them here." Camille pointed to a
chair at the next table.

"Fine." Sandrine shimmied them off, one after another, and sat back down, wearing only her chemise and
stays. "You going to play standing up?"

"What game?"

"Vingt-et-un."

It took until the third round before Camille caught Claudette. A
small pile of coins, including the gold louis, had grown in the middle.
But neither Claudette nor Sandrine had lost a single hand; even more
suspicious, their cards consistently beat hers. In front of Claudette lay
an eight and a seven. Fifteen.

"Another card?" Camille asked.

"Think about it carefully," Sandrine said.

As Camille pretended to consider the dresses, Sandrine pulled a card—a ten—from her sleeve to switch it for one of the cards in her hand. Quick as thought, Camille grabbed the girl's wrist.

"Tired of your cards already?" Camille snapped.

"This?" Claudette simpered. "I must have dropped it."

Caught red-handed and yet she'd deny it? "How dare you—"

Sandrine's eyes glinted. "Play our way or don't play at all, mademoiselle. We at the Palais-Royal have our own rules, n'est-ce pas, Claudette?"

Camille gritted her teeth. What else had she expected? It wasn't as if she could call on some authority to help her.

"If you say so." Releasing Claudette's wrist, Camille tossed her last ten livres on the pile. Her determination dipped when the coins settled, but she pressed on. "A side bet, then. I'll keep playing, but if I catch you again, all this is mine."

"Fine," the girls said in unison as they tossed more livres onto the pile. Thirty livres. Another six in the main stake, along with the three gold louis, each of those worth another twenty-four livres. Rent was two hundred livres—even if she won all of this she would not even come close—but it would be something, at least, to hand to Madame Lamotte to show that she didn't have to throw them out.

But by the end of the next round Sandrine had scooped all the coins into a pile next to her. Claudette didn't seem the least bit concerned—more confirmation that they were planning this together. Worry coiled in Camille's gut.

"We're done then, aren't we?" said Sandrine. It was hardly a question.

"The cheat stake—" Camille said, her hand closing on it.

Sandrine slapped her away. "I cheated? How, pray tell?"

Camille had no idea how the girls had done it. It was one thing to have a card waiting in one's sleeve, another to hit twenty-one like this. Camille bit at the edge of her fingernail and felt the despair well up in her. This was not just a loss. It was a staggering one. She would have to go back to Sophie with nothing.

"Ah, she doesn't know!" Claudette laughed, showing the few good teeth she had. "Go home, little fool."

The rasp of Claudette's laughter woke Camille from her fog. She was not ready to give up yet. "I won't leave without the dresses."

"Losing badly and she still wants to play," Sandrine said, scooping up the cards and handing them to Claudette. "Want to win them back, m'selle? All right. You deal."

In the other room, the roulette wheel ticked like a clock.

Camille dealt and again—somehow—the girls bested her. Sandrine had nineteen and Claudette eighteen. Either of them could win, but both would be unlikely to take a third card. Camille had an eight of spades, which lay hidden, facedown, and a ten of hearts facing up. Eighteen.

On the nearby chair lay the dresses. The pretty hems Sophie had pleated with Maman's help were already grimed with dirt. Her throat tightened when she remembered how, at the draper's shop, her mother had held a length of mint-green silk to Camille's face and nodded approvingly. *This will be like magic on you.*

She exhaled, steadying herself. To win, she needed a three. It would be easy to go over. "One more."

Claudette took a card from the deck and placed it faceup in front of Camille. The ace of diamonds.

Her blood went cold. Counting the ace as one only gave her nineteen. And with a tie, the dealer won. "Will you take another hit?" she asked.

"Perhaps," Claudette lisped. "First tell me what happened to your face. Your husband beat you? Or your father, peut-être?"

"I bet it's that lout of a brother of hers," Sandrine said. "I bet he takes whatever she makes and drinks it away. N'est-ce pas, m'selle? And if you say anything? It's like this." Sandrine smacked her fist into the palm of her other hand.

"It's not like that at all." Camille's voice trembled. But of course, it *was* like that. Her mind spun back to the clouded blankness in Alain's eyes when he'd shouted at her, the way the cords in his neck tightened and bulged, how she fell, so slowly, so slowly, the crack of her head on the floor. Her body still ached, but woven into the pain's fabric was fear: the broken strongbox, the worry that she would never escape.

"In that desperate place he is, family doesn't matter." Behind Sandrine's earlobes, dirt speckled her skin gray. "Drunk on cheap wine and laudanum, what does he care? Bah! Not his problem. I know someone who sold his daughter to get out of debt."

No.

"Or that monsieur who shot himself, remember? In the Bois de Boulogne?"

Despair and hopelessness clenched Camille's throat. Had it really come down to this, a card game? Why didn't she have the ten of spades instead of the eight? She could see it in her mind, how eight of its pips were arranged like two walls facing one another, the other two pips in the middle. Like she and Sophie, trapped.

She shook her head. "My brother wouldn't do those things." He wouldn't go that far.

Sandrine pressed her hand to her mouth in pretend shock. "You came here thinking he'd give you back everything he'd taken, didn't you? And now you think he wouldn't do worse than what he's done?" Her laugh was harsh. "I pity stupid girls like you."

"You going to hold?" Claudette said, elbowing Sandrine. "I've got eighteen, and you've got nineteen, Drine. Chances are, m'selle is under. You want the rose dress or the green?"

Blood thrummed in Camille's ears. This was not the world she wanted: dank gambling dens and pain and these girls laughing while they cheated her. Damn them to hell.

She flipped her last remaining card faceup and waited for their jeers.

Silence. Their mouths fell open.

"Merde! How is it possible?" Sandrine swore.

Next to her two red cards—the ace and the ten—lay a ten of spades. So much like the eight, but with two wonderful pips in the middle. The eight of spades seemed to have—vanished? Tentatively, Camille touched her fingertips to the ten. It felt as real as any other. But she knew it wasn't.

She had *turned* it.

Just as if it were a scrap of metal.

Quickly, she scooped up the coins, shoving them into her purse.

"Wait! One more game!" the girls shouted as Camille snatched up the dresses, hugging them close. She had staked everything and won. Her pulse jumped in her throat, keeping time with the question that raced through her mind: how? How? How? But she knew.

She'd thought la magie ordinaire could only turn coins.

Apparently it could do so much more.

The girls pushed away from the table. Claudette jabbed a wine bottle at Camille. Her voice was hard. "Sit down and play, m'selle. This isn't close to over."

"Désolée," she said, though she wasn't sorry at all. Camille backed away toward the door. "I've had enough."

Her mind blank with fear that the girls would catch her, she elbowed past the gamblers watching the roulette wheel while the croupier cried, "Les jeux sonts faits!" No more bets could be placed now. As the wheel spun, the ball slipped from its position on the rim of the wheel and began to race, red blurring into black as the wheel whispered its promises: riches, luck, transformation.

Dodging a pair of the duc's guards, Camille vanished into the crowds.

14

C ount it," Camille said as she tossed her purse on the kitchen table. The back of her dress was soaked with sweat. She'd come home from the Palais-Royal running the whole way, as if the two girls would come after her, their dirty fingers reaching into her purse to take back what they thought was theirs.

Sophie began sorting the coins into piles. "There's not so very much," she said, a tiny *V* forming between her eyebrows. "Only sixty livres. Alain didn't give you any more?"

"Alain was dead drunk," she said, wearily. "There were two girls there—"

"What girls?"

"The kind of girls who gamble with people like Alain."

Worriedly, Sophie rearranged the coins on the scarred surface of the table.

There was no use pretending, not any longer. "Alain gambled away all he'd taken from us and our dresses, too."

"He didn't," Sophie said, but the downward arc of her mouth showed she knew it might be true.

"He took all the money we'd saved for the rent." Camille paced to the window that gave out over the tilting roofs and chimneys of Paris. Down there, somewhere, was the running girl Camille had seen the night Alain pulled his knife, the girl Camille would do anything not to be. Perhaps she was safe, hiding in a hole with her crust of bread. Or perhaps she was caught, in prison, plagued by rats and cold puddles and hard, grabbing hands. Who would help you when you were brought that low? No matter how hard you toiled, you would never rise, never have enough for a safe bed, a loaf of bread, a pair of shoes. Because in every instance, the cards were stacked against you. When you were that poor, no one cared if you lived or died. Not even magic could save you then.

Fierce tears trembled on Sophie's eyelashes. "How could he think he could make money at cards?"

"That doesn't matter now. He lost." Unlike Camille, who could find no printer willing to take her on, even for the smallest tasks, or Sophie, whose work at Madame Bénard's shop earned her only a meager salary, Alain had a job. He should have been collecting a salary from the Guards, and the knowledge that he threw this away made her insides burn. "And the rent is due."

"What should we do?"

"What those girls did." They'd tried to cheat her and she'd bested them at their own game. All the way home, running along the river, she'd been buoyed by the thought of it. Her mind had built the idea, tested it, polished it. It wasn't perfect, but it was something. A chance.

"You mustn't, those men at the Palais-Royal—" Sophie's voice quavered to a halt.

"What?" Camille pretended to be shocked. "Oh, not *that*."

"What then?" Sophie's thin shoulders hunched as if she were readying herself for more bad news. "Tell me."

On the mantel sat a stack of playing cards, tied with a scrap of ribbon. Papa had made them when Camille was a little girl; she remembered how quickly he'd painted the cards, sketching the girls' faces as the queens. *What kind of queens would you be, mes filles?* he'd wondered aloud. *A beautiful and kind one*, Sophie had said. *And you, Camille?* he'd asked. *I'd be a just and righteous one who helps her people*, she'd replied, very serious. Papa had turned away so she wouldn't see his tears.

Scooping up the worn, familiar cards, Camille sat down at the table with Sophie.

"Cards?"

Camille nodded as she began to shuffle, hand over hand until the cards blurred. Years of playing with her sister and Alain had made her fingers sure and deft, the softened cards slipping through her hands like water. Playing cards and gambling was one thing. To turn the cards as she'd done at the Palais-Royal was another. Excitement throbbed in her chest—fear, too. If she couldn't get coins to keep their shape, how could she keep the king of clubs that she wanted from turning into a four of spades that she didn't want at all?

Cutting the deck carefully three times, she stacked the cards. Her fingertips rested on the top one for a moment as she tried to sense its shape and color. Absolutely nothing appeared in her mind.

Frowning, she placed the deck in front of Sophie. "I'll show you," she said, with more confidence than she felt.

Sophie sighed. "What are we playing?"

"Vingt-et-un. You deal."

Sophie dealt Camille two cards, one facedown, one faceup: the ten of spades. Then she dealt one for herself, faceup: the eight of hearts. "Hearts is my favorite suit."

"How am I not surprised?" Camille teased. Stealthily she bent a corner of her facedown card. The six of diamonds. Sixteen points in total. Even if Sophie took another card, the highest value it could have would be eleven, if it were an ace, which would put her at eighteen points. It was a risk for Camille, too. Unless, of course, she had la magie at her disposal. Determined, Camille took a coin from the small pile on the table and laid it in the center. "I'll bet a livre."

"Oh là là," Sophie said with a smirk as she tossed another livre in the center. "How high we play today." She dealt Camille another card, faceup: the seven of spades.

Merde—at twenty-three Camille was well over. She was disappointed but she mastered it: this was the moment. The precipice. She would turn the six of diamonds to a four of diamonds to make vingt-et-un.

Camille placed her fingertips on the card. "Your play."

Next to her eight of hearts and ten of spades, Sophie placed a two of diamonds. "Twenty! Can you beat that?"

Bien sûr. Her fingers on the six of diamonds, Camille cast her mind back to the Palais-Royal, the way those girls had treated her as if she were prey, Alain's slumped shape on the table, running the memories over and over in her mind until the bitter trickle of sadness welled up inside her. Holding that sorrow, she saw in her mind the four of diamonds, the symmetrical arrangement of the red pips, each little diamond in its own corner. And smiling a little to herself, she turned the card.

The *six* of diamonds.

"You're over!" Sophie crowed. "I win!" And she scooped up the two livres and set them beside herself.

Camille stared at the unchanged card. If her plan was to succeed, this could never, ever happen again. She'd imagined the card as vividly as she could. Which could only mean she hadn't brought up enough sorrow to fuel the magic. She had to try harder—hurt more—or else her plan would fail.

"Encore une fois, Sophie?"

"Prepare to lose," Sophie said as she squared the cards, shuffled them, and dealt. She started with an ace of diamonds, a seven of hearts. Camille had two elevens, one facedown. If she could turn one eleven into a face card, she'd have a "natural": twenty-one without taking a hit. An immediate, instant shock of a win.

In the apartment, the light was changing. At this time of day, Camille couldn't *not* see the dark rectangles on the walls where Maman's paintings had once hung nor the black soot along the fireplace and ceiling that she couldn't scrub away, the way that everything in the apartment had been thinned down to just one thing for each of them: one chipped glass, one cup, one plate, one chamber pot, one book. Maman had insisted magic would save them, but Papa had tried to solicit help. Not from strangers, but from people, like their grandmother, who could have helped. *Should have helped*, Camille thought, anger and sadness unfurling in her chest as she remembered her father's humiliation.

She needed a face card. *A dark knight to carry me away*, she wished, holding onto the welling sorrow as she pictured Lancelot, the knave of clubs. He resembled Lazare with the gloss of his thick black hair and the hooded falcon on his shoulder. Then she turned the card.

Lancelot's brown eyes met hers.

"Vingt-et-un!" Camille shrieked. "I did it!"

"You need not shout," Sophie sniffed. "Encore?"

Again and again they played, and each time Camille brought forth the winning card. She had it now. She practiced winning with three cards, and with two, claiming the natural four times in a row.

After the last one, Sophie slapped her hand down over the cards. "How are you doing it?" she demanded. "I thought you hated using magic."

"It's just like turning coins—nothing more."

"You're going to go back to the duc's and play cards like this? Trick people? Don't you think someone will know what you're doing?"

The knave of clubs continued to stare up at her with his unfathomable eyes.

One magician knows another, Maman had said patiently when Camille asked once again why she—and not Sophie or Alain, who tried so hard to do it—had to work magic, when it hurt so much and was so hard. *You are one of very few, mon trésor.*

But how many was *very few*? How many magicians, if any at all, were there in Paris, and what were the chances she'd be seen through?

Maman had been a magician. Her mother, Grandmère, had been, too. Was it passed through families by blood? Stung by regret, Camille wished she'd asked these questions while Maman still lived. Before, when there was still time for asking questions. Perhaps Maman would have relented and told her what she wished to know.

Camille met her sister's gaze. "I'm going to Versailles."

"The Palace?" Sophie scoffed. "You won't be able to get in."

"But at the Palais-Royal, it was easy to—"

"Versailles is not the Palais-Royal."

Camille couldn't stand the way Sophie was looking at her: knowingly, as if hiding a sly laugh. This was Sophie's forte, after all—court ways and etiquette, fashion and rank—and in her dream to eventually become an aristocrat, she'd learned as much as she could. From Maman, who'd grown up at court but renounced it all when she fell in love with Papa and his revolutionary ideals, from the courtly invitations Papa printed to bring in money, from the customers Sophie waited on at Madame Bénard's.

"But we went to Versailles for the balloon launch with Papa. And you've been there with Alain, haven't you?"

"We were only visitors then, and the private rooms were roped off, guards posted at doors and stairs. It's the home of the king and queen. The Hall of Mirrors, the gardens—there are hundreds of rooms, suites, hallways. Most of them *private*." With her hands, Sophie traced labyrinths in the air. "You won't be able to simply slip in there and play cards."

Camille didn't wish to play cards. She wanted to steal things. She wanted to cheat, and not care—take as much as she could, pawn it all, and get away from this place and leave behind the cracks in the plaster, the empty fireplace, her numb fingers, her hunger. Most of all—though she couldn't think of it without guilt—she wanted enough money to get away from her brother.

"I must find a way," Camille hissed. She was horribly gratified to see Sophie flinch.

"What about Grandmère? Couldn't she help us? I remember she let me play in her jewel box when we visited her, when I was little. She had an enormous house," Sophie said, warming to the subject. "You're certain that Grandmère is . . . dead? When Maman told us stories of when she lived in a grand château and went to court, wasn't that with Grandmère?"

"I suppose." The stories of Maman's childhood, told while she brushed their hair or tucked them into bed, had felt so real. Costly dresses, a tiny lapdog, a diamond-fretted bracelet she was allowed to wear when she was six. Beautiful stories as if cribbed from Perrault's fairy tales. But Maman had willingly given all that up when she met Papa. In the end that fantasy childhood was nothing but sweet and fleeting dreamstuff, like the fluff Alain fed Sophie now. "I wrote to Grandmère, you know."

Sophie stared.

"After Maman and Papa died. I found a letter from her, from before we were born." Camille had unearthed it at the bottom of her mother's bureau. Written in an exquisite aristocratic hand, on thick paper, the letter informed Camille's mother that since she had disobeyed her own mother's wishes and married a printer—the word underlined so savagely Camille could feel the gouge with her finger—she was to consider herself cut from the family. "I hoped she would help us," Camille said as the old hurt resurfaced, its nails still sharp.

"She said no?"

"The letter was returned, unopened. Maybe she sent it back, or maybe she's dead," Camille said, taking a shaking breath. A memory surged back: a closed door, a crowded street, her father's shattered face.

"But Alain—"

"Forget Alain! If you had seen him, Sophie—" The Alain who had been her brother, juggling plates to make her laugh, was gone. "He can't help us. He can't even help himself. The rent is overdue. Madame Lamotte said she would throw us out. Now she will. I know it. Sophie, there are girls on the street, younger than you, selling themselves in a doorway for a livre or two," she said grimly. "That cannot be us."

"Then what?" Tears hung in Sophie's blue eyes. "What will we do?"

It was easy, and it was not. "We will survive," Camille said. "I'm going to Versailles to gamble." Seeing Sophie's shock, Camille pressed on. "The man who holds Alain's debts is from Versailles. That's where the stakes are the highest, that's where people play the richest games. And there are no duc's men ready to throw me out."

"At Versailles, you must be an aristocrat—and you can't pass for one."

Couldn't she? Putting her hand to her throat, Camille pulled a fine gold chain out from under her chemise. A tiny golden key swung on it.

"Not the glamoire." Sophie shook her head. "Maman said it was wrong. Too dangerous."

Nothing was more dangerous than the path they were on. They'd first put their feet on it when Papa began to print his revolutionary pamphlets. At night, in secret. The money he made by printing invitations and cards and books for the wealthy men and women of Paris paid for all of it. And for a long time—long enough for Camille to learn how to help him print those pamphlets—it worked. He'd pulled the wool over the eyes of the aristos, and he reveled in the deception. He had not, however, expected to be seen by the Vicomte de Parte as he nailed up a pamphlet outlining reasons for abolishing the aristocracy. The vicomte told everyone. Papa's rich clients vanished without paying their bills. Then the shop disappeared. And soon after, Papa and Maman too were gone.

What Papa had done was right. It was the world that was wrong.

But she'd not walk this crooked path any longer.

She would change it, just like she changed the cards and the scraps of metal she dug from the dirt, until it no longer resembled anything she knew.

She would change herself.

15

Camille pulled hard at the lid of the charred wooden box. It refused to budge.

In the room under the eaves, the whispering was insistent, impossible to ignore.

A dark and tricky magic, Camille's mother had called the glamoire. In their magic lessons, she'd deflected any questions about the burned box. If Camille pressed her, she would say, pitching her voice so no one else could hear: *If you don't like working la magie, you will not like that at all. Stay away from that box.*

The candle Sophie carried threw strange, leaping shadows onto the walls and ancient beams of the attic space. Where the roof slanted down to meet the floor, black piles of mouse droppings lay; in the far corner, under the eaves, something scratched. Bats.

"I'm afraid," Sophie said in a small voice.

"It's just a box." It smelled of scorch and it had a kind of warmth to it that made Camille's skin crawl. But glamoire was just another kind of magic, wasn't it? Stronger, perhaps, than la magie ordinaire she used to turn cards or nails, because a glamoire turned oneself. Still, the glamoire wasn't their enemy, whatever Maman had said. She would open the trunk and see what was inside.

"But Alain didn't take it. What if he knew it was bad luck?"

"Alain knows nothing about magic." This trunk would be their escape. It *had* to be.

"If you can't open it, maybe it shouldn't be opened," Sophie cautioned. She was holding the candle as near as she could without stepping any closer.

Sinking back on her heels, Camille dragged the box into the candle's wavering circle of light. The box's surface was blistered and ridged, as if someone had shoved it into a fire and then—for whatever reason—regretted it. It had no lock, no visible hinges, only a seam the width of a hair running all the way around the top. Camille worked her fingernails under it, running them back and forth until she felt the lid loosen. As she shoved the lid up, the smell of ashes hung in the air. The hair on her nape tingled.

"Camille, I think you should close it."

"I'm not afraid," she said to Sophie—and to the box. The box remained as it was, leaking magic. "Bring the candle a bit closer, would you?"

With a little whine of worry, Sophie held the candlestick over the open trunk.

In the half-light, something glimmered: wide lengths of folded fabric stippled with gold threads. Camille reached in and pulled the bundle out. It was much heavier than she'd thought it would be, the silk threatening to slither out of her hands. And longer, so that she had to take several steps backward before it slid fully from the trunk.

"Oh," said Sophie in a hush, her hand pressed to her mouth. "It's a grand habit!"

Such a gown was worn only at the most formal court occasions. Weddings. Easter. All the important events of the court calendar. It wasn't designed to be beautiful, necessarily, but to be costly, to show how rich the wearer was.

Camille shook out its wide skirt. She coughed as dust—as well as a thick fug of magic—rose into the air. Made up in cloth-of-gold, it was embroidered with bronze ferns that twined among flowers and down the train. Camille removed a matching bodice from the trunk; between the ferns' curving leaves, crystal anemones glowed.

"This belonged to Maman?" Camille stared at the garlanded and beribboned skirt. What would her mother have done with this?

"Maybe it was Grandmère's? She lived at Versailles, when Maman was a little girl."

Camille held the dress up. In her arms it rustled, whispering. Tears in the fabric showed where the trimmings had ripped away; several embroidered garlands dangled sadly from threads. Many of the silk roses edging the hem were dirty, the train's creamy lining grass-stained.

"It looks like it's been stepped on by horses." Sophie rubbed the old silk between her fingers. "It's so old and worn, it's practically falling apart. Why ever would Maman save this?"

In Camille's hands, the skirt felt dangerously alive. As if it had ideas, memories. She blinked and they passed through her in a blur: dewed grass, the press of a man's body in a dance, the wicked flame of a candle, the black loneliness of the box. "It's la magie bibelot—magic caught in an enchanted object. I think I'm supposed to wear it."

A miniature had tumbled out of its folds and lay on the floor. It was so small she could have enclosed it between her forefinger and thumb. Set in a frame of false diamonds, a woman gazed out at Camille with blue, wide-set eyes that could have been Sophie's. Above her rouged cheeks her hair was tightly coiled and powdered, fat rubies gleaming around her neck. Her crimson lips were parted, as if she were about to speak.

"Who is it? Grandmère?" Camille said, as old resentment flamed to life.

"That's not Grandmère. Her hairstyle is a hundred years old. One of Maman's family, I suppose. Back in the time of Le Roi Soleil, Louis XIV?"

"So long ago, during the Sun King's reign? Whoever she is, she looks just like you." Camille turned the miniature over and there, in faded ink, was scrawled a name. "'Cécile Descharlots.' I can't read the title—'Baroness de la Fontaine,' I think." An aristocrat. "You think the dress was hers?"

Sophie nodded as she edged closer to the box. "They were all magicians, weren't they? Our ancestors?"

"I suppose," Camille said, slowly. Her idea of what she'd once thought la magie to be was changing. When she was little, she'd thought it was just something her mother did and something she'd learn from her, the way that Sophie learned needlepoint and singing. But it turned out to be worse than needlework, and much harder. There was so much about it she had never been taught. She imagined the world of magic stretching away from her, far into the distance, like a long shadow just before dusk.

"How beautiful it all is!" Sophie said as she peered into the box. "Can you imagine how our ancestresses lived, with all of these lovely things?"

They lived by magic, Camille thought as she removed a silver-edged mirror and a folded fan trimmed with feathers. Its plumes waved lazily, as if in a breeze. She took out a pair of curved-heel silk shoes, embroidered to match the dress. And at the bottom of the box, cushioned by a woolen cloak, lay a brooch and small makeup box, a nécessaire. Darkened by age and smoke, its lid was decorated with shepherds and shepherdesses dancing around a fountain. In the clouds was painted a Latin phrase: *Tempus Fugit*. Time flies.

Her hands clumsy, Camille fitted her tiny key into the nécessaire's lock. When it opened, it made a noise like a chime. Where fingers had brushed against it, the soft nap of the lining was worn thin. The compartments held tiny crystal jars, an ebony comb, and several brushes, including one made from a white rabbit's foot. As she touched each of the objects, warmth surged against her skin, as if she were putting her hand to a flame. With this makeup—she was certain of it—she was supposed to paint her face. To *turn* it.

The mirror had lost most of its silvering; she saw herself in it as if underwater. Or only half-there. Her startled gray eyes, the pale brows above them, the mouth her mother called stubborn, her constellations of freckles, the fox-red of her hair. She took a deep breath and watched her collarbones rise like wings, and settle. Shadows collected in the hollows of her neck and under her cheeks.

"How thin I am," she murmured. Sophie squeezed her shoulder in sympathy. "Do you remember how Maman used to tease me, saying I couldn't leave the house because my curves would make the boys follow me home?" Not anymore. Her thinness said hunger. Hunger, and sorrow. Waves of sadness lapped at her.

Bien, she told herself, *let it come.* There was no room for fear.

"What are you going to do?"

"Paint myself." Camille picked up the rabbit's foot, and, opening one of the containers, dipped it into the white face powder. As she stroked it across her skin, her freckles faded—and then vanished. Her skin became luminous, snow-white. She ran the brush along her forehead and her cheeks; her purple bruise dimmed, then disappeared. If only she'd known how to do this before she'd gone to the Place des Vosges, Lazare would never have seen her eye. Camille allowed herself a wicked smile. What if he could see her now?

Sophie gasped. "Mon Dieu."

With a thrill, Camille ran the brush along the tops of her hands, and there, too, the skin whitened, its redness fading, her cracked fingernails growing whole and smooth and clean.

"Incroyable," she said, examining her hands in the candlelight. "It's as if I've never washed dishes or scrubbed the floor." As if the lean years after Papa lost his business were themselves disappearing. She touched her palms together: her skin was so soft, like a small child's. With a narrow sable brush, she darkened her eyebrows; from a pot she rubbed on rouge.

"Not too much," Sophie warned. "Only the old court ladies still wear those big red circles on their faces."

"You know better than I do." Camille couldn't tear herself away from her reflection. "Ma chèrie, would you put up my hair?"

"I thought you'd never ask," Sophie said as she set down the candle. Deftly she gathered Camille's chestnut hair into a subtle pouf like the marquise had been wearing at the Place des Vosges. She coiled a few curls at the nape of Camille's neck. "And now for hair powder."

Sophie opened the box; a cloud of powder danced in the air. "But where's the little bellows for blowing it on? And the cone?"

Then Camille remembered: the ebony comb. In her hand, its fine black teeth were smooth and warm. As she'd done with the rabbit's foot, she dipped the tips of the comb's teeth into the powder and touched them to her hair. Instantly, her unfashionably red hair whitened to frost.

"Dieu, that's even better than powder," Sophie said, pinning a jeweled ostrich feather so it curved across the crown of Camille's head.

The cloth-of-gold dress still lay draped over the trunk's lid. Again she had the distinct impression that the whispering was coming from the dress. "I suppose I should put it on."

"Don't ask me—you're the magician."

Camille stripped down to her chemise and pulled the skirts of the cloth-of-gold dress over her hips. The whispering stopped, as if it were waiting for something else to happen.

Sophie shook her head. "Even if it weren't falling apart, you could never wear that to Versailles."

Camille spun; the skirts clutched at her feet. "I can't even walk in it! And it smells like I've been sleeping in a fireplace."

"Try these." Reverently, Sophie set the embroidered shoes in front of Camille and held out a glass bottle filled with amber liquid. Once the shoes were on her feet—only a little too small—Camille touched the perfume's stopper to her throat, then to the dress, the scent of orange flowers blooming to mask the stench of smoke.

"That's better. And now," she said, taking hold of the clothes brush, "I believe I'm to use this to turn the dress." But when she ran the brush across her dress, nothing happened. She tried again, sweeping the bristles over the fabric more slowly this time, and still—nothing.

What was it?

With a stab of unease, she realized that it had to do with pain. Or the lack of it. She'd been so pleased with her transformation, she'd forgotten. Taking a deep breath, Camille began to search her memories, traveling underground through dark, cold tunnels. The familiar ache of sadness coursed through her as she saw again Alain's grimy hand wrenching Sophie's hair, heard her own head snap against the floor.

Lace, she urged, as she ran the brush along the dress's neckline. Lace, delicate as moths' wings.

Nothing.

"Why are you being so stubborn?" Her voice was small. In the mirror, her bone-white face stared at her like a stranger's.

Maybe she hadn't imagined it hard enough. Or maybe she had to focus on the fabric itself.

Camille thought of silk the color of the sky when she first saw the balloon. Oyster-shell storm clouds, Lazare in the chariot. As soon as she thought of him—the ultimate impossibility of him—the feeling dissolved into an ache of sadness. Riding the wave of sorrow, she swept the brush from shoulder to neckline: lace frothed along it. She ran the brush down the bodice of her dress, the dress changing as if she were painting the worn fabric with ink made of sky. The hem rose and the skirts swagged up behind like a modern gown. Something like a sigh set the silken skirt rustling, and as the magic crept like searching fingers between the dress and her skin, she sensed its dark might was hers for the taking. She had only to be strong enough to let it in.

Sophie jumped up and down. "You did it! You did it! Now, who will you be? What's your name?"

Camille's eye landed on the miniature portrait with its knowing eyes. She remembered the faint scrawl on the back. "Cécile Descharlots— the Baroness de la Fontaine?"

It felt right—a name her ancestors had used.

"Why not?" Sophie bubbled with enthusiasm as she looked Camille up and down. "I can't believe it! No more freckles, no more hollows in your cheeks, no bruise. And the dress. I couldn't have designed one better. C'est parfait!"

It *was* perfect. But as the words were leaving Sophie's mouth, Camille's reflection dimmed.

"No!" The lace neckline vanished as if an invisible seamstress were ripping it out, the bronzy gold of the old dress seeping into the blue, the red of her hair flaming beneath the powder. "It's fading, Sophie! Help me! I don't know how to make it stay!"

Sophie flung herself at the box and rummaged inside. "Have you used everything?"

In the mirror, shadows rose to gnaw at Camille's cheeks. She pressed her hands to her face as if she could stop them. "What else is there? What can I do?"

Sophie held up the brooch. "What about this?"

Camille thrust out her hand. It was shaking again.

Tears of frustration pricked at the corners of her eyes. Not now. Not yet. All magic faded, but this was too soon. She didn't want to go back to the way she was before: starved, worn-out, exhausted Camille. She couldn't. There was too much at stake. Sophie handed Camille the tear-shaped brooch. Studded with the tiniest shards of diamonds, it glimmered like a real tear.

"Quick, Camille, pin it on!"

Fingers trembling, Camille unclasped the brooch. As she steadied the needle against the fabric of her dress, it wobbled and pierced her finger. Three drops of crimson blood welled up and slipped onto the fabric of her dress.

"Merde!" she swore as she clasped the brooch into place. "I've ruined it!"

But the drops of blood disappeared into the dress, as if it had licked them up.

"Look, Camille." Sophie's voice quavered. She pointed at the mirror.

Where the blood had spilled, the dress had begun to change again, its stormy blue spreading like a wave, until the fabric and Camille were once more transformed. And when she took a step back from the mirror, the magic held. She ran her hands along the dress's silky folds, touched her powdered hair. The hollows were gone from her face, the shaking in her hands stilled.

"It was the blood." Sophie shrank away, her face waxen. "That's horrible, Camille! The glamoire needs blood."

The dress was ravenous. Camille could feel its hunger, its desperation to be freed from the box. Did it sense what she was willing to give it in exchange for its help?

Camille pressed her shoulders down and stood straight. The dress responded, the bodice tightening around her like an embrace. It was somehow—pleased. All this time, it was the dress that had been whispering to her, calling her. It had known what she needed. Her new face, the clothes, her steadiness, all of it was armor fashioned especially for her. A new and perfect self.

And, if she was lucky, a new life.

She tossed her head so that the plume in her hair danced. The mirror was clear as if it'd been newly made, all its underwater blurriness gone. The girl she saw reflected in it was as sleek and hard as the diamond brooch she wore. Like her ancestors before her, she would use this dark and creeping magic to go to court, to glitter, to win.

"Dis-moi, Sophie," she said, admiring the glow of candlelight on silk. "What are a few drops of blood?"

16

Camille was determined to hate it.

The gold, the glass, the impossibly high and lavishly painted ceilings. The carpets, the chandeliers, the mirrors, the windows upon windows upon windows, each one costing a fortune, gleaming spotless in the sun. The posing statues, the miles of parquet, the dancing water in the fountains. The whole gaudy place, crawling with aristocrats who'd willingly step on her if it was to their advantage.

But she didn't. She couldn't. Despite her best intentions, it dazzled and seduced her.

She felt its pull as soon as her hired coach rolled to a stop at the edge of the enormous cobbled forecourt of Versailles, the Cour d'Honneur.

All around her, coachmen jostled for position in the flood of horses, riders, and people, on foot and in palanquins, streaming through the gilded gates and into the palace. Nobles in their finery as well as commoners in their drab, rented swords at their sides, ambled toward the palace, its every surface beckoning with gold. It was a small, shining, mazy city, where thousands of the grandest nobles lived in imposing apartments or cramped closets, all so they might be near to the king. Louis XVI was an actor upon a stage, and he and Marie Antoinette played their parts for both the aristocrats and the commoners, who could enter the palace's public rooms at will and watch the king and queen eat or take their exercise in the gardens.

Part of Camille wanted to sneak in, grab something—a costly knick-knack, a watch, a necklace—stuff it in her skirt's hidden pocket, turn the coach around, and return to Paris. The longer she stayed, the greater the danger of being found out. Who knew what they did to thieves caught in the king's own palace?

But perched at the very edge of the carriage's seat, the crowded court-yard ahead, her humming dress in her hands, her fear disappeared. *This was it.*

The carriage door swung open and a coachman extended a gloved hand to her. She pressed her fingers lightly against his and stepped out, her skirt following behind her like a mermaid's tail. And as she smoothed the silk of her gown, she felt it crackle against her hands. The wrinkles fell out of the skirts and the bodice snugged closer. The dress offered her its protection, but in exchange, it wanted to go in.

The coachman cleared his throat. "When shall I return, madame?"

A clock above the courtyard pointed its sun-ray hands to three o'clock. "Eight." That should be enough time.

The man bowed. "Oui, madame."

Camille pressed two real livres into his hand. "Don't be late."

Leaving the carriage, she joined the crowds funneling toward the entrance. A guard dressed in the white and blue livery of the Bourbon kings ushered the commoners inside, and she would have followed them had it not been for a footman who bowed and opened another, grander door. Instinctively, she swung around to see the fancy aristocrat he was admitting to the palace before she realized: he was opening the door for her.

With a rush of pleasure, she realized she'd done it. She was in.

Smiling to herself, she was ushered by another footman into the Hall of Mirrors. Before her lay an expanse of honey-colored parquet floor so long she couldn't see the end of it. Gold-framed mirrors on the interior wall spangled the room with light; sun through the windows set the crystals in the chandeliers aflame. Among the gilt busts or by the windows, courtiers stood gossiping in groups of two or three. In their silks of lavender and rose and cream, subtly whitened faces and powdered hair, the aristocrats were another exquisite decoration. The mirrors multiplied their jewels, their clothes, the men's red-heeled shoes, their swords, and the three-cornered hats crowning their watchful faces until they seemed to number in the thousands.

As the hall pulsed with flirtation and braggadocio, talk of debt and power, hairdressers and lovers and parties, the dress came to life. It trembled against Camille's skin, as if it yearned for the press of other bodies, for the click of heels on the parquet floors, for the extravagant everything that made Camille's pulse race. She steeled herself against trusting any of it. She could not let herself forget that under the glamoire, her hands were chafed red and dirt lingered under her fingernails. She could not let herself forget where she had come from just this afternoon: the scraped-bare pantry, the dizzying hunger, and only a few steps away, the running girl on the street a warning of what could come.

Taking a deep breath, she entered the Galerie des Glaces, mingling with the crowd as the courtiers contemplated her, nonchalant. No surprise, no recognition. Doing her best to imitate their disdain and the ladies' gliding walk, she passed a delegation of copper-skinned men in turbans and long white robes, a gaudily dressed French courtier prancing alongside them. As she made her way down the long room, she looked for a staircase to take her away from the crowds.

"Madame!"

Camille froze. Already? She'd been found out before she'd gotten inside, before she'd had a chance to find a card game?

An older woman approached, a bird's nest Sophie would have laughed at perched in her powdered hair. "Tell me, how long has it been?"

It's now or never, Camille told herself, as she faced her.

"Oh," said the woman, her face quickly brightening from disappointment into politeness, "I thought you were someone else!"

And she was. In the wall of mirrors, Camille spotted her own reflection among the crowd of courtiers. No wonder the noblewoman had been mistaken. In the glass, the bruised, freckled, red-haired girl was gone. In her place stood a lovely and haughty aristocrat, her skin creamy pale, her storm-blue silk dress magnificent, her ruby lips curved just as they should be. Footmen bowed as she passed, men nodding as if they knew her, until she reached the end of the room, where she found an empty staircase and began to climb, not rushing, as if she did it every day.

The hum of the crowd faded as she reached the first floor, where, on the landing, under a set of open windows, Camille stumbled onto a rumpled matelassé quilt. A wicker picnic hamper anchored one corner; scattered across it were small pink-and-green Limoges plates, half-filled wineglasses, a dish piled with blushing strawberries and pastries, a platter of cold chicken. Camille's stomach rumbled. The candles in the silver candelabra had gone out; among the forks and napkins lay an abandoned fan and a jeweled snuffbox. But there was no sign of the picnickers.

From the next floor, a man's voice drifted down to her, followed by a woman's rippling laugh; somewhere nearby, a door snicked closed.

Statue-still, her muscles aching, she waited until she was sure they weren't returning. There were so many valuables at this ridiculous picnic—who picnics on the stairs of a palace?—that she wouldn't have to search elsewhere. Imagine if she could grab the corners of the quilt and haul it away over her shoulder.

She picked up the silver snuffbox. On its lid shone a star picked out in diamond chips; a huge pearl gleamed in its center. It had to be worth a thousand livres. *Five months' rent.* With a quick glance behind her, she dropped it into her pocket. She smoothed her skirt and felt how the snuffbox hung heavily underneath, reassuring as a promise.

And then there was the food. She heard Papa's voice in her ear: *See how the aristos waste good food, leaving it for rats to gorge on!* She could even imagine herself setting type for the pamphlet he'd write, one with an etching of the half-eaten picnic. The title would condemn them all: *Nobles Feast While Our Children Starve!*

Not this child, she thought ruefully, not when these riches were laid out before her. Kneeling on the coverlet, she snatched up a half-eaten pastry and stuffed it into her mouth. A dazzling hit of sweet marzipan danced across her tongue. Next she gulped down a handful of tiny strawberries, then an herbed chicken leg, salty and rich. The wineglass had a smear of lip paint on it but she was thirsty and did not care; the strong red wine burned as it ran down her throat.

As she set the glass down, Camille heard music from upstairs. Violins singing high together. Could it be? She stood up, pressing her skirts straight. Somewhere upstairs, another door opened. Laughter spilled out—and something else. The clickety-clickety-clickety of a roulette wheel.

17

At the top of the landing was a set of double doors. One of them stood ajar. Beyond it, in a grand, high-ceilinged room stuffed with mirrors and paintings and gilt everything, aristocrats clustered around green baize-covered tables or sat in chairs listening to the final strains of a string quartet playing Mozart. The gaming tables were crowded, two rows deep, the faces of the players flushed pink with heat and excitement. Not to mention their rouge. On every surface, wax candles burned bright; between the guests, footmen strolled with trays of sweets and canapés and swaying glasses of champagne. One of the ladies gave a shout; the whole room watched as she gleefully raked up her winnings.

That could be me, Camille thought. She had only to get inside.

And then, opportunity presented itself: a couple were on their way out. Just as they were leaving, she would sneak in. No one would notice; it could not be easier.

The couple passed Camille, nodding in her direction. She dipped her head in return, slipped around them, and was nearly through the doorway when from nowhere a footman stepped forward, a piece of white paper in his hand.

"Invitation?" he said.

"I haven't got it with me," she stammered.

"For you, madame, it's no trouble; what name?" He peered at his sheet.

With a sinking feeling, Camille realized it was hopeless. There was no way to guess a name off that list, and even if he were holding it so she could read it, the chance was too great that she'd pick the name of someone already inside.

"It's nothing," she said, waving her hand as if swatting at a fly.

"No name?" Realization spread across his face. Stepping outside, he pulled the door closed behind him. "Then I can't let you in."

Merde. Even the servants had hierarchies here.

Keeping her back straight and proud, Camille crossed the landing to a pair of windows that overlooked an orangerie, where potted orange trees had been arranged among curving gravel paths. Several gardeners moved between them with watering cans. Beyond the trees glimmered a lake, hazy in the afternoon sun.

She tried to tell herself it didn't matter.

But it did. Sophie had been right about Camille's idea to come to Versailles. It was destined to be a failure. Outside, the gardeners struggled to move one of the orange trees. Under their coarse shirts, their shoulders strained.

"Showed you the door, did they?" said a voice behind her. "It's insufferable when they do that."

Camille startled away from the window. Slouching against the wall was a boy about her age, seventeen or eighteen. He wore an elegant lavender suit embroidered with silver flowers and red-heeled court shoes.

He was not especially tall, but handsome nevertheless with his square jaw and teasing hazel eyes. His pale skin and flushed cheeks made a contrast to his wavy, walnut-brown hair, which he wore faintly powdered and pulled back with a black ribbon. A dimple curved in his cheek as if he were trying not to laugh.

Distractedly, he patted the pockets of his jacket. "Snuff?"

The snuffbox she'd found lay deep in its hidden pocket. "No, thank you."

"I meant, do you have any?" The boy heaved a theatrical sigh. "I suppose the answer is no." He pulled a fat gold watch from his pocket and frowned at it. "I must run. Are you still determined to attend the Comte d'Astignac's party?"

Heat flamed up her neck. "It wasn't that—"

He lowered his voice. "I only ask because that idiot guard is plodding over to us and he's brought a friend. I believe they may throw you out." Camille was about turn around when the boy closed his fingers around her wrist. His grip was surprisingly strong. "Don't look at them."

She tried to pull away. "What are you doing, monsieur?" she hissed.

"Saving you from those wretched guards."

"Monsieur!" the guard called from behind them. "A word!"

"Come on!" Her hand in his, the boy in the lavender suit whisked her across the landing and into a gloomy hall. Endless rows of doors, portraits, damask wallpaper, and curlicued gilt sconces unfurled in front of them. "Down here! Hurry!" He raced along the parquet, holding the pommel of his sword so it wouldn't bang his leg. Camille ran beside him, the snuffbox jouncing in her pocket. Finally, he slid to a stop in front of one of the doors.

Camille pulled her hand free. Though he was charming—almost as irresistible as Versailles—she knew better than to go into a room with a strange boy, especially an aristocrat. "Thank you for saving me, monsieur. I can find my own way out."

"Those guards are slow, not stupid, and you'd have to fly over them if you wanted to get downstairs. You'd better come in. I saw the way you tried to brazen your way into the comte's party. You'd most certainly be wanted."

He'd seen that, too? "What would I be wanted for?"

"Isn't it enough, to know you'd be wanted? I must confess, it's usually enough for me."

"Oh?" What was he talking about?

"Alors, what could one be wanted for?" Rings flashing, he nonchalantly ticked off reasons on his fingers. "Treason, perhaps? Forgery? Love? Foul play? It's none of those, at least not at the moment."

Baffled, Camille asked, "What, then?"

"Cards, madame! You wished to play, and our fourth is late. He always has more pressing engagements. But tell me, what could be more important than cards?"

"Nothing, apparently." Exhaling, Camille felt some of the tension leave her body. *He wanted her to play cards. Cards!* It was just what she had been seeking and here it was, in the palm of her hand. For once Fortune's wheel was spinning in her favor.

"Bien! I see we're of like minds." He held out his ringed hand to her. "Come, we're playing lansquenet."

She hesitated. She needed a game where she could turn cards, and lansquenet was not it. Still, what other chance would she have? She did not dare to throw this one away. And whoever the players were, surely they would eventually tire of lansquenet and want another game.

"Perhaps," the boy said in an undertone, "you've come unprepared to play? Because if that's the problem, not to worry. I'll front you some livres to start."

What would a baroness say if she had no money to play? Camille realized she had no idea. "You mustn't think—"

"Oh, I hardly ever think," he said cheerily. "Though I may regret it this time. I bet you'll be a ruthless player. A veritable shark."

"Not at all. But on those terms, who could resist?"

He clapped his hands together. "Excellent! I would kiss you! But perhaps we don't know each other well enough for that? At least, not yet." He bowed low. "Étienne Bellan, Marquis de Chandon."

Camille swallowed. A marquis? So young? But what else had she expected—this was Versailles, after all. Everyone would have either money or a title. She dropped into a curtsey, willing the name she'd stolen from the portrait to glide off her tongue as nonchalantly as the boy's had. "Cécile Descharlots, Baroness de la Fontaine."

"Incredibly wonderful to meet you," he said, flinging the door wide open. "Après vous!"

18

The room he led her into was strangely made—oval, without any corners. Where corners would have been, marble statues lounged in niches built into the creamy-white walls. Gilded flowers ran along the seam where the wall met the ceiling and the floor was covered in a rose-colored carpet. Under the chandelier, in the center of the room, four chairs were pulled up to an oval table strewn with cards and heaps of coins and candy-colored betting chips. A boy in a military uniform reclined in one of the chairs, his chestnut-brown hair tied with a dark-blue ribbon; next to him lounged a raven-haired girl, her feet on his lap, lazily fanning herself. When she spotted Camille, she snapped her fan closed. "Mais, c'est merveilleux! Chandon, you are a genius!"

"I *am* exceptional, am I not? We needed a fourth, and voilà! Here she is!" He gave Camille a dazzling smile. "Madame la Baroness, may I introduce you to my friends? This gorgeous creature is Aurélie—Madame de Valledoré."

As the girl turned around, Camille froze. It was the marquise from the Place des Vosges. The one who'd been in the carriage that had nearly hit Sophie. What were the odds that of all the young aristocrats in Paris, she would be here? As before, she was dressed in a simple but unbearably rich lilac gown, her dark hair unpowdered and pinned up except for one gleaming curl that lay gracefully on her shoulder. Around her neck she wore a necklace made of three strands of pearls, the largest the size of grapes.

"You say *everyone* is gorgeous, Chandon. It doesn't mean as much when you toss compliments around like confetti." Her clever green eyes met Camille's, but there was no recognition in them. "Call me Aurélie. Thank God you've come—we're absolutely exhausted from having nothing to do."

"That's an under-exaggeration," Chandon said. "We're not exhausted—we're nearly *dead*. This handsome boy is the Baron de Foudriard," he continued, as the uniformed boy stood. He wore his regimental colors with careless ease, like a second skin. Curving across his freckled cheek, from the corner of his mouth to his right ear, was a thin, white scar, but it only added to his dashing good looks.

"Delighted, Baroness," he said with a bow. "Your timing is exquisite."

"Enough talk!" said Aurélie, shoving her skirts out of the way to make room for Camille. "Come and sit, madame. My fingers are positively *itching* to play."

Chandon sat down next to Camille and slipped her the promised money. Lansquenet was a game of luck and high stakes, and it was easy to play. Foudriard acted as the dealer and managed the keep—rows of beads strung in a box like an abacus—which was used to keep track of the cards that had already been played. At first Chandon lost and the others' stacks of coins grew. It wasn't difficult to throw a coin or two onto the pile when she had such a solid stack of them in front of her.

When play slowed, Foudriard pressed a button on the mantel that sounded a bell; five minutes later, a bottle of champagne rose miraculously up out of the floor on a dumbwaiter. The others drank and laughed, and Aurélie de Valledoré bet wildly, shouting gleefully each time she won.

Once a servant came in to lay a fire, and once the door was flung open by a pair of girls dressed as shepherdesses. One of them, pretty with a halo of white-blond hair, asked, "Have you seen Sablebois?"

Her question was followed by a nasal bleat as a curly haired lamb on a ribbon nosed its way past the girls' skirts to peer at the card players.

"He's probably at the Trianon—all the way at the *other* end of the gardens." Aurélie held out her glass for Foudriard to pour her some more champagne.

"Too bad!" the blond one sighed. "We'd hoped to find him here."

"I'm sure you had," Aurélie said under her breath. "Au revoir!"

"Yes, good-bye, then." The blond cast a longing glance at the gambling table before her friend pulled her back. With a violent rustle of silk and stiff petticoats, the girls stepped backward, their lamb's little hooves sliding on the parquet.

Chandon leaned in as the door clicked closed behind them. "Why did you tell her that?"

Aurélie's cheeks pinked. "I should help her find a husband? She never gives me the time of day. I'm not the daughter of a comte, so I'm beneath her notice."

"You've got money, though." Chandon glanced down at his cards. "Bien, she doesn't need our help. With her fortune and title, she'll marry well."

"Bah," Aurélie said. "She's a simpleton. Come, what shall we play?"

Just like that, the interruptions were forgotten and the game went on, but after an hour or so, it was as if someone had simply decided enough was enough and Chandon started to win. Each bet he placed won big, and soon Camille was nearly back to what she'd started with. She had to be more careful. The idea was to win enough to drop a purse with two hundred livres in Madame Lamotte's astonished hand, not throw it all away. "This is too much, monsieur!" she said. "We'll be beggars if your luck continues."

"Not at all. Fortune favors the brave. Flip the last card, Foudriard, and then I'll stop." Foudriard swore softly as he did so; Chandon exulted. "All mine," he cackled, pulling the coins toward him.

Aurélie threw her fan onto the table in disgust. "You've bankrupted me, Chandon."

"Hardly." He grinned, his dimple showing. "I may have taken *this* week's pocket money but there's a lot more where that came from."

"You know too much," she said as she popped a bonbon into her mouth. "One day he'll cut off my allowance, and then what will become of me?"

He? Camille wondered.

Chandon snorted. "He'd never do that."

Watching them go back and forth was like spectating a game of tennis. Desperate to say something, Camille asked Aurélie, "Do you mean someone objects to your playing?"

Counting his winnings, Foudriard seemed oblivious to what they were saying. Did Aurélie mean him?

"*Object* to playing? Who would ever do that?" Aurélie followed Camille's glance to Foudriard. "You don't mean to say—him? Foudriard?"

"I thought—" Camille stared at them all, bewildered. "Isn't he your husband?"

Aurélie burst out laughing, high like crystals clinking. "You are too much, madame! The Baron Foudriard is my dear friend, and—"

Foudriard stiffened. His gaze met Chandon's, watchful, guarded.

Aurélie hesitated. "Pardon, mes amis—have I gone too far?"

Chandon seemed to consider and then waved the concern away with a flick of his fingers. "Go on, Aurélie. I hate hiding. Besides, the baroness isn't the type to spread rumors, is she?"

Aurélie raised a daggerlike eyebrow at Camille. "It's the court's favorite pastime, isn't it? But you won't find a welcome from me if you do. Foudriard isn't *my* husband—he's Chandon's lover. Frankly, it's an injustice even to compare them. My husband isn't brave and dashing like our handsome Foudriard."

Foudriard ducked his head, a smile tugging at the corners of his mouth.

I am an idiot, Camille thought as her cheeks blazed. How could she have made such an error? Now they'd think her a fool, a bumbling girl from the provinces. She knew she shouldn't care about impressing them—she was there to rob them. But now she wished she could vanish through the parquet floor.

Chandon tried in vain to keep a straight face. "Still, Aurélie, you do have the best *kind* of husband, don't you? Isn't he a hundred years old and staying obediently in the country, breeding prize piglets or some such?"

"One hundred?" Camille's voice came out as a squeak. Aurélie didn't look any older than Camille.

Aurélie snickered, which made Camille feel only more lost. Everything she said was wrong.

"Hardly," Aurélie said. "He's fifty-four, which is quite old enough. And it's prize chickens, Chandon, not piglets. It's just a typical court marriage, non?" she said kindly to Camille. "He doesn't care much what I do, as long as he hears glowing reports of how lovely and charming I am from his acquaintances at court. If no one sees me misbehave, I can keep my rooms in the palace and my allowance."

"Your very nice allowance," added Chandon. "And lovers, if you want them. Though I assume one lover at a time is enough, n'est-ce pas?"

Aurélie mock-frowned at him before she asked Camille, "But what of your husband, madame? He doesn't like to play?"

Everyone's attention swiveled to Camille, all three of them regarding her with open curiosity. What an idiotic faux pas she'd made, to bring up the husband, and now this. She had to put it to rest. "He's dead."

"Truly?" Foudriard said, rising from his chair. "I'm terribly sorry—"

"Don't be," Camille said quickly. "It's nothing. I mean—" Worse and worse. She should have said nothing at all.

"Well, then!" Aurélie applauded, her rings clinking. "You win, madame! *You* have the very best kind of husband there is!"

Foudriard raised his glass. "To convenient husbands!"

"To lovers!" Chandon added, clinking glasses with Foudriard. As they toasted, Camille allowed herself a smile. Somehow, she'd saved herself.

"Now we know where all the money comes from. Thank God that's taken care of!" Chandon pretended to yawn. "Come, mes amis—more cards, more cards! What shall it be?"

"Vingt-et-un?" When the tide had turned against her, Camille had started watching the game closely. There were ways to cheat at lansquenet, though no way she could think of that she could do with magic. But from her game last night with Sophie, she knew that she could win at twenty-one.

The others agreed. Foudriard pressed the button and plates of macarons and strawberries came up in the dumbwaiter. The games went quickly, the betting high and fast. All the best cards came to her and she played so well she had no need to turn any cards with la magie. When the last game was over, she was surprised to see that she had more coins than anyone else. How surprised Sophie would be when Camille spilled the gold and silver out onto the kitchen table! Enough for food, rent, medicine. The near-relief of it was almost overwhelming.

Foudriard rose to light the candles. "You're not upset your luck has changed?" Aurélie said to Chandon.

"How could I be? The joy is in the game, not winning or losing." He gathered up the cards and shuffled them so fast that they blurred in his hands. "Maman always reminds me an aristocrat never thinks of money."

"I'm not too elevated to care," Camille said. *It's all I think about.* She slid twenty livres over to him. "This belongs to you. Thank you for the loan."

"It's nothing, madame. I'm beginning to see it was a very fine moment when I found you trying to trick your way into that party. But now," he said with a devilish grin, "I am going to take all your money."

"I can't let that happen," Camille said as she pushed back her chair.

A quick calculation revealed she had close to one hundred and fifty livres. Not enough for the rent, but close. Close enough that Madame Lamotte might give her more time. And then there was the snuffbox.

Chandon fixed her with a sharp look. "It's bad manners not to give me a chance to win it back." But his voice was light when he said, "Do stay for one more game."

She thought of the mix of livres and louis she had, how good her luck had been. Perhaps she might win even more? What could it hurt? The tug of the game was hard to resist, like a sweet rush of sugar. She'd play one more round.

The cards were dealt, bets placed, and play began. But it was as if, until now, Chandon had been letting her win. His pile of coins grew and grew while Camille's flattened to nothing. She kept on betting, determined to win it back. After a devastating loss, in which she'd wagered almost everything, she realized what a fool she'd been—she was no better than Alain.

She rubbed at her temples as Foudriard tried to cheer her up. "Come, come, live for today," he said consolingly as he tipped more wine into her glass. "That can't be the end—not for you. I bet you've got something up your sleeve."

She had almost forgotten.

She'd use magic to turn the cards and win it all back and more. She'd staked all at the Palais-Royal and won. She'd do it again, and savor the shock on the aristocrats' faces.

Then it would be her turn to smile knowingly. "D'accord, one more time."

The cards were dealt and Foudriard started the betting high. Chandon scrambled in his vest pocket and pulled out his fat gold watch, which he brought to his lips before adding it to the pile.

"How rich the stakes are!" Aurélie gave a little shriek of excitement. "I'll see you," she said as she pulled a bracelet off her wrist and tossed it onto the pile.

All Camille had left to wager was the snuffbox.

It was worth at least a thousand livres. Five months' rent. Or last month's and this next month's, she calculated, and then enough to move, to find another apartment. But if she used magic—and won everything on the table—not only could they move, but she could stop working magic. Forever.

She reached into her pocket, grasped the reassuring weight of the snuff-box. For a brief moment, she feared it might belong to one of the aristos. She must take the risk, though, and she must win. Quickly. Decisively. She wouldn't turn just one card; she'd do both at once, make twenty-one. And why not? She'd done it last night, over and over again with Sophie.

"I'll raise you this," she said as she set the snuffbox on the table.

Chandon whistled. "Well, well. That's much nicer than any I have."

The little snuffbox looked vulnerable in the middle of the table. While the others waited for Foudriard to decide if he was in, Camille touched her fingers to the backs of the cards in front of her. Briefly, her eyelids closed, and she stepped backward into sorrow.

The room grew distant, the voices of her fellow players muted, as if dampened by water, as she disappeared into the memory well of sadness. Back, back, her mind traveled, calling up pain. Her parents' death three months ago, Sophie's weeping face, Alain's fear and rage as he hit Camille. As sorrow wound its way through her, she imagined the cards she wanted—two of diamonds, nine of spades—and pressed her fingertips against her cards.

"Baroness?" Foudriard asked. "Will you flip your cards?"

Camille blinked. The room swelled into clarity: the flames of the candles on the table, violet evening outside the window, the half-full glasses, the glittering piles of money and jewels and chocolates, the young nobles' animated faces, waiting for her.

"Daydreaming as usual," she said in a way she hoped was self-deprecating.

Her hands trembling, she flipped her cards.

The two of diamonds and the eight of spades. "Twenty!" she breathed. Not exactly what she'd imagined, but certainly good enough.

Faster than she could think, Chandon flipped his. "Twenty-one!" he crowed. He scooped everything on the table toward him: the pile of coins, the bracelet—and the snuffbox.

"Damn." Foudriard tossed his cards on the table. "And I had such a good feeling about that one."

"Your feelings are good, but mine are even better," teased Chandon.

Camille sank back in her chair, pressed the heels of her hands to her eyes. She had failed. At the moment when she'd needed it the most, magic had deserted her. Chandon had been extraordinarily lucky.

But luck didn't hold forever.

She sat up straight, felt the bodice of her dress support her. "One more game," she said.

"Spoken like a true addict," Foudriard said. "Brava."

"You want your dead husband's snuffbox back, I'm guessing?" Chandon said cheerily. "Well, I can't say no to that." He held out his hands to take the cards.

She'd do it this time. There was no way the odds could favor him again. As Chandon shuffled, Foudriard laughed at a joke Aurélie made. Chandon was smiling, too, his hazel eyes on Foudriard, but he did not stop shuffling the cards. They hissed as they slid through his fingers, arcing and slicing. A dazzling display, like fireworks. He was about to deal the first round when Aurélie held up her hand. "Attendez—someone's coming."

Chandon said, low, "Don't be nice to him, Baroness, whatever you do."

Outside in the hall, heels clattered on the parquet. The door crashed open and a young man stepped into the room, his sword swinging from its sash. He was no longer at the Place des Vosges, where his carriage had nearly hit Sophie, but Camille would have known him anywhere. The long, aristocratic nose, the heavy-lidded, golden eyes accentuated by a beauty mark, the fair skin, the hair like spun gold: the Vicomte de Séguin.

"Damn my servants!" he said. "I'd swear it takes them several days to dress me."

"Dismiss them, then." Aurélie tossed him a faint smile.

"While you were *getting dressed*, the Baroness de la Fontaine so kindly filled your spot," Chandon said. To Camille, he added, "Do you know this dishonorable gentleman, madame? If not, we don't need to include him. We only tolerate him because of his money."

Foudriard coughed into his cravat. Camille shook her head. She didn't trust her voice.

"Your face is so very familiar," the vicomte said in a low, rich voice as his eyes flicked lazily over her face and down to her hands. "But I can't place where we might have met. You'd think I'd remember such a lovely girl." At her chair, he stooped into a bow. "At your service, madame."

"Monsieur." The less she said, the better. She tried to tell herself that even this close, so close she could see the fine film of powder dusting the planes of his face, the glamoire would protect her, like a shield. Its power was in its perfection, the subtle erasure of her freckles and the hungry tightness around her eyes, the illusion that darkened her lashes and her cloud-gray eyes, added curves to her cheeks. Still, the way he scrutinized her, as if she were a counterfeit coin, made her wish she were somewhere else. He sensed *something,* she was certain of it. She forced herself to smile when what she wished to do was to shrink back into the stiff shell of her stays.

Séguin straightened abruptly, and just like that, the line of tension between them snapped.

His thin mouth curved when he saw the pile of coins and jewels. "You play high, mes amis." Opening a purse, he pulled out a handful of gold louis, which he dropped carelessly in front of him. Camille had never seen so many, all at once.

Chandon put his mouth to Camille's ear. "Careful," he said. "Séguin cheats."

Now that Séguin had arrived, she saw what a terrible mistake she'd made to stay. He made it hard to concentrate, but the snuffbox—on top of the glittering pile—she could not leave without it. She had no choice but to trust the glamoire, work her best magic with the cards, and then leave as soon as she had even a hundred livres.

Over Chandon's shoulder, through the tall window, the sky above the gardens of Versailles was darkening to purple. It was growing late. *Too late.* With a start, she remembered she'd told the coachman eight o'clock. Quickly, she rose from her chair.

"Madame," Aurélie said, frowning. "You've spilled something on your dress. I'll ring for a maid?"

There was no maid at Versailles who could help her. For there, on the bodice of her dress, was a scattering of drops—just like spilled wine. But it wasn't wine. The dress was changing.

"It's nothing," Camille said, fear snaking along her skin. She had to go. The snuffbox—she could still feel how reassuringly it had lain in her pocket—she would have to leave behind. Taking a step backward, Camille pulled her skirts free of the table. There was more damage: along the hem of her skirts ran an irregular seam of dark gold, creeping up like mold.

"My apologies," she said quickly. "I've overstayed my welcome. It's much later than I thought."

"*Later?*" asked Chandon. "It's not even late."

"Was it something I said?" The Vicomte de Séguin mock-frowned as he rose. Chandon and Foudriard stood up, too, their swords clattering against the furniture.

"Bah, it's too bad!" Aurélie pouted. "It was so fun to have you with us, madame! And now the evening is popped, like a bubble!"

Camille's throat burned with shame. Not only had she lost the snuffbox, but if the dress's enchantment continued to fade this might be the last time she came to Versailles. She wished desperately they would all leave so she could sneak away unseen.

"Ah, it's not that bad," Chandon said, putting his arm around Aurélie. "Your special friend, the Baron de Guilleux, is sure to be playing paille maille by torchlight in the gardens. Let's join him, non?" Everyone agreed it was a fantastic idea; Foudriard blew out the candles.

At the door, Camille tried to hide her fading dress, willing the magic to hold. The boys bowed to her; Aurélie kissed her on the cheek. "Next time we won't let the boys win. It'll be you and I, invincible." Aurélie was kind, but her words did nothing to make Camille feel any better or to stop the refrain jangling in her mind: *you lost it all.*

Last to leave, Chandon paused beside her. All the amusement had vanished from his face; without it, his hazel eyes were surprisingly somber.

"Séguin takes a toll, doesn't he?"

"I'm not sure I know what you mean."

"No?" Chandon raised an eyebrow as he polished the snuffbox on his coat. "You'll forgive me that I didn't give you a chance to win this back."

Her fingers longed to wrest it from him and run. But as the others drifted down the hall and on to their next game, Camille was beginning to see another path. Another way to win. This palace might be the home of Marie Antoinette and Louis XVI and the French court, but it was also a gambling hall of immense proportions. These aristos would play any game and bet on anything.

She could see it unfold ahead of her.

If she could master the magic of turning cards, she might make much, much more than a few months' rent. She could make her and Sophie's fortune and step into a new future. She had only to be assured of another chance to play.

"Perhaps another time?" she murmured.

Again, the dimpled smile. "Of course! Still, you mustn't leave empty handed—here, take what I have left." He slipped the little box into his vest pocket and, from another pocket, pressed eight heavy gold louis into her palm.

She hardly dared breathe: there was the whole rent in her hand.

"Next time, come to the Petit Trianon, won't you? We need more people like you there," Chandon said. "We play on Thursdays."

"Oh?" She had no idea what the Petit Trianon was. Or what he meant by *people like you.*

"That's where the queen hides from old age and etiquette, bad press and debts, people who beg her for help." Chandon examined his nails. "I suppose she deserves it. After the dauphin died."

Camille had never thought of the queen like that, as a person who needed to escape—but all the gold louis in the world hadn't saved the queen's son.

"Still," Chandon went on, speaking faster as the others ambled away, "she's lonely at the Petit Trianon without anyone to flatter her, play music or cards. That's why pretty young things such as ourselves get invited. It's a select group, I might add. We're all terribly louche." A square, pink card appeared as if by magic in his hand. "This will get you in. And I can promise you money and strawberries."

Money and strawberries—and a bright, new chance to make up this loss. Those gold louis on the table, the jewelry and shiny trinkets in a pile—it'd only take a handful of Thursdays before she had all the money she and Sophie would need. To eat until their bellies were full. To move to another place. To be safe.

She reached out and took the card. "Merci."

"It's nothing," Chandon said with a quick bow. He walked away, sword swinging from its sash. "You'll have to practice, madame, if you wish to beat me!"

She had been so close. Playing at the Palais-Royal, and with Sophie, it had seemed so easy to use la magie to turn cards, but this was a new lesson: there was no guarantee.

Hanging back in the shadows, pressing her skirts to the wall, she watched the aristocrats saunter away: Foudriard with his arm slung over Chandon's shoulders; Aurélie with her right hand tucked into the crook of Chandon's arm, Séguin one step behind. Chandon made a joke and Aurélie giggled into his shoulder.

They made a pretty group, a gaggle of young nobles straight from a Fragonard painting. They were figures in a most foreign world, so unfamiliar to her it might as well be China. It had its own rules and prejudices and was filled with so many, many things they took for granted—things she'd only dimly glimpsed today. She could play, yes, and cheat, but she needed to know the rules of the game. She couldn't afford to make any more foolish mistakes. And the thought of beating them? Their pretty mouths falling open, cards sliding from their soft hands? The knowledge that this time, it would be *their* pockets that were empty? She could almost taste how sweet it would be.

She tucked the pink card into her sleeve. *Soon.*

Her dress looked as if someone had spilled bronze ink all over it. There was no time to waste.

She picked up her skirts and ran.

19

Down avenues of parquet, under jangling chandeliers, past innumerable marble rooms, Camille ran. She raced past white-faced statues and portraits of men on horseback and more mirrors than she had ever seen in her life.

In each one, she couldn't help but look.

Invisible hands were erasing the glamoire. Stubborn freckles rose up through the white on her cheeks, red hair seethed through the powder's film, the bruise purpled again. Her hairpins would no longer hold and her locks tumbled down around her shoulders. Her stormy-sky dress had completely faded to worn gold, its trims flapping loose. And each time she caught her reflection, the more the hungry hollows gaped under her cheekbones and around her throat. The bruise made her remember how Lazare had startled when he'd seen it. It wasn't just the dress and her hair—she needed to get away before anyone else could see her *face*.

The halls were empty of day-visitors; somewhere, far off, she heard the click of heels and laughter, someone shouting, "To the fountains!" From an upstairs room, a blurry snatch of music. Camille fled down a narrow stair and surprised a servant carrying a laundry basket. Through a window she glimpsed the pale rectangular shapes of the parterres and then—with a relief so profound she wanted to cry—she came to a door that opened to the outside. The footman who should have been waiting to open it slumped against the wall, snoring.

She let herself out into the cool evening. She paced through the shadowy gardens, through the park, and out to the Cour d'Honneur where the coachman would be waiting.

Except he wasn't.

There was no sign of him or his flea-bitten gray.

After scouring the courtyard, swearing under her breath, Camille pulled off her shoes and started to walk. The summer sky was growing dark, and it was hard to see what lay ahead of her on the road. Leaping aside to avoid a speeding cabriolet, she'd nearly stepped on a dead cat. She hoped that one of the fancy coaches driving past her on the avenue might take pity and stop, but none did. Not only had she lost the snuffbox, but she had also lost the illusion that she was anything more than a starving girl in a ruined gown who'd foolishly thrown away her prize.

Bone-weary and miserable, she'd walked for nearly an hour on the road to Paris when a cart, drawn by a draft horse, drew up alongside her. The horse's legs were muddy to the knees, the back of the wagon stacked with sacks of grain. The farmer held up his lantern and tipped his hat to Camille. His face was kind. "It's late to be out walking, mademoiselle. I've got daughters no older than you. Where might you be going, ma fille?"

"Paris—the rue Charlot."

"I can take you as far as the Hall des Blés." The farmer pulled his horse to a stop and patted the bench beside him. Grateful, Camille took his rough hand and swung up, tucking her skirts around her legs.

"Merci, monsieur. You're heading to Paris to sell grain?"

"Barley—and some wheat," he added in a low voice. "I put *those* sacks underneath; no need to advertise it. Wheat's like gold to people and I'm liable to be robbed. Or accused of hiding it to sell to the rich. Not sure which is worse. My friends say I'll be rich, too, with wheat prices climbing to the sky. But I don't like it. I'd rather get less and not be afraid."

"People would steal from a farmer?"

He shrugged his big shoulders. "Can you blame them? Criers on the streets shout that aristocrats make cakes from wheat and children's blood. They don't know any better."

"Those things—they aren't true." Papa had printed provocative pamphlets but nothing like that. The rule, he'd said, was to explain, not inflame.

"Bien. You and I know that," he muttered. "But when people don't know what's really happening, rumors start. And that's when you've got to be careful." The farmer reached behind him and pulled out an empty sack. "Wrap this around yourself, mademoiselle. You've hardly got any clothes on."

The old court gown had a deep neckline, she remembered with a twinge of embarrassment. She tugged the sack around her shoulders.

"You work at the château?"

She shook her head.

"I suppose if you did, you'd know better."

"Know what, monsieur?"

He gave the reins a shake. His hands reminded her of her father's: strong, capable. "Girls shouldn't walk along the road so close to the palace. I'd never let my own daughters flounce around Versailles."

"Oh?" Imagine if she told him what she'd just done. "Why is that?"

"Good thing I'm here to tell you."

"Go on, then." Camille settled against the rough board that served as a backrest. From her shoulder she unpinned the diamond brooch and slipped it into her pocket with the eight gold louis and the card Chandon had given her.

"First the men. All they want is . . ." he said, ticking off on his fingers a list of all the things they wanted that put young girls like her in peril. Camille rubbed her neck. The rolling of the cart and the farmer's comfortable voice made her limbs heavy. She felt as if she'd been awake for days. Now that the glamoire was gone, her body was becoming her own again, thin and shaky. The dress's troubling aliveness was fading, as if it too were tired, ready to sleep.

"And the ladies?" Camille asked.

"They'll wear you to the bone with all their demands, the fetching and carrying. Even if they give you their castoffs." The farmer frowned pointedly at her tattered gown. "Be on your guard, mademoiselle. Rakes and hooligans, all of them, in that château." He waggled a dirt-caked finger at her. "You never know what they might do."

"C'est vrai." You never knew. She'd gone to Versailles hating the nobles for their riches, their arrogance, the way they believed France and its people existed just for them. To serve them, or to crush if they chose. Certainly that was what Papa would have seen, tonight, in their manners and their idle games. But—and she was suddenly glad that Papa had not seen this—she'd liked the play and the players. It was an uncomfortable feeling.

She did know, however, that when she got back to Paris, before she snuck into their apartment on the rue Charlot, she'd count out the louis in her purse and slide them under Madame Lamotte's door. One month's rent, one month's more time.

It was already very early on Tuesday morning. Tomorrow would be Wednesday, the day she'd been invited to the aeronauts' workshop. It had been less than a week since she'd met Lazare. She thought of how, after she'd agreed to come, he'd walked away backward, smiling. A promise.

Above Paris's western gates, the evening star glinted like a silver coin.

20

Camille woke halfway through the afternoon to find Sophie poised at the foot of the bed. Waiting. When she started asking questions, Camille flung her arm over her eyes and begged for coffee. Sophie huffed that Camille was developing very refined tastes but agreed to go, taking with her a hat she'd finished trimming to Madame Bénard so she could get paid. The apartment was quiet, Camille's only company Fantôme, a black comma curled on the wooden floor.

She felt under her pillow for the two pieces of paper she'd hidden there. On one she'd inked the address of Lazare's workshop and a day: *Wednesday*. Tomorrow. The promise of that day was like a louis d'or, gleaming in her hand.

The other was Chandon's pale pink card. A pass into fairyland.

Camille jumped when the door swung open and Sophie came in, a fist-sized bag of coffee in the crook of her arm. "I must say, you look terrible."

"How kind of you to say that. I feel as if I've been run over by a dray wagon."

"Is it the glamoire?"

"A little." Camille dragged herself out of bed and dropped into the good chair. "It was a long night."

"I'll boil the coffee," Sophie said, "if you tell me what happened. Immédiatement."

When the coffee was ready, thick as tar and nearly as sticky, Camille gulped it from the chipped cup. She told Sophie about the gold that shone everywhere, so much of it she wished to pry it off and sell it. She described the lavish costumes of the courtiers and the plainer clothes of the visitors, the marble stairs that led to the abandoned picnic, the food that had been left behind, the snuffbox, and impulsive Chandon, dragging her into the game.

"What was he like?"

"I hardly knew what to think at first," Camille mused. "He has a quick wit and pretends he doesn't care about anything. But underneath, I think he does." She thought of him pressing the gold louis into her palm so she could not refuse them, the way he'd persuaded her to come to the Petit Trianon, as if he knew she needed another chance. "And his lover the Baron de Foudriard is a cavalry officer. He certainly looks the part—tall and handsome, with a scar. You'd think he'd be formal and severe, but he's soft-spoken and kind."

"His lover is a *he*?"

"And what of it? The boys were more in love than the girl was with her husband."

"And who was that?"

Camille relished Sophie's surprise when she told her that the aristos from the carriage in the Place des Vosges had been there, too, and she related what she'd learned about Aurélie and her old husband and his chickens.

"And the vicomte?"

"The others don't seem to like him very much." She recalled Aurélie's barely-there smile, Chandon's jest about the Vicomte de Séguin's wealth. "I was terrified he'd recognize me."

"That's impossible. You were nothing like yourself—"

"You're full of compliments this morning," she said, a little hurt. But wasn't that what she'd intended, after all: to reinvent herself? On the floor by her feet, Fantôme's paws twitched in a dream.

"And the snuffbox?"

"Gone," said Camille miserably.

Sophie slumped back in her chair. "What about the rent?"

"As it happens, I came home with eight louis, which I gave to Madame Lamotte before I went to sleep." She allowed herself a look of triumph.

"That's fantastic!"

"We've still got nothing to eat." If she'd only taken some of the forgotten picnic home with her. There was nothing for it—she would have to turn more coins. Camille cleared her throat. "I'm going back, you know."

"Alone?"

"How else?"

"You might take me," Sophie said wistfully. "I might wish to go."

"Absolutely not." She couldn't keep Sophie safe on top of everything else.

"Don't tell me it's because I'm ill. I'm getting better, little by little. I'm almost well again."

Sophie was still too pale for Camille's liking. And only better food would help that. "It's not that—"

"I would be so good at it! How I would love to be there—"

"It's not a party!" Camille picked up her cup, irritated to find it empty.

Sophie scowled. "It certainly sounds like it. It's not fun to be the one who's left behind, you know."

The hurt and the envy in Sophie's voice tugged at Camille. This was, after all, the life Sophie had always imagined for herself. But what if something happened to her? On her deathbed, before fever rendered her senseless, Maman had entrusted Sophie to Camille's care. *Whatever you do, take care of your sister.*

She clasped Sophie's hand. She didn't wish to quarrel. "Forget Versailles. Everything will be so much more fun from now on. We'll have new clothes and plenty of food. Once we have enough, I won't have to work magic." The thought was a profound relief. "Then we'll go out in an open carriage at Longchamps, we'll drink hot chocolate and wear furs and whatever else you want."

"Even in summer?" Sophie said archly.

Camille kissed her sister's hand. "As you wish. And we'll move. To a nicer place, with bigger rooms." A safe place with no forwarding address.

"Without Alain?"

It felt like a test. She steeled herself. "Without Alain."

Sophie sat still for a moment, her face keen with thought. It lasted only a moment before she nodded. "When will you go?"

"The day after tomorrow. They play on Thursdays."

Sophie squeezed Camille's hand. "And tomorrow's the workshop."

21

Camille hesitated, then rapped on the cobalt-blue door of the large building.

No answer.

She'd woken too early that morning, her head burdened with dreams. In the last one, Lazare's balloon descended from a stormy sky, but the boy in the gondola wasn't Lazare but the Vicomte de Séguin. As his spyglass swept a circle over the ground, she fled. She didn't want to be seen. Clawing with her fingers in the black dirt, she dug a scrape to hide in, like a desperate rabbit. The balloon sailed right over her; but whether the vicomte saw her or not, she did not know.

Next to her, Sophie slept on, Fantôme rounded against her stomach.

Careful not to wake her sister, Camille wrapped her shawl around her shoulders and slipped out through the window to clear her head. From the tiny slant of roof, the streets of Paris mazed out around her. When she'd been up here last, she'd been looking for Lazare in the air, hoping for something to change. Now she knew he was somewhere in the streets below and change felt closer than before. The address he'd given her put the workshop not too far from the rue Charlot, though she couldn't pick it out from the mass of tilting roofs and crowded houses.

It was still early when she left. Sophie was fussing too much about Camille's hair and wanting her to wear the mint-green dress she'd rescued from the girls at the Palais-Royal. The lace on the hem needed cleaning, but Sophie argued that it would have gotten dirty anyway, as Camille was not planning to take a carriage, was she? She wasn't, of course. As she'd settled her wide-brimmed straw hat over her hair, she sighed at the bruise over her eye. It had faded to violet, tinged with yellow and green, but it was in no way *gone*. Camille stuck out her tongue at her reflection.

Walking past the Bastille, the old prison, she made her way through morning crowds, keeping toward the river. She stopped to ask a grocer's boy where she could find the rue de la Roquette. Following his directions to take a left at the next corner, she found herself suddenly in a familiar street. Straight in front of her was the building where Papa had housed his printing shop. It seemed forever since he'd sold off everything, including the press, but now, as if in an unsettling dream, the storefront was once again a printer's shop.

The sight of it was a physical hurt. It radiated through her, leaving her stunned. Lost. How could the shop still exist, without Papa? Without her?

She crossed the street and pressed the tip of her nose against the window. The shop hadn't yet opened but inside the printmaker and his apprentice were hard at work, the apprentice setting type by the light of several candles, the printmaker leaning on the press handle to print the sheets. Overhead, from the same hooks she and Papa had used, hung lines of printed sheets, drying. If not for the aristocrats who'd betrayed Papa as easily as they threw away their gloves, she'd be in there, with him, printing. Maman would be alive.

The apprentice saw her. He started to come to the door, wiping his hands on his apron, but Camille shook her head and moved down the street. The dream-spell shattered. That life was gone. But she hadn't managed to snuff out her hope that she might somehow do it again. Every day, reasons to keep printing confronted her. The terrified running girl with her stolen bread, the skeletal paupers picking through horse dung for food, the pain that poverty scratched into all their faces. Those were the good reasons to have enough money to start a press: to tell their stories. Darker, much deeper than that was the righteous revenge she wished to wreak on the aristos Papa had been obliged to bow to. The ones that had ruined everything.

Approaching the well where she was supposed to turn again, Camille imagined telling the aristos she'd met at Versailles that she hoped someday to become a printer. *A printer of what?* she could hear Chandon asking. *People's thoughts,* she'd answer, *the truths they want to tell the world.* Chandon would wonder why she did not just do it, then, if she wished it—as a pastime. And she would answer, scornfully: *Because of* your *people.*

Standing in front of the big blue door, biting the edge of her thumbnail, Camille wondered if she'd remembered the address correctly. She knocked again, louder this time. From deep inside the building, someone shouted. A clang of metal rang out. Another clang, and a thud. But no one came. Camille tilted her head to better see the faded letters painted across the building's façade: L'École de Dressage. A horse-riding school? Glass ran across the top part of the door, but someone had rubbed hard yellow soap across the panes to make them opaque. She scratched at it with her fingernail. It didn't budge.

Just as she was wondering where the aeronauts might be, the door swung open and Camille fell forward, catching herself against the doorjamb.

"Mademoiselle!" Charles Rosier beamed. His curly hair was covered by a strange hat, slouched like a nightcap, and in his hand he held a curved pipe, unlit. "You did in fact decide to come."

"Didn't I say I would?" Now that the door had opened, now that she was actually going to go in, she felt a little sick. What if, when Lazare saw her, he realized he'd made a mistake?

"Lazare wasn't sure." Rosier blinked at her. "You're perfect."

"How?"

"To be the heroine of this story, of course."

"I told you before—I'm no Jeanne d'Arc, monsieur."

"Bah! Does anyone know what their future may bring?"

Camille crossed her arms. "I don't believe in fate."

"Oh?" Rosier sucked thoughtfully on his pipe. "Who said anything about fate? We make our own futures, non?"

"It's true," she said, relenting. "Monsieur Rosier, may I come in?"

"As long as you don't call me 'monsieur.'" He stepped back as she entered. "Here I am, philosophizing and you're on the doorstep. I'm rude, rude, rude—I know it. Lazare tells me all the time. It's my English blood." He waved his pipe in the air. "Mother's side. Come along." He led her into a tiny corridor with sawdust on the floor. A large barn door hung at its end. "This way." In an undertone, he added: "Lazare's been waiting for you. I swear, he's checked the calendar every morning since he saw you. Counting the days. But don't tell him I told you or he'll finish me off."

"Pardon?" she asked, incredulous. He'd been thinking of her? All these days, just as she had?

Rosier winked. "Don't mind me. It's my role in life to exaggerate."

The creaking door slid open to reveal a vast, high-ceilinged room. It was an old riding ring, with a viewing stand trimmed with faded bunting and full of something that looked like furniture. Where the ceiling met the wall ran a row of clerestory windows. They were dusty from years of neglect but let in enough light. Pigeons nested in the rafters, cooing and occasionally startling across the empty space. Tables of different sizes stood haphazardly on the dirt floor, paper littering their surfaces, as well as large felt-lined boxes of instruments, their lids splayed open. All of this Camille could have imagined, based on her father's shop and his various inventions. But she hadn't imagined a group of older women, mobcaps covering their hair, sitting at a huge table in the corner, sewing together long pieces of fabric. One of them tsked loudly at Camille.

She flushed and pretended to be invisible. And in turning her back to the seamstresses, she saw Lazare.

He was standing by one of the long tables. He wore no coat over his vest, only a white shirt underneath, open at the neck. He was not looking at the drawings scattered on the table beside him but up, through a spyglass, at pigeons resting in the rafters. With his left hand, he scribbled notes on a piece of paper, not taking his eyes from the birds. The rapt way he looked at the ordinary pigeons, as if there were nothing in the world that was beneath his notice, made her smile. It reminded her of the way he'd looked at her when they'd stood by the balloon's chariot. As if she were the only still point in a spinning world, the only thing that mattered.

Rosier cleared his throat. "Look who's come to pay a visit."

Lazare lowered his glass.

His face changed when saw her; she felt his recognition like a stab of joy.

When she'd been up on the roof on the rue Charlot, hoping for a glimpse of his balloon, she'd never truly believed she would see him again. When once more he appeared out of thin air at the Place des Vosges and invited her to come here, she'd feared it was to be kind, because of her eye. She'd even worried she would come to the workshop and it would be closed. Or the address would be wrong. It was hard to hope when things hadn't gone well for such a long time. And yet, here they were, she and Lazare, standing in this strange room, dust motes dancing overhead. It was suddenly beautiful to her.

"Et voilà," Lazare said, beaming. He grabbed his coat from a chair and shrugged it on, apologetic. "We're a bit informal here, as you can see. The ladies don't seem to mind."

Camille guessed that they didn't mind at all.

Lazare bowed low, adding an elegant flourish of the kind she'd seen the courtiers use at Versailles. "Would you like a tour, mademoiselle?" He stepped next to Camille and for a moment she thought he might take her hand. He didn't—probably worried she'd hide her hands as she'd foolishly done before.

Rosier trailed after them as they walked. "Wait until you see what we've been doing," he said. "C'est magnifique! And why shouldn't it be? Aren't we living in a time when anyone might try his hand at anything?"

Maybe we are, Camille thought as Lazare stood next to her, so close that his sleeve brushed hers as he pointed out how the seamstresses shaped the rubberized silk that made up the balloon's membrane. The women beamed at him, called him their brave boy, but had only frowns for Camille. She could guess what they were thinking—a girl among all these boys—but she didn't care. Not now, standing here with him.

When she asked Lazare what was in the jumbled heap in the viewing stand, he sighed. "Do you truly wish to see? They're the worst."

She did. The winglike oars poking out of the heap had been intended to help with steering, he told her, as had two rudders, one the size of a small boat's, the other bigger than Camille.

"What's wrong with them?" she asked.

Lazare squinted at the strange machines as if trying to see them better. "They're all mistakes. I have a book by Leonardo da Vinci that shows how water is full of currents. We thought we could steer through the air the same way." He shook his head regretfully. "Absolutely wrong." He gestured at an object that resembled a miniature windmill. "And that one's called a moulinet. It's supposed to help with navigating the air currents. That didn't work, either." Lazare rubbed his forehead as if just thinking about them gave him a headache. "Failures, every last one. You must think me a fool, mademoiselle."

"Hardly." She thought of all the botched prints she'd made when she first worked as her father's apprentice, the ones that became fuel for the stove—or folded bagatelles—once she'd ruined both sides. "I did the same when I first learned to print—"

"You print? Paper?"

Camille bit her lip. Having just passed the shop, it was more in her mind than usual, but also more fraught, like a hole in the ice she didn't want to go too close to. "I did, before. My first attempts were worse than any of those windmills. And I was just trying to do something that had already been done! I wasn't inventing anything." What she'd wanted to say was getting away from her, now that he was looking at her so intently.

"Everything here was intended to make the balloon better, somehow?" she asked, hoping to turn the conversation.

Lazare nodded at the pile of balloon parts. "Sometimes it seems rather hopeless."

It was a familiar thought. The constant effort, and then, when it was finished, the realization that she was no further along than she'd been before. "Why, then? I understand why you need to add a release valve and learn how to steer the balloon. But after that—what will you do with a better balloon?"

"People asked the American, Benjamin Franklin, the same question," he said, thoughtfully.

Papa had told her about America's former ambassador to France, who'd been a printer like they were. "And Monsieur Franklin said?"

"It doesn't matter what it's used for. It can just exist. I like that, don't you? Not having to *be* something?" A dreamy smile tugged at his lips. "I'd fly away, of course."

It was as though a hand squeezed her heart. "Where would you go?"

"Over the Alps," Lazare said, watching her expression. "Can you imagine? To fly above Mont Blanc? To be so high?"

Camille thought of the view of Paris from the much lower roof of 11 rue Charlot, laid out below her like a map, like something that might finally be known. "How much you would see! Or perhaps," she teased, "it would be only snow and ice."

"It wouldn't matter. For me, at least, it's about the flying." He nodded at the pigeons roosting in the rafters. "As it is for my friends up there, who are born knowing what I'm desperate to learn."

"They can fly," Camille said, "and yet—"

Rosier cleared his throat. "They just sit here cooing and crapping."

"But they *could* fly away, if they wished," Camille said.

"Perhaps." Lazare fiddled with a loose button on his coat.

"There's one thing you've missed," Rosier said, as the birds murmured above. "Pigeons don't need money to fly. Aeronauts do."

"But you have the balloon already," Camille said. "What else do you need?"

"I'll tell you." From his pocket, Rosier produced a notebook and flipped through it until he found the page he wanted. "Et voilà! A new balloon means—everything new. A bigger balloon, sewn by the ladies. Bigger basket. Maybe even a new kind of air, Armand tells me, such as *hydrogen?* Who knows what it will take to Ascend the Immeasurable?" He snapped the notebook closed. "The point is, it is going to take a lot of louis and livres that we do not have."

A familiar problem. "And how will you get them?"

Lazare looked sternly at Rosier.

"Sell tickets! Let the public watch!" Rosier jabbed the bowl of his pipe at Lazare, then waved it angrily in the direction of the table where Armand sat. "But no one listens."

"Ah, poor Rosier," Lazare said, gently. To Camille he said, "We can't seem to agree on this—yet. But we're not a circus, are we? Astley's Marvelous Aeronauts? We're natural philosophers. Explorers."

Papa had believed in a kind of honor in only printing what he liked. "My papa was the same way."

He would have loved to see the aeronauts' workshop, she knew. The gleaming measuring instruments in their cases, the scribbled papers and plans, the failed experiments on their way to becoming successes, the oddities, the seamstresses' hands like determined birds swooping over the silk.

With a sudden pang, she realized: she missed all this. Time working together in the print shop with her father. And at home: her father sitting by the fire in winter or by the open window in summer, after supper, folding the paper bagatelles. *I am testing a thought,* he'd say and invite her to come and watch, or to help him crease a fold with her little fingers. It was a kind of companionable work that was nothing like working la magie.

Camille saw from their somber faces they'd figured out that Papa was dead. "I shouldn't have—"

"Not to worry, mademoiselle; fathers are always problematic. Lazare here, for example, wishes his father—"

"Enough, Rosier, or I'll ban you from the premises." Lazare gave Rosier's shoulder a shove. "Come, I'll show you what Armand's doing."

"Wait, I also have something I'd like Mademoiselle's ideas on," Rosier said, but he stayed where he was. Apparently his feud with Armand continued.

On the other side of the workshop, Armand sat at a long table. He half-lay across it as he scribbled rows of numbers next to a complicated diagram.

"What are you calculating?" Camille asked.

Armand didn't look up, just crooked his shoulder so it hid the drawing from her. "A better balloon."

"The Next Best Thing," Rosier called from the other side of the room.

"I won't steal your idea, you know." Camille desperately wanted to see the drawing but there was no way she was going to give know-it-all Armand the satisfaction of asking.

"Show her," Lazare said, tugging at the sheet of paper. Armand kept his elbow planted on it but let Camille see.

The paper was covered with numbers written so rapidly the ink had blurred as he had calculated the figures, changed a variable, and then recalculated, over and over again. Arrows pointed from the clusters of figures across the page to drawings of two balloons: one that, with its stripes, resembled the balloon Camille had seen; the other one was slightly smaller, with a more rounded top.

"You're building a different kind of balloon?" Camille asked. "For the Alps?"

"We are," Lazare said, slowly. "The first balloon—the one you rescued—is a hot-air balloon. This one," he said, tapping the drawing of the smaller balloon, "is a hydrogen balloon."

"Is it better?"

"Good question," Armand said, reluctantly. "The balloon would be smaller, because the air—which we would make here, in the workshop, before bringing the filled balloon to the launch site—can get much hotter. And you don't need to have a fire in the chariot, or fuel. You can't, in fact. You'd explode. But it's less easily controlled. I'm not sure it can sail the Alps, as Lazare wants to do." Armand stared at her through his smudged glasses, as if daring her to ask another question.

"Imagine sailing over the snow-topped peaks, Armand! But as Rosier said, it takes money." Lazare smiled ruefully.

"Speaking of money," Rosier said, "I have been trying to convince Lazare that a poster will not ruin our honor nor create any difficulties. As a printer, I'd like your opinion." From a table he grabbed a sheet of paper where he'd sketched the poster's layout, with the words TRIP TO THE HEAVENS marching across the top, the balloon's gondola at the bottom. "What do you think? Your professional opinion?"

Camille took a breath. It was awful.

"You don't like it?" Lazare asked her, hanging on Rosier's shoulder.

"It's just—the way it's arranged could be better. If you put the balloon at the top, there? That gives a feeling of space. If your printer could do it, the title could even curve around the balloon. But if not, you put the words here," she said, pointing to the left side of the page. "That's where the viewer's eye will naturally go—after looking at the balloon, of course."

Both boys were staring at her. "What?" she asked. "You don't like the idea?"

"It's not that at all," Rosier said. "It's perfect. I'll take it to the printer's now and get them started."

The ladies looked up from their sewing. One of them tsked again at Camille.

"I suppose I should go, too," Camille said, though she didn't wish to.

"Au revoir," Armand called from the desk. He didn't want her here, either. And Lazare? The time had passed too quickly, but as he walked with her to the door, he said nothing about her staying longer.

"Au revoir, then," Camille said.

Lazare leaned against the doorjamb, his face thoughtful. "Thank you for coming, mademoiselle. I hope you enjoyed the tour of our failures. Or our dreams, as Rosier would call them."

"They are your dreams, and I love them. It felt like home here, a little. Which is nice, especially," she added in a rush, "when one's home doesn't truly feel like home." Instantly, her cheeks flamed hot: why on earth had she said that? She was making no sense.

His long, elegant fingers had found the loose button and this time, he snapped the thread and twisted the wooden button free. He spun it in his fingers, around and around. "That's a kind thing to say about a bunch of failed experiments taking place in an old riding stable that still stinks of manure."

Camille laughed. "You're quite welcome. Adieu then, monsieur." She put her hand on the doorknob. She didn't want to go but she couldn't think of anything else to keep her there.

Suddenly the button spun out of Lazare's fingers, hit the floor, and rolled to a stop by her feet. Camille stooped to pick it up.

"I've got it," said Lazare, dropping to his knees next to her.

So close.

Camille scooped the button off the floor and held it out. As he reached for it, the tips of their fingers touched. The shock of it was like grazing her fingers against a hot stove. He was so improbably close, all tawny skin and black lashes over his impossibly brown, gold-flecked eyes. For an unbearably long moment, they held hers, while she tried to remember to breathe, and then he was standing, his hand under her elbow, helping her up.

"I should be going." Before she made an utter fool of herself.

"One moment—mademoiselle?"

Camille stopped. Waiting. "Yes?"

He lowered his voice. "Your bruise—you've had no trouble since? With the person, I mean?"

She pictured a drunk Alain, slumped over the dirty table at the

Palais-Royal, her money gone and her dresses in the hands of those filthy girls. "Not at all."

"Grâce à Dieu." He sighed. He tapped his fingers distractedly on the doorjamb. "There's something else. I've been thinking of a way to thank you for saving the balloon. And for saving me, and Armand, of course, though sometimes I wonder if he's worth saving. In any case. There's something I have in mind."

"Oh?" Camille's heart started thumping ridiculously again.

"It's a surprise."

Secrets were heavy, unruly things. But it was impossible to resist his smile, the way one corner of his mouth rose higher than the other. "I'm intrigued."

"Where shall I find you, when it's ready?"

She winced. Once again, the thought of Lazare Mellais coming to their bare apartment on the rue Charlot was unthinkable. That might very well undo this new thing, as if the shadow of her life were to spill into this sunlit space. "Might I come here at an appointed time, instead?" she asked. "Wouldn't that be easier?"

"Absolutely not," he said, as charming as ever. "I'll come for you in a carriage. Tell me your address." He looked at her, expectantly, as if this were the most normal thing in the world.

She felt the precipice ahead of her, her toes on the edge. She could say it wasn't possible. It would be easy to curtsey and smile and mumble something polite about having to go, or perhaps another time, and escape into the street. She'd be safe.

But that was the rub. The hesitant, shimmering feeling of *what if.* Like a playing card that hadn't yet been flipped to reveal its face. A gift that hadn't been opened. She wanted to reach out her hand and take it. But what if she missed?

Lazare's smile faltered. "I promise I won't lurk outside your door." He seemed to be struggling with something and it made Camille feel better. Less alone in her fear. Less *outside.*

"Listen, mademoiselle," he said, "despite the awkward thing of almost crashing the balloon, I am fairly reliable." He put his hand on his heart. "I swear."

He was so vulnerable in that moment her fear disappeared.

"The tall house with the gray door in the rue Charlot, number eleven." And before he could say anything more, she opened the door and went out into the street.

22

When Camille stopped in at Madame Bénard's to tell Sophie how the visit to the workshop had gone, she did not get a warm welcome. Ushering Camille away from her wealthy clients as if she might dirty them just by being in the room, Madame informed her Sophie had already gone home. Camille couldn't believe it.

"Oh, but she has! She finished her work—What speed! What delicacy! What fantasy!—before leaving with a young man. Not a client, bien sûr, someone else." Madame Bénard raised her eyebrows meaningfully. "Or maybe a brother?"

Impossible, Camille thought as she let the door swing closed behind her. Sophie would have told her if she had seen Alain, or met someone.

Wouldn't she? A year ago, yes. Camille was certain of that. But now? She didn't know. Not to a certainty. Two days ago, when they'd talked about Alain, Camille had the creeping sensation that Sophie didn't look like her sister at all. In the way a mirror can be tilted to show another part of a room, Camille had looked at her sister and seen someone else. Someone *different*.

But when Camille ran up the stairs and through the door, Sophie was there, her golden hair spilling loose around her shoulders, her feet in their cotton stockings up on the chair, an enormous silk chapeau in her lap. "How was it? Tell me now!"

After Camille described what had happened and was crossed-examined about every detail of expression and conversation, Sophie shook her head wonderingly. "It's like something from a fairy tale."

"It is not," Camille protested. As if good things happened only in stories. "Lazare is nothing like a prince and I am nothing like a princess."

"True," Sophie mused. "Maybe it's a different type of tale. You're more like the pathetic little sister, sorting flax seeds while blind or some other impossible task."

"Lest you forget, I'm the older sister."

"That doesn't mean you know everything." She set the hat aside and fixed her eyes sternly on Camille. "For example, how will you succeed tomorrow, at the Petit Trianon?"

"As I showed you. I'll use la magie to turn the cards."

"I meant in terms of the Rules of the Game."

"I know the rules to every card game there is."

"Not *those*. How to behave. Etiquette. Maman taught me and I can teach you. If you ask nicely."

Though she didn't want to admit it, she did need Sophie's help. She winced when she thought of how she'd not only mistaken the Chevalier Foudriard for Aurélie's husband, but actually said it out loud.

"There are so many things I don't know. It feels hopeless. You'll help?"

"Sit up straight, then," Sophie said imperiously. "We begin immédiatement."

For the rest of that day and into the next, Camille didn't leave the apartment. She gnawed on day-old bread and nibbled bits of cheese, feeling like one of the gray mice in Perrault's story before it was transformed into an elegant horse. There were so many things to learn it made her head ache. How to sit, how to stand, how to walk as if floating. How to address strangers, how to address the king and queen. How to speak to servants. How some of the people who behaved like servants were in fact aristocrats and had to be treated as such. Which doors to knock on with her knuckles and which doors she should only scratch on, with her fingernails.

"Really?" Camille asked.

"Some courtiers grow an especially long nail for it," said Sophie.

Camille listened carefully to stories about the old king's mistresses, the hierarchy of the court, Marie Antoinette's favorites—everything Maman had told Sophie in their nightly tête-a-têtes, Sophie now told Camille, and pushed her to practice.

In its own way, etiquette was just as exhausting as magic.

Thursday afternoon, Sophie gave her approval. After Camille put on the cloth-of-gold dress, she took Chandon's pink card from its hiding place.

On the front was printed: *JEUX ET JOIES*, and below it, *At the Queen's Pleasure*. A pretty circlet of roses framed the words.

On the back, in turquoise ink, Chandon had scrawled:

Jean-Marc Étienne de Bellan, Marquis de Chandon
Thursdays after eight
Madame du Barry's rooms

Please come was underlined twice.

With her finger she traced the words, *GAMES AND PLEASURES*, feeling where the type had bitten into the heavy paper. It was beautifully and expensively made. In her hand, the tiny square felt curiously alive, substantial but almost weightless. She lifted it to her nose.

It smelled of vetiver and, faintly, of blown-out candles.

She slipped it into her pocket. From the room under the eaves, she took the little painted nécessaire from its burned box and propped the foggy mirror on her bureau. The apartment was quiet; Sophie had left for Madame Bénard's and though Camille couldn't say why, exactly, it felt better that Sophie wasn't here. Working the glamoire felt almost shamefully private.

When she heard the coachman shouting from the street, she took the brooch from its place on her bureau. Instead of worrying about how the dress appeared to relish her blood and seemed in fact to be lying in wait for it, she let her mind go to the pure heedless thrill of winning, the cool stacks of louis d'or piled on the gaming tables, and—though she'd intended for them to be her enemies—the young aristocrats she'd met last time. With that churn of conflict in her mind, she steadied the point against the skin on the inside of her elbow, hidden beneath her sleeve, and pushed it in.

23

She'd shown the pink card to a footman who told her the rooms in question were on the top floor, and directed her to go down one corridor and along another. Empty wine bottles, each with a sunny daisy in its mouth, had been left behind on a window ledge; by a closed door lay a pair of peacock-blue shoes, kicked onto their sides. In the wainscoting, mice scratched and squealed, the hallway's floorboards creaked, and on the ceiling, paint was peeling, but she ignored it, focusing on the laughter and shouts of the gaming party drifting toward her.

In an instant, the hall's dimness gave way to a series of cream-and-gold rooms, full of nobles in their fine clothes, trembling with feathers and ruffles, rich in lace and glinting with diamonds. The rooms buzzed with conversation and laughter; hundreds of pale pink candles—in the chandeliers, on the tables—burning as brightly as the animated faces. Camille suddenly wished she were outside in the garden, inhaling the cool evening alone, and not here in the crush. She did not belong here.

But the ancient magic in the dress refused to listen. It urged her on, its pleasure at being among the glittering crowd a steady thrum in her blood. It murmured to her of the seductive pressure of legs against petticoats, the rustle of hot breath across silk, and warned her of coming too close to the candles. Most of all, though, it showed her coins nestled in her lap, cool against its fabric. Camille touched a hand to the bodice and felt it tighten around her in response. She was here to win. All the rest meant nothing—or so she told herself as she wove her way into the first room.

Pausing on the threshold, she took in the unfamiliar, polished faces. There was only one she recognized at first glance: the queen's, sitting at a far table, dressed in the deceptively simple white dresses she favored. A ribbon twined through her hair, her face was lightly powdered; she wore jewels at her throat and on the fingers that held her cards. The king was not there; his lack of interest in gaming was well known. But there were plenty of handsome men at her table, and women, too, including the blond one with the nearly white hair and good marriage prospects. She'd left her lamb elsewhere tonight.

All of this was just as Chandon had promised. Still, that didn't make it any easier to enter the room, to pretend that she belonged. What had she been thinking? That Chandon would be waiting for her by the door? Casting about the room for a familiar face, she wondered if she would even recognize him. Like half the men there, he had light-brown hair, but he didn't wear his heavily powdered. At least he hadn't the last time. She had no idea what he might look like tonight.

Settling her shoulders, she moved farther into the crush, begging pardon as she went, lifting a glass of champagne from a tray that sailed by on a footman's palm. In the next room, shouts erupted, followed by a ripple of applause. "Encore une fois, Chandon!" someone called out.

"Just once more!" Camille found a space between two courtiers and slipped through.

She found herself in a large room with painted panels of mythological scenes fitted into the walls. The room was filled with green baize-covered tables surrounded, several rows deep, by aristocrats who watched the games unfold. An older man pushed away from the card table, shaking his head. "Pas encore," he muttered. "Who can play with the likes of you young people?"

Chandon, wearing a wildly patterned waistcoat and a beauty mark next to one of his lively hazel eyes, tipped back in his gilt chair, beaming with triumph. Camille could have thrown her arms around him, so relieved she was to have found him.

"Suit yourself, Monsieur le Comte," he laughed. "There are plenty of people who will play with us. Aren't there?" A few courtiers shuffled away from the table, smiling and shaking their heads. Chandon nodded to the boy sitting across from him. "I do believe they're afraid of us."

"Of *you*, perhaps," the golden-haired Vicomte de Séguin replied. Neither of them had noticed her. She stood frozen, waiting. Perhaps they wouldn't remember her. Nor would it matter if they did, she scolded herself. This was not about making friends. It was about making money.

"They're afraid of *you*, Séguin," Chandon said as Camille drew closer. "You strike fear in all but the bravest gamblers. Or the most foolish." Chandon winked at Foudriard, who lounged next to him, his elbow propped on the back of Chandon's chair. Next to him, in a froth of feathers and primrose-yellow satin, sat Aurélie, gossiping behind her fan into Foudriard's ear.

"Me? I've the worst luck of anyone tonight," Séguin said as he pulled handfuls of chips toward himself. Guffaws and a smattering of applause from the observers drew a meager smile from his face. He was doing very well. Camille remembered how much he was willing to play for last time. A player running on his luck was dangerous.

Then Chandon saw her. His whole face brightened. "Et voilà! It's the Baroness de la Fontaine! Shall I make a wager?" he said to the crowd. "I bet she's come specially to play with us."

Camille bowed, secretly happy. "What does that make me then, brave or foolish, monsieur?"

"It makes you gorgeous," he said. "Now make way, mes amis," he cajoled, and the courtiers around the table stepped back.

"Madame," purred the Vicomte de Séguin, rising from his chair. Expensively dressed, he wore a black silk suit with copper-threaded embroidery twining around the cuffs and up the front. Camille was struck again by his bronze-colored eyes, watchful as those of a bird of prey. "There's a seat for you next to me."

There was no polite way to refuse that would not test her newly learned rules of etiquette, so she sat down, unfurling her fan and letting her skirts drag on the floor. *A rich woman cares nothing for her gown,* Sophie had told her. *Don't protect it. You'll look like you care too much.*

Séguin ordered a footman to bring some bonbons as the high notes of a violin soared over the din. Camille tried to rein in her excitement, but it wasn't easy. Now that she was here, at the table, the candles and the blue-and-gold-patterned cards in front of her, anything could happen. Each card was a possibility; with a little luck, a little magic worked discreetly, there was no limit.

"What are we playing?" she asked.

Chandon swept several decks' worth of cards together and rapped them against the table. "What do you like, madame?" He tapped the table, pretending to think. "I seem to remember you are a devotée of vingt-et-un, n'est-ce pas?"

"Yes, yes!" exclaimed Aurélie. "We must foil the Vicomte de Séguin in his plan to take over the world."

Séguin said nothing but stacked his chips in candy-colored piles.

"Count me in," Camille said, with a quick glance at Séguin. "We cannot let him have even Versailles."

"We'll see about that. I've been waiting for the chance to play with you, madame," the Vicomte de Séguin said languidly. "The pleasure was denied me last time." The way he lingered on the word *play* made Camille's skin crawl. *Ignore him and fix your thoughts on winning,* she told herself as she opened her purse. "I'm happy to play vingt-et-un, as long as no one else objects?"

"Who could possibly object?" said a boy slouched on Camille's other side. His fashionable stand-up collar was crushed, his light brown hair mussed, eyes bloodshot, and white skin ashy, as if he'd been awake for days. "Just let's get on with it, shall we?" He snapped his fingers over his head and a footman approached. "Again some wine, my man," he said in awkward, English-accented French. "In case," he said to the other players, "blows need to be blunted, et cetera, et cetera."

"Allons-y, then, Lord Willsingham," Foudriard said. He called for chips for himself and Camille, and Chandon began to shuffle.

He cut the decks several times against his palm, and then, smiling to himself, he made the cards fly, one after another until they twirled like a strange snowstorm around his hands. For a moment, one card would seem to catch on a fingertip, frozen and gravity-defiant. Another would balance on its edge on the back of his hand, but then, just as quickly, the pirouetting cards would fall back into the deck and vanish from view. And as the cards danced around his hands, they created a tiny breeze that ruffled the candle flames.

"Bravo!" called one of the onlookers.

Yet.

The more she watched, the more Camille was certain that there was something peculiar about the cards. Some moved slower than others. Others moved faster, so fast that no one could possibly follow them. It was as if Chandon were manipulating them, sliding certain cards under others, different ones on top, all in full view of the players. She watched, fascinated. Did no one else see what he was doing? It seemed that they did not. But it wasn't with her sight that she knew, suddenly, what it was. It was with her nose. For with each flourish, each planted card, an invisible breath of smoke escaped his ringed fingers.

Chandon was working la magie.

The skin on her scalp tingled. Another magician. Here, opposite her at the gaming table. Here, at court.

Why had Maman had never told her anything? Wasn't this important information to give to one's child, especially when she was being trained in magic? All those lessons with Maman, her voice barbed as she told Camille to try again, to practice more—never once did she tell Camille that la magie wasn't a special trick only the Durbonnes had up their sleeves. But why hide it? It made no sense.

Pretending to count her chips, she watched Chandon under her eyelashes as the cards danced in his hands. It was like watching a lightning strike illuminate the landscape: what had previously been only darkness was suddenly revealed to be full of trees, grass, buildings, people. He'd shuffled the same way last time, in the oval room. He must have been working la magie then, too. And she hadn't even guessed.

Not only had he beat her with magic, but he was clearly a thousand times better at it than she was. With a sick, sinking feeling, she understood that if he was using magic, he must know that she'd been using it, too. He'd probably realized it the very first time she'd worked it.

Chandon was cutting the deck now, laying down stacks of cards and piling them on top of each other. Each cut felt as if it were reducing her chances to nothing. He tipped his head toward her and winked. "Bonne chance, madame."

Throwing herself into the game, Camille won several hands by luck alone, and when her luck abandoned her, she started turning cards. Each time she won, she tried to judge Chandon's reaction. But he was a consummate actor, a perfect courtier: nothing showed on his face that he wished to hide. Next to her, the Vicomte de Séguin sat so close Camille smelled the sweet pomade in his fair hair, the dry wood scent of his strong cologne, and, more unsettlingly, felt the pressure of his calf against her skirts. Was this normal for court? All this flirting and innuendo? Sophie hadn't said.

There was something about the way he watched her that made her worry he would catch her cheating. Or recognize her. At the other end of the room, the music crescendoed. "Madame," he said softly, "I'd advise you to be careful."

Camille's unease worsened. "How, monsieur?" she asked as if she cared nothing for the answer. "Is there some danger at Versailles? A monster? A plague?"

Séguin smiled, but Camille sensed it was not at her jest. "Madame is new to court, non? There are many ways to find fame and fortune at Versailles. You know how sometimes it happens that you can go quite a long way down a path before you realize it's not the right one?" He leaned closer, his tone brotherly. "I might be your friend, help you avoid the traps."

Exactly what she needed, but from him? She could not put her finger on it—for he was handsome and rich and, she thought, not harmful, exactly—but Camille didn't want his help. What would Aurélie say? Camille tried to imagine the girl's voice in her own throat, Aurélie's confident, teasing expression on her own face. "But aren't traps part of the fun?"

Séguin straightened slightly in his chair. "Ça dépend," he mused. "It depends on whether you are the hunter or the hunted, n'est-ce pas? Or it might depend"—his voice softened into silk—"on how promising the bait is in the traps."

Camille had no idea how to respond to that. "How do you know, monsieur, what the traps are baited with?"

"I hope you're not conspiring with the enemy," Aurélie interrupted. "Even if you are, we must stop for a moment." She held out her arm to show how her diamond bracelet dangled loose. "Chandon, close this for me, will you?"

Play paused while Chandon worked the tiny clasp. Camille fiddled with her chips, wishing she were at another table, one where he wasn't working his magic and she might better work her own. She needed to win this game, and to do that, she needed to turn her cards. But she didn't dare when Séguin was watching her so intently. She swiveled away from him to better hide her cards.

Irritatingly, he tapped her on the shoulder. "Perhaps you're already well equipped for this adventure. Shall we find out?"

"How?"

"Give me your hand," he said, and before she'd decided what to do, he had taken it in his. His hand was smooth, heavy with rings. As she tried, decorously, to pull away, the dress rustled around her, distraught. Painful visions rushed through her: a tipped candle, flames hurtling over silk, burning so hot that the fabric blackened and lifted off as ash. It was the dress's nightmare: a warning to be careful.

Next to her, the tired English boy was opening his snuffbox and putting a pinch of tobacco in his nose.

"Now?" Camille said. "I must focus on the game—"

"Rest easy, Madame de la Fontaine. There's plenty of time." His voice in her ear was cool as stone. "Release your fingers and I'll tell you your fortune."

Across the table Chandon, vexed, still tinkered with Aurélie's bracelet.

Camille exhaled. "Go on, then."

Séguin peeled her fingers open, one by one. With his forefinger, he traced each line on her palm. Involuntarily, she shivered.

"Ça va?" he asked.

Letting him touch her palm was like letting a spider scurry across it. "It's nothing."

He held her hand toward the candelabra to see it better. "Now show me the other one, madame."

Lord Willsingham sneezed.

Camille laid her cards facedown on the table and held out her left hand. She tried to hold it still, but it shook. His golden eyes narrowed, but he said nothing. *It's because of la magie,* Camille wanted to say. *It's not trembling because of you.*

"Shall I tell your fortune now? Here," he said, languidly tracing one of the lines as it curved around the base of her thumb, "is your life line. Long, though not always strong. See those bubbles? Difficulties."

There was no end of difficulties in her life, but none that she would tell this aristocrat. Mentioning death had thrown the others last time, so she played that card again. She dared him to say something about *that.* "The death of my husband, perhaps?"

"Peut-être," he said, though he did not sound convinced. "Maybe. Now this line, which curves up to your fingers—that's your love line."

"What do you see for me there, vicomte? Another husband?"

He gave her a quizzical stare. "Oui. The Line of Love shows you cannot be alone for long. But the Line of Fate presents more problems." He ran the tip of his index finger down the center of her palm. There was something about his touch that burned. "Most people have only one Line of Fate, madame. But see here, you have two: you and your shadow life. One path is thin, but whole. The other is broken. It is crossed with a triangle, and a star." He touched the crisscrossing lines in the center of her palm.

Either he was good at invention, or there was something to this palmreading. "What do they mean?"

"Secret knowledge. Or a warning."

"A warning not to wear rouge if I visit the queen's rooms?" she said, lightly. "To not be alone with the Comte d'Astignac of the Roving Hands?"

Séguin reclined in his chair. Again, she smelled his heavy cologne, and something else—something familiar Camille couldn't place. "Bah, the Comte d'Astignac has nothing on you. It's fate that interests me. Isn't it reassuring to know it's written in your hands?"

Under the table, out of sight, Camille wiped her palm on her skirts. "I don't believe in fate, monsieur."

"What else is there?"

"Freedom, perhaps? Choice?"

Séguin's bold stare faltered for a moment. "Freedom is chaos, non? I don't like disorder."

Disorder is the beginning of change, Papa had said. *When taxes rise, when the harvest fails, and bread prices rise: see what happens.*

"Slap me, marquis!" Lord Willsingham cried in his atrocious French. "One more card and damn me, I'll make twenty-one."

Everyone roared with laughter; across the table, Chandon was snapping his fingers at her. "Madame de la Fontaine," he said, his voice brisk, "attention, s'il vous plaît! Would you like another card?"

All the players waited, expectant. But Camille had lost her bearings completely. She could only stare back. She touched her fingertips to her cards, trying hard to read their hidden faces. Nothing came to her.

"I don't know," she said, haltingly. Had she successfully turned the card before Séguin had interrupted her? Startled, she realized she couldn't remember. And if she had, which card had she turned? What had been her plan?

"Perhaps not," she said, biting the edge of her fingernail.

"Come on, madame," cried Chandon, "live a little!" As he stretched across the table with a card for her, drunk Lord Willsingham assumed it was for him and reached for it. Doing so, he upset a glass of red wine, which spilled wide across the green baize, the playing cards, and into Camille's lap.

24

In a moment, Chandon was at her side, pulling out her chair, helping her up. Under her elbow, his hand was like iron. As if he were *forcing* her to leave. With a deft movement, he picked up her purse and chips and guided her away, his arm now around her shoulders. Her skirts caught on a chair and tumbled it to the floor, but he would not let her stop to right it.

"What are you doing?" Camille seethed.

"Saving you," Chandon hissed in her ear. Then loudly, so everyone could hear, he added, "Come, madame. I'll find you a maid to blot your dress. Red wine makes such an unfortunate stain." Obediently, the crowd parted as Chandon led her out of the cream-and-gilt room, down a servants' stair, to a seemingly unused hall, where a frowning portrait of the old king hung crooked in its frame.

"How exactly are you saving me?" As she stood there with the magician, a finger of fear crept up her spine. "What do you want from me?"

"Isn't it clear? We must talk." He glanced down the empty hallway. "We haven't much time."

"Why drag me out of the game? Unfair, monsieur—I was sure to finish big."

Out of nowhere, he produced her purse and handed it to her. "And here I thought you were enthralled by the Vicomte de Séguin," Chandon challenged. "You're not worried about the wine that spilled on your lovely dress?"

But the plum-colored skirts of her gown were once again spotless. The crimson stain had vanished.

"Your dress is very thirsty, madame," he observed.

"There must not have been much wine, after all—"

"Or your dress is fashioned from magie bibelot, n'est-ce pas?"

Camille froze. "Magie bibelot?" she said, doing her best to feign ignorance.

"The magic of enchanted objects," he said. "And I bet you're working a glamoire. People rarely look as dazzlingly perfect as you do."

"And what of it? You're a magician, too," she dared. "I saw you manipulating the cards. Is your plan to expose me?"

"What? Never!" Chandon said, alarmed. "What is there to expose? All the world comes to Versailles, hoping to be someone else. Who really cares if you're not noble? Or a widow?" He blinked, as if he could peer beneath the glamoire's polish. "You were never even married?"

Camille shook her head.

"Well done! As our alarmingly clever Aurélie said, a dead husband is the best kind a woman can have. You've chosen wisely." Chandon crossed his arms. "But that's neither here nor there. We must be quick—everyone who wishes to travel unseen uses this hallway, so we could have company at any minute. I want to warn you."

Another warning? "About what?"

"The dangers of doing magic here, what else?"

"I was so easy to see through?"

He produced the snuffbox he'd won from her and flicked open the lid. "Snuff?"

She shook her head. Chandon took a pinch and inhaled it. "One magician always recognizes another," he said. "I could tell the first night we played together."

"But how?" She'd hardly known what she was doing. She had worked the glamoire, turned the cards, but with no understanding of how it worked, or why. It had been like grasping at something in a pitch-black room. And yet, he'd seen it?

Chandon sneezed. "How you do tease, Baroness!"

"I'm not teasing."

"You really don't know?"

She shook her head. There was so much she did not know.

"There's a certain fog around a magician, especially one that's working a glamoire. Usually a sign of someone completely untrustworthy—or utterly desperate. Also, I count cards. I noticed there were suddenly twins of cards we'd already played." He wagged a finger at her. "Cheater."

"I cheated less than you did!"

"Ha! That's why I like you. Still, it's altogether too much magic." He drew closer, as if the shadows were listening. "That's why I tricked Willsingham into spilling wine on you. You *must* be more careful. Not everyone at court is as kind and charming as I."

"I will try, I promise." She'd studied so hard to learn all of Sophie's etiquette, and now there were more rules, magical ones she didn't understand. "The only magician I knew was my mother. She told me almost nothing."

"Not proud of her heritage?"

It was true. Maman had been happy to marry Papa and leave her noble life behind. Until she needed the magic again. "Why do you say that?"

His mouth fell open in mock-horror. "How surprising you are! You *really* don't know anything."

"Tell me, then, monsieur." No matter how many doors she passed through, how many rooms she entered, how hard she worked, she was still *outside*.

"Only if you call me Chandon, as everyone does."

"Chandon."

"That's better." Taking another pinch of snuff, Chandon slouched elegantly against the wall. "Shall I tell it as a fairy tale?"

"If you wish."

"Once upon a time, two kings before our present king, there was a particularly greedy one named Louis XIV. He demanded to be the center of the universe, the Sun King.

"Not everyone went along with this idea, however. First, he got rid of the treacherous nobles." Chandon made a slicing motion across his throat. "After he tamed the defiant ones, he wanted the tricky magicians under his thumb. He invited them all—your ancestors and mine, for magic is in the blood—to come to the palace he'd thrown up at Versailles. A ramshackle place, really. He demanded the magicians weave webs of protection around the château, so none of his enemies could attack it, and to work glamoires to make it more beautiful than any other palace that had ever been."

Versailles *was* enchantingly beautiful. The way the gardens looked as the sun sank low and set the faces of the statues to flickering, as if they might speak. The way the Hall of Mirrors multiplied light to forever. The dancing fountains, the silver stretch of the Grand Canal and its black-prowed gondolas, the mournful hush of doves in the trees at dusk. It was all extraordinary, all magical.

But under the surface of the glamoire there was rot. The mice in the wainscoting, the courtiers' lapdogs who shat in the corners, the stink of urine and decay in the less-used hallways where drunk or lost visitors relieved themselves. Suddenly she understood: the magic of Versailles was like the magic of the turned coins in her purse.

"It's been more than sixty years since Louis XIV died, even longer since he built Versailles. The enchantments are fading, aren't they?"

"Bien sûr. It's the royals' own fault. Louis XIV wasn't particularly protective of the magicians. Once they were here, all the nasty, greedy courtiers—desperate to rise, desperate to be in favor with the Sun King—wanted la magie." Chandon's voice rose to a pleading, nasal squeak: "'Please, dashing magician, make my enemy sick and make my friend forget a debt'; 'please, charming magician, make me beautiful forever and ever.' 'Magician, make this person fall in love with me and I will make sure you are handsomely rewarded.' Can you imagine how tired those magicians were?"

Somewhere, a door opened and closed. Chandon fell silent. He listened intently, his hazel eyes narrowed, then shook his head.

"And that's when it all went wrong. One of the king's mistresses bought a love spell to use on the Sun King, and when he found out—mon Dieu!" Chandon pretend-glowered. "How dare anyone attempt magic on the person of the king! Inquisitions! Torture!" His voice dropped, a note of real fear in it. "Then came the burning of the witches, as he called them."

Why had Maman never told her this terrible history? As the skirts of her gown rustled uneasily, Camille shuddered to think what her ancestors had gone through. "But those magicians did nothing wrong! They only did what the king and the other nobles compelled them to do."

"That's one way to think about it," he said carefully. "But you can see why the magicians who escaped never renewed the glamoires or the protections at Versailles—and now the whole place is crumbling like old cake. After the love potion inquisition, magic fell out of favor at court. Though the nobles wanted our magic as desperately as ever, they were frightened of us. Not simply because of the magic we worked, the magic that seemed to make all their desires possible—the magic that made the hair stand up on their necks. But also because they saw what we did to achieve it. What we were prepared to do to ourselves." A shadow fell across Chandon's face. "I'm certain you understand."

She did. She had seen the blank revulsion in Sophie's face when she realized the glamoire needed both blood and sorrow, and that Camille was willing to give it. She was no longer simply working la magie ordinaire, using her sorrow to turn coins or even cards. By working the glamoire and using the sinister, magic-threaded dress, Camille had stepped over some kind of dark and desperate threshold.

Now she stood on the other side. It was a lonely place.

There had been a time, before the smallpox crept into their house, when Camille had seen Maman standing at the mirror over the fireplace, her hands gripping the mantel's fluted edge to stop herself from shaking. Not that she could. The fine trembling showed itself in the lace on her sleeves and the ends of her hair. In the mirror her face was wan and etched with fatigue, too old for her thirty-six years. Liver spots Camille had never seen clustered on the backs of her hands and tarnished her cheekbones. And Camille had been oblivious to anything but her own anger with Maman for favoring Sophie and forcing Camille to work la magie.

Suddenly, Camille saw what she hadn't seen then. Before, she'd thought the glamoire a frivolous thing, something for dressing up and being pretty. But Maman had been working a glamoire so she could use turned coins closer to home without being recognized. The fatigue and the wear of it finally made her so weak that she succumbed when the pox came.

If you don't like working la magie ordinaire, she had said, *you will not like the glamoire at all.*

Maman had never intended to be cruel. She had only ever asked for Camille's help, not demanded it. Perhaps she too had felt there was no other way.

Camille's voice was thread-thin when she said, "More and more, I think I do understand."

"And therefore I'd say, if I were to be blunt—which I hardly ever am—stay clear of anyone who asks about magic. Favors and other such things. As for the other magicians—"

Her throat tightened. "There are others? Here?"

With a creak, a door opened and Foudriard's tall silhouette appeared at the end of the hall.

"It's time for me to go," Chandon said, straightening his cravat.

It was too soon. There was so much more she needed to know. "I'm frightened, Chandon. I'm not really an aristocrat, and I'm certainly not a courtier. I only came here to gamble at cards. I can't be found out. I need to stay at least a little longer. Please help me—what should I do?"

Chandon bent his head to hers, his words tumbling over themselves. "You must be the Baroness of Pretend. Give absolutely nothing away. Watch carefully how much you win. Remember to lose every once in a while. Stay clear of traps! Next we meet I'll tell you more, I promise." He took her hand and squeezed it. "Fear not. We'll stick together, we *nice* magicians."

When he reached them, Foudriard bowed and handed Camille her fan, which she'd left behind. His kind brown eyes were full of concern. "That Willsingham is fun to have around but sometimes he really is a fool," Foudriard said. "You found someone to dry your dress, madame?"

Camille nodded. "Merci."

Foudriard put a hand on Chandon's shoulder. "Shall we go? I have to be up at dawn with the new recruits. They still haven't understood that the horses are smarter than they are."

"Silly cavalry officers." Chandon suddenly looked tired, shadowy, just as he had the last time she'd seen him, as if it cost him to play the games court life required. "Au revoir, ma petite," he said to Camille, blowing her a kiss. "I hope to see you soon. If not here, then at the big palace. I am there most nights, like a ghost that can't stay away."

"Like a gambler," Foudriard said tenderly.

Camille curtsied, her hand on her heart. "Thank you for everything, both of you. I'm in your debt."

"Hardly," Chandon replied. "I'm not *that* kind of magician. I'd much rather be your friend." Before he left, he said, a warning in his voice: "Remember—magic is a cheater's game, and everyone who sees it wants to play."

25

Camille pushed her needle through the silk and pulled so hard the thread broke. "Merde," she swore, frowning at the court dress.

"Manners, Camille." Sophie was sitting with her by the window's bright light. She had half the dress's skirts in her lap, working to repair a tear that had proved too tricky for Camille.

"Manners are for Versailles," Camille said, impatient. "In Paris I'm allowed to be as crass as I please." Several lengths of trim remained on the floor, waiting to be reattached to the skirt. The matching dancing shoes lay under the chair where she'd kicked them off this morning. Their curved heels were stained grass-green.

Camille's fingers trembled as she picked up the end of the thread.

She tried three times before she was able to slip it through the needle's tiny eye. Part of it was exhaustion from working the glamoire—that she knew from the smaller magic of turning metal scraps into coins. To turn herself and the dress was magic of a magnitude she'd never worked before. Since Chandon's warning, she saw it was no longer an isolated thing, but part of magic's twilight history.

Realizing that this was her own history felt as if a shadow were burrowing under her skin and making itself at home. *They were frightened of us then*, Chandon had said. *Because they saw what we did to achieve it. What we were prepared to do to ourselves.*

"When we've finished these repairs, we'll pack," Sophie said.

"Why?"

Sophie groaned. "Aren't you finished with Versailles?"

"Because of what the Marquis de Chandon told me?" Camille touched the seam she was working on. The stitches were crooked and would have to come out. "I just need to be careful, that's all. The court both loves and fears magic. And I must guard myself against the unfriendly magicians, whoever they are." In the moment, her conversation with Chandon in the dim hallway had seemed so necessary, everything he told her so dangerous. But in the end? He'd only meant she needed to be more circumspect. Less obvious. His warning wasn't enough to keep her away when she'd come home with such a full purse and there was still more to be won.

"Perhaps the marquis means that the magicians are unfriendly because they're territorial." Sophie took another stitch. "Like dogs?"

In the wall behind Camille, something scratched. A crack snaked from the floor to the window where they were sitting. It had been there for months; Madame Lamotte never made repairs. Soon, the crack would widen and become a throughway for mice. Or worse. How big did a hole have to be before rats shouldered their way in?

Camille wanted three months' rent safe under the hearthstones before they searched for another apartment. She might ask Aurélie if she knew of one—Aurélie seemed to know everything. But what would that rent be, somewhere nicer? Twice as much, four hundred livres? She had twelve hundred now. Three times as much? Six hundred? Or even more, so much so that she could no longer count it in livres but would have to count in louis d'or?

Irritated, she ripped out the stitches, rethreaded her needle. Once again, she dipped the tip of her needle in and out, catching the satin edge of a ribbon of roses and sewing it to the skirt while trying not to compare her long, impatient stitches to Sophie's invisible ones. As she was pushing the needle in for another pass, Sophie pulled at the skirts and made Camille prick her finger.

"Ouch!" She stuck her finger in her mouth to stop it from bleeding. The dress shifted uneasily in her lap—as if it wanted a taste—and a heave of repulsion turned Camille's stomach. Sometimes she wished she could quit magic. And she would, as soon as they had enough. "Watch what you're doing!"

Sophie didn't seem to hear. She was peering out the window. "There's a carriage in the street."

"And?"

"I've never seen it before."

Down below, a carriage, its brass fittings gleaming, had appeared. As Camille watched, its wheels rolled slowly through the mud.

"Probably a new customer for Madame Bénard, no doubt come to buy one of your fantastic hats."

"Hush, someone's getting out."

With a sigh, Camille pushed herself out of the chair and peered down, her stomach tightening at the drop. Someone *had* stepped out. A boy in a plain brown suit, a spyglass leaning precariously from his coat pocket. Tawny skin, dark hair tied back with a black ribbon. "Oh," she breathed.

"I told you. I bet he's come with the surprise."

Camille gripped the windowsill as, down in the street, Lazare strolled to the next building to check its number. Even from this distance, his movements were lithe, confident. "Dieu," she said. "He came."

"That's usually how it works." Sophie said, a twist of envy in her voice. "When a boy likes you."

"How would I know?" Camille said. The last three months had been a fog of hunger and death and dwindling in the slow, stifling grip of not having enough to eat. When she thought back to that time, and even before, when Papa lost the printing shop, she could not recall one promise kept, except the bad ones.

But here Lazare was.

She could watch him all day.

In the street, he pivoted on his heel and walked back to number 11 rue Charlot. He rapped on the heavy courtyard door. And waited. He poked at something in the street with his shoe; he took a notebook from another pocket, hesitated, and put it back. He looked over his shoulder at the coach and shrugged.

Then he tipped his head back and shouted, "Mademoiselle Durbonne! Does anyone know where I may find Mademoiselle Durbonne?"

"Oh là là!" Sophie exclaimed, laughing. "He certainly is impatient."

"And loud." Secretly, though, she didn't mind. If anyone were to be calling her name, she was proud to have it be this handsome boy.

"Soon busybody Madame Lamotte will be down in the street, curtseying and squinting at him. Better hurry, Camille."

The less Madame knew of Camille's affairs, the better. She unhooked the latch, felt the window frame tilt unsteadily around her, and leaned out. "Monsieur!"

He looked up. "Mademoiselle Durbonne!" His voice bounced against the buildings on its way up to her. "I've come with a surprise!"

Etiquette said she should ask why, delay, pretend that she was doing something he'd interrupted, but all she could think of was taking her cloak and hat and racing down the seven flights of stairs.

Sophie gave her a little shove. "What's wrong with you? Say something!"

"Oh? What is it?" Camille called back, flinching at the foolish words as they came out of her mouth.

"Bien sûr, to fly!"

"Oh, Camille," Sophie gasped, "he wants you to fly in his balloon!" She squeezed Camille's hand. "Say yes!"

Fly? Sweat pricked on Camille's back. She could barely manage to go out on the roof. To fly in the sky? She thought of the way the ground had dropped away under her when she'd caught the balloon. That had been only a tiny distance off the ground and she'd thought she might die. "I can't go up—in the balloon," she said to Sophie. "I'll fall out."

"Is the great magician, Camille Durbonne, *afraid*?" Sophie said gleefully. "Afraid to fly through the air? Afraid to say yes to a boy?"

She was. And what if it was more than that? What if, when he got to know her better, she was nothing like what he imagined she might be, like a coin turning back to a nail? Or, what if she cared for him and he did not feel the same? What if she lost, again?

Lazare stood, waiting. He was waiting for *her*.

Sophie gave Camille a little shove. "You'll never know unless you say yes."

"Monsieur, tell me this first," Camille called. "Have you found a better kind of ballast?"

Lazare looked puzzled, then threw his head back and laughed. "Of course! No problems with the landing this time. I promise."

So many promises.

Camille took a deep breath. A breeze from the street lifted the ends of her hair and twirled them around her face until they flew like banners. *Yes*, something deep inside her demanded. *Say yes to this.*

"Alors, if you've solved that problem, then yes. I'll come."

"Fantastique!" Lazare stretched out his arms like wings, as if he would lift off right there in the street.

26

She found Rosier waiting in the carriage when she came down to join Lazare.

"Mademoiselle!" he said, his words tumbling out. "You will make us a part of aeronautical history! A girl, in a balloon, in the air! Who else has done it? No one, that's who," he said, before Camille could respond. She didn't care one whit about aeronautical history. At this moment, all she cared about was remaining in the balloon without her body flinging itself over the basket's wall.

"Just imagine the poster we will print!" Rosier sketched a rectangle in the air. "You in the chariot, soaring above the waters of the Seine. Perhaps next time your sister will join us. *Sisters Soar Across Paris!*"

"Please," Camille said from between clenched teeth. "Don't speak of it."

"What?" Rosier said, chastened. "Have I offended?"

"C'est rien," Lazare said. "Just leave Mademoiselle be."

Camille was finding it hard to speak. Her mind hadn't stopped racing since she'd seen Lazare in the street, and now he lounged on the seat opposite her. Though he'd bent his long legs at an angle to make room for her, his knees still pressed against her petticoats. It felt too hot in the carriage. She wanted to lower the window.

Rosier tapped on the glass, startling her. "Could you draw a map, mademoiselle?"

She shifted in her seat, which only brought her closer to Lazare's legs. "Why?"

He appraised her, like a thief casing for a heist. "It's Armand. He doesn't want you on the balloon, especially his balloon. I've tried to tell him that your being there will be a boon to our finances—First Girl in the Air!—but he has no vision."

"It's not his balloon." Lazare tucked an arm behind his head and stretched back against the upholstery. "Not even close."

"He thinks it is. Therefore, I scheme. If Mademoiselle were to draw a map, one that we might use to raise money for the balloon flight over the Alps—"

"That's all?" Camille asked. "He won't have any other objections? Say, that I'm a girl and not a boy?"

Rosier made an irritated noise. "Bah! That you're a girl? That's precisely the point! Armand is a fool. His brain's been addled by fumes. And numbers."

"He's not the only one whose brain's been addled," Lazare said. He'd thrown his head back against the top of the seat, and Camille tried not to stare at the curve of his throat, the tender spot under his jaw where his pulse beat, slowly, slowly. He was so at his ease and she was so utterly unsettled. It wasn't just the idea of going up in the air, though, that was her most pressing concern. There was also *him*.

He was looking directly at her, his gaze a caress on the side of her face. She wondered if a boy—if anyone—had ever looked at her like that before. It was so different than the hungry eyes of the boys on the streets, with their whistles and their fast, rough hands, different than the cool stares of the courtiers at Versailles, who hid their feelings behind double entendres.

Lazare's gaze was nothing like that. It felt honest. True.

She flushed. She found a spot of dirt on her skirts and rubbed at it with her thumb.

Rosier was still fuming, loosening his cravat and scribbling notes for a conversation he was going to have with Armand that would put him in his place.

"Almost there," Lazare said. "See?"

The carriage window no longer showed Paris's gray buildings, but instead, a green field, its brightness topped by a sweep of watery blue sky.

Camille bit the edge of her fingernail. What if the balloon had problems again? What if there was no one like herself waiting around to save them? What if she fell out?

"Have people died?" she asked. "In balloons?"

"People have died sitting in their armchairs," Lazare said.

Her stomach flipped. She smiled as bravely as she could, and clutched the edge of the seat more tightly.

27

Now that she stood in the woven chariot, gripping a sketchpad tightly in one hand and the chariot's railing in the other, she felt sick.

When Rosier had handed her into the balloon, Armand had ignored her offers to help or her questions about where she should stand. As she watched him test the ropes and check the fire in the brazier, she felt more out of place than she had at Versailles. What had she been thinking? She shouldn't be flying in a balloon at all, she told herself, as hot panic spread under her skin. She should be back at court, fleecing the nobles for all they were worth. She should be saving her money, hiding it under the bricks so that Alain could never get it again. Or at least mending her dress. Not sailing *in the air.*

"Ready?" Lazare beamed at her, the lead-ropes taut in his hands. "Watch your dress, mademoiselle!"

In the center of the gondola, the brazier sparked, the air above it shimmering with heat. Gathering her skirts, she stepped away from the stove, only to feel the hard line of the gondola's edge against her back. There was nowhere safe to run to, she thought, as she wiped her sweating palms on her skirt. Either she'd be burned alive by the fire or she'd plunge over the edge.

Above her head, the silk of the balloon trembled as if it were alive.

Rosier stood on the rough grass outside the basket, furiously sketching the balloon and its crew. "Do something exciting when you're up there," he said. "Anything, really, except falling out. Then come back and tell me all about it."

Peering up at the underside of the balloon, Armand called, "It's time to go! The sky stands open!"

"Let us go that way," the other boys responded in chorus. Rosier rolled his eyes.

With a nod at Camille, Rosier tucked his notebook under his arm and stepped away from the basket. "Bon voyage!"

She hadn't forgotten when the balloon dropped out of the sky like a shot bird. Nor what it felt like to stand on her roof, only the little railing between her and death. Her hands clawed tight onto the basket's edge. She had no sense. Why ever had she listened to Sophie?

The basket sloped drunkenly as one set of ropes was released. Camille choked down a scream. The boys who'd come to help were whooping; Lazare pushed past her to do something at the other side of the balloon. One of the ropes had hooked itself on a stake and he worked hard to tug it free. The basket shook.

She shouldn't be here at all. She might vomit. Or jump out. Because if she died, who would take care of Sophie? If Alain was the only one left, he'd marry Sophie off for money and—Camille stepped across the basket and unlatched the door.

She froze when Lazare yelled, "Don't leave us now, mademoiselle! We're going up!"

Beyond the perilously thin edge of the basket, the grass plummeted away. The balloon rose. On the ground, the gang of boys cheered and, hands shielding their eyes from the sun, watched the balloon climb. "More fuel!" shouted Lazare, and Camille dropped to her knees before the little stove and pushed straw and small logs into it until the fire roared.

In a heartbeat, they lifted past the green tops of the trees. In another, they passed the spire of a stone church. Lazare fed the fire as Camille edged away from the center of the basket, pulling her skirts clear of the sparks. Standing at the lip of the wicker basket, Camille dared herself to look down. Below her, Rosier and his helpers' faces dwindled to nothing larger than stones. Then they were small as pebbles, grains of sand, dust.

The world blurred. Camille gripped the edge of the chariot so hard her arms ached.

"We're going so fast." Her voice came from far away; pinpricks of black winked at the edges of her sight. She felt herself swaying but she couldn't stop herself. Her cold fingers slipped.

Lazare was suddenly next to her, his hand under her elbow, holding her up. "Steady now," he said, his breath warm in her ear. "It's the ascent. Breathe as deeply as you can."

Camille inhaled, her ribs straining against her stays as she filled her lungs with cool air. Then she exhaled and felt her shoulders uncrimp. She breathed again and again until the world below stopped getting smaller. Now that the balloon had achieved its intended altitude, Armand began taking measurements from the barometer.

"We can go through the clouds, if you like." Lazare seemed to want her to say yes, but Camille shook her head, once. It was all she could do to hang on.

They were sailing above Paris. There was the river Seine, a dazzling silver ribbon winding through the city. There, the two islands, where the sun flamed in the stained-glass windows of Sainte-Chapelle. In the other direction, the hilly vineyards of Montmartre, where once she'd picnicked with her family.

"It's all so far away," she said. "So small."

"You might have told me you were afraid of heights." Lazare rested his elbows on the railing, so close to her that she saw the day's growth of beard on his cheeks, the inky tilt of his eyelashes. "I wouldn't have thought any less of you."

Mademoiselle, your disregard for your own life is apparently equal to mine, he'd said when she saved the balloon. Then, and now, she wanted it to be true. She didn't want to be afraid.

She tried to loosen her grip on the chariot's railing. "I'm not frightened."

He looked away, as if to hide a smile. "Watch now. Everything's going to change. I'd start sketching before Armand notices that you're not doing anything," he said, too low for Armand to catch.

Camille rested the notebook against the gondola's rim. She stood closer to the edge than she would have liked—it was, in fact, The Edge—but there was nowhere else to go. The wind snatched at the paper. Taking a deep breath, she began, sketching quickly, loosely, as she tried to capture an impression of what it was that lay below.

Paris had become an unfamiliar city. The dark, dank alleyways she ran through were now just lines, the awe-inducing cathedrals of Notre-Dame and Saint-Eustace shrunken small as wooden toys. She rendered the Place des Vosges with its crisscross of paths, thinking, *There by the apothecary I ran into Lazare.* She drew the mesh of streets around it, and then traced the network of lanes running from the rue Saint-Antoine toward the river. She drew in the landmarks of the grand hôtels, their names those of the noble families who had lived there: Soubise, Sully, Carnavalet.

When she walked past one of these imposing houses, she couldn't see the whole thing: they were simply too big, their walls too high. Instead, she might glimpse through their iron gates fine horses hitched to gleaming carriages or hear the drift of music from some inner room. But from the air, she could see them—whole, not a world away but side by side with the rue Charlot. "How strange it is, monsieur."

Lazare came to stand next to her. "What is?"

"On the ground, all the quarters of Paris feel so separate, like foreign countries. The aristocrats in their own fine neighborhoods, we in ours. But up here, it's different—no one could deny that the houses touch each other."

"Of course they don't!" shouted Armand.

"Things are different in the air." Lazare lowered his voice. "Sometimes I wish I could stay up here forever."

"With Armand?" she teased. His face was a hand's width from hers. If the balloon tipped—what would happen? What would it be like to touch him? She was in terrible, wonderful danger: her toes right at the precipice.

Lazare shook his head. "I'm here with you."

A thrill of happiness ran through her. "Me?"

On the other side of the gondola, Armand snickered. "It's obvious what he means."

"Stop eavesdropping!" Lazare called out. "Or I'll throw you overboard." He began to shrug out of his coat. "You must be cold."

"Not at all!" she said, not wanting to be lesser, frailer, more *in need*.

But Lazare held the coat out and she relented. As she slipped her arms into the too-long sleeves and pulled the collar up around her neck, she caught the scent of leather and horses, the bright note of his cologne, and under it, the warm musk of his skin. Heat climbed Camille's neck. Wearing his coat was almost like touching him.

Casting about for something to say, she focused on his face: "How did you get that scar? The one in your eyebrow?"

Lazare raised it high. "This? In the country, when I was a child."

"What happened?"

"A waterwheel I'd put into the stream snapped and one of the blades cut me. I almost lost my eye." He glanced at hers, where the bruise had been.

"But you didn't."

"No. Instead, my tutor, Monsieur Élouard, was punished. His pay was docked, reduced to that of a kitchen maid. My parents hoped he would leave on his own after that."

The sun-dappled stream she'd imagined was now tainted with shadows. Aghast, she said, "But it wasn't his fault! You were experimenting—"

A muscle worked in his cheek. "My father always tells me how important it is to be honorable, how that's the most important quality a person can have. My father is—how can I explain?"

His grip tightened on the gondola's railing.

Camille waited. Below them, Paris dwindled, insignificant.

"Are you certain you want to hear this?"

"Of course."

He took a deep breath. "My mother was an Indian woman, in Pondichéry, where I was born. She was beautiful, my father said, and clever. He also told me that *she* chose him." The wind pushed a few strands of Lazare's hair against his forehead; he brushed them roughly back. "I try to imagine that place sometimes—the heat, the hue of the ocean—but I can't."

"You resemble her?"

"My coloring. But I have my father's features." He ran a finger along his eyebrow, thinking.

It hit her then, the sadness. "Why did you say 'she was'?"

"My mother died of malaria."

She wished she dared to comfort him, put her hand over his. "I'm sorry."

"I never knew her. When we returned to France, my father remarried. He wishes me to be French, with a Frenchman's sense of duty and honor, whatever that may mean," he said, scornfully. "My father paid my tutor Élouard to teach me Italian, Latin, horsemanship, dueling. All the things a *French* boy such as I should know."

Below them, thin clouds obscured the city. Even the river had disappeared.

"Despite those things, Élouard showed me it was important to dare, to experiment. To forget the rules. It almost drove me mad, his always asking: why? Why this and not that? He took nothing for granted. A different kind of honor, I suppose."

Camille nodded. Élouard sounded a lot like Papa.

"It was Élouard, not my father, who took me to see the montgolfière, at Versailles. Then back at home, we made our own balloon, a little one." Lazare paused. "Is any of this interesting?"

"Yes, tell me." It sounded as if he hardly spoke of this to anyone.

"He wanted to send up a kid goat, but the thought of the goat getting hurt brought me to tears. Élouard teased me for being sentimental, but in the end, I was right—the balloon got stuck in an oak and we couldn't get it down again. After that, it was all I wanted to do. Build a balloon, get up in the air."

"To fly away," Camille said, almost to herself. Hadn't she thought the same thing?

"Exactly." His hand moved next to hers on the rail. They were nearly touching.

Camille did not dare move.

"Lazare!" shouted Armand. "Stop talking nonsense and help me release some air! We've got to start our descent!"

"I never got to ask you—" Lazare said.

Armand's scowling face appeared next to Lazare's shoulder. "Quit your gallantry or we're going to end up flying to England. If we run out of fuel and fall in the water, just know I didn't bring a cork vest for *her*."

Lazare held up his hand. "Calme-toi, my friend. If we fall in the water, she can have mine." He flicked open the silver case of his pocket watch. "Armand's right. We've got to get going."

Behind her, Lazare and Armand pulled the rope tied to the release valve. The balloon began to sink almost immediately. Lazare threw a heavy horse blanket over the brazier to dampen the fire. Smoke swarmed out from underneath it, hiding him and then revealing him. He knelt by the basket of instruments, consulting their faces and taking notes on their numbers. He was a long time at it, his back to her as he jotted numbers with a stubby pencil in the notebook he kept in his pocket.

As they sank, the earth rose to meet them. They flew over a pasture, the balloon's shadow racing along the ground below them. Wild-eyed sheep scrambled ahead of the dark shape, their worried bleats floating up to Camille. Now the brazier smoked worse than ever; Paris disintegrated in a haze of blurred buildings and towers.

She did not want to go back. Not to 11 rue Charlot, not to all the problems that awaited her there. If she had her wish, they *would* sail all the way to England.

Her stomach clenched as they dropped. Closer and closer, until she could see rocks and footprints in the soil below. "Where are the others?" She tried to sound nonchalant.

"There," Lazare said, pointing to a cluster of houses from which two boys on horseback emerged at a gallop, one of the steeds Rosier's tall gray. "They'll try to catch us now."

The balloon swept down, the ground rushing closer. Rosier was yelling; the other boy urged his horse on with his heels.

"Come, Armand!" Lazare called out. "We can't let them get to us before we're on the ground!"

Armand released the last gasp of hot air. They sank to the earth, touched once, twice, and were still. Rosier flung himself off his horse and ran toward them, already shouting. "What a landing! What skill! The Prince and Princess of the Air!"

"And me?" said Armand, tossing Rosier a rope. "Don't I warrant a mention?"

"Bah, you're not in this story!" Rosier pulled back on the line, holding it tight. "My story is full of passion! Poetry! Danger and thrills! But, if I ever write something in praise of tiny little numbers in a row—then, Armand, you will be the hero."

Lazare hopped over the edge of the basket and Rosier embraced him, kissing him on both cheeks. "Formidable, formidable! Get Mademoiselle out of that basket—not that she doesn't look well there, not at all—and I'll uncork the wine!"

Before she could step out, Lazare put his hands on Camille's waist and swung her over the basket's edge. She stumbled a little when she landed and fell forward into his arms. For a moment, he held her close to his chest. His heart against hers thudded once, twice, and then he said, softly: "You liked it?"

"I loved it," she replied.

"Bravo!" cried Rosier, clapping his hands.

From his saddlebag Rosier produced a bottle of wine and Lazare poured quickly, sloshing the golden liquid into their outstretched glasses. As they stood around the basket, Rosier scribbling on a piece of paper, Lazare toasting Armand's scientific prowess, everyone laughing, Camille sipped her wine and studied them. They were all so alive. She wanted to hold on to *this*—the boys' laughing faces, the feeling that she might now be included in their group, what Lazare had said to her up in the air, the way she found him looking at her—all of it.

It was like trying to grasp sunlight itself.

28

Back at Versailles, she won.

As May spun into June, she returned again and again to the palace to play, and she won. At piquet, at lansquenet, at cavagnole. At roulette, its little ball rushing around the ring, she won by luck. At vingt-et-un no one could beat her; she could turn the cards without anyone noticing, raising and lowering the number of pips that graced their faces as required. Still, she needed a bit of luck not to turn a card into one already in someone else's hand, but it hardly mattered. The tables were wild and raucous, the players giddy on wine and the pursuit of a win. Everyone wanted the same thing: luck and money, luck and money.

She sewed new pockets into her gowns so that she could slip her gold louis inside. People sometimes forgot who won and who lost at the tables, and she never wanted to leave with too obvious a purse in case they were reminded. And at the back of her mind, in a corner she didn't think about when she was shaking the dice in her hand, a voice insisted, *The court fears and worships magic. Be careful.*

Working la magie ate away at her, little by little.

She would come home at dawn, and as the glamoire seeped out of her body and the shaking fatigue took hold, she would struggle up the stairs of the building, one hand after another on the wobbling wooden banister until she could open the door to her bedroom, strip off the dress, and fall as if slain onto her bed. Camille's head ached and her limbs were as sore as if she'd hauled buckets of water all day.

She'd promised herself and Sophie that once they had three months' rent for a new apartment, she would stop. But once she had that, she realized she needed even more: eighteen hundred livres. A staggering sum. Or perhaps they needed even more. Because if she were to stop working magic, once and for all, they had need of some other way to live. Perhaps Sophie should have a hat shop of her own. And Camille her own printing press . . .

Soon, she would stop. Soon.

Until then, she watched those at court who shone the brightest and did as they did. She never gloated, only celebrated; she was courteous to everyone she met, and everyone at court wanted to know her. When she walked down the long halls of Versailles, courtiers bowed. Her name was on their lips and in their ears: la belle veuve Fontaine, the lovely widow Fontaine. In her silk purse she carried Chandon's pink card that gave her entrance into the queen's sanctuary at the Petit Trianon, but she never showed it. The guards simply bowed and waved her through.

Camille had money for food now, but no matter how much she ate, she could not fill out her dresses. For what the glamoire gave her, it also took a little for itself.

When Camille first told Sophie about her trips to Versailles, she listened as if hearing a tale of wonder: face alight, hanging on every word.

But later, as the stories piled up, Sophie crossed her arms, or didn't ask, as if Camille had stolen something that rightfully belonged to her.

She hadn't forgotten the balloon flight. How could she? Her fear, the exhilaration of being in the air, what she saw below—and the achy flame of happiness she felt each time she thought of Lazare next to her, his coat around her, his words in her ear: *I'm here with you.*

But Lazare did not come back to the rue Charlot.

It was easier, then, to be at Versailles.

Sometimes Camille strolled in the gardens with Aurélie and other young women at court, gossiping as they walked on lawns sheared by hand by an army of gardeners. The girls wore the pale-colored gowns and straw hats the queen preferred. With Chandon and Foudriard she drifted on the Grand Canal in a curved black gondola, one hand in the water, the other dropping cherries into her mouth. She tried to discover from Chandon more about the other magicians at court, but he seemed unwilling to speak about it when Foudriard was nearby, and they were inseparable. Still, she listened with interest as Chandon told her about all the improvements—a new system for growing grapes, better houses for his tenants—he was advising his father to make at their estate, where he would go when he was no longer wanted by the queen.

She didn't know what to say: she didn't hate Versailles as she'd thought she would. When she left the palace at night, walking on gravel paths in the moonlight, the linden trees fragrant with flowers, she wondered about Maman and how she'd felt about this place. Of course, she'd left it for Papa, but before? Perhaps she'd loved the grandeur and her pony and her little dog on its red ribbon but then, slowly, realized she didn't want it. Camille wondered if she was taking the opposite journey: from disgust to something else—acceptance? Perhaps it was even a dark kind of love. But when, at dawn, the peacocks cried mournfully from the rooftops of the Trianon, she wondered how it might be if she were to stop all this, to stop the blood and the magic and the hollowing out of herself. When was enough going to be enough?

That was when she thought about Lazare, the balloon, and the person she was there. That was her true self, separate from all of this.

Sometimes, though, she felt as if the magic now clung to her more tightly, as if the tiny threads of the dress were working their way into her skin. Being with Lazare—even thinking of Lazare—kept Versailles and magic at bay, but three long weeks had passed since the balloon flight and there had been not one word from him.

Yet at Versailles, with the familiar cards in her hands, and the louis d'or in her purse, she felt safe enough. Or that was what she told herself: that it was for the money, for the new apartment where they would forever escape Alain.

Back in Paris, her winnings paid for food and clothes. Now that they had a steady supply of food, Sophie gained back much of her strength. Her cough disappeared; the laudanum bottle no longer needed replacing. Developing ideas for hat designs from Camille's dreamy descriptions of Versailles's gardens, Sophie became an asked-for designer at Madame Bénard's, and the prices she commanded rose.

Soon they'd have a maid to dress them, a cook to make their food, and scullery maids and housemaids. Now that they paid their rent on time, Madame Lamotte did all she could for the girls. As if she knew they had a foot out the door. When Camille stumbled home at dawn, weak and shaking as the glamoire leaked out, she sometimes found Madame Lamotte drowsing outside her apartment door, waiting.

"And where have you been tonight?" she'd say to Camille, her voice dim with sleep. Her great-grandfather had been a nobleman's companion during the Years of Gold, in the second half of the seventeenth century when Louis XIV was the Sun King and Versailles the center of Europe. When she learned Camille was going to court—Camille never told her how she went, not exactly—Madame told her stories her great-grandfather had told her, of when an elephant escaped the king's menagerie, or when miniature armadas battled on the Grand Canal.

"How was the Life," she asked, voice quavery, "the glory of it all?"

"Incroyable as always, madame." Camille smiled wanly, pulling her cloak over her tattered dress. What should she tell Madame? Something pretty. "When I was leaving, the nightingales were singing in the linden walks. The queen had hung Chinese lanterns in all the trees around the Petit Trianon, as if fairies danced among us."

"I hope you did not gamble too much, my dear. My great-grandfather didn't like it. 'Only death and duels will come of it,' he would say. 'Death and duels.'"

"No, not too much gambling," she replied, bobbing a curtsey before she scooped up her skirts, heavy with hidden coins, and climbed the rest of the stairs.

She was rising, and it was glorious to rise.

29

Coming home late from the dressmaker's and wearing a leaf-green silk dress she'd bought with her own earnings, Sophie flung herself into a chair and kicked off her shoes. Fantôme wound around her shins as she massaged her feet. "All that standing is making my feet grow."

"Madame Bénard's working you hard, now that you've been feeling better?"

"Pas de tout. She could hardly care less about my health. It's the customers. The husbands want me to model the dresses so their wives can decide. They want me to walk back and forth in front of them."

"And you think it's so they can see the dresses?"

"Very funny." Sophie frowned.

Camille remembered the time she'd stopped by Madame Bénard's and Sophie had already left, with a man—or so Madame had said. "Do they ever want to walk you home?" Camille asked.

"The customers?" Sophie bent to pull off a stocking. "Never." She flung it over the arm of her chair and started on the next one. "By the way, someone's downstairs charming the wrinkles off Madame Lamotte."

Camille looked up from the ledger in which she kept their accounts. Sophie's gossip was usually about Madame Bénard's and which dashing gentleman had paid Sophie blush-worthy compliments. "Someone you know?"

Sophie smiled as if she had a secret. "Shall I give you a hint?"

"Please," Camille said, rubbing at her eyes. She'd returned to Paris in the small hours of the night, stumbling from the carriage and pulling the hood of her cape over her head to hide her red-rimmed eyes. It was always this way after the glamoire. A fatigue she felt deep in her bones, an ache at their very centers. And it only became worse, it seemed, the more she did it.

Only coffee ever helped.

Sophie cleared her throat. "The one downstairs. He's very handsome."

"And?" Camille placed her finger on a column of numbers. She wasn't about to be goaded into curiosity by Sophie's tales.

"He likes redheads. And balloons."

Camille shot up from the chair. "He's come for me?"

"And why not? You'll only see him if he's in a balloon?"

"What will I wear?"

"It's nearly dark. He'll hardly see you. Though you may wear my petal-of-rose cloak hanging by the door if you wish. What?" she said as Camille paced the room. "All he wants is a walk. He hasn't asked you to *marry* him."

As if marriage were the most important thing. On her way out of the apartment, Camille rubbed some color into her cheeks. Her skirts in her hands, she raced down the stairs. One flight from the bottom, he called up to her. "Mademoiselle Durbonne!"

He was waiting with a foot on the first broken step, his cocked hat tucked under his arm. His tawny skin was burnished, as if he'd been out in the sun. "You are something to behold," he said.

Camille flushed.

"A new dress?" He hesitated. "I didn't know if you'd come—it felt like centuries were passing, mademoiselle."

For someone who'd grown up in the country, he had a pretty way with words. "It has been a long time, monsieur."

"Regretfully, I've been away from Paris." He smiled then, holding out his arm. "Take a stroll with me? I've something to show you. Tonight's the perfect night."

30

"Where are we going?" Camille asked. They had left rue Charlot and were heading toward the Seine. It was that time of night when the sky brightened into an impossible blue and the crowns and branches of the trees made dark, sumptuous shapes against it. It did not feel the way Paris normally did to Camille. It felt newly made and rather fascinating.

Ahead lay the Pont Notre-Dame. Only a few months ago the houses on the bridge had been torn down. Some rubble remained; here and there a bent nail lay embedded in the dirt. She didn't give the nails—or the soldiers loitering in the streets—a second glance. She didn't need any of them. Usually the city felt dangerous in the evening, set with threats and obstacles. A wilderness. But walking in the dusk with

Lazare at her side as he told her about the history of all the ancient things they passed, Paris felt new.

"Isn't the bridge lovely now, open and wide?" she said. "When I walk across it, I can almost imagine I'm—"

"Flying?"

"How did you guess?"

"Your face." He walked backward in front of her, beckoning her on. "Come, mademoiselle. We're nearly there."

Once on the other side, they arrived quickly at the broad square in front of Notre-Dame. Above them, the old towers hulked against the dusky sky. "Et voilà," he said.

"But the cathedral isn't open at night."

"Ah, but it is for us. I know the night watchman," he said, mischief in his voice.

A quick knock on a side door let them into the church. Camille blushed when the watchman doffed his cap at her. He went ahead of them, holding his lantern high.

"Do you bring many girls here?" she said to Lazare, keeping her voice light.

Lazare seemed oblivious to her innuendo, focused as he was on finding his footing on the stairs. "You're the first person I've thought might care to come with me."

Camille was glad of the dark, cool as a hand over her hot cheeks.

They climbed a quick flight of stairs, coming out onto a narrow gallery overlooking the cathedral's cavernous nave. Like tiny ghosts of flame, candles burned in the side altars, though where their light didn't penetrate, the cathedral was grave-dark.

The watchman unlocked a stout wooden door. It creaked as he pulled it open. "Quick now, monsieur. Stay too long and people will notice." He handed Lazare a lantern and descended into the dark, whistling.

Above her, in the tight coil of the tower, the stairs were pools of shadow, flowing up into an even denser darkness. Somewhere higher she heard a rat scrabbling against the wall. "On second thought, I'd rather not." She tried to turn around and bumped into Lazare.

"It's too beautiful to miss, really. I promise." Lazare didn't move, just gave her the lantern. "You hold the light and go first. It'll be easier than following me."

Again, going up—and first, this time. She heard Sophie laugh at her: *Camille Durbonne, afraid?*

Holding the lantern aloft, she placed her other hand on the wall to steady herself. As she went, the stairs flared into existence, each stone step hollowed in the center by hundreds of years of bell-ringers and night watchmen. Something flew toward her, squeaking. She ducked and covered her hair as the bat swooped past.

"Watch out, monsieur!" she laughed. Behind her, Lazare swore.

Now was her chance to get to the top before she thought too much about the steep stairs or what would happen if she fell. She grabbed her skirts and ran. Up. Up. Up.

"Wait!" Lazare cried.

"Catch me if you can," she called over her shoulder. And kept going.

The lantern swung wildly in her hand, she stumbled once or twice—feeling a lunge of fear when she nearly fell backward and could have killed them both—but then, suddenly, she reached the landing. Lazare was close behind and bumped into her when she slowed down.

"You'll knock me back down!"

"It wouldn't be my fault if I did," he laughed, catching his breath. "The way you ran. Like when you caught the balloon. Did you forget you were holding the lantern?"

"I'm sorry!" But she wasn't. She'd run and he'd been right behind. Maybe he'd only been trying to stay in the light of the lantern, but the feeling of him following her, of being the one to catch, was very pleasing. Now they stood close together in the darkness of the cramped landing, the flickering light catching in the hollows of his throat, his eyes.

"Is this all?"

"You think I'd bring you up here to stand in this stone box?" He reached around her and pushed open the door. "Walk out into the night."

The door swung open into the stars.

The tower's parapet surrounded them at waist-height. From its walls and from the bell tower, chimères loomed, horns curving from their beastly heads, their beaks and cackling mouths gaping. One of the creatures crouched nearby, its head in its hands. "How sad he seems!"

"I suppose he does," Lazare said. "Why, do you think?"

Camille touched the statue's melancholy wings. "His feathers are made of stone. He can't fly, so he's trapped, non?"

The lantern light flared as Lazare shifted behind her. "It's not his fault."

What did he mean? How could it be the fault of the chimère?

He cleared his throat. "Remember, in the balloon, how you said Paris looked so different from above?"

Camille nodded.

"Come see this Paris," he said as he set the lantern down and moved toward the parapet.

Standing at the edge, gripping the stone wall, Camille held her breath. Below them, the city spread out, closer than when they'd been up in the balloon. And now it was night, the windows of the dark houses lit by candlelight; the bridges gleaming with torchlight; barges and boats on the Seine, the flambeaux at their sterns reflected in the inky water. Looking out at the lights of the city—a reflection of the star-flung sky—she felt Paris, her own world, was new to her. The games she played at Versailles—the gambling and the cheating, the magic and the flirting and the conversation—she didn't have to play them here.

"It's almost like flying, being on the tower," she said. "Though not quite as terrifying."

"No." His voice was very close in the darkness.

"Is that why you come up here? Because it's like being in the balloon?"

"Nothing is like that," he said. "But being here, I feel different. Freer, with fewer rules to follow."

A breeze pulled at Camille's cloak and this time she let it, opening her arms so that the pale pink silk winged out behind her. "What if I stepped up on the parapet and launched myself into the air?"

Lazare grabbed her arm. "Don't."

"I only mean I wish I could."

"And leave me here by myself?"

"I thought you knew how to fly, monsieur."

"That's what the balloon is for. Which reminds me," he said quickly. "I have something for you, mademoiselle."

A package, clumsily folded in brown paper and tied with a slippery silk ribbon.

"Did you wrap this?"

"Yes, why?"

Camille shook her head. "No reason." It was comforting to know that not everything came easily to him. While he watched, she slipped off the ribbon—nicer than any she or Sophie had worn in their hair before la magie—and folded back the paper.

It was a balloon, hardly bigger than her hand.

Its chariot was fashioned of woven wire, thin silver threads like ropes running to the balloon, its oilskin surface painted blue like the midnight sky and scattered with silver stars. "Oh," she breathed. It was one of the most beautiful things she had ever seen.

"You don't like it?"

"Oh, monsieur, it's—" She swallowed hard. "It's ravishing. Where did you find such a beautiful little balloon?"

"A jeweler friend and I made it."

For me? She wanted to ask, but she couldn't bear it if he said no. "It's an automaton?" she asked instead.

Lazare reached into his pocket and pulled out a little brass key, which he threaded onto the silk ribbon and gave to her. "A music box."

Camille fit it to a keyhole in the chariot and began to wind it. In her hand, she felt the spring tighten; when she stopped, the balloon began, slowly, to twirl. A tinkling music poured out of it. As the balloon spun, the stars on it shimmered.

Was it meant to be a souvenir of their flight? It had to be. She couldn't speak.

"If you put a candle near it—it's difficult to see it here, in the dark."

"It's not difficult at all. It's absolutely beautiful, monsieur."

"Please call me Lazare."

Camille's stomach danced. "Lazare." Wonderingly, she traced the pattern the stars made. "Does it have a name?"

"Heart's Desire."

Beyond the dark curve of his head, stars dusted the sky. He was standing very close now. His eyes searched her face, catching first on her cheeks, then on her mouth. She reached up, tentatively, and put her hand on his shoulder.

"I've missed you," he said, low in her ear. Camille's heart beat so loudly she knew he must hear it.

She started to ask him where he had been when he bent and kissed her. His lips were soft, asking. Her mouth against his was an answer, her whole being rich and alive, weightless and full of stars, tethered to the only thing that now existed. Gently, his hand caressed her jaw, his fingers twining in her hair. She wanted nothing more than to be here, at the top of the world, kissing him.

And then the night watchman flung open the door.

It was over. They broke away, stepping apart, catching their breath.

For a moment, she saw herself as the old man must see her: her hair half-tumbling down, her face and throat flushed with heat—another foolish girl up in the tower at night.

"Monsieur," he grunted, "you must descend now, or I will lose my position. This is a church, not a—"

"Of course," Camille said, moving toward the door. "We've finished gazing at the stars."

They walked home, side by side, fingertips almost touching. She was afraid to look at him, afraid of what she might see in his face. What if that kiss had meant nothing? What if it was—just a kiss? She wanted it to mean more, but was afraid to hope it did.

When they reached the courtyard door of 11 rue Charlot, Lazare said, "I'll wait here until you're inside."

"Weren't you the one who said my disregard for my own life was equal only to your own?" she teased. "Merci, but I'm perfectly capable of walking these last few steps on my own."

"Of course you are." Lazare paused. Waiting. "You've utterly bewitched me, you know."

Camille fiddled with the cuff on his sleeve. "Does that mean I'll see you again? You won't fly off somewhere?"

"Is tomorrow too early?"

She laughed. "It doesn't have to be tomorrow."

"Oh yes, it does."

Lazare looked as if he might say something else—*do* something else—but he simply bowed. "Until then."

31

She watched him walk down the street until he melted into the darkness, and she pressed the music box to her lips, as if somewhere on the star-scattered oilskin there might still be a faint trace of him.

"Camille."

A shadow separated itself from the gloom.

Camille stumbled backward, her hands scraping against the courtyard wall. She felt for the door, but could not find it. Where were all those soldiers she'd seen before?

"Wait."

It was Alain. She shrank back against the wall. *Please*, she begged silently, let him just leave her alone.

Instead he ambled closer, taking his time. His black cape hung too large around his shoulders, his cocked hat pulled low over his waxen brow. His face was haggard and Camille could find no kindness in it at all. Beneath his hat's brim, his blond hair hung in greasy strands, as if he'd had neither water nor inclination to wash it. His coat was missing buttons, his boots filthy as a soldier's returned from war, and one of his fingers was inexpertly bandaged. The wrapping was rusty with blood.

Camille's hand tightened around the metal balloon.

"Overjoyed to see your brother, as always, non?"

Slowly, carefully, she edged toward the gate. When she found it, she jabbed at the lock with her key, but in her shaking hand it skittered uselessly against it.

"I'll open it for you." Alain was by her side, too close, his breath dank, his clothes reeking of sweat and strong cologne.

Camille tried again. This time, she heard the thunk of the bolt as it slid back. She willed her voice steady. "Leave me alone, Alain."

"I need money."

"For your debts?" she asked, her voice caustic. "No more of your sisters' dresses to gamble with? Or have you completely stopped being a soldier?"

"Bah, I wasn't made for it. They wanted to send me to the country. I was to guard the nobles' bread carts from hungry peasants."

It was a terrible thing to have to do. But it was his job, just like she had hers. "It's better than starving, as those poor people do—"

He put his hand on her arm. She tried to pull away but his grip was strong. "I wouldn't have come but for the man who holds my debts. You have no idea what he'll do to me if I don't pay up."

"He'll speak to the police? Surely you have figured out how to escape them by now?"

Alain persisted. "What about some jewelry, something of Maman's?"

Anger flared inside her. "You sold it all, remember?" Everything but the diamond tear-shaped brooch, and he had been too stupid or afraid to search the burned box for it. "Even the miniature of Sophie and me that hung on Papa's watch chain—you gambled that away, too."

He paused a long moment, and when he spoke his voice was distant, melancholy. "Remember how we used to pretend we were in Astley's?"

The Englishman Astley had opened his Ampithéâtre Anglais in Paris when she was nine years old. Extravagant posters had advertised its miracles. MAN RIDES FOUR HORSES ABREAST! JOCKO THE MONKEY SMOKES A PIPE! CLOWNS! JUGGLERS! DANCING DOGS! After weeks of enduring her relentless begging, Maman and Papa gave in and took them all. They had money then, but the tickets weren't cheap, and their seats crouched under the ceiling at the back of the smoky second tier. Under the blaze of two thousand candles, the lively crowd applauded and sweated. The rope walkers crisscrossed the air, wobbling on purpose to make the audience shout for them to stop. White horses in blue harnesses flashed by. Straddling their backs was a rider holding a banner that spelled out ASTLEY'S in gold. But when the dancing dogs came out, they were too small for Camille to see. Sophie was already up in Papa's arms, clapping her little hands. Though Camille strained on her toes to look over the silhouetted heads of the crowd, she couldn't. It was so unfair!

Then Alain said, *Don't you worry. Put your arms around my neck and I'll lift you up.* He was only twelve, but he was tall, and when he pulled her onto his hip the world of the theater unfurled for her. In ecstasy she watched as Delilah's Dancing Dogs capered across the backs of twenty chairs, yipping happily and catching morsels in their mouths. For weeks afterward, she could not let the entertainment go. Not Alain, either. He'd loved it as much as she. Inspired, he juggled lemons—then plates— for her and helped her prance along the thick rope they stretched across the salon carpet. He even let her ride on his back, balancing on one shaking leg, like her heroes in the ring.

Sorrow swept through her as she remembered what he had been. How much she had loved him, her big brother. Again she took in his dirty, torn clothes. What had happened to him?

"Have pity, Camille!" he begged. "If I have nothing to give, he'll take my soul."

Alain was not prone to nightmares and fancies. Or he hadn't been, before. Was it drink or laudanum that made him think his creditor could take his soul?

"Please," he begged. "Only ten thousand livres and he'll let me go."

"*Only* ten thousand?" she said, coming back to herself at the mention of such a great sum. It was more than twice the amount she and Sophie had saved. "That's more than Papa earned in a year!"

"I won't tell my creditor where you live."

"And if I don't give you the money, you *will* tell him?" Camille snapped. "You'll sell us as harlots—as you threatened before? You may not care for me, but think of Sophie!"

"I don't want to do it." His voice in her ear was a rasp across stone. "Anything you can give me, just so he stops hurting me."

Something cold slithered across Camille's back. If this was true, this person—the man Alain was in debt to—was not a normal man. She gestured to his bandaged hand. "Did he do that to your finger?"

Alain said nothing, but Camille saw it in his face. This man *had* done it. And if he succeeded in breaking him? What would her brother tell him to avoid more pain? Here, in the suffocating dark, he seemed terrified enough to say anything.

It was dangerous, the idea she now had. What if she gave him some money? Just this once? If she did, he might stay away long enough for her and Sophie to escape the rue Charlot. Tomorrow.

"What if I gave you—" What was the right amount? She and Sophie still needed enough to get away. "One thousand?"

Alain clasped her hands and kissed them, his shoulders shaking.

How had it come to this? Her brother, once so handsome and clever and strong, teaching her to play cards and juggle, was now a raving drunkard. Addicted to gambling or laudanum or both. She still remembered the light in Maman's face when he had first come home in his uniform, the buttons on his coat gleaming like tiny suns. With Maman gone, who was left to believe in him?

"I've been waiting for you every night, ma soeur. This is good, a good start, but I'm going to need a lot more to appease him."

"I don't have more—"

He crushed her hands. "I *see* you when you go to Versailles. I know you go there to gamble. Work magic, too, non? What if I told the constable you use counterfeit coins? Told someone at Versailles?"

Fresh anger crackled through her. It always came back to this—no matter everything they'd shared, she was no longer a person to him but a way to get money. He'd been hiding in a doorway, watching as she stumbled exhausted to the courtyard gate, and never lifted a hand to help her. Where was the brother who had pulled her up, shown her the dazzling world she couldn't see?

Utterly gone. Now she too had to get away.

"Constable!" she shouted, adding a tremolo of fear to her voice. "Police! Aidez-moi!"

People in the street, who had ignored them until now, stopped, stared, waiting for something to happen. One of them passed on her call: "Police! Dépêchez-vous!"

The crowd rumbled closer, angry.

His back to them, Alain grabbed Camille's arm and shook it once, hard, like a dog shakes a rat to break its neck. "I won't forget this. This will cost you."

"It's already costing me," she said bitterly. But tomorrow they'd be gone. "Promise you'll never bother me again and I'll leave the money for you with Madame Lamotte."

"Fine." He let go of her arm.

"Stay away from me and Sophie. Understand?"

But Alain had already disappeared into the dark.

32

Hôtel Théron was a beautiful fortress. A high wall protected the house from the street, the only entrance to the courtyard an iron gate topped with spikes. Through the black bars Camille glimpsed a mansion of pale stone, its windows reflecting the hot June sky. The house itself was serene and unconcerned. Alain's appearance at the gate had been the final warning, one she could only disregard at her peril. They had to find another place to live.

"Truly, that's the one?" Sophie asked. "It's so—"

"Imposing?" Even after Camille's time at Versailles and all its blinding excesses, it was a different thing altogether to imagine living in such a place.

Sophie sniffed. "Modest. I thought Aurélie would have recommended something much finer."

"You know, I haven't actually become a wealthy aristocrat," Camille said.

"We *are* aristocrats. At least half-aristocrats. And I thought you said—"

"I *asked* for simple." Camille checked the address Aurélie had scribbled on a receipt for hair powder. "This is the one: rue Saint-Claude, near the church."

"But I wore my best dress." Both of them had. Camille had planned to work a glamoire, but Sophie convinced her it was best not to: did she want to have to work magic every day, to disguise herself from their landlord? She did not. They'd laced themselves into their finest silk dresses, trimmed with ruffles and lace. Camille had chosen a ribboned cloak, while Sophie's cartwheel of a straw hat—one of her own very popular designs—slanted becomingly over her forehead.

The bell in the nearby church began to toll. "It's time." Camille took a deep breath. "Let's knock."

A maid showed them into the quiet house. In the grand entrance hall, a floor of patterned marble led to twin staircases circling to the second floor. On a side table, peonies curved from a vase. A clock ticked somewhere upstairs.

"May we see the rooms?" she asked the maid.

"Of course," the maid said as she led them up the stairs to a set of double doors. Fishing a key from her pocket, she flung them open. In the salon, sunlight streamed through windows and bounced off the high ceilings. The sofas and chairs were freshly upholstered in pink florals and stripes; they perched on plush Savonnerie carpets. She longed to reach down and run her hand through the carpets' dense pile. Off the sitting room, the two bedrooms were less grand, but just as comfortable. Sophie trailed behind the maid, her hand pressed over her mouth in astonishment.

Downstairs, Madame de Théron emerged to greet them. She was

probably close to sixty, wide, and along with her powdered wig, she wore a bright circle of rouge on each cheek. She cast slow, careful looks over their dresses, shoes, their bare hands. Camille resisted tucking them away in her skirts.

"You liked the rooms?" Madame de Théron said finally.

Sophie curtsied. "Very much, madame."

"The rent is thirty louis?" Camille held out a bulging purse. "Here's two months' worth."

"Hélas!" Madame de Théron shook her head, back and forth, back and forth like a pendulum. "I wish I could accept payment from such lovely young ladies, but I cannot! Such a shame! There is, as it happens, someone ahead of you. She liked the rooms very much."

Suspicious. "But she did not take them?" Camille asked.

The old lady waved her hands. "Not yet. She wasn't prepared—financially—to fall in love with my little rooms."

Madame was lying, Camille knew suddenly. The other woman—if there was one—hadn't come with ready money. And here Camille stood, holding out two months' rent to Madame de Théron. If they didn't need the rooms as much as they did, Camille would have snapped. As it was, she tempered her speech. "If she changes her mind, madame, you will let us know, won't you?"

"Of course, of course," she said, all politeness. "I will send a boy to fetch you back."

Once they were out in the street, Camille took Sophie's arm. "Come, I'm sure she's watching from behind the curtains."

Sophie squirmed. "How could Aurélie be so wrong? Didn't she say Madame de Théron had found no one to stay with her?"

"Aurélie was not wrong." Camille led Sophie down the street, away from the windows of the Hôtel Théron. "We were seen through, that's what happened. Madame needs money but she doesn't want ours."

Sophie frowned. "But we're nice people. What could she possibly object to?"

"She wants money, but more than that, she wants a good name. *Quality.* Which apparently we can't offer." Camille had witnessed enough snubs at court to know what this was: all kindness on the surface, silk over unyielding iron.

Sophie managed a smile. "Don't take it so hard. It doesn't matter. There are other rooms, other places." She was working hard to conceal her disappointment, but Camille saw it—a little downward tug of her mouth.

"It isn't fair, or right," Camille said. "We have the money, we played our roles. Why shouldn't we have it?" She had worked so hard to reach a place of safety, only to see it snatched away. Hôtel Théron had everything they needed. Its walls were high, the iron-studded gate unbreakable. Unslip-throughable. There were maids at the doors and gatekeepers to keep out Alain.

"What about another house in this quarter?" Sophie asked. "There have to be other widows with too many rooms."

"They're all the same," Camille fumed. "Aristos who think they're better than everyone else because an ancestor fought a battle in the thirteen hundreds or because their grandparents did a service for the king. With their duels and their titles, they think they're above the law. It's ridiculous."

As they walked slowly down the street, Camille's mind raced through the possibilities. There had to be a way. She simply needed to find it. She might write again to Aurélie. She might try to find something in their own neighborhood. It wouldn't be as nice, but it would be elsewhere—at this moment, an apartment's most important quality.

Sophie had come to a stop and was staring at one of the houses on the street. "Do you recognize that one? It seems so familiar but I can't think why."

Right away Camille knew the one Sophie meant: tall and severely elegant, with menacing black ironwork below the windows. The curtains were drawn, just as they had been before. She'd hoped never to see it again. "Grandmère once lived there. I visited her almost two years ago. With Papa."

Sophie's voice was small. "I didn't know that."

"You were only thirteen, Sophie. I was the age you are now." Papa had known what the visit would entail, and he had spared Sophie the anguish. Camille had known to do the same, and said nothing.

They had gone in secret. Papa wore his finest suit, she her best dress, a dusty pink one of Maman's that she'd made over and a hat she'd trimmed with a new brown ribbon. He smiled vaguely when she asked him where they were going. "You'll see when we arrive," he said. "It's not far."

The stern old house stood before them, the panes in its windows narrow as eyes. She and Papa were ushered into a formal salon. The furniture was stiff and painted with gold, souvenirs of Grandmère's time at Versailles. On the wall hung a small portrait of Louis-Dieudonné, the Sun King, astride his horse. He watched Camille from the painting: dark-eyed, arrogant, knowing.

Grandmère came in and both Papa and Camille bowed deeply, Camille nearly to the floor. "Only a queen deserves such a curtsey," Grandmère corrected. But Camille saw she was flattered.

She did not invite them to sit. "What do you wish, monsieur?"

"I've come without Anne-Louise's knowledge," he admitted. "You know she would never consent to my coming here."

Like a statue, Grandmère waited. A clock ticked in the hall.

"I regret to tell you this, but I was obliged to close the printing shop," Papa said into the heavy stillness.

"It is old news, monsieur. You are lucky the others did not run you out of Paris."

"Your fellow nobles?" In his voice was an edge like a blade, and it frightened Camille.

"You might have been arrested for libel—those anti-Royalist things you printed."

Papa said smoothly, "Perhaps those things were true, and needed saying. Perhaps a new world is on the horizon."

Grandmère looked at Camille to see if she was listening. "Only through my intercession were you and my daughter spared a court case. Prison."

Papa inclined his head. Camille noticed for the first time that a few silver strands laced his hair.

"But you have come for something else, I see," she said imperiously. "Out with it."

Papa took a deep breath. "Money for our family, for your daughter and your three grandchildren, to take us through the winter." Camille stepped closer to him, but he held out his hand for her to stay where she was. Her father's face, Grandmère's tone, the suffocating stillness of the rooms—Camille wanted to rush out the door and disappear.

Haltingly, Papa added, "We don't have enough for wood, or food."

"My daughter would never have been in this situation had she married as I chose for her. She would be at Versailles, an ornament to the court. She would want for nothing."

"I regret—"

"You regret *nothing*." Her voice was biting and cold as ice. "And because of that, I will never give you a sou."

Camille's breath caught as Papa dropped to his knees on the carpet. *No! Get up, get up!* she wanted to shout. She wanted to pull him up and away from this place. Everything was upside down. She could not bear to see her proud Papa on the floor, begging, as if he had nothing, as if they had no other choice, while Grandmère stood over him and gloated.

"I beg you to reconsider, madame. I fear Anne-Louise's—work—will weaken her to the point of exhaustion. Or death."

"You mean, her magic?" Grandmère's mouth was hard. "What of the girls? How old are you, mademoiselle? Do you work la magie?"

"I'm fifteen." The words stuck in Camille's throat. "I'm learning."

Grandmère looked at her more closely then. Camille drew herself up tall, as she knew her mother would want her to do.

Grandmère said, "She might live with me."

Camille shrank back. *Never*. She would starve first.

"We might go to court," Grandmère went on. "I could not give her a title but I might make her a good match. Pity she has red hair." She sniffed. "It's unfashionable, but that's what powder is for, I suppose. But there is another girl, isn't there? Blond, like my daughter? Pretty?"

"Prettier than I," Camille burst out.

"Stop," Papa said, warning in his voice. "My girls have no part in this. Ask what you wish of me, but leave them alone."

Grandmère put her ringed hand to the bodice of her dress and laughed. The sound was like the scratch of dry leaves across cobblestones. "There is nothing I wish of you, monsieur, except that you had never delivered those printed invitations to my door. Could you grant me that wish? Or this one: that my daughter had never deigned to speak to servants—especially not an upstart printer of cards and invitations who convinced her that her own noble privilege was something corrupt. She ruined her life by marrying you—and for what, exactly? Ask what I wish of you? I wish, monsieur, you had never been born."

Camille clenched her small fists. How could Grandmère say that to Papa? Her dear, kind, brilliant Papa, who was full of life and ideas and would do anything—even subject himself to this—to keep them all safe?

Papa rose to his feet. In his best coat, shiny at the elbows from too much use, his back straight, he stared at Grandmère. Camille stepped close, took his hand. It was damp with sweat, cold and hot at once.

"Adieu," he said to Grandmère. He did not bow. "May your pride keep you company when your family is dead."

And then they walked through the hall and out into the street, the crowds moving around them like a river. Camille was terrified to see her father's shoulders shaking. He wiped his tears away. "I wish you had stayed back with Sophie. Did I do wrong to bring you, mon coeur?"

Camille pressed her face into his coat. "You have never done anything wrong, Papa."

She would never forgive her. She vowed it, there on the street. She would never forgive the aristocrats who doomed the print shop, and she would never forgive Grandmère for thinking of Papa in terms of what he lacked. The only things that mattered to Grandmère were the things that Papa did not have. Power, money, a title—Grandmère's aristocratic obsession with these *things* erased him. She could not see him for who he truly was. Camille, too, had come up lacking. It was only magic that gave her any value at all.

Camille had known even then how wrong Grandmère was, though her prejudices were a sticky web, difficult to get rid of. And this new widow—Madame de Théron—she was just the same. This time, though, Camille had the means to change the game.

She straightened her back. "We'll put on something else."

"It won't matter. What else can we do? Our dresses are perfect—"

What had Chandon said? *You must be the Baroness of Pretend.* "We must be even more perfect."

Their apartment in the rue Charlot had shrunk while they were away, the rooms dwindling to cupboards, the chestnut-beamed ceiling bearing down on them.

After Camille told her what she intended, Sophie gamely stepped into another dress and ran out to Madame Bénard's for a wig. "If I wear a wig," she said, "and you change your hair—but not your face—she will have no idea what our true hair color is. Once we move in, we will be free to wear it as we want." It was a good idea—it meant Camille wouldn't have to work the glamoire as often.

When Sophie went out, Camille opened the wardrobe in which the enchanted dress hung. Waiting. She reached out to touch it and felt it shift against her hand, unnervingly alive.

Once she had the dress on, it laced itself up her back. From the shoulder of the dress she took the teardrop brooch and pierced her skin. One, two, three: the drops of blood slid off her arm onto the tattered cloth-of-gold. *Gaudy*, she thought to the dress. *Costly*. A dress only the wealthiest aristocrat could afford. Its power returning, the dress rustled back to life. A wave of purple silk—an expensive color to dye— swept from the hem to her chest. She touched the ebony comb to her hair, fading the red. And though Sophie said Camille should not change her face, she couldn't help covering the freckles on her cheeks and hands, then brightening her lips.

Back at the Hôtel Théron, they gave different names to the maid— the Baroness de la Fontaine and her sister, Mademoiselle de Timbault—

and were shown in once more. Again, they walked through the lovely rooms, though this time Sophie didn't coo. Like Camille, she was grimly determined to act disdainful. And again, Madame de Théron waited for them in the black-and-white entry.

"We liked the rooms, madame," Camille said, her voice diamond-hard, "though they were smaller than we had been led to believe. I could only offer one month's rent at this time."

Madame batted her eyelashes. "It's not really necessary! You are just the kind of young ladies I wish to live here."

The girls nodded slowly, not chancing to say anything that might break the spell.

"Well," said Madame, taking their hands and patting them, as if Sophie and Camille were her granddaughters. "It will make me so happy to have some pretty faces around me." She went on, in a stage whisper, "You wouldn't believe how many undesirables have inquired. It's all the rabble on the streets, calling for this right or that, hanging effigies of our tax collectors in the square—can you imagine?"

Not your tax collector, Camille thought. Noblewomen didn't pay those kinds of taxes.

Camille held out her purse, and this time, Madame de Théron took it, smiling at its weight. "Come as soon as you can, mesdames." And she *curtsied*.

They moved that evening. Camille left their new address with Madame Lamotte, along with strict instructions not to share it with Alain. There was not much Camille wished to take with her in the dray wagon that followed behind them. Among their trunks of dresses and the big basket of Sophie's trims and notions, Camille packed the burned box, her books, and Fantôme in his wicker basket. She also took Papa's bagatelles—the ship, the dragon breathing fire in the word LIBERTÉ!—as well as a well-worn pamphlet Papa had written about the education of girls. He'd called the imaginary heroine Camille. The driver and Madame de Théron's outdoor servants—now *Camille's* outdoor servants—carried the trunks up the stairs; a maid came to help them unpack.

As night crept in, Camille stood by a window, looking down to the street. Somewhere nearby stood Grandmère's house, still and watchful. In the window's glass, Camille's reflection was her own, and even though the glamoire was fading, her face was prettier than it had been, before. The hollows lurking over her collarbones and under her cheeks had all but disappeared. That's what food would do for a girl.

Still, her dress was made of enchantments and her hair shone with magic. Who was she without it? She was a girl with hands still red around the knuckles, hands she'd have to disguise—even from the maids—as long as they lived at the Hôtel Théron. She had hoped to at least stop pretending. But in taking rooms in a noblewoman's house, she traded that freedom for safety. She was protecting herself and Sophie from Alain, she knew. That's what she'd wanted to achieve, after all. But she had thought she would leave la magie behind.

Not completely, of course. Still, she had dreamed she could step out of the wearing-down life of magic and into a new one as easily as stepping into a new pair of shoes.

Not yet.

33

"Do you intend to auction your card?" Camille asked an inebriated Lord Willsingham as he threw back another glass of wine.

"I know not," he said, flummoxed. "Should I, yes, Monsieur le Comte?"

Tediously, the Comte d'Astignac began to explain how auctions worked in the game of speculation. At the palace, midnight had come and gone; among the players shouting and crying, the footmen moved noiselessly from table to table, replacing the guttering candles. Gazing around the packed, thrumming room, familiar cards in her hands and louis d'or in her purse, Camille felt safe. *Safe enough.* Like two sisters in a fairy tale, she and Sophie had escaped from their prison. The beast who'd kept them there hadn't been able to follow. For the moment, they'd slipped away.

Still, however safe the house, there was always the street.

Anyone might come along a street.

Camille had taken one giant step forward by securing them a house with fortress-high walls and an iron gate. Now she needed more, money that would never be taken from them. Money for a shop of Sophie's own. She remembered the printer's apprentice in Papa's old place, wiping his hands on his apron, and she wondered: if she had enough, could she buy her own press? She was a girl, but—could she not, if she tried, continue what Papa had started?

As soon as she had enough for all their dreams, she would stop work-ing magic. The problem was she didn't know how much it would take. And until then, didn't she deserve to have fun? Turning her three of diamonds into the king of spades while keeping watch on the devious Comte d'Astignac under her eyelashes, Camille sighed. She knew it was more than that which brought her back to Versailles.

No sooner had Lazare dropped into her life, than he had dropped out. Now all of Paris felt as an empty house does, lonely and full of echoes. She'd reminded Madame Lamotte to tell only Lazare her new address. For three days she waited for him to come and see her. Hadn't he said tomorrow wasn't soon enough? She wanted to bask in the warmth of his smile, that one corner of his mouth curling up as the light danced in his eyes.

But he never came.

So tired of waiting that her own skin felt too tight, hungry for some-thing to happen, she'd gone to back to Versailles. She almost fright-ened herself at how easy it'd become. Each quiet dawn her hired carriage clattered to a halt outside the gate of the Hôtel Théron. Each afternoon, when she woke, Sophie was gone. Camille ate alone at the polished table. The rooms seemed too big without her sister's conversation, her teasing. While Sophie charmed customers at Madame Bénard's, Ca-mille wandered, restless, among the arcades at the Place des Vosges, hoping for a glimpse of Lazare.

"Madame?" Lord Willsingham said.

Camille startled back into the game and flipped the magicked king faceup. Across the table, the Comte d'Astignac groaned. "You don't make it easy, Madame de la Fontaine." He snapped his fingers for more gambling chips. "Pas de tout."

Willsingham called for more wine. Neither the comte nor Lord Willsingham was good enough to match her. There was no question that she would win, the question was only when. As she watched the comte organize his chips, something soft brushed Camille's left cheek. It was Aurélie's fur-trimmed cloak.

"Darling!" she breathed. "I haven't seen you in centuries! Come quickly, won't you? We're playing cache-cache at the Green Carpet!"

D'Astignac scowled. "What are you saying, Madame de Valledoré?"

"Hide-and-seek on the Green Carpet?" Camille said to Aurélie behind her fan.

"On the lawn that leads to the Fountain of Apollo. Hurry! The sun's nearly up and then all the fun will be—pouf!"

Out of nowhere Chandon appeared, his hazel eyes feverishly bright and his cheeks flushed. He threw her cloak over his arm. "It's hardly a lawn, nor is hide-and-seek a proper game. Still, it's bafflingly amusing."

"But what about all this?" Camille gestured at the teetering stack of chips in the center of the table.

"Give someone else a chance," Chandon said as he tossed her cards on the table. "Come!"

"But I'm not finished!" Camille laughed as she tried to shake off Aurélie, who only pulled harder.

"Eh, Monsieur le Marquis, have a care! The game's not over," the Comte d'Astignac said, half rising from his seat. "I've staked too much for her to go now."

Chandon assessed the stack of chips in front of Camille. Grabbing half, he stuffed them into her purse; the rest he divided between the remaining players. "Ça va? My apologies, Monsieur le Comte, for taking the baroness, but we cannot delay one more moment. She's agreed to help me tend the sick." He raised an eyebrow. "Who are dying of terrible diseases."

D'Astignac blanched. "Go then, and God be with you."

"How ever did you do that?" Camille asked as she followed Chandon outside.

"He's notoriously afraid of any kind of sickness," Chandon said. "Mention it and he'll run the other direction."

"Still, one minute more and d'Astignac would have wagered the lease for his house!" Camille said.

"Bah! He only mentions it to lure unsuspecting ladies into his trap," said Aurélie with a smirk. "Then, he trounces you."

Camille frowned, half-serious. "No one trounces me."

"Not yet. Besides," Chandon observed, "too much winning isn't good for anyone. Remember?"

Camille ducked her head. She'd been unwise. In the thrill of the moment, it was all too easy to forget. "I'll be more careful, I promise."

"Careful about what?" Aurélie asked.

"Allons-y!" Taking a lantern from a table, Chandon ushered them through the doors. "Cache-cache awaits."

The moonlit night was cool relief after the heat of the gaming rooms. Their pastel-colored clothes glowed in the darkness as they ran between the pools of the Water Parterre and down the stone steps to the next parterre, where a party was taking place under a large silken tent, glowing with rose-colored candles. In the vague darkness, it shimmered like a moth's wing. The queen and her friends were dining at a long table, jumbled with glasses and plates and food. Stumbling around the edge of the tent, a blindfolded courtier fell into a man's lap; Marie Antoinette and her favorite, the Duchess de Polignac, burst out laughing. Next to the queen, a man in a foreign uniform poured champagne until it frothed over the lips of the glasses.

"Something new, those tinted candles?" Chandon asked idly as they went by, keeping well away from the party.

"All the rage, mon ami," Aurélie said, linking arms with Camille and Chandon as they headed down the slope. "If you want them, you must order in advance, and after you order, you must wait. Can you imagine: a queue for candles?"

It is nothing compared to a queue for bread, Camille thought, but she kept it to herself.

Two soaring walls of yew trees—so tall they blocked out the stars—edged the stretch of lawn known as the Green Carpet. Against their plush gloom, marble statues of Roman gods and goddesses glowed eerily white.

"They're like ghosts," Aurélie said with a shiver.

"Shh, the real ghosts will hear you." Chandon stared down the expanse of shadowy green. "Where are the others?"

"There." Aurélie pointed straight ahead. "Someone's coming out of the trees."

Two figures stepped out of the hedge: one wore a crown of flowers; the other one, golden-haired, stopped and raised his arm. "Dépêchez-vous!" the Vicomte de Séguin shouted. "The game's nearly over!"

"Séguin," muttered Chandon. "Always appearing where he's not wanted."

"Some may want him," Aurélie said, squeezing Camille's arm. "Even though he's not a marquis like you, Chandon, he is terribly rich and handsome, if you like your lover to resemble a gold statue. I've caught him looking at our baroness with something very much like longing."

"Hardly," Camille said, though she knew what Aurélie meant about the way he stared. "More like he's hoping to catch me cheating."

When they reached the middle of the lawn, Séguin had already disappeared into the hedges and Julien Aubert, Baron de Guilleux, strode up to them. Strikingly sunburned, as if he spent long hours out of doors, with a beaky nose like a Roman emperor, Guilleux was all warmth and smiles. Against his golden-brown skin, his sea-green eyes nearly glowed. He had a tumbler of red wine in his hand, which he finished off and then set neatly in the grass.

"Bienvenue à nos jeux!" He beamed. "Everyone, welcome to our entertainments!"

"Julien's an officer in the navy—and our host," Aurélie said in Camille's ear. "The midnight garden revels, including this game of cache-cache, are his invention. Isn't he terribly clever?"

Greeting them all with kisses, even Camille, he crowned them with wildflower circlets like his own. Only Aurélie's was fashioned of tiny pink roses that gleamed against her ebony hair; by the way the baron looked at Aurélie with unabashed admiration, Camille suspected he'd planned it.

"You've come just in time, mes amis," Guilleux said. "The others have already taken their hiding places. Per our usual rules, the person who's le loup—the wolf—guards the Fountain of Apollo—the one with the bronze horses and chariot. Put your hand in the fountain's water and you are safe. Be touched by le loup, however, and you must hunt with le loup."

"Hunt with the wolf?" Camille laughed.

Guilleux pretended to launch an arrow from an imaginary bow. "To help him, bien sûr, and find all the others who are hiding."

"And what's our prize? If we're the last to be found?" Aurélie asked.

"A gondola ride on the Grand Canal." Guilleux smiled when he saw their surprised faces. "My valet arranged it." He waved toward the Apollo fountain, where a shadow stood out against the water, waiting. "Count again, will you?" Guilleux shouted to the boy standing there. "We've three more who want to play."

While the boy counted, his voice muffled, the others scrambled into the maze of hedges and topiary surrounding the fountain. Camille had hoped to hide with Chandon, but he vanished quickly into the maze of yews. Ducking as branches scratched at her face, Camille ran on. Behind the statues, shadows deepened: good places to hide. She squeezed in behind a figure of Proserpine. No one would see her; she could barely see her own hand. But she could see the fountain, and the shape of the boy who was le loup, straight ahead of her. As soon as he went to look for the others, she'd run to put her hand in the water.

She stooped in the hedge for what seemed like hours. Field mice scratched in the leaves nearby, and she tucked her dress closer. She felt it resist; it didn't like to be cramped. She slapped at midges biting her neck. Behind her, the bushes crackled as Aurélie bumbled in.

"I found you!" She crouched down beside Camille. "Isn't this a charming game?"

"It might be, if your skirt wasn't suffocating me," Camille said as she pushed some of the flounces away.

"What? There's nowhere else to hide."

"We're in the gardens of the palace. There must be a hundred places!" But secretly Camille was glad Aurélie had sought her out.

"And be too far away? I don't know what I'll do if Guilleux doesn't find me. I might expire." She rested her head on Camille's shoulder. "I'm so desperately in love with him."

"He's certainly besotted with you."

"You think?" Aurélie sighed. "My husband won't care, as long as he never hears of it. But it's hard to be discreet here. Everyone loves rumors and if you are young and pretty—as we are—they're thrilled if the rumors bring you down. Maman warned me that at Versailles, the men hunt in the forests and the women hunt in the palace." She peered through the rustling bushes. "Voilà! Here comes Julien. I hoped he was following me."

Soon the Baron de Guilleux was kneeling under the yew branches next to Aurélie. They grinned at each other. "This is fun, isn't it?" Guilleux said. "All crushed in together like this?"

Camille laughed. But underneath her smile, the sight of the two of them—pressed close in the underbrush like child-elves from fairyland—made her ache with envy.

"Hush!" Guilleux said. "The wolf will hear us."

"Look there." Aurélie pointed out into the clearing. "He's moving."

Having left his post by the fountain, the figure wandered off to the right, where he disappeared in the shadows of the trees. Overhead, a nightingale trilled.

"I'll go, then," Camille said. "Bonne chance." She peeled back the branches until she stood, listening, in front of the hedge. Now was her moment. Picking up her skirts, she ran toward the fountain. It was not far, and she was almost there when she heard something crash out of the trees. Then the wolf caught her, grasping her shoulder.

"Got you!" he shouted.

"You sneak!" Camille said, pushing his hand off. "The wolf isn't supposed to hide!"

Behind her, he was breathing hard. "All's fair in love and cache-cache."

She spun around to face him.

He looked as if he'd stepped out of a woodland scene in a play: deep-green suit, a heavy crown of fern and daisies in his hair. In the dark, lace gleamed white at his throat and around the hand he still held suspended in the air. A diamond ring on his finger caught the starlight. When he saw her expression, he laughed, his teeth a flash in the tawny brown of his beautiful face.

It was Lazare.

34

He was dressed like every aristocrat in the palace.

She struggled to take it all in: the suit embroidered in silver that hugged his shoulders like a second skin, its pockets empty of packages or spyglasses. Fashionable breeches ran tight down his thighs; the buckles on his shoes glittered with white stones. Even his cravat—usually a messy afterthought—was snow-white and meticulously tied.

And the drumming thought in her mind: how?

Even his ink-black hair was faintly powdered, she saw now. Apart from his clever, long-fingered hands and his golden skin, he could have been anyone else. *Like me*, she thought—perhaps he too had disguised himself to come here? A tiny spark of hope flamed to life. She'd thought him a member of the bourgeoisie, but he too might be a thief and a gambler like her, come to prey on the aristocrats.

"You?" she gasped.

"Why not?"

"That's all you have to say?"

Lazare stared. "Forgive me, have we met before?"

No shock of recognition. He did not see her.

From the time when she first came to Versailles and the Vicomte de Séguin didn't recognize her, she knew that the glamoire would shield her, as long as the magic lasted. That was what the glamoire was supposed to do. Hide her.

And yet.

She'd been herself with him, in Paris. She'd been someone else here, and until now, she'd managed to keep her worlds distinct. Separate. But Lazare had stepped from one to the other and now she was lost. It was as if she'd marked her path through the woods with bread crumbs, only to find the path utterly gone.

Her snare-drum pulse beat faster and faster, but she willed herself calm.

He bowed, deeply, making a flourish with his hand. "Lazare Mellais."

"He's also the Marquis de Sablebois," Aurélie called as she burst out of the bushes and threw her arms around his neck. "Unlike me, he never mentions his title unless he has to."

No. He could not be. Not one of them, not Lazare with his lazy smile, his graceful ease. He smiled at Aurélie—a kind smile, a brother's smile— as Camille's mind reeled between opposites: revulsion that those hands were ones that could write letters asking for favors from the king, and spinning desire for those same hands, the ones that touched her.

Between herself and these aristocrats she'd built a fine wall in her mind: they might come this far *only*; she might walk to that border, but she would not wholly cross it nor dismantle it, brick by invisible brick. There was too much safety in it. Aristocrats had been the enemy for too long to let her guard down. Grandmère; the clients of Papa's who turned on him and made him go bankrupt for his political views. The rich who stood on the backs of the poor and bent them to the ground.

Now an aristocrat stood *inside* her wall.

"My title is a suit that doesn't fit," Lazare said, quickly, but she couldn't tell if his nonchalance was real or pretend. "Will you introduce me to your friend?"

"Isn't she the loveliest? This is Cécile, the Baroness de la Fontaine."

"Enchanté," Lazare said, bowing again.

Camille flushed as she curtsied.

"She's recently come to court," Aurélie went on. "Her husband's dead."

"Aurélie, what are you saying?" Lazare said, as if offended on Camille's behalf.

"She doesn't care. Husbands aren't any good unless they're gone— which you would know, Lazare, if you were required to have one."

His face clouded. "My apologies."

"Not at all," Camille said, using her best imitation of Aurélie to cover the confusion she felt. "But I wonder if it's not time for me to go." She counterfeited a pretty yawn. "It's almost morning and I've a long ride back to Paris."

"But you mustn't, not yet—"

A shout cut Aurélie off.

Out of the hedges on the other side of the fountain, Chandon emerged, followed closely by Séguin. As they came closer, Camille saw that Chandon was injured, a livid scratch across his cheek.

"You're hurt!" she cried.

"It was Séguin who did it," Chandon snapped. "He forgets himself and behaves like the ruffian he is."

"Blame it on me, of course," the vicomte said silkily. His face wore its usual sneer. "It was the way you were scrambling through the shrubbery."

Angry color flared in Chandon's cheeks. "I was hurt trying to get away from *you*."

"You're bleeding." Séguin stepped close to Chandon as he dug in his pocket for a handkerchief.

Chandon flung off Séguin's hand. "Leave me!"

"I only wish to help. What ails you?" he said, his voice mocking.

In answer, Chandon drew his sword with a hiss of steel.

Instantly, as if he were Chandon's mirror-image, Séguin drew his own weapon. In the moonlight, its blade gleamed, a cold smile. A line of energy sprang up between the two sword-points, racing up the boys' arms to their shoulders, necks, and their tense, terrifying faces.

The line crackled with heat.

Desperate for them to cease, for there to be no more fighting, no one hurt, Camille cried out, "Stop it! Please don't—"

"I told you to stay away from me," Chandon growled. Blade up, he circled closer.

"You forget yourself," Séguin hissed, the tip of his sword leveled at Chandon's throat. "You cannot tell me what to do."

At the malice in his voice, Camille's dress stiffened, uneasy.

"No?" Chandon laughed grimly. "You think you have so much power? I outrank you in every way possible, *Vicomte*."

"Hardly," Séguin snapped. "Rank means nothing when you are—"

"Enough!" Aurélie dashed between them and held her hands up, her palms only inches from their swords' points. Her chest rose and fell. "What will you do? Fight until first blood, when one of you is cut open? Then call for the court surgeon to come and sew you up? Or will your honor only be satisfied with death? The king forbids dueling and will throw you in prison, titles or not," she stormed. "Besides, you're behaving like idiots."

The tip of Chandon's sword wobbled.

"Don't have what it takes, Chandon?" Séguin sneered.

"You know it's not that." Under his breath, he spat: "*Cheater*."

"What did you say?"

"Come away, Aurélie." Guilleux's throat worked. "And both of you, put down your swords. You're frightening the ladies with your foolishness."

Drawn by the shouting, Foudriard had emerged from his hiding place and come to stand by Chandon. He said something to him, but Chandon shook his head, coughing. "Tell him to keep his hands off me," he said.

Séguin laughed. "Most people want my hands on them, but, as you wish." Sheathing his sword, he strode away.

Chandon and Séguin had nearly dueled over a scratch. Camille had thought duels were fought for love, or honor—not something as trivial as that. Unless it wasn't trivial? Perhaps there was bad blood between them. Some old grudge?

"Are you cold, madame? Take my coat," Lazare said, shrugging out of it. "Please." He must have seen something in her face, because he added, quietly so only she might hear, "You're Chandon's friend, non? Don't worry about him. He and I played at duels when we first came to court, as children. For all his wit, he has a quick temper. But rest assured, in dueling, no one's his equal."

It didn't do much to reassure her, but it was something. Lazare held his coat out behind her, just as he had in the balloon. When she stepped backward into its warmth, his hands brushed her bare neck, just as they had when as they'd sailed over Paris. She'd thought then that he'd done it because he cared about her, because he wanted to have the excuse to touch her. But now? Why did he do it now if he hadn't recognized her?

Perhaps—a prickling, painful thought—he was this kind to all the girls he met. Perhaps he did take other girls up in the tower at Notre-Dame and tell them, too, that they'd bewitched him.

She did not know anymore.

He went to where Foudriard stood with Chandon, his face still white and flat as a sheet. Lazare bent his dark head to Chandon's walnut-colored one. She couldn't hear what they said, but eventually, Chandon laughed, gripped Lazare's shoulder. He was kind; she could not deny it.

At the far end of the linden walk, a flutter of movement. "Someone's coming," she said.

Led by a boy holding a candelabra of ice-blue candles, Marie

Antoinette, in a simple white dress, strolled toward them. Next to her, a man in a foreign uniform walked languidly, picking wildflowers.

"How lovely she still is," Aurélie murmured. "Can you believe she is thirty-four? Some say she drinks secret potions to keep her complexion. Arsenic—or magic."

"Arsenic, most likely," said Chandon. He raised his eyebrow significantly at Camille.

Did he mean the queen used magic?

"Of course it's arsenic! Magic doesn't exist," Aurélie protested. "Not anymore. Everyone knows that."

"Do they?" Chandon's voice had an edge she hadn't noticed before. "Magic built the Palace of Versailles. What makes you think it's gone?"

"Wouldn't we know if it was still here? For myself, I'd love there to be magic all around," Aurélie said with a glance at Guilleux. "Love potions, especially."

Chandon coughed. He was trying to tell Camille something, she was certain of it. "What sort of magic does the queen use?" she asked him, under her breath.

"A kind of disguise. But she is no magician."

A glamoire? But if not a magician, how could she work one?

Lazare overheard them. "If it *is* magic," he said, "then I have even less respect for her than before. Taking blood from others and using it to enrich themselves—why should the magicians have been allowed to stay at court after the things they did?"

Camille stared at Chandon. Taking blood from *others*? What did Lazare mean? Was this something else Maman had never told her?

"The magicians were bloodsuckers?" Aurélie asked, a thrill in her voice.

"That and worse. La magie is detestable," Lazare said, coldly. "It was one of the tools of the ancien régime, the old days. Magic has no place in this age of Enlightenment."

A tool of the old way of ruling that had been in place for hundreds of years, magic was part of the system by which nobles had everything, the people nothing. What grim work had they done, her magician ancestors? Had they truly drained people of blood, like vampires in folktales? If so, they'd wanted the power that came from working blood magic—but not to suffer its cost. It was terribly wrong. She was repulsed that it might even have been possible.

"But why—" Camille began.

"Hush now, my revolutionaries, here they come," said Chandon.

As the entourage drew close, Aurélie, Camille, and all the boys bowed deeply.

The queen paused before them and smiled. "Up, up, everyone! Etiquette holds no sway in my gardens. It is refreshing to see young people out in the greenery. Soon the sun rises," she warned, as she swept away. "Be quick with your games."

Foudriard threw his arm over Chandon's shoulders. "We must hurry, the queen commands it."

Camille watched the queen glide back toward the palace. The uniformed man handed her the bouquet he'd picked and her ladies ambled behind her, the hems of their dresses soaked with dew. As the group headed away, the boy with the candelabra of sky-blue candles ran to catch up and, in that instant, Camille knew him: the chandler's apprentice with the fancy airs, the one who'd taken her turned louis without a second thought. He cast a glance at Aurélie, then Camille, before rushing past them, candle flames wavering. They were all court ladies to him—once again, she'd gone unseen.

Aurélie sighed. "The queen has the dashing Count von Fersen at her beck and call—*and* that poor chandler, the one whose candles are impossible to buy! How he stares at her! Perhaps she will make him Court Chandler." She cast a teasing glance at Guilleux. "He is not bad to look at, either."

Guilleux crossed his arms and started walking away, his good humor gone. "You cannot make me envious of a chandler who waits on the queen, hoping to rise."

Coming from the other direction, Séguin bowed as he passed the queen, who stopped and exchanged a few words with him.

"Who could possibly envy the poor?" he called as he strode closer. "They are a repulsive lot."

"I hate to agree with the vicomte but it's true—the poor are dreadfully boring," Aurélie said. "Let's speak of something else!"

Camille flinched as if she'd been hit. "Do you truly mean that?"

"Of course she does," Séguin said. "What are they but starving mice, living in our grain houses?"

"Mice?" Camille's voice climbed. Any benefit of the doubt she'd given to Séguin was completely gone. "The poor don't steal *your* grain—they are the ones who grow and harvest it! How do you think you—we—have all this?"

"Bah," said Séguin scornfully. "In Paris the streets are full of poor people doing absolutely nothing. They are filthy, lazy—"

"Don't say it," Lazare interrupted, his voice like ice.

"Tell us," Séguin said, "how is it on the other side, Sablebois?"

"What do you mean, the other side?"

Séguin shrugged. "The *dark* side. La vie sauvage."

Cold anger rushed through Camille as she watched Lazare swallow hard, look away. How dare Séguin imply that there was something wrong with Lazare because of the color of his skin? She did not know how far she could go, but she had to say something. "The dark places are in our own hearts, isn't that so, monsieur?" she said, her voice cutting. "Isn't it our duty to help others?"

Séguin regarded her carefully before his hard, golden gaze twitched to Lazare. "What were we talking about?" He yawned. "Baroness, care to take a turn in the shrubbery?"

"No one is safe in the shrubbery with you," Chandon snapped. "Stay with us, Baroness."

Foudriard put his hand up. "Before more swords are drawn," he warned, "does anyone wish to take a boat ride?"

On the Grand Canal, the curving, black silhouette of a gondola cut through the silver water. A lantern light winked at its prow. "Guilleux's boat approaches," Chandon said. "Coming for you, Aurélie, I suppose. None of us will get a ride before the sun comes up."

"Well then," Lazare said, "I must be going. Good night, everyone."

"So soon?" Camille heard herself saying. She wanted to pinch herself.

"He must return to his balloons and whatnot," Séguin answered. "Pointless, futile, and utterly childish experiments."

Ignoring him, Lazare began to walk toward the palace, his head up. When the dawn breeze billowed the sleeves of his chemise, Camille realized she still had his coat. "Monsieur!" she called, running a few steps to catch up with him.

"I'm loath to take it from you," he said. "You'll be cold."

When she tried to slip out of it, he came forward and took it off her shoulders. As he did so, his fingers again brushed the bare skin on her back, between her dress and her neck—and then were gone. It was perfectly respectable, but its effect on her was decidedly *not*. She exhaled. "I wish the Vicomte de Séguin had not said those things."

Lazare startled—a flash of deep brown eyes, a black sweep of lashes. "That's kind of you."

Down by the water, Guilleux started to sing a bawdy sailor's song that made Aurélie shriek with laughter.

"What's wrong with Séguin, that he behaves that way?"

"He believes he behaves perfectly," Lazare said, exasperated. "He's been that way since he came to court three years ago. Along with Chandon, we were all under one fencing master. One day, after our lesson, Chandon challenged Séguin and won handily. Embarrassed, Séguin thought to vanquish me. I'll admit it to you, madame—I brought him to tears." One side of his mouth curled into a smile. "He's never forgiven me for being who I am, and beating him."

"But it's pathetic, non?" It stung to think of anyone being against Lazare.

For a moment, she thought he might say something in response, but he only shook his head, as if he'd answered a question he'd been asking himself. "I must go—my balloon, the one Séguin's always harping on—awaits." And then it was over. With a wink, he said adieu, asking her to give his best to the others.

As he strode easily up the inky green slope, his sword swinging, he looked back at her over his shoulder.

Their eyes met.

Something flickered in his face—what?—but it vanished as quickly as it came. He continued to the palace.

Her shoulders sagged with relief. He did not suspect.

Camille pressed a hand to the bodice of the dress, felt its fibers shift and meet her palm. The glamoire had perfected her to the point at which she no longer resembled herself. She knew how she looked in the mirror: illusion erased the hollows of her face, her freckles. Certainly Sophie recognized Camille when she was glamoired—but Sophie was her sister. She knew who Camille was on the inside. And Sophie had watched her put on the glamoire's mask. She knew what was under it.

Lazare, luckily, did not.

"Someone caught your fancy?" Aurélie called out.

The last thing Camille wanted was for others to suspect there was something between them. "Not at all."

"Come, then, Cécile. Let's go watch the sunrise! There's room in the boat with me and Guilleux."

With the two of them, in the boat? She felt suddenly very much outside of it all.

"You go," Camille called out, waving her and the others on. Her heart hurt. She tried to understand what Lazare was doing at Versailles, but she could not. Why was everything so hard?

Chandon stayed behind, flicking at the grass with the toe of his gold-buckled shoe. "Something on your mind?"

She blurted out, "I don't belong here. And nothing is as it seems." Though she was one of them by blood, the horror of what Lazare had said haunted her: one of her aristocrat ancestors in her finery—perhaps in this very dress—slicing open the arm of a peasant and putting it to her lips. "Is it true that aristocrats used the blood of others for their magic?"

Chandon rubbed the back of his neck. "I wish it weren't, but I know it to be so. They often preyed upon the poor, sometimes even their own servants. After all, who has more sorrow than the poor?"

She had nothing to say against that.

"What happened, in the shrubbery?" she asked, recalling Chandon and Séguin with their swords drawn, tethered by anger and that erupting line of energy.

His hands shook as he adjusted the lace at his cuffs. "Séguin? He wished to remind me of my place, as he sees it. He is a cheat, Baroness, and he is very clever." He glanced down the lawn to the others. They were out of hearing, but still he dropped his voice. "This is what I have needed to tell you for all these weeks, but couldn't find the right time. And now with his talk of strolling with you in the shrubbery, I can't stay silent. I wish someone had warned me." He lowered his voice further. "Séguin is a magician. And unlike us, he's not a nice one."

"A magician?" she stammered. How had she met him all these times and never known?

"You didn't guess?"

"How should I have?" she said, uncertain.

"Have you never noticed how a magician smells? Like burned wood? Perfume helps, of course. But Séguin works so much magic he positively reeks of it."

She recalled the card game, the scent she couldn't place lingering under his cologne. "But before tonight, he seemed so helpful. And then with the Marquis de Sablebois—"

"That's precisely it!" Chandon's voice hardened. "Sablebois is noble and honorable and he doesn't give a fig for Séguin's feelings. Séguin is beneath him, and Sablebois decides to shrug. But *we* may not. That is what I meant when I said you must be the Baroness of Pretend," Chandon added, urgently. "You must not reveal *anything* to him, for he will use it against you. Don't even show him your wariness, vous comprenez? Promise me, you won't let on?"

"Come on, you two!" Aurélie sang out.

"Of course, I promise. But—is it not safe here? Because of Séguin?"

Chandon cocked his head. "I for one cannot stay away. And it seems, neither can you."

"I won't be here long," she said, though she hardly believed it herself. "Soon I'll have enough louis that I can stop gambling."

"How many louis is that? I'll admit, I've never seen a number that satisfies." Chandon smiled wanly. "It's hard to stop gambling, and harder even to stay away, if you're a magician. Don't you see? Versailles is one enormous, fantastical magical object. Every roof tile and doorknob and armoire bristles with magic. And—I'm guessing your dress is the same— those threads of magic grasp at us like tiny hands, or fishhooks. It is very difficult to tear yourself loose."

"Thank you," she said, wearily. Everything had become so complicated.

A shadow slid over Chandon's face. "Why thank me? It's a warning, madame. The best I can do, considering. As for belonging at Versailles, you know that you—we—of all people, belong here. We made this monster."

In front of them, the long rectangle of water had turned to gold. Inside the palace, servants would be stumbling awake as nobles tripped from gaming tables and secret trysts into their beds. In the orangerie, gardeners would be harvesting fruit for the queen's breakfast; in the royal stables, the king's horses would be snuffling at their grain.

"It's so beautiful," Camille said, and was surprised by the catch in her voice. "This monster."

"It's a pretty prison, no more." Chandon gingerly touched the scratch on his cheek. "I'd rather be home in Normandie, drinking cider in an orchard with Foudriard, not a care in the world."

"Why stay, then?"

Chandon gazed down the lawn to the shimmer of water behind Foudriard's broad-shouldered silhouette. "For him. He loves what he does. As long as his post with the cavalry keeps him here, this is the best place for me to be. Imagine if he were sent elsewhere, and I not allowed to go—" He sighed, his breath ragged. His hazel eyes were bright with tears. "Am I being foolish?"

"Not at all." Camille took his hand. It was strangely hot. "Are you not well, Chandon?"

"As well as can be expected, Baroness Whoever-You-Are."

"You must call me Camille."

"A bientôt, then, Camille, mon amie," Chandon said. "Until next time?"

"How did you know I was leaving?"

"You'd better," he said, sotto voce. "Your dress is turning."

35

As Camille returned to Paris, the sun rose above the horizon. The carriage trundled past open fields and vineyards and small towns, their stone houses crowding the edge of the road as if they wanted to see inside the passing carriages. She sat with her elbow on the window's edge, watching the countryside go by.

Lazare was an aristocrat.

So much money, so much privilege, so much noblesse oblige toward the poor. Had he included her in his noble kindness? Or did he care for her as she was?

The carriage picked up speed. A broken-down manor house flashed by. A milkmaid in man's shoes poking thin cows with a branch.

And Séguin a magician.

She thought of the time he'd offered to help her avoid the traps of court. She was sure he'd meant it as a kindness. But the way he'd read her palm, the fire in his hands when he touched her, that was something else. Were the intense looks he gave her—the ones that made her want to pull her cloak up to her chin to stop him from seeing *into* her—those of a magician? Or were they the looks of someone who wanted to trap her in an empty room and push her against the wall, his hands shoving up her skirts?

Bile rose in her throat. There was something brutish about him, used to getting his way. But whether that was because he was an aristocrat or because he was a magician—or both—she did not know.

She lowered the carriage window and inhaled the cool morning air. Either way, she needed to be careful. And to pretend she wasn't. Was Séguin somehow interested in Chandon, too, because they were both magicians? That charged line vibrating between them and their swords. Where had she seen it before?

Rows of unripe grapes on a hill. Ducks flapping from a pond.

And then, as if in a darkened salon someone had held up a candle and suddenly everything in the room could be seen, if only dimly, she realized: she'd felt that same line of energy between him and herself the first time she'd come to Versailles.

But what did it mean?

Did he want something from her beyond what any rake in the palace wanted? It was close, the answer. She could feel it, a pulling certainty in her fingertips. But she could not grasp it.

Whatever it was, she was not relinquishing Versailles to Séguin. She would not be frightened away. Not when there was so much she still wished to do.

36

Sunlight flared in around the edges of the bed curtains. Camille blinked, rubbed at her neck. She'd fallen asleep so fast that she'd slept on it twisted. It was crooked and stiff. Her whole body ached from the glamoire. She wanted nothing more than to forget what had happened last night and sleep for another day or two.

"You awake?" Sophie called though the bedroom door.

Wrapping a shawl around her shoulders, Camille walked numbly out into the salon, where Sophie stood by the fireplace, reading a letter.

"Partially," Camille said, rolling her shoulders. "You've been out already?"

Sophie slipped the letter into her sleeve. "Not everyone keeps such hours as you, ma soeur." She removed her hat—a tall, mint-green confection trimmed with swooping egret feathers, a wide, striped ribbon, and silk camellias dyed scarlet—and laid it reverently on a table. "I took a walk with some girls from the shop. We wanted to show off our hats, see if we might drum up some business."

"And did you? It's quite something."

Sophie laughed. "I made it in honor of a new kind of pastry from Sweden, if you can believe it. Ladies practically threw themselves at me on the street, begging to know where I'd bought such a wonder."

"Madame Bénard is lucky to have you." Camille found the teapot, poured herself some tea. It was lukewarm. She set the cup down so hard it rattled on its saucer. "Why doesn't she *pay* you more? It's not as if she doesn't have the means."

"Bah! She doesn't think she *needs* to." Sophie dropped into an armchair, pulled her workbasket closer. "Wait until I set up my own shop and she discovers I've become her competition."

Camille kept silent as Sophie rummaged through her basket, searching until she held up a hodgepodge hat ornament made of lace, feathers, and something like straw. "Isn't this hideous?"

"Charming," Camille muttered.

"I'm going to take it apart." Sophie pried loose a tiny papier-mâché bird from the hat ornament and set it aside. "What's made you so cross?"

Oh, a hundred reasons. "The dress turned too early, again." She glared at it where it hung lifelessly from its hook.

"That's all?"

"Perhaps." There was Chandon's revelation about Séguin, of course. She'd decided to be on her guard at the palace, and not mention it at home, as there was nothing she could say to Sophie without alarming her further. Sophie had already become disenchanted with Camille's visits to Versailles. Mentioning that Séguin was a magician would only make things worse.

"Tell me, Camille—what's wrong? Something's happened, anyone can see that."

She took a deep breath, exhaled. "Lazare was at Versailles last night."

Sophie sat up straight. "Really? What was he doing there?"

"I don't know."

"You didn't talk to him?"

"I did."

"And?"

"Sophie, he was dressed as an aristocrat! He *is* an aristocrat!" Camille paced to the fireplace and back to the window.

"Are you sure he wasn't pretending? Like you?"

"He has a title! He's the Marquis de Sablebois."

"Oh là là!" Sophie laughed. "You're being courted by a marquis!"

Camille leaned her forehead against the window's cool glass. "Don't you see it's a problem? Why did he never say anything to me?"

"Perhaps he thought you wouldn't like it. And he was right. Even if you are an aristocrat yourself."

Sometimes Sophie was too perceptive. "It's about how you behave, not your bloodline."

"The aristos don't see it that way." Sophie began to unravel a long length of silk ribbon. "Alors, what will you do?"

"I don't know. Why has he kept this hidden? Why is he at court now? He knows all the same people, Sophie. It's beyond strange." Unsettled, she remembered how—slowly, slowly—Alain had changed and become someone else. A stranger in her brother's body. How she'd counted on him for so long and then one day, the person she knew was gone. She wasn't sure she could endure that happening again. "I want the truth, that's all."

"You do realize you are also using a disguise. A magical one."

"It's not the same! I can't afford the number of dresses one needs to be a courtier at Versailles." She held out her hands. "The redness is still not gone from my fingers, even though we have someone to cook and clean for us." The longer she held them out, the more they trembled. She let them drop. "I could never pass for an aristocrat without magic."

"Perhaps he needs the disguise."

"Why would an aristocrat need to do anything he didn't wish to?"

"Why don't you ask him?"

What would she say? She imagined seeing him again at Versailles, crossing paths in front of the mirrors in the Galerie des Glaces, calling out to him, "Pardonnez-moi, Monsieur le Marquis!"—and then what? She would have to reveal herself as a magician, and after what he'd said about magic last night, she did not wish to at all.

That kiss at Notre-Dame, among the stars. Those moments in the air, in the balloon, soaring over the city. He was becoming something to her, and now that she knew he was an aristocrat, she was afraid. Afraid that there would be, somewhere inside of themselves, a fundamental mismatch. Afraid that he had a *reason* for not telling her. Because why would an aristocrat pretend to be someone else, when his position gave him such privilege and power? What could be so terrible that he wished to hide it?

She needed to know.

Whistling out of the summer sky, a pigeon dropped onto the windowsill in front of her and ensconced itself there, shuffling and settling its wings. A second bird came. And then a third, and a fourth, until the sill was full of steely gray birds, cooing.

She knew where to find him.

37

The blue door to the aeronauts' workshop yawned open.

"Bonjour?" Camille called into the cool, dim hallway. "Anyone there?"

From deep inside the building, a boy shouted, "Come in!"

Camille stepped out of the warm June sun and over the threshold. "Hello?"

Pressing her skirts close, she made her way down the narrow hall, where, in the murky half-light, she promptly stumbled into Armand, jacketless in his shirtsleeves. He skittered away as if she'd bitten him.

"Mademoiselle!" He crossed his arms over his chest. "You weren't expected!"

"Pardon—I'd hoped I might see—"

"Lazare isn't here."

She tried to smooth the disappointment from her voice. "And you don't expect him?"

Footsteps echoed from behind Armand. "Who are you talking to? Mademoiselle Camille?"

Elbowing Armand aside, Rosier came forward, beaming. His curly hair was even more disheveled than usual. "You are *always* expected, mademoiselle!" he said, beckoning her with his pipe. "Entrez, entrez!"

As they entered the riding ring, the pigeons rose from their roosts in a thunder of wings, careening through the space before settling on the beams on the ring's opposite side. Camille was surprised to see the striped balloon, lifeless and strangely small, lying on the floor. Two seamstresses bent over it, each of them sewing an endless seam that ran along one side. A third worked to attach a large, irregularly shaped piece of fabric to the balloon. A letter.

"What's happened to the balloon?" Camille asked.

"Mice," said Rosier, crossly. "They chewed up two entire panels of fabric, which now must be treated with rubber and resewn. A foolish expense, when we could have imported a cat instead."

"Cats make me nervous," Armand said.

"As if he wasn't already nervous," Rosier said, waving his pipe at Armand. "Bah, things are not well in our world of balloons, mademoiselle."

"Don't," Armand said.

"What?" Rosier retorted. "It's none of your business." He turned his clever black eyes on Camille. "As I was saying, our balloon adventures have reached a nadir."

Apart from the balloon that needed mending, everything in the workshop seemed to Camille just as it had the last time she was there. "Why, what's happened?"

"When you and Lazare went up in the balloon, and were so magnificent? Well, no one came."

"There was to be an *audience?*"

Rosier shrugged. "Une très petite audience. Not one that would have bothered anyone, not even Lazare with his scruples about a natural philosopher's honor and all those things I never can fathom. Besides! What's the harm with a very small, very quiet *paying* audience?" He made a tiny space between his thumb and forefinger to show how small it would have been. "Because balloons—especially Alp-ascending balloons—cost a lot of livres."

How much *did* a balloon cost: as much as six months' rent at Madame Lamotte's? A year's rent? "Lazare mentioned you needed money for the new balloon."

Rosier acknowledged this with a fierce nod. "Lazare himself has supplied most of the money, so I do my part by scheming. I printed up posters—the ones you helped us with—and plastered them all over Paris. But only two people came." He pulled at his hair, making it even wilder. "I was furious! Dumbfounded! But I see now why we failed."

"Don't!" shouted Armand.

"Ignore that fool. He should know by now to stick to calculations. In the end, we failed because we didn't take advantage of what was right in front of us!"

"Which was?" Camille said, not following his train of thought.

"You, mademoiselle! A balloon flight? It's already been done. It's passé! But a flight by a girl—now *that* is something else." He took a drag on his unlit pipe. "I mentioned it before, didn't I? But it was too late. Next time, we'll advertise that you're going up."

"Going up?"

"You're not afraid anymore, are you?" He regarded her quizzically. "Not with your intrepid aeronaut beside you?"

"He's not my aeronaut," Camille said. After last night, who or what he was, she could not say.

Rosier's eyebrows jumped to his hairline. "Well. In any case, I'd like to do a sketch. Of you, in the gondola, if it's not too much trouble. We'll put it on the posters before our next flight."

"Lazare didn't wish you to do it?"

"He didn't. Doesn't." Rosier threw up his hands in exasperation. "Lazare doesn't want to do a public launch, with people gawping and shouting things and waving commemorative handkerchiefs. He thinks the balloon should be used for testing the winds and the pressure of the air. For exploration! Knowledge! Which of course it can be. But without an endless river of money—and Lazare's money is nearly finished—to the public we must appeal. Plus," he sighed happily, "the people of Paris love a spectacle."

Here was something interesting. An aristocrat with no money? "Lazare's money is gone?"

"I didn't say gone. Nearly finished."

Could *this* be why he'd never mentioned his title and all that came with it? It was certainly possible. "Where does his money come from?"

"I'm afraid I don't know. He never speaks of it."

Camille suppressed a sigh of frustration. Getting at whatever lay behind Lazare's decision to hide his noble birth from her might be more difficult than she'd first imagined.

"May I direct your attention this way?" Rosier said, pointing to the balloon's gondola, which rested on the floor beneath the largest window. It was perfectly placed for a portrait, Camille realized.

"You've been waiting for me to visit the workshop!"

"I hoped. And was lucky, as usual." He smiled as he unlatched the wicker door. "Please? It won't take long."

After he told her where and how to stand, with one arm up as if holding onto one of the balloon's ropes, he took out his notebook and a piece of charcoal. "Now, the drawing! Chin up! Imagine the wind!"

Feeling a bit foolish, Camille stood in the balloon's gondola while Rosier sketched, talking to himself while he drew. "Bigger!" he said under his breath. "More shadow here! No, no, this way."

He'd sketched for nearly ten minutes and Camille had begged for a pause to rest her arm when, from the hallway there came the sound of rapid footsteps. Camille tensed as the steps came closer.

Lazare was dressed once more in a plain brown suit, the powder brushed from his ebony hair. His face was flushed, as if he'd been running. Under his arm he held a rectangular wooden box; when he set it unceremoniously on the ground, the top slid off and sawdust rained out of it. "Couldn't the man have nailed the lid down?" he said, exasperated, as he bent to retrieve it.

Rosier coughed. "We have a visitor today."

Lazare stood, followed Rosier's gaze. "Mademoiselle!" For a moment, Lazare only stared. "You're here?"

"Apparently," she said, pleased that she'd surprised him for once. "I thought I'd pay a visit."

When Lazare reached her, he sketched a deeper bow than was truly necessary, his hand grazing his leg in a courtly flourish. She couldn't help wondering if it were like a gambler's tell, a sign that he was something other than a boy from a bourgeois Parisian family?

"It's been too long," he said with that easy smile. "It's fantastic to see you again. And in the daylight, too."

For a heart-thudding moment, she thought: *He means to compare last night with today.* But then she remembered that the last time she'd seen him as Camille, as herself, it had also been dark on the tower at Notre-Dame. She swallowed. "I heard you didn't want me to sit for a portrait? Armand seemed determined to prevent it, on your behalf."

"Armand might have his own, suspicious reasons, but I thought *you* might not wish it." Unself-consciously, he began to loosen his linen cravat.

"Mademoiselle!" Rosier chided. "Please; look straight ahead."

Reluctantly, Camille faced Rosier.

"I have a better idea," Rosier said. "Lazare, get in the basket, too. It will look very well, trust me!" Rosier waved him on.

For a moment, he simply stood next to Rosier, watching her, with all his lanky grace. Camille's eyes went as if magnetized to the golden skin at his throat as his deft hands undid the knot of his cravat. Those hands had stroked her cheek, tangled in her hair, on the tower of Notre-Dame. . . .

He saw her looking, raised an eyebrow. "It is a warm day, non?"

If he took off his coat, she might expire.

"Hurry up," Rosier said. "My drawing is waiting."

And then Lazare was letting himself into the gondola, and she was making room for him, the gondola wobbling a little so that he reached out a hand to steady himself on her shoulder. It was only a moment, it was nothing, but it felt like everything. How could a touch be both intoxicating and reassuring?

"Pardon," he said, as he settled in next to her, but there was something in the way he said it that suggested he'd meant to touch her all along.

"Now, mademoiselle," Rosier said, "arm up once more, and Lazare, stand right behind her, so I can see your face over her shoulder."

He did. He was very near, so near she felt his breath on the side of her neck, the heat radiating from him, the rustling of his shirtsleeves against her back.

"Is this close enough?" Lazare said, very seriously.

"Parfait!" Rosier turned to his sketch, his hand shifting rapidly over the paper.

Her intention was to get answers to her questions, but with him standing next to her, she felt less clearheaded and more distracted than she'd imagined she would. She had no idea where to begin her investigation. *Start somewhere*, Papa had always said, so she took a deep breath and plunged ahead.

"It's been a while since we last met." She wanted to add: *when we said good-bye outside the courtyard gate on the rue Charlot, you asked me if tomorrow was too early for us to meet again. And that tomorrow never came.*

He leaned closer, his elbow brushing against her waist. "Not for lack of trying," he said. "I went back to the rue Charlot, the very next evening. But your landlady told me you'd moved."

Camille half-turned, astonished. "What? She didn't tell you where we'd gone?" All that time she'd spent wondering why he never came: it was because of stubborn, misguided Madame Lamotte?

A smile twitched at his lips. "I was quite persuasive," he went on, "throwing compliments and money at her, but she refused." His voice climbed an octave, became wheezy and indignant: "'I can't give Mademoiselle's address to every boy that comes calling!'"

"Mademoiselle! Face front!" Rosier admonished Camille. Reluctantly, she did as he asked.

"I specifically told her—" Camille began.

"That I might be allowed to know your new whereabouts?" he teased. "If so, I'm relieved. I got the impression she'd been warding off a herd of boys, and I was only one of many. Indistinguishable from the rest."

Whatever he was, he could never be that. "You've been in Paris, then?"

"A bit," he said slowly. "My parents wished to go to Versailles, so I took them there."

His aristocratic *parents,* she thought, but she wasn't supposed to know that. "As tourists?" she asked.

"To visit friends."

Was there a strained note in his voice?

"Do you often visit the palace?" she asked, as nonchalantly as she could.

A hesitation. "Sometimes."

She was getting closer to learning why he was so determined to keep his noble birth a secret, she was certain of it. Versailles was somehow implicated in it.

"And what do you do there?"

"Balloon business, mostly. You know how relentlessly Rosier hounds me to raise money."

"Unfair!" Rosier exclaimed.

She turned, saw Lazare's dark brows swoop into a frown. "That's all?"

He shook his head. "My parents wish it. They think I should make my living at court." He sounded so stricken by this that she reached out—and took his hand.

My title is a suit that doesn't fit.

She tried to imagine him in the fine court clothes he'd worn the night before. It was nearly impossible. Apart from that tiny flourish in his bow, there was nothing—no sign whatsoever that he had been at Versailles, disparaged magic, argued with the Vicomte de Séguin, or told her about it. Rien.

"Face front!"

Chagrined, Camille dropped Lazare's hand and turned around. Lazare said nothing, but she could hear the rise and fall of his breathing behind her.

"Why?" she asked.

"Their reasons don't matter," he said, roughly. "It simply *is*. Did no one in your family ever wish you to do something you didn't want to do?"

She thought of Alain, Sophie, Maman with her insistence that Camille master la magie, even though she had to draw on her own sorrow to do it. Now she could see that Maman had forced her to practice because she was terrified her children would starve. But Camille still smarted from the pain of not being given a say in what was happening.

"Yes."

He swallowed. "Then you understand."

No. She did not understand why his parents had anything to do with his sudden appearance at Versailles among her new friends. She did not understand why this fact of his birth, his station in life—this yawning chasm between his place in society and hers—was not something he would mention, even as their conversation circled at its edges. There was too much pretending for this to be nothing. Her frustration mounting, she tried another tack. "Perhaps you'll take me to Versailles sometime?"

Something shifted. Lazare stepped back. "I couldn't do that," he said.

"Why not? Would I not like it?" she pressed.

"I don't think you'd like being there with me," he replied. And before she could say anything more, he called out, "Rosier, are you almost finished? I have more business with the instrument-maker."

What had she said that was so wrong? She had stepped over some line she hadn't seen, and now he was retreating. "You're not going, are you?"

"I'm afraid so," he said, letting himself out of the gondola.

"Your timing is perfect, Lazare," exclaimed Rosier, leaping out of his seat to show them his drawing. "See? All finished. I've captured you with the dreamiest expression, mademoiselle. It'll be perfection on the poster. Girl Ascends the Heavens!"

"You've made me more mysterious than I am," she said, but she was secretly pleased. He had given her big, visionary eyes and not emphasized her childish nose.

"And I?" Lazare asked. "How is your drawing of me?"

"Less successful," Rosier said.

Rosier tore out one of the pages from his notebook and folding it, gave it to Camille. "Off to the printers," he said, and with a quick bow, he left, the street door banging shut behind him.

She expected Lazare to make some excuse to go with him, but he did not. Nor did he put on his coat, retie his cravat. His river-brown eyes were shadowed with worry. It hurt her to see it. "I'm sorry if I said something wrong."

He shook his head. "It's nothing."

"Will you come see us," she persisted, unwilling to let this be the end, "in our new place at the Hôtel Théron?"

Lazare nodded. He paused, as if calculating risk. "Before I go, there was something I meant to ask you. Why did you move?"

Did no one in your family ever wish you to do something you didn't want to do?

She remembered how Lazare had stared at her bruise in the Place des Vosges, how broken she'd felt knowing he'd seen it, what he must have been guessing. She hadn't wished to be seen *that* way. So exposed. She'd tilted her hat, turned away.

But now it felt as though there were too many secrets, too much hiding. And if she wanted him to tell her what she wished to know, how could she defend a decision not to tell him? She exhaled, tried to keep her voice from shaking. "My brother—I didn't feel safe with him any longer."

Lazare's face hardened. "He wasn't the one who—*hit you?*"

Camille bit her lip to stop it trembling. Somehow the furious shock in Lazare's face was almost too much to take.

He took a step back and his right hand went, in a ghostly gesture, to his left hip, where his sword would, at Versailles, have hung. "I should have done something earlier," he fumed. "Why did you not tell me?"

"I didn't wish you to know." She blinked to keep back the tears. "I was so ashamed."

Slowly, tenderly, he straightened a wayward ruffle on her cloak. "You saved me, once. Or have you forgotten? Might I not have a chance to save you?"

Camille smiled as best she could. "I'll endeavor to do something dangerous. Soon."

"Come up again in the balloon, then. Though it's only somewhat risky."

"I don't know about that."

Together they ambled down the dark hall and out into the street, the liquid June sunshine thick as honey, and said their adieux.

He hadn't recognized her at Versailles, she was sure of it. And the rest? This secrecy had something to do with his family, but she still did not understand why. Did he not trust her? What had she said that had been so wrong?

It didn't matter, she told herself. She'd gone too far. They had parted as friends, but it did not feel as easy as it had before. There was now a crack in it.

One winter it had been very cold in Paris. Winds blew in from the north with ice in their mouths. Weeks and weeks passed huddling by the fire, her hands too stiff to help Papa sort type into boxes. When the Seine froze, she and Alain walked out onto the ice. They shuffled their feet at first, then took bigger steps, running a little before sliding to a stop. Daring each other, they did it over and over until she went too close to the river's center. Her foot punched a hole in the ice's skin and disappeared. She remembered her fear, the numb shock, how her stockinged leg shot down into the black water as if it had been pulled.

Sometimes the fragile places were impossible to see.

She came to a church and paused in its cool, deep shadow. In her hand she still had the drawing Rosier had given her. Unfolding it, she took care not to smudge the network of charcoal lines.

In the drawing, Lazare was not looking straight ahead, at Rosier. He was looking at her.

38

Despite her best intentions, Camille could not give up Versailles. For it turned out that even when she had shelter and food and money, those things were not enough.

There were other kinds of hunger.

Weeks and weeks ago she'd told herself that as soon as she could, she would stop working magic. Stop wearing herself thin, stop coming to Versailles. But, as Chandon had foretold, the palace's magic had fastened its hooks in her and she could not stay away. Versailles was the only thing that eased the gnawing emptiness she was desperate to fill.

In Paris the news was of the National Assembly, which was meeting at Versailles to write a constitution, and of the angry riots that raged as bread prices soared. At Versailles, the talk was of the queen's lover and the Turkish fashion in hats. She knew it was trivial, fluff and glitter, and she was glad she didn't have to explain her feelings to Papa. She couldn't quite explain them to herself, but it was somehow a relief to escape the struggle and striving of Paris for the palace's glint and flash.

When she entered the lavish rooms set up for gambling, she wanted nothing more than to pack her purse with coins, like sand piled behind a defensive wall. She was remorseless in her card-turning, but not foolish. Changing tables often, she made sure to lose every once in a while, and kept up a constant flow of banter and eyelash-fluttering while remembering to call for plenty of wine for the others to drink. She hadn't played this hard or ruthlessly in a long time, and as she excused herself from the table, a fig tarte in her hand and the sum she needed—plus more—safely stowed in the seam of her dress, she stumbled, a wave of la magie-weariness swelling over her. A courtier caught her by the elbow. "Are you well, madame? Shall I escort you?"

"Quite well, thank you," she said, and made her way out of the room. They all probably thought her a terrible drunk. Well, let them. Better that than knowing what she'd really been doing. Savoring the sweet tarte, she went through the glass doors and out to the parterre. It had been a beautiful day when she started gambling but now rain clouds crowded the lapis sky. A summer storm was blowing in.

"Cécile! Over here!" Aurélie stood at the top of the stairs that led to the orangerie, wind tousling the skirts of her pale blue dress. She wore an enormous straw hat that curved around her head like a snail's shell. Two puffs of white ostrich feathers perched on its crown; between them, a long iridescent feather swooped down to curve along her cheek. From behind the hat, Chandon emerged and waved.

"You've had quite a morning," he noted when Camille reached them.

"How did you know?"

"You seem tired, ma belle," he said, kindly, but there was a warning in his eyes. What he really meant was that she hadn't been careful with her magic. Somehow, he could tell.

"As do you, mon cher." Chandon's appearance was worse each time she saw him. His cheeks were even more flushed, yet all the time his skin grew paler. More translucent, as if made of glass.

"Bah, I'm fine. We'd been planning to walk out to the Temple of Love—that little folly in the middle of the stream, near the Petit Trianon?" Past the Grand Canal, the clouds had darkened ominously; Chandon frowned at them with the same vexed look he gave to people he found unbearably dull. "But the sky is being troublesome."

"Are you worried about your hat, Aurélie?" Camille asked.

"Don't you adore it?" She tipped her head to show off the back. "There's a girl at Madame Bénard's who designs the most divine chapeaux. I wonder if I should become her patroness. What if her hats become le dernier cri and it's like the chandler and I have to wait in line?"

Camille smiled to herself. She could not wait to tell Sophie.

"It'll be fine," Chandon said. "The others have gone to find umbrellas."

No sooner had he said this than Foudriard—and right behind him, Lazare in his fir-green silk coat, with his night-dark hair—appeared at the edge of the lawn, having come from the palace's east wing. In each hand they carried an umbrella.

Lazare waved, the flash of his smile against the amber of his skin dazzling.

Him.

Everything to do with Lazare was a tangled skein of questions she could not answer, full of her own tightly knotted doubts. But amid that confusion there were also things that had happened, things she told herself *were* real: the music box, the kiss at Notre-Dame, the balloon. How angry he'd been about Alain. And how strange he'd been when she'd asked about Versailles.

Yet, the truth of her heart, despite all of this confusion? That gnawing emptiness lessened when she saw him.

"Something's happening!" Lazare shouted as he ran toward them. "Hurry!"

"What?" Aurélie said peevishly. "I had my heart set on visiting the Temple of Love."

Foudriard pulled up, breathing hard. "But this is important! France is changing."

"Not for the better, I'll hazard." Aurélie smirked. "Please? I just wish to stay here."

"Tomorrow," Lazare said. "*Today* the National Assembly has been locked out of its meeting place, perhaps by the king himself, and they're convening at an old tennis court in the village." His easy grace was gone; he burned with eagerness. "Baroness, you'll come, won't you?"

If things were truly changing in France, she wanted to see it happening. She held out her hand to Aurélie. "Come, mon amie. We'll be safe, won't we, dressed like this?" she asked the boys.

"No one will touch either of you," Lazare said. "But come—time is running out!"

Once Aurélie was persuaded, they left the palace, hurrying through the gold-tipped gates and into the town of Versailles. Soon they found themselves behind an enormous crowd chanting "Vive l'Assemblée!" as it passed down the rue du Vieux Versailles to an indoor tennis court where the National Assembly, the people's representatives, were holding a meeting.

"History is being made, Baroness," Lazare said into her ear as they came to a stop outside the weathered building. "Can you not feel it?"

She could. The crowd of people radiated purpose and hope. And Lazare, she was beginning to suspect, was not wholly on the side of the aristocrats.

Slipping through the mass of cheering people, Camille, Lazare, Chandon, Aurélie, and Foudriard found a spot by the windows overlooking the scene. The huge room, with its coffered ceiling painted blue and adorned with gold fleur-de-lis, was crowded with men. The roar of their conversation filled every corner.

Aurélie tapped an older man on the shoulder. "What's happening, monsieur?"

The man gave their clothes a hard look before answering. "The assembly was locked out of their meeting rooms by the king and his sycophants." Another severe look. "Undaunted, one of them—I heard it was

Dr. Guillotin—led the rest here. They have been discussing their demands and how best to have them met. The king is reluctant. Someone proposed the National Assembly withdraw to Paris."

Lazare took in the crush below. "What have they demanded of the king?"

"That there be no taxation without representation," said the man proudly. "To get rid of those damned lettres de cachet that, with a scribble of the king's signature, can throw a man into prison—without trial or appeal. And of course, freedom of the press."

A thrill ran through Camille. If Papa could have stood here beside her, how righteously happy he would have been! He'd abhorred those restrictions. *When a writer—a printer!—can be imprisoned for libel*, he'd said, pacing the room in frustration, *for upsetting the peace, criticizing the church, or besmirching someone's honor, what else is left? There will always be something that offends someone. Bah! One day I will print what I like.*

He had, but the cost had been great.

All Papa's clients had considered him a great printer, but in the end it had become too dangerous to associate with him. Imagine if they were accused of also being against the monarchy? Or for a constitution, like the Americans? His clients had dropped him like a fruit that they'd bitten into only to discover it was rotten. After that, he never printed one of his own pamphlets again, because—Camille realized now—he was afraid. All sorts of inflammatory pamphlets and posters were printed and circulated in Paris, but each printer did so knowing he might find himself manacled in a dank prison. Papa had been afraid not for himself, but for his family.

If these demands for freedom of the press had come only five years earlier, Papa might still be alive. Still printing.

But change was coming. All the people in this room, all of them wanting the same thing—they were part of an enormous wave that could alter the world. She could feel it racing through her, rushing to sweep away injustice.

"And will they get these concessions?" Lazare asked.

"Doubtful. The king will do what he can, as long as he can, to hold onto his power. Et bien! We must persevere."

"Who's that speaking now?" Aurélie asked. "He's terribly handsome," she added as Camille tried to shush her.

The young man called out: "Even if the king makes things difficult for us, we must not return to Paris. We must stay together. Let him not part us from one another! We must not disperse until the new constitution is drawn up. We owe it to the people of France!"

To cheers and applause, another man, tall and thin, was helped up onto a table made of a door recently ripped from its hinges.

"That's the astronomer and president of the assembly, Jean-Sylvain Bailly, who's been in charge of the debates," the older man said. "They've given him hell these past weeks, shouting and arguing and getting nothing done."

As Bailly stood up straight, the representatives fell silent. Outside, thunder rumbled.

Slowly, Bailly held out his right arm in a salute. In his left, he held a piece of paper from which he read a formal oath. Before he had even finished reading, the arms of the men in the room rose, one after another, all of them pledging not to disband the assembly, to keep working for the rights of the people.

With a mounting sense of excitement, she knew she too would be part of this wave. She *had* to be. Not just because Papa surely would have, but because she wanted to be part of this—this surge. She needed to do something that mattered.

Slowly, Camille raised her arm.

One of the representatives on the floor saw her and pointed, and those around him applauded. Lazare nodded at Camille, and his hand went up, then Foudriard joined them. And then, a bit shamefacedly, Aurélie and Chandon raised theirs, too.

Lazare hadn't sided with the aristocrats at all. He was with her, with the people.

"Et tu, Brute?" Chandon frowned at Foudriard. "Supporting the rebellion only means a mob will come, divide my father's estate—which will be mine someday—into tiny pieces, and give it away to the farmers. I will inherit nothing, we will be ruined."

Foudriard clapped a hand on Chandon's shoulder. "You and your father treat your farmers so well they'd have nothing to gain by it. But for the others? The ones who demand so many taxes—the cens, the champart, the banalités—even in years of drought and killing frosts?" Foudriard's voice was raw, angry. "The people who speculate in grain and hoard it? They deserve what they get."

"That's what I tell my father—treat everyone well and you won't have any problems." Lazare shook his head. "Not that he listens to me."

She didn't wonder at that. It had been Lazare's father who'd docked his tutor's pay for daring to think differently. The father who thought money could control everything. The father Lazare was always trying to please, who wanted him to be more *French*, whatever that was.

Camille said to Foudriard, "But you're in the king's cavalry. Don't you support the monarch?"

"Bien sûr, if he serves the people. If he's only out for himself? Never."

Next to her, Lazare leaned over the balcony. "See, Baroness, the people getting what they want? It's possible all of us will be thrown from our gilded perches."

Thunder rolled outside; the long curtains in the windows billowed. A cool wind swept into the room, catching at the lace on her dress, lifting a few strands of Lazare's glossy dark hair. When he turned to her there was a question in his eyes. "Will it be a struggle, do you think?"

"I wouldn't mind if it were," she said.

His eyes gleamed. "To tell the truth, neither would I."

In that moment, everything seemed possible.

Down on the floor below, the representatives lined up to put their names to the document. There were nearly six hundred of them; it would take time. Outside, the crowd cheered as the rain poured down. As she filed out with her friends and the boisterous crowd of onlookers, Camille felt something had changed. *Shifted.* Without bloodshed, the people had spoken back to their king, a king so worried about losing his absolute power he'd filled the streets of Paris with foreign mercenaries. If the National Assembly could make sure the people's demands were met, so much would be possible.

If things in France were going to change, it would happen like this. People talking to one another. People arguing with one another, convincing one another. Camille had seen it at the Palais-Royal, men and women, up on tables, giving the royals hell. And if the press were free?

Paris would need all the printers it could get. Printers who would tell the truth, reveal the injustices, so the king and the nobles and all those in power could no longer ignore it. Printers who could change France for the good.

Camille planned to be one of them.

39

The warm air in the small rose-and-cream-striped shop tasted like sweets.

It had previously been a confectioner's shop, and as Camille and Sophie walked through the echoing, empty space, assessing its possibilities, their shoes kicked up a fine layer of powdered sugar, which drifted in the air like sparkling dust. While Sophie peered into storerooms and display cases, asking the landlord if they could be refashioned to show off a line of staggeringly beautiful hats, Camille watched with quiet pleasure at Sophie taking charge. Camille stayed silent and only offered her opinion when it was asked for.

Standing at the sugar-coated windows, she absently traced a spade, then a diamond, in one of the windowpanes. Rent for this shop was fifteen louis a month, and they almost had that to spare.

Camille exhaled. It felt as if she were shaking off a shadow that had followed her too long.

Alain was wherever he was, and to Camille it didn't really matter *where* he was, so long as he was not here. Paris was endless crooked streets, mansions and cramped attic spaces—and more than six hundred thousand people. Alain might well try, but he would never find them.

Where that shadow had once been, there was now a tiny spot of light. She might dream again. Not the dreams that had fueled her for so long, the desperate need for a full belly and shoes without holes and *safety*, but dreams of things that might be. After the meeting of the National Assembly at the tennis court, she saw how she might have a role to play in the changes that were coming. She dreamed of a printing press with which she could publish people's thoughts, tell the truth of what was happening.

And she dreamed of the balloon. She could write about their preparations, their hopes and their disappointments, their final triumph when they sailed over the Alps as no one had ever done. In secret, she let herself imagine such a life: each day something new, another adventure, she and Lazare together.

In the dream, the secrets they were keeping from each other did not exist.

In her waking life, she couldn't reconcile them. But perhaps it was possible. A balloon might be big enough to carry all their hopes.

"Camille?" Sophie said. "Are you ready to go?"

Having given the landlord a deposit, Camille and Sophie left the sweet shop, their clothes scented with almonds and vanilla, and returned to the Hôtel Théron. It was early in the afternoon, but Sophie was already getting ready to go out for the evening. She'd promised to dress a visiting countess from Bavaria, who was staying with one of Madame Bénard's best customers, for a party. Sophie would be at the fashionable lady's house well past midnight, but Sophie's face was bright as she prepared to leave. She nearly hummed with happiness. "I'm going to charge her double for every feather and scrap of lace I stitch onto her. And do you know what?" Sophie said, as she kissed Camille good-bye. "She will happily pay. If I charged her less, she'd feel cheated."

Camille listened to Sophie's light footfall as she went down the marble stairs and said good-bye to Madame Théron. The great house fell silent. Camille picked up a book—*Les Liaisons Dangereuses*—and thought about beginning it again, but none of the characters appealed. Instead she wandered to the mantel in the salon. Tucked behind the carriage clock was a folded note the size of her palm.

It had arrived yesterday. She unfolded it again and glanced over the words, though she already knew what they said:

> *Ma chère Cécile!*
> *Paille maille in the afternoon—meet us at the back*
> *steps of the Grand Trianon at three o'clock.*
> *Don't say no!*
>
> > > *Je t'embrasse*
> > > *Aurélie*

Of course she would go.

What had she to keep her here, in Paris? Surely she could stop using magic another time. Perhaps Lazare would be there. Perhaps she might learn the reason he had kept his noble birth a secret from her. Perhaps, among his friends, he might let something slip.

Perhaps, perhaps, perhaps.

40

Chandon was waiting by the high yew hedge, swinging two mallets like windmills.

And next to him, in the cool of the shadows, Lazare.

The lush green branches cast complicated patterns on his skin, rendering him mysterious, half-seen, and her first thought was that she had dreamed him there. After what he'd said about only *sometimes* coming to Versailles, why he was here again?

He was trying to balance his wobbling mallet on the palm of his hand, taking steps back and forth to keep it from falling. When he saw her, he caught it neatly and bowed. Once again, he seemed completely at home at the palace, in his suit of pale yellow silk, green embroidery scrolling down the front of his coat. If he was unhappy to be here, forced by his parents to come to Versailles, as he'd claimed, he didn't show it.

A finger of unease curled up her back. She thought she'd wanted revelation, but now she wasn't sure. What if she learned things she didn't actually want to know? Flustered, Camille curtsied to the boys.

"As always, I'm thankful you've arrived. Otherwise Aurélie complains about being outnumbered," Chandon said, grinning so that his dimple showed in his cheek. "Here's yours," he added, handing her one of the mallets and tossing a wooden ball, painted with blue stripes, across the grass. It rolled to a stop against another ball, this one mint striped. "That green one's mine—careful you don't hit it."

The rules of paille maille were simple. Hit the ball down the lane of grass, smacking others' balls out of the way when it was possible and generally creating chaos. The first ball through the iron arch was the winner. She shaded her eyes, squinting to see it. "You've put the arch very far away."

"So we can play forever," Aurélie smirked. "Or at least until Guilleux arrives from Paris." She waved at Camille's ball. "Go on, give it a try."

Camille smiled to herself. Setting her embroidered shoe on top of her ball, she thwacked her mallet into it, the force of her blow jettisoning Chandon's ball across the lawn so that it bounced into the high grass, where it promptly disappeared.

"What have you done?" Chandon sank to his knees. "I am finished!"

"Oh, come," Aurélie said as she dragged him up. "It's only paille maille, not the end of the world. Fetch a gardener to trim the area around your ball and voilà, you can hit it out."

"And if I can't find a gardener?" Chandon bared his teeth. "I suppose I'll have to chew it off?"

Lazare laughed. "Or get one of the queen's sheep to do it for you."

"We'll let Chandon have an extra turn, won't we, Aurélie?" Camille said.

"Bien sûr." Aurélie strolled to her ball and slammed it so hard that it

scudded violently down the long stretch of grass. She smiled trium-
phantly. "As long as we're *winning* he can have an extra go."

Chandon waded slowly into the meadow. "I don't see it."

"Can you believe," Aurélie called out, "a grand mansion in Paris was
set on fire by a mob? The lady of the house ran in to save a trinket and
nearly lost her hair."

"What was she thinking?" Camille said. "To have escaped with her
life and then to run back inside?" In her mind, she recalled all the things
in their new apartment. She found most of them not worth the trouble
of saving. Except the burned trunk. She would have gone back for that—
as someone once, in the past, probably had. But that was not something
she could mention.

Chandon looked up from the long grass. "Except for Foudriard,
there'd be nothing else I'd be that desperate to save. And I think he'd
get out on his own."

Aurélie swung her mallet idly at a patch of golden-eyed daisies. "I'd
take my jewels and my dresses."

"Nothing sentimental?" Lazare asked. He had found his ball and was
sighting the final hoop.

"Bah! I'm as hard-hearted as they come." Aurélie winked. "Though
there are some letters, tied up with a blue ribbon, from a Monsieur de
G—what about you, Cécile?"

A gloomy magical box that whispers at me? "I'm not sure," she said.

"No jewels?"

Settling his feet in the grass, Lazare raised his mallet for a hard strike.

Suddenly, Camille knew. "A music box!"

With a clunk, Lazare's ball curved wide of the wicket and sank into
a wet little hollow in the lawn.

"Tant pis!" Aurélie called. "Sablebois isn't usually one to miss his
shot."

Lazare looked back at Camille over his shoulder. "What kind of
music box?"

Camille swore under her breath. She could not believe she had said
it, completely without thinking. She'd come to play paille maille with

the intention of finding out something about him, but if she continued like this it would be Lazare who found something out about *her*. She struggled to keep her face blank, as if it'd meant nothing at all. Lazare kept staring, his eyebrows tilted up, baffled.

She'd slipped. But she wasn't going to cower.

She beamed at him.

Chandon hit his ball hard. It sailed up out of the rough grass and onto the lawn. He followed after, coughing.

Worrisomely, Chandon's cough reminded her of Maman's, the way it had lingered and not improved. If anything, it was getting worse. Still, he was, as usual, full of wit and high spirits. "Are you not well, Chandon?"

"Fine," he said. "Too many late nights."

Aurélie frowned. "Then get some sleep, darling. Or I'll be forced to send my physician to you. He's very strict, you know, and his medicines are absolutely vile."

"Please, not that," moaned Chandon. "It's your turn, Cécile."

She settled her foot on her ball, wriggling it into place, and wished Lazare weren't watching her so intently. She raised her mallet and swung.

"Your music box," he said, "is it one of those new ones with a melancholy tune?"

Her mallet hit the ball hard, but at the wrong angle, so instead of scudding down the lawn it ricocheted away and blundered through the hedge.

"Oh, too bad!" Aurélie said. "You were so close."

"I'll fetch it for you," Lazare said, leaning on his mallet. "You'll have to pay a penalty, though, if I do."

"What kind of penalty will that be, Sablebois?" Aurélie said, a wink in her voice.

"You're a neutral party," Lazare said. "You decide."

"A kiss?" Aurélie suggested.

"If you insist," he said, smiling. He raised a hand to shield his eyes so he might see Camille better and in the shadow his hand cast, she could see the keenness in his face. "Baroness, are you in?"

She flushed. And she nearly said yes.

It was *Baroness* that stopped her. With all the talk about the fire and the objects they'd save, and the slip she'd made, she had completely forgotten the other game she was playing, the game in which she was a pretend baroness. The important game she must not lose. With a creeping sense of dismay, she realized that Lazare wasn't asking for a kiss from Camille—he was asking for a kiss from the Baroness de la Fontaine.

It was one thing to be confident and safe in her disguise, but it was another thing entirely to imagine the disguise was so perfect—so enthrallingly beautiful—that Lazare was ready to kiss this girl he hardly knew.

He could not be falling for the baroness.

"Well?" he said.

Could he?

She desperately needed a moment away to gather herself. "How cheaply kisses are traded!" she said, taking cover beneath her best court manner. "I'll find it and hit it out myself, thank you."

She did not wait to see Lazare's reaction but headed for the yews lining the lawn. Her friends' bright voices faded as she plunged into the hedge's shadows. On the other side, a fountain purled, cool and sweet. Peering through the dense branches, she saw gravel paths marking off a basin of water, rows of dusty pink roses, a building of golden stone. Finally she found a narrow tunnel cut into the hedge.

Branches caught at her clothes, and more than once she had to stop and unhook a piece of lacey trim from a twig. In the center of the hedge it was murky and still, except for the scrabbling of birds in the upper branches. She tried to push away her feeling of unease, but it persisted.

In her quest to find out what lay behind Lazare's secrets—what reason he had for not telling her that he was an aristocrat, why he kept returning to Versailles—she was in danger of revealing her own. She thought again of the frozen Seine, its uncertain safety.

Even if he hadn't recognized her when she'd mentioned the music box, it was dangerous. And to imagine he might be interested in her shadow self, the Baroness de la Fontaine, was to imagine labyrinths of trouble and misunderstanding and heartache.

She'd gone too far. She needed to be more vigilant, to maintain somehow the distinction between her two selves. When she first came to Versailles, she'd never dreamed that she would need to create a self so different from her own. If she'd thought at all about it, she'd imagined the baroness would be like her own self, but better: perfected by the glamoire and polished by etiquette.

And of course, she thought, as she shoved through a break in the hedge, she'd never dreamed Lazare would be here to witness it.

Her ball had come to a stop at a rose bed. She was so intent on grabbing it and making it back to the game that she did not hear anyone approach until she stood up and found the Vicomte de Séguin standing in front of her.

Camille stiffened.

"Bonjour, madame," he said, smoothly bowing. "Fancy seeing you here."

Camille curtsied, the threads in her gown agitating against her skin. "Monsieur le Vicomte."

As always, the Vicomte de Séguin appeared supremely confident, dressed in a costly, dark-blue suit: everywhere there could be a gold thread or glass bead, there was. Though it had not rained in days, and the garden paths billowed with dust, his clothes had not a speck on them. A thread of richly scented cologne hung about him, frankincense and cold marble, and under it, the faint smell of smoke. The skin on her neck prickled.

Magician.

Séguin works so much magic he positively reeks of it.

What did a magician like him do with his magic, when he was already so powerful, so rich? Certainly not pretend to be someone else, as she did. As far as she knew, Chandon used his magic for cheating at cards, but what Séguin did with his, she could not guess. A small voice inside her said: perhaps you do not want to know.

"Surprised to see me?" he said.

"A little." She showed Séguin her ball. "We were playing paille maille on the other side of the hedge. I missed my shot."

"Or you were fated to see me today." He raised a perfect eyebrow. "Despite my not being invited to play."

"I'm sorry—I didn't know."

"It's nothing new," he said, as if regretful. "Sometimes I say the wrong things. Do the wrong things. It's not always easy to be oneself, n'est-ce pas?"

"No, it isn't," she agreed. She was torn by the desire to get away from him with his unnerving stare, and not to reveal that he unsettled her. "What do you have there?"

Séguin opened his hand: in it was a fresh plum. In the dappled light, it glowed a deep amethyst. "I spoke to the king just now, in his fruit garden. He loves to see what his gardeners grow at Versailles. He yearns for the simple things, did you know?"

She shook her head. On the lawn, the others were waiting. "I must be getting back."

"Stay a moment—it won't take me long to peel this." From his pocket, he removed a knife. Camille flinched. Setting the blade to the fruit, he remarked, "Remember when we played cards, when you first came to court? You never took me up on my offer to help you with the traps."

"I didn't find them to be so terribly dangerous after all."

"Oh?" His knife gleamed as he tossed a peel into the rose bed. "Some are so finely woven you cannot see them, like magic. Court gossip has you engaged to half a dozen people. I thought I'd missed my chance."

He was jesting—wasn't he? "Hardly. I much prefer to keep control of my money. Husbands tend to get in the way of that."

His bronze gaze flickered over her face. "And if you could guarantee that wouldn't happen, would you marry?"

Camille took a hesitant step backward. This was not at all what she'd expected. "Monsieur—"

"You and I, for example. We would be magnificent together."

Two *magicians*, was that what he meant? "And how is that?" she asked, pointedly. "When I am only a simple baroness from the provinces?"

His thin lips twisted into a smirk. "Some things are more than what they seem, aren't they? The way sand becomes glass. A piece of grit becomes a pearl."

Transformations.

As close to saying *magic* as one could come without speaking the word. Séguin must suspect she was a magician. And he wanted her to know that *he* knew, and that he thought her magic a prize.

Something he wanted.

Her dread was paralyzing, a rush of icy water before drowning. She tightened her grip on the ball in her hand. "I'm sorry to say, monsieur, that as much as I'd like to be, I'm not any of those things."

A half-laugh, as if he couldn't believe she'd deny it. "One bit of advice, madame."

"Is it about the traps?" she said, as lightly as she could.

He inclined his head, as if to say yes. "I've learned that the worst thing at court is to be seen."

What a strange thing to say about Versailles, where not to be noticed was to be forgotten. Doomed. "Everyone at court wishes to be seen. Isn't that the point?"

He shrugged. "Coming out of the hedge as you did, fetching your ball, and returning to your game before I could see you—it was like a game of hide-and-seek. As if you'd wanted to remain invisible."

That was exactly what she had wanted. Instead she stood there as if compelled, paralyzed like prey under his golden eyes, watchful as a hawk's. All-seeing. As if he were telling her: *even in your glamoire, you are not invisible to me.*

The knowledge was a pulse of fear. *Steady,* she told herself. She needed to go, and quickly. "The others will wonder where I've gone."

He flicked the last plum peel into the flowers edging the path. Juice dripped from the knife and fell onto the ashy gravel in tiny dark spots.

"Adieu then, Baroness." Something raw flickered in his eyes. "Patiently or not, I'll be waiting."

Camille bowed and ducked into the hedge, clutching the ball in her hand.

What had just happened? The Vicomte de Séguin had suggested—marriage? Some kind of partnership? But why would a magician need a partner, a partner who was also a magician? For she felt quite certain now that Séguin suspected—if not knew outright—that she, too, was a magician.

She'd thought magic a simple thing, once. Magic was the way one turned useless scraps into useful coins. It was difficult, and it hurt on the inside to work it, but it was manageable. Now magic seemed a vast and trailless continent, only one very small part of its landscape familiar to her. There was so much she did not know.

Nothing seemed right: not Versailles, with rot crumbling at its edges; not Séguin, with his watchful eyes and his talk of invisible traps and magic; not even Lazare, with his lazy smile, willing to bestow a kiss on a baroness he hardly knew. In the space of one bright afternoon, she was in grave danger of her disguises failing, the boundaries between her two selves collapsing.

She had to be more careful.

By the time she'd finally made her way through the yew hedge, her friends had advanced down the lawn. They seemed tiny next to the wind-ruffled hedges, beneath the wide dome of washed-blue sky. They were as painted figures in a model of Versailles, placed there by some larger force. And just as easily knocked down.

Lazare must have wandered off in search of his ball, for she could not make out anywhere his lanky shape, the ink-black of his unpowdered hair.

The dress shifted restlessly against her skin.

As she watched, Chandon hit his ball squarely, though not very far. The effort made him double over, coughing. The raspy sound echoed toward her.

Aurélie rubbed his back. A breeze caught at her skirts and then, as if she could feel Camille's gaze, she tipped her hat back and waved.

"Hurry up!" she shouted. "You'll miss your turn!"

41

"Viens ici," said Sophie, her blue eyes sharp with concern. "I want you to come here and really look."

"I'm reading," Camille replied, carefully turning a page in her copy of *Les Liasons Dangereuses* so as not to reveal how it trembled in her hand. Late afternoon light warmed their sitting room at the Hôtel Théron; Fantôme lazed in a golden splash of sunshine, licking his paw. To be a cat, she thought, and not have to worry about being caught out as a fraud, or a magician. A simple, snare-less life.

"I'm very serious," Sophie said.

Camille lay her book down over the arm of her chair. "You won't leave me alone until I do, I suppose?"

Sophie said nothing but waited, with her hand on her hip, next to the large mirror above the fireplace. Camille was exhausted, la magie-worn— and she suspected she knew what Sophie wished to show her.

"Come," Sophie said, waving Camille closer to the long mirror. It reflected back at them the salon's wallpaper and curtains, the unlit chandelier.

"What is it?" Camille said, warily.

"Stand by me, and look at your reflection."

Camille did as her sister asked, fixing her attention on the mirror's curlicued frame.

"First me. The more money we have, the better I look," Sophie said. "See?"

Avoiding her own reflection, Camille looked at Sophie's. Her sister's blond hair gleamed with health. There was a pretty flush in her round cheeks and her blue eyes shone brightly. "It's true. You're very pretty," Camille acknowledged.

"And you?"

"I don't wish to analyze myself at the moment." She pulled the collar of her robe around her throat, over her collarbones. "I've only just woken up."

"Camille," Sophie warned.

Reluctantly, Camille shifted her gaze from Sophie's reflection to her own. If she didn't look too closely, she did resemble herself. The dusting of freckles across her nose, her serious gray eyes, the copper lights in her hair. She was no longer as gaunt as she used to be and the hungry tightness was gone from around her eyes. "Well enough."

"Truly?"

She'd seen it enough in Chandon to see its shadow in herself.

Sometimes she'd catch a glimpse of herself at Versailles, reflected in a mirror or a window, and be struck by how *thin* her skin seemed. The way a chemise would wear away to holes, the more it was washed. Or the way a piece of paper, scraped over and over to remove old ink, slowly became translucent.

Ghostly. Spirit-thin.

"It's because I was at court last night. It takes time to recover from the glamoire. It's always been that way. As you know." Which was true, as far as it went. The aching weariness in her bones, the sensitivity of her skin, the slaying fatigue were as they had been the first time she'd gone to Versailles. But now there was something more. It took her longer to recover her strength, as if the glamoire took more from her than it had in the past. It had a constant hunger.

"I'll stop la magie soon. I'll even stop going to Versailles," she said, though it didn't sound as convincing she'd hoped.

Fantôme pressed against Sophie's skirts and she picked him up. "Do you go to see your friends?" she asked. "Chandon, Aurélie, Foudriard? And the other one, Séguin? Do you see him very much?"

"Not very." The less that was said about Séguin, the better. "Bien sûr, it's my friends. It's hard to give it all up." When she'd first pulled up to Versailles in her rented carriage, she'd been determined to hate it. Instead, the palace had sunk its million tiny claws into her—and offered her the unexpected freedom of being someone else. "It gives me so much, Sophie," she faltered.

"And it takes."

Sophie didn't say it, but Camille could almost hear her think it: *it doesn't just take from you. It takes from both of us.* Out of the corner of her eye, Camille saw Sophie turn something in the palm of her hand. Something violet. A card. A folded letter.

"Is that from Aurélie?" Camille gasped, reaching for it. "Were you hiding it from me?"

"I was waiting for the right moment," Sophie conceded. "Take it."

Camille broke the seal. Aurélie's note was a baroque scrawl of loops and dashes.

"What does it say?" Sophie asked.

Camille read aloud: "It says, 'The Paris Opera. Tonight! We have a box and miss you terribly—'"

Sophie's smile wobbled. "How lucky you are! A night at the opera."

It did feel like a bit of luck. Beneath her weariness, she felt the itch of magic under her skin, the whisper of the dress in her ear, but she didn't want to go back to Versailles. Versailles felt haunted, strung with snares in which she might get caught. And she felt like a fool after the way she'd behaved the last time she'd seen Lazare.

The opera in Paris would be perfect. Safe.

"I think I'll go," Camille said slowly. "Though attending the opera without working a glamoire is not an option, not tonight."

And if she were being completely honest: perhaps not ever.

Sighing, Sophie set the cat down. "If you insist on going, make your dress a pale, sea green. And don't put too much powder in your hair—it's no longer done in Paris."

"Thank you, ma chère," Camille said, embracing her sister. As she did, she felt again a wave of fatigue sweep over her, the magie-sickness.

"Camille, you're shaking," Sophie said. "Why not stay—"

She shook her head. She did not wish to stay at home to rest. She knew that as soon as she worked the glamoire, the tiredness would disappear. "Off I go then."

As she rang for the maid to order the carriage, Camille's gaze snagged on the little music box balloon, sitting silently on the writing desk.

"Why can't you let yourself love him?" Sophie said, quietly. "Lazare being a marquis—how can it matter so much? I hate to disabuse you of your high-minded ideals, but they're our people, too."

"It's not that." She struggled to explain. "How can I trust him? When we played paille maille, he asked me what kind of tune my music box plays, as if he were *reminding* himself of a girl he gave a music box to"—Camille's voice wavered—"a girl he's in danger of forgetting. And then he called me baroness and gave me these *looks*." As if he had forgotten Camille.

Sophie's smile curled. "I thought looks were what you wanted?"

"Not like that! This is serious! Sophie, what if there's something about the baroness that reminds him of the real me, so much so that he's fallen for her instead? She's prettier than I am, more sophisticated, with a better wardrobe and more money—"

"Why would those things matter to him?" Sophie said. "He likes *you*."

"I'm afraid he won't, not if he knows who I am. What I do. He dislikes magic, even more than you do." Camille understood why. She often felt the same way about it, with its gruesome tithe of blood and sorrow. The way it wore at her, until she felt as though she were less and less *Camille*, and more and more magic. Illusion. If he disliked magic, how could he like her? "I'm afraid. Things haven't worked the way I've hoped very often."

"You're in love, that's all."

"Is it that obvious?" Camille picked up the balloon and turned its tiny key. It began to play its lilting, melancholy tune.

"It is," said Sophie. "And you know what? Take my advice: kill off that baroness sooner rather than later."

42

But not tonight.

Once she arrived, she was certain: better to be at the opera, where life was a giddy, spinning top that ran on rumor and innuendo, on desire and lust for all that sparkled, than perplexed and wondering in her rooms. This evening, Camille and Aurélie shone; as they climbed the stairs to Chandon's uncle's box in the balcony, people bowed low and remarked on them behind their fans.

Aurélie tucked her hand around Camille's elbow and squeezed. "I can't believe you haven't seen Mozart's opera yet! *The Marriage of Figaro* isn't even his *latest*. There's a newer one, if only I could remember the name." She waved to a friend as they merged with the crowd streaming upstairs.

"Isn't the opera based on a play? I think my father saw it." Camille remembered how much he'd liked it, especially the speech Figaro the servant makes to his master, the count, about how nobles were born into everything they had, while servants had to use their wits to survive. Sophie had asked, *Are we noblemen or servants?* And Papa had answered, *We are neither. We are citizens.*

"Lucky him! That play was a *scandale*," Aurélie said in a stage whisper as a grand duchess passed them in a froth of yellow silk. Aurélie's head followed her for a moment before snapping back to Camille. "Did you see her? In the daffodil-colored gown? Talk about scandal! Her husband and her lover dueled over her—and the duchess was ecstatic when her husband won! Who ever heard of such a thing?"

Camille tried to smile.

"I wish you'd tell me what's troubling you." Aurélie missed nothing. "You've been so strange lately."

"It's nothing, ma chèrie," Camille said. "Séguin won't be here, will he?"

Aurélie raised her dark brows. "He hasn't been bothering you?"

Camille nodded to the Comte d'Astignac and his party as they passed them on the landing. She dropped her voice. "In a way."

Aurélie stopped dead. "He hasn't proposed?"

"Not really—he never said the words." Camille bit the edge of her nail. "He said everything but."

"Oh là là, when did this happen?"

"When we were playing paille maille and I went to find my ball."

"Did you give him any hope?"

Camille shook her head. "It was strange—I was so frightened. How can one be afraid of someone about to propose?"

Aurélie squeezed Camille's hand. "You were right to be careful. He's ridiculously proud and treats a refusal like an unscrubbable stain on his honor. I don't know what it is with these boys. Probably something they get from their fathers. In any case," she went on, as they reached the top of the stairs, "you were right to tell me. I'll keep Séguin away as much as I can."

It was his magic that unsettled her most, and even Aurélie couldn't help with that. "Will the Baron de Guilleux be here tonight?"

"I hope so," Aurélie said with a smirk. "Is there anyone you're hoping to see?"

She was as relentless as Sophie. "Let's find the box."

There were many people Aurélie had to greet and the orchestra was already playing the overture when they found it. Over the door hung a crimson curtain that Aurélie lifted with her fan as she went in, beckoning Camille to follow. The little room that opened out to the stage was like a jewel box, the seats plush, a small candelabra illuminating the walls.

"Oh, look who's already here," said Aurélie as they swept in. With a clanking of swords and bumping of shoulders, Chandon and Foudriard stood up. Both were all smiles, but Chandon was pale, as if he'd been up for days.

"Lovely to see you both," Aurélie said. "Where's Guilleux?"

"He sends his regrets, mon étoile," Chandon said. "Something with his frigate and a storm at sea?"

Aurélie made an impatient sound as she dropped into a chair. "Not only do I have to manage it so that my husband doesn't come to court but also, apparently, I must manage the weather. Sit with me, Cécile?"

Camille tucked herself into a spot between Aurélie and Chandon. Chandon kissed her on the cheek and squeezed her hand. His skin was dry, and feverishly hot.

Aurélie shook out her fan. "How warm it is! Such a crush!" Beyond the box's ledge, the theater was filling up: a mix of nobles, wealthy Parisians, commoners standing on the floor. The place thrummed with excitement. "All because the opera's in French, I suppose."

"French?" Chandon groaned. "It's in Italian. Despite your pretty face, you really are a barbarian. Did you never have a handsome Italian music master?"

"I suppose you did?" Aurélie cracked her fan on his arm in mock indignation. "Maman would never have let a handsome Italian enter the house! Besides, who needs to know what they're saying? It's all about the *feelings*, n'est-ce pas?"

"Hush, you loudmouths," said Foudriard over the last notes of the overture. "It's starting."

All around them, people quieted. Beyond the constellation of blazing chandeliers, the curtain slowly swayed open to reveal a half-furnished room. The servant Figaro was kneeling on the floor, measuring stick in his hand, while his fiancée, Susanna, arranged her wedding bonnet.

Camille shifted closer to Chandon. "How are you?"

He smiled wanly and batted his eyelashes. "In love, as always."

"Not that. Are you any better? You still look so—"

"Awful? Don't I know it. No longer can you call me the dashing Marquis de Chandon."

"This is serious! Aurélie said she'd send her physician to you. Why not see what he says?"

"No physician can help me, my sweet. I'm too far gone." He put his mouth next to her ear. "It's too much magic."

"Then stop," she said, her voice low.

"It's not easy to do, is it?" he said pointedly. "And it's not for my own sake, which makes it harder." He put up his hand. "No more, please, I've come to be distracted."

She wished he would let Aurélie—or herself—help him. But if he wished to speak of something else, she could at least try to cheer him up. "Will you tell me what's happening as we watch the performance?"

"Of course, ma petite. There's not much I love more than the opera." And he was true to his word. At every important moment, Chandon explained what was happening or what the aria was about.

Camille watched in rapture. The problems of the characters were so familiar, but the singing elevated their concerns, their foolishness, and their heartache until those things felt larger than life—which is how feelings felt. Too big for speaking, they could find their perfect shape in song.

At the end of the second act, after the singers had hidden in closets, jumped out of windows, and come in and out of every door on the stage, the curtain dropped and Chandon stood up, clutching his throat.

"Foudriard and I must get some air," he croaked.

"Do, darling," Aurélie said, concerned. "You look terrible."

It was true. Now that he'd confided in her, she could see it: too much magic. From where she sat, the fine shaking in his hands that came from working sorrow was all too obvious.

"It's a suffocating tomb in here, that's why." Holding onto Foudriard as he went out, Chandon promised to send in some lemonade.

The audience came alive at intermission, people standing up, some waving at their friends. Men left their boxes to call on friends or family sitting elsewhere, food was brought in. Peering at the crowd through her opera glasses, Aurélie spotted the ambassador Thomas Jefferson, in his drab American clothes, and the chandler's apprentice.

"What circles that chandler moves in, eh?" Aurélie said, gleefully. "Nothing can keep him down!"

Camille cringed. If Aurélie only knew she was sitting next to a printer's daughter, an apprentice less experienced than the chandler she laughed at, what would she say? Camille asked, "May I borrow your glasses?"

Once Aurélie handed them over, Camille could spy on the commoners, drinking wine and chatting. As fine as everything was in Chandon's box, she'd have given anything to be down there with Papa. He would have loved this.

Aurélie tapped Camille's arm. "I think I see someone we know. On the left."

Camille moved her glasses up and over. "Where?"

"The box where someone's stood up. Isn't it the Marquis de Sablebois?"

Here, too?

Her fingers suddenly awkward, Camille fumbled with the glass's rings.

Lazare was bowing to the others in the box, preparing to leave. He wore a close-fitting suit, its pale blue silk a gleam against his skin. A haze of powder tamed his fiercely dark hair and expensive lace frothed at his wrist and throat. His face, as he said his adieux, was kind. Happy. As if he did not wish to go.

"Dreamy, isn't he?" Aurélie sat forward, her décolleté on full display. "See his parents? They're at the front of the box."

Now, Camille thought, she would have a chance to see the people that compelled Lazare to come to court, the father who'd both traveled to India and, in a fit of anger, had docked the wages of Lazare's tutor. Through her glasses she saw they were powdered and haughty, though there was something in his father's straight nose and easy posture that was very much like an older Lazare, though he was white-skinned where Lazare was tawny brown. And next to him, Lazare's stepmother: disdainful, dripping with jewels. She frowned at the commoners on the floor as if she wished they would be swept away. Camille knew that stare—she had seen it on Grandmère's face.

"C'est pas possible!" Aurélie gasped. She grabbed the glasses from Camille's hands. "Do you see who's in the box with him?"

"Who?"

"That blond ninny, the one who's practically paved with diamonds. She's been flaunting her wealth at Versailles while her parents search for a husband." Aurélie lowered her opera glasses in disgust. "She might as well stuff her dress with gold louis—it'd be more subtle than what she's up to."

Aurélie reached across Camille and waved determinedly at Lazare with her fan.

"What are you doing?" Camille protested.

"Not letting that blond fool get the best of me," she said cheerfully. "Besides, wasn't it sweet that he offered to get your ball for you at paille maille?"

"In exchange for a kiss? It seemed too easily won."

Aurélie laughed. "It's the thought that counts. He was dreadfully sentimental about the constitution at that old tennis court and does tend to go on about how awful and terrible we aristocrats are, but underneath? He's wonderful. Really, he's just your type—ready for anything."

As Lazare was leaving his box, the blond girl tipped her face up to him and smiled, as pretty and self-assured as an angel. While Camille herself felt so out of place that she needed Chandon to translate for her. How fervently she wished that she could see Lazare—elsewhere. Not here, but somewhere in Paris—a boat on the river, the workshop, the Place des Vosges—anywhere she was Camille and neither of them were wearing disguises or webbed in secrets.

"I must get some air," she said.

"What are you thinking?" Aurélie asked, astonished. "The best part of the opera is yet to come, and Lazare's on his way to see us."

But Camille couldn't face him again. To see him and not be able to truly speak to him—to know what he was thinking—it was too much. She recalled the frank stare he'd given her on the lawn at Versailles, and how she'd almost given herself away. "Forgive me, I cannot stay."

"But Cécile! Are you ill?"

If not ill, very close to it, Camille thought as she pushed through the chairs to the curtain at the back of the box. She was halfway there when the velvet panels parted.

43

"I hope I'm not intruding, mesdames," Lazare said, coming into the box and nearly bumping into Camille. He grasped her hand to steady her, but it did nothing of the kind. She had completely lost her bearings and all she could think was, *He is holding my hand.*

"Not at all," Camille managed to say.

Below, the orchestra tuned their violins.

"Intrusions such as yours are most welcome." Aurélie fluttered her eyelashes at him. "I know Cécile was hoping to see you again."

Camille glared at her. Of course it was true, but why did she have to say it? Was it so obvious?

"You were?" Lazare faltered. "Even though you would not let me fetch your ball in paille maille?"

She took a deep breath and felt the answering embrace of the dress, steadying her. However he behaved, whatever he did, she must continue to play the game. Court manners, she reminded herself. Court guile. "You've recovered from your trouncing, I see."

"Have I?" he teased. "We'll have to play again. Double the penalties."

"Enough, mes amis!" laughed Aurélie as she patted the empty place next to her. "Come, Lazare, sit by me. Chandon and Foudriard will be thrilled to see you. You know Chandon fears one day you will fly away and never return."

"In my balloon? Not without the rest of you." He hesitated, his hand on the back of the chair. "But that's the baroness's spot, isn't it?"

Camille froze. Sit next to him? For the remainder of the opera? "I was just leaving."

"You are always going," Lazare observed.

"Nonsense," Aurélie said. "You sit here, and Cécile will sit on your other side."

After the chandeliers rose and the curtain swung away to reveal Count Almaviva considering the charges brought against Figaro, Chandon slunk in. Foudriard was gone; instead the Vicomte de Séguin— her breath caught—followed Chandon into the box. It was clear that Chandon was trying to get away from him. His face was flushed, his eyes red. Séguin wouldn't have hurt Chandon, would he? Here, at the opera?

But her own experience whispered that it was not at all unlikely.

Séguin took the last seat in the box, behind Camille. He sat so near, she could smell his heavy cologne, and under it, the drifting smell of ash. She resented that he was here, suspicious of her secrets. Closing her in.

Next to her, Lazare stretched his long legs out in front of him, his elbow propped carelessly on the arm of his chair. The candles' glow caught on the edges of his cheekbones and the curve of his mouth, outlining them in gold. The air between her and Lazare felt like a living thing whose every curve and indentation she was aware of.

As if spellbound by the performance, he faced the stage. But when she resumed watching the actors, she felt the heat of his gaze on the side of her face, as charged as a touch.

He was looking at her.

On the stage below, a long recitative punctuated the drama. Camille had lost track of the story; the poor countess, whose husband no longer loved her, was terribly upset. Chandon now sat in front of her, too far away to ask. The countess approached the front of the stage, handkerchief in her hand. As she began to sing, her face took the shape of anguish and pain. Chandon's shoulders began to shake. Camille put a comforting hand on his back. "What is it, Chandon?"

He shook his head and waved her off. "It's nothing, nothing. Just the music."

What was the countess singing that was making Chandon so sad?

Turning to Lazare, she asked, "You speak Italian—what's happening? What is she singing?"

"You know I speak Italian?" he said, surprised.

"Didn't your tutor teach you Italian?"

He stared. "Élouard?"

Merde! He must never speak of Élouard to anyone at court, or he wouldn't be so taken aback. Playing these roles, being two different people—she was losing track of what she knew and what she was supposed to not know, who knew what about her.

She pretended nonchalance. "Oh, that was his name?"

Lazare nodded slowly, his brows drawn together. Wondering. "You know him? I've mentioned him before?"

Camille clutched the arm of her chair as if it would keep her upright. "I assumed you had an Italian tutor, like everyone else."

Only as Camille—not Cécile—had she heard him mention Élouard. Only in confidence. She'd made another slip, this one more perilous than the last. If he did not know who Cécile was by now, he must at least suspect there was something more to the Baroness de la Fontaine than met the eye.

Her thoughts ran on, shaky and unstoppable. If he suspected, what exactly did he suspect—that she was in disguise? For that might be explained, though it wouldn't be exactly comfortable. Still, it would only be as bad as what Lazare himself was doing by not telling her he was an aristocrat.

But if he suspected she was working magic? She thought again of Sophie's horrified face when Camille had first worked the glamoire. She'd looked at Camille as if she were a monster.

If Lazare knew what she was doing, would he feel the same?

She wanted more than anything to push her way out of the box and disappear.

At that moment, he shifted in his seat and the side of his hand touched hers. He did not move it closer nor move it away. Their two hands, each one on its own armrest: one white, one brown. Camille tried to breathe as if everything were ordinary. But it wasn't. It was as though the infinitesimally small place where their bodies touched was the only thing that existed, as if all the candles in the opera house had been blown out except one that flickered between them.

"The countess is desperate and angry," Lazare said quietly. "She's wondering what happened to the count's love."

Camille pressed on, reckless, as if she felt nothing. "Oh? What is she saying?"

Lazare's breath was electric in her ear. "She says, 'What happened to the promises that came from those lying lips?'"

Did he mean she was lying? Or that he was? But all she managed to stammer was, "Lips?"

Instead of replying, he leaned in and kissed her.

His mouth was soft against hers, honey sweet, searching. Before she understood what was happening, she was kissing him back, her neck curving to bring him closer.

Lazare inhaled—then pulled abruptly away, as if he could not believe what he had done. "Pardon, Baroness! It must have been the music—I don't know what came over me—I would never—"

Stunned, Camille pulled her hand from his. What a fool she was to have kissed him back!

He knew. He must. Or worse, he didn't know. Utterly bewildered, she said, "What do you think you're doing?"

Lazare's voice shook. "I'm terribly sorry. I—I don't know what happened—How—"

From the stage, the singer's voice soared to an aching crescendo, but all Camille could think of was Lazare. Being with him was like standing in the Hall of Mirrors—between the two of them there were so many selves that she didn't know which one was real, and which one a reflection. At the end of the aria, everyone in their box stood, clapping, except Chandon. He was coughing and shaking. Before she could say or do anything, Lazare squeezed past Camille, put his arm around Chandon's shoulders, and led him out of the box.

When Camille had finally elbowed her way into the crowded lobby, Lazare and Chandon were nowhere to be seen.

44

Late June grew hot, the river stank. The city held its breath. A restless week had passed since the opera. Camille had tried to occupy herself with reading, or shopping, but those pleasures felt hollow. Following Sophie's lead, she considered buildings where she might set up a printing shop, but her heart was not in it. The king had not granted true freedom of the press. And she was tired of striving.

Wandering the streets, she hoped to see Lazare.

She'd even walked past the workshop, but its high windows were dark. Disappointing. Of course, she'd seen him at the opera. And before that, playing paille maille. She'd stood with him and cheered as the members of the National Assembly took their oaths. But she hadn't *really* seen him, had she? Since that time when Rosier had sketched her and Lazare at the workshop, she'd only been with him as Cécile.

And the more she saw him as Cécile, the more desperately she longed to see him as Camille. To talk with him about ideas, to share her concerns about buying a press, to look into his eyes and see reflected there only herself. She was so tired of her own questions, of not knowing, of being double.

When she returned to the Hôtel Théron, she played the music box balloon he'd given her and watched the balloon spin. She waited until it wound down, then put it away. Its tune was too mournful.

Perhaps the kiss at the opera house was nothing, she told herself. But it could *not* be nothing. Either he had kissed her as the baroness, in which case he did not love her, that is, Camille—or he had kissed her as Camille, which meant he had seen through her glamoire and she was found out. Trying to work it through made her grind her teeth.

Except for the kiss itself, there was nothing good about it.

Perhaps he was not in Paris at all, but at Versailles. Expecting to see her—or not. She'd stayed away, apprehensive of Séguin.

Since witnessing the oath in the tennis court, she waited eagerly for the news that France was changing. The king had agreed to some of the National Assembly's requests, but his concessions were so full of exceptions they meant nothing. That wave she'd imagined at the tennis court, the one that would sweep away all injustices? The one she'd pledged to support, that would vindicate Papa and give purpose to her own life? It now felt like one of her false coins, dissolving back to scraps.

But the people of France did not give in. In the newspaper she read of angry demonstrators by the Tuileries palace who'd thrown garden chairs at a troop of foreign soldiers. Two companies of soldiers who'd pledged to protect the people had been imprisoned, only to be released by a Parisian mob. Unrest in the countryside grew worse as the price of bread doubled; any landowner suspected of hoarding grain might find his house on fire or his family dead.

Unsettled, uneasy, unsure.

That morning, the suffocating weather broke with early rain. Camille and Sophie were at home, doing nothing but relishing the cool air coming in through the windows, when the maid delivered a folded, violet-colored note on a silver salver. "This just came for you, madame. Footman brought it."

Joy burnished with relief flooded through Camille. At last: *something*. "It's from Aurélie!"

"Maybe it'll be some news about Monsieur le Ballon," Sophie said. "Then you won't have to keep flailing around Paris looking for him."

"Hush." Camille mock-glared at Sophie. "I don't flail. I—swan."

"You swoon. Open it. Or I will."

Camille unfolded the cover. A small card, shaped like a beech leaf, tumbled into her lap. On it were written a few lines, followed by Aurélie's flourish. It was a clever invitation, the date and time and place radiating out like veins. In the center it said, *Fête Galante*, and along the stem was written: *woodland dress*. "What in the world is 'woodland dress'?"

"Oh, it's a masquerade!" Sophie started bouncing on the sofa. "Please, Camille, me, too! Can't I come this time? I'll be disguised—no one shall know me."

Perhaps, perhaps. The waiting and the silence from Lazare was wearing at her. She could not be at peace. Sophie seemed to be drifting from her; Chandon did not answer her letters. She felt isolated, cut off. "The second of July—that's in three days."

"Lucky for us, you can work magic and I'm clever at sewing. Three days to us is a hundred to mere mortals. I see you as a magpie, all black and white. And I will be a pretty little dove. We will be utterly enchanting."

"I thought you preferred I not go to Versailles anymore," Camille said, almost serious.

"Can I not change my mind?"

"You're feeling well enough?"

"I haven't felt better in ages!"

Camille reminded her, "You haven't even been presented at court."

Sophie shrieked with laugher. "Presented at court? Do you hear yourself? And who, may I ask, would have done the presenting?"

Camille glared. "You know what I mean."

"You were never presented, Widow Fontaine. Nor widowed. Nor even married, come to think of it. As for being too young, think of the queen, when she first came to Versailles from Austria. *Thirteen*." Sophie dropped prettily to her knees. "S'il te plaît!"

She did not wish to see anyone on their knees. With a pang, she understood how Sophie must feel: left out, ignored, forgotten. She'd hope for the best.

"If you insist," she conceded.

Sophie shrieked with joy. "You are not to worry about anything, ma soeur! I promise to be completely forgettable."

45

The Grand Trianon shone like a fiery lantern.

And she, a winged creature to its flame.

She'd come for a frivolous distraction from the empty ache of waiting and not knowing. But as she and Sophie entered the colonnade packed with courtiers, the air crackled with uneasy energy.

The revels were underway. Laughing men with antlers branching from their heads passed women masked with feathers or moss, delicate wings harnessed to their shoulders. A costume of organza leaves, a furred bear; girls in the gauzy dresses of woodland sylphs, veils hiding their faces. Some masks were elaborate confections, outstanding examples of the mask-maker's art, but others were simply bands of sheer silk tied behind the head, with holes cut for seeing.

And everywhere, there were eyes. Glinting in the masks' recesses, stealing glances, searching, appraising. Underneath the masks, crimsoned mouths curved, laughed, tightened. *Eyes and mouths and teeth*, Camille thought with an unpleasant shiver.

In the whirling revels, she and Sophie were a small, still spot. Sophie squeezed her hand. "Where are your friends? Aurélie de Valledoré? Monsieur Ballon? The other one you're always talking about, the Marquis de Chandon?"

"Somewhere, no doubt." Camille tried to shrug off her growing sense of foreboding. "It's just—there are so many people, and they're all in disguise. It makes it difficult to recognize anyone."

Joining the stream of partygoers, they were swept into a long gallery that had been transformed into a wooded grove. Birch trees mingled with boxwood in planters, crowded thickly to make a forest. High above them, dark blue crêpe de chine swathed the ceiling, so that the candles in the chandeliers burned like stars. Green walkways of turf zigzagged across the floor; tame rabbits and deer nibbled at the grass, their long ears twitching. In the trees, finches warbled.

"Isn't it enchanting, Camille? If Madame Bénard could see this, she'd faint with happiness at how beautifully everyone's gone along with the theme. Well, except that one there." She made a moue of distaste. "He's not wearing any kind of a costume, unless you consider a plume stuck in your hair to be something."

Camille realized she knew him. "Lord Willsingham!"

Willsingham straightened his cravat and stalked over to them. He wore a strangely flattened wig, pierced with a bent peacock feather. He hadn't even reached them before he burst out: "Damn me, I'm at the end of the wits! Tell me, my lady, have you seen the marquis? The one with the blond hair?" He peered at her. "Blue, like me?" His French was terrible.

"Blue eyes, do you mean? The Marquis de Chandon?"

Willsingham nodded emphatically.

"I haven't. Have you?"

"Obviously not. I was hoping to get up a game. I'm terribly in debt, you know, and need to ah, improve my situation." Willsingham scanned the crowded room, as if Chandon might suddenly appear. "They say he's ill."

Still ill? A finger of worry ran up Camille's spine. "He isn't any better?"

"Last I saw him he looked as if he'd aged twenty years. I thought he was pretend. Apparently I was wrong." He bowed abruptly and moved off into the crowd, lost as always.

"How rude," Sophie said.

"It's just because he's English," Camille said vaguely, following Willsingham's progress through the crowd. "Chandon seems only to get worse. Aurélie promised to send her physician but Chandon didn't think he could help."

Too much magic. And the uneasy feeling that Séguin had something to do with it.

She needed to find Aurélie.

As they passed among the revelers, servants offered silver trays arrayed with glasses of lemonade and champagne, tiny canapés shaped like acorns, clusters of grapes dusted with gold. Standing under a haze of birch leaves, she sipped champagne, trying to appear as easy and nonchalant as everyone else. It was all very beautiful, but standing at the edge of everything, surrounded by beauty and laughter and twirling motion, Camille felt very alone. At first, the magic had been a way to beat the aristocrats at their own game, to punish them. But after all these weeks playing at being one of them, she wasn't so sure. She'd become an imposter, both here and at home.

Dancers swept past, none of them her friends. Why had she bothered to come? She'd wanted to please Aurélie, who'd invited her, and to give Sophie a treat. But deep down, she knew. Despite her attempts to scrub her confusion over Lazare from her mind, it remained, darkly impervious to all her deliberate forgetting. And the kiss at the opera had only made things worse. Sophie insisted that his being an aristocrat did not matter, and maybe it didn't. But the gnawing secrets did. She wished he would say *why* he had not told her.

Both of them were impostors. She had her reasons. But his? They were unguessable.

An accordion player joined the orchestra and played a few bright notes. It would be a country dance—Marie Antoinette loved to pretend she was a simple country girl. Camille felt a surge of resentment at a queen who could pretend whatever she wanted while everyone else followed happily along.

"Camille!" Sophie whispered. "I think we have partners!"

Two boys, dressed in the blue and white of the King's Guard, were making straight for them. Over their faces they wore strips of white silk with holes cut out; their only other concession to the masquerade was a sprig of apple leaves pushed through their buttonholes.

"How seriously they've taken the theme," Camille said under her breath.

"Hush." Sophie's face glowed with anticipation. "I won't dance without you, so be nice and say yes when they ask."

"Sophie—"

But when the guardsmen stopped in front of them, bowed low, and asked for the dance, Camille gave in and took the taller one's hand. For a moment they stood, holding hands, in a circle of other dancers. He asked her if she was much at court, but before she could answer, the violins joined the accordion and the dance sped into motion. As they promenaded forward, and then backward, his hand lightly holding hers, he said, "You make a very fine magpie, madame."

"What if I stole the buttons off your coat?"

"You have already stolen my heart," he flirted, as they stepped together, shoulder to shoulder. "Isn't that enough?"

It was all a dance. Things were said that had to be said, things were done that had to be done, like steps in a dance, a pattern that everyone followed because—because if they didn't, what would happen? No one wanted to know. It would mean chaos, collapse. No rules would mean the end of the nobles' power—so they followed them, assiduously, and laid mighty punishments on those people, like Papa, who didn't.

Forward and back they went until he spun her away to the man dancing behind them. "When you come back to me in the dance," the guard said, "I'll toss salt on your tail. That's how you tame a magpie, isn't it?"

"You'll have to catch me first." She ducked under his arm and away, clasping hands with her next partner. This one was tall, dressed in black silk, wearing a raven mask and a short cape of glossy dark feathers. He wore his hair fanned over his shoulders and held her hand high between them.

"Madame Magpie," he said, tipping his head to her so that the feathers on his mask danced.

Lazare.

"Monsieur Raven," she said, endeavoring to be witty. "Two thieving birds, aren't we?"

"I stole a kiss," he said, as they took two steps forward. "It was wrong of me."

Perhaps. "And what did you think of it, once you had it?" she dared.

"I shouldn't say."

"Why not?" They came together, shoulder to shoulder.

"It might be too revealing."

All these double entendres! Knowing and not-knowing, saying things but not saying them—it was a torment. But she replied, sweetly, "Revealing what?"

The raven smiled. "Myself."

The mood of the dance swept her up; emboldened, she asked, "Are you planning to kiss me again?"

"Is that what you wish?" His voice was honey rich in her ear.

They pressed their palms together.

"What kind of kiss would it be? Raven and magpie?"

"Marquis and baroness?" He turned his head and met her gaze. His dark eyes in the darker mask gleamed. "Or—something else?"

What did he mean?

They were walking backward now, hands clasped; they would face each other only once more before they changed partners. Her time with Lazare was slipping away.

As they stepped backward with pointed, measured steps, heads up, side by side, a moving part of the great wheel of dancers spinning under the blazing chandeliers, all Camille wanted was for it to be finished. She wanted the confusion and guessing to be gone, the masks and disguises to be stripped away—even her own. Once, she'd been safe, hiding in her glamoire, but the girl who'd come to court to gamble and flirt and fill her pockets with louis was gone. She didn't want to be a magpie any longer, nor the Baroness de la Fontaine. She wanted to be herself, to hear Lazare to say: *I know you.*

At the last moment, he spoke, low and earnest. "Tell me," he began. "At the opera—"

But before he could finish, the dance propelled him away.

Why all these riddles? Why could no one say what they meant? Frustrated, Camille took the hand of her next partner. He wore a fox mask of glossy fur, his lips red over white teeth. When he spoke, she answered by rote, watching Lazare move on without her in the dancers' circle.

Dutifully, she gave her new partner a small smile. "How many foxes there are in the king's forests this evening!"

"I'm pleased to see you, Madame la Baroness. Did you enjoy the opera?"

That melodious voice, the burn of incense and smoke. *Séguin.*

She was grateful that in this movement, the dance let her turn her face away so he could not see her apprehension. "Did you?"

"From where I sat," he said, his voice slippery as silk, "I got quite an eyeful."

"The opera was beautiful."

"I meant the kiss."

Camille bit her lip.

"Though somehow I don't think you're the kind of baroness he wants," he added. "He's searching for one a bit more—how shall I say?—authentic. Madame—careful you don't stumble!" he said as he caught her up, holding her tightly by the hand.

Camille tried to pull free. "Let me go."

"I didn't mean to tease you. Besides, our dance is nearly finished." He held her hand high for the promenade.

She wrenched her hand from his. "It's finished now." As she stumbled away from him, the toe of her shoe caught on the hem of her dress and she nearly fell.

"In case you are dealt cards you don't like," Séguin called after her, "you know you can change them."

"Mademoiselle?" she heard a man saying. "Do you wish to sit down?"

When he'd found her a seat by a potted birch, she asked him for lemonade—*just go, leave me*, she wished at him—and he vanished into the crowd. She could no longer doubt that Séguin knew she was a magician. And that he wanted her to know that he knew. But why? Her head ached.

Near where she sat, groups of courtiers bent their heads together, gossiping.

"Dieu," exclaimed an older woman. "Have you seen young Sablebois tonight?"

Camille froze.

"Who could miss him?" said her companion in a high, nasal voice. "He's a glorious dark angel."

"Do you see how he dances with the white-blond daughter of the Comte de Chîmes? Money and a title."

"They're dancing together now! Even his parents watch with approval."

As in a nightmare, she felt her head swivel like a puppet's on a string toward the movement of Lazare's black cloak in the mesh of dancers. She had to look.

The blond one wore a moth costume, her hair coiled down her back to where her white wings flared out. Blonder than the queen had ever been, a kind of northern beauty, she moved with fairy grace. As she danced with Lazare, her white hand intertwined with his brown one, her face was radiant, as it had been at the opera.

And Lazare?

His back was to Camille, so she could not see his face. But whenever he said something into the curve of the girl's ear, the pretty play of emotions on her face made Camille sick. And there, at the edge of the crowd, stood Lazare's parents, with alabaster faces and crimson-painted smiles of approval.

The dance spun, its wheel turning, and Lazare and the daughter of the Comte de Chîmes were lost from view. She told herself it meant nothing. The court loved to spread rumors—she knew that. She tried to let the worry go but it persisted, a heavy hand on her shoulder.

Why could she no longer tell what was real and what was not?

Her hands trembled in her lap, as if her glamoire were fading, and, sure enough, the black-and-white-striped gown had taken on a grayish cast. Unpinning her brooch, she thrust the needle into her arm. Blood welled up, red and alive as always, and dropped onto her skirt. Almost instantly, fresh black bands raced up from the hem as if an invisible hand were stitching it anew. Revived, the dress drew in protectively around her, giving her strength to stand up. The glass doors to the gardens beckoned and she shouldered her way through the revelers to reach the parterres.

In the gardens, she stopped, caught her breath. Compared to the hectic burn of thousands of candles, here it was cool inky darkness, the moon a scimitar in the sky. The clipped yews at the edge of the Grand Trianon had ceased to be trees and become pointed tips of a deeper shadow. The stars were out, fierce and knowing, as if they had been watching dances and lost loves for thousands of years. Over the Grand Canal, fireworks shot up and bloomed into bluebells, then sprouted into vines of wild eglantine.

It was all so beautiful, and none of it for her.

She strode out onto the gravel path. But the farther she went from the Trianon, the more the dress rustled. Warning her. Urging her to return.

She was halfway to the lower parterre before she remembered Sophie.

Camille gathered her skirts and ran. Back up the stairs, along the paths, through the open doors, she plunged back into the sea of silk and tulle and feathers—all the masked faces spinning blind in the dance. She saw the queen, dressed as a berry-picking maid, her basket filled with raspberries; the king clothed as a woodsman, an axe poised on his shoulder. Fears of something happening to Sophie—a darkened room, a chair against the door, rough hands—kept her searching the crowd. *Where is she?* Camille wanted to shriek for the musicians to stop playing, for everyone to stop dancing, so she could find her.

And then she did.

Sophie was dancing with the Vicomte de Séguin. As they came together, Séguin bent his head toward Sophie's, his fox-ears pricked, as if he were about to devour her. She ducked her head and smiled.

Camille's pulse raced as she neared them. How dare he? She tapped Séguin on the shoulder. He spun around, and where the long, toothed smile of the fox should have been there was instead his own thin mouth, curving up at the corners as if he scented something good to eat. His strong cologne burned in her nose.

"Madame la Baroness," he said, in that low, thrilling voice. "You never told me you had a sister."

Sophie smiled knowingly.

And in that silence, Camille realized she was perilously close to being unmasked. Séguin might know she was a magician, a fraud—but he did not know she was Camille Durbonne, the girl whose sister he'd nearly run over in the Place des Vosges. She clung desperately to this last scrap of self and would not let it be taken from her. "My sister is in fact too young to come to court," Camille said, grabbing Sophie's arm so hard she winced. "And it's late."

"But—" Sophie shook off her sister's grip. "I don't wish to go. I wish to dance and speak with the vicomte."

"Any later and our carriage will become a pumpkin," Camille said through gritted teeth.

"What a pity," Séguin said. He took Sophie's hand and pressed it to his too-red lips. Sophie flushed. "I will live in hope of our next encounter," he said.

"You were ruder than that Englishman to drag me away," Sophie complained as they left for the colonnade where Madame de Théron's carriage would be waiting. "He said he would live in hope of our next encounter. Isn't that polite enough for you?" She glared at Camille. "Can I not be my own judge of character? I see nothing wrong in it. Would it have been so terribly unbecoming if *I* had said I could not wait until next time?"

"There won't be a next time." Camille hated how cruel her voice sounded, how mean and unfeeling, but she couldn't shake the picture of the fox and his prey. Those watchful eyes behind the mask.

Sophie's voice was hard. "He's a rich nobleman, Camille. He likes me—perhaps he's the one, n'est-ce pas? Isn't he everything I've been wishing for? Why is it that you can take what you want from the nobles and I can't?"

Camille shook her head. It wasn't the same. Was it? "The difference is I don't like doing it."

"If Alain were here," she grumbled, "he would have congratulated me on my conquest."

"Of course he would have. He thinks that's the best we can do, we girls—marry a man with money."

"But that's what I want," Sophie countered, hopefully. "Don't you see?"

It was useless to try to convince her.

Once in the carriage, they untied their masks. "How ravishing everything was," Sophie said as the carriage rolled down the linden tree allée, her anger at Camille seemingly forgotten. "The ladies' dresses, the costumes, the men in their masks—so mysterious! I had many partners besides Monsieur le Vicomte. And what they murmured in my ear! The things the men will say—c'est incroyable."

"At court, no one means what you think they mean," Camille said, tossing her mask to the side.

Lazare, least of all.

In the tower of Notre-Dame, they stood so close under the stars, and everything was as it should have been—except that at the center of it were their secrets. She saw how he'd danced with the daughter of the

Comte de Chîmes, how prettily she'd flushed and laughed. Wasn't that the way Lazare once smiled at her, before, under the stars? Wasn't that how she'd flushed, too, in his arms?

She had perhaps lost him with her pretending.

Camille sank back in the seat, her mask next to her. It stared up at her as the carriage jostled across the cobbles of the grand court and through the palace gates.

Sophie murmured, "It was perfect, except for the candles. Someone should have taken better care of them. What's the point of all the lovely flowers if they can't cover up the smell of the candles? Couldn't you smell it, Camille?" She yawned and snuggled her head against Camille's shoulder.

"Smell what?"

"Snuffed candles." Sophie's eyelids fluttered. "When I was dancing with the vicomte, all I could smell was the stench of snuffed candles."

"Like the smell of the glamoire box, Sophie? Like fireplaces? Burned wood?"

Did her sister know the smell of magic? Had she realized what Séguin was?

But Sophie was fast asleep.

It doesn't matter now, Camille thought, as she slipped off her cloak and tucked it around Sophie's shoulders. Her cheeks were flushed, her mouth slightly open, like a child's. Against her best judgment, Camille had let her go to the masquerade. Grâce à Dieu nothing had happened to her. It would have been Camille's fault and she never could have forgiven herself.

Séguin had come dangerously close.

And she had been too caught up in her own agony to notice.

46

"What's this?" Camille said when the maid came in the next morning. She and Sophie were drinking chocolate in their dressing gowns and Camille was rubbing her aching forehead, trying not to think of the masquerade, Lazare's talk of kisses, the blond girl—or Séguin's predatory smile. It was not going well.

"A delivery for Mademoiselle Durbonne," the maid announced.

A footman in navy-and-citron livery stood on the landing, his face hidden by the potted orange tree he was holding. The maid waved him forward.

Sophie sat up expectantly in her chair. "This is early, isn't it?" she said.

"With all respect, I do not make these decisions, mademoiselle," the footman said as he staggered in.

"Is there a card?" Sophie asked.

"I must set this down. Immédiatement." The servant lunged forward, the pot braced against his hip. "Where?"

"By the window will be best," Camille said. They both watched as he lowered it to the floor and spun the gilded pot so that its prettiest side faced them.

"It's lovely," Camille mused. It was clearly a costly gift. The tree glowed with tiny fruits the size of a baby's fist. She recalled her first day at Versailles, when she'd looked out over the orangerie where the gardeners were working. Now she knew firsthand how, when the trees bloomed, their sweet perfume made the palace a paradise. A gift from someone at Versailles, then?

"Who—?"

From a pocket, the footman presented Camille with a small, folded note. The thick paper was pale gray, her name curving across it in black loops: *Mademoiselle Durbonne.*

"At your service, mademoiselle." In a moment he was gone, the door clicking shut behind him.

"Do you know, I dreamed of oranges last night?" Sophie squeezed in next to Camille on the sofa. She ran her fingers across the swirling letters. "Oh, how romantic, Camille! To have something from Lazare!"

Camille held the note out to Sophie. "You open it."

"Why? It's for you."

With slow fingers, Camille lifted the wax seal and unfolded the paper. The handwriting was unfamiliar. She cleared her throat and read.

> *Mademoiselle,*
> *No blossom could smell as sweet, nor any fruit, entice*
> *as sweetly as you.*
> > *In memory of that enchanted evening—*
> > *Your Most Ardent Admirer*

Sophie gasped, her hand over her mouth.

Camille frowned. "What does it mean?"

"Oh, Camille, I'm so sorry," Sophie stammered. "I think it's for me."

"For you?" A hot blush crept up Camille's neck. "But how?"

Sophie reached for Camille's hands and clasped them tight. "Don't be angry, please."

"What evening could this boy possibly be talking about?"

"The ball?" There was a sudden edge to Sophie's voice.

She hadn't seen all of Sophie's partners last night, but she'd seen the one who mattered. Only Séguin would do this, trying to turn a girl's head. "You may absolutely not accept his gifts. He will get the wrong impression—"

"What a fantastic idea!" Sophie crowed. "The more I refuse, the more intrigued he will be."

"That is not a fantastic idea!" *Séguin cheats*, Chandon had said. She thought of the time that Séguin had suggested—hadn't he?—that Camille marry him, on that warm afternoon when they were playing paille maille. She felt again the deliberate, repulsive caress of his fingers when they'd danced. What game was he playing with Sophie?

"He's not to be trusted. Once, at Versailles—"

"I've heard enough about your *experiences* at Versailles. What I say to the vicomte is none of your business." Sophie crossed her arms. "You're simply jealous it's not from Lazare."

Her words were a slap. Camille felt the blood rise in blotchy spots in her cheeks. "You have no idea." She wished desperately to tell Sophie all the things that unsettled her about Séguin, that Chandon had warned her about him. But what good would it do to tell her he was a magician? Nothing could overturn her belief that money and a title were what mattered in a husband.

"Don't I? Everything is for you. *Everything.* You have magic, I trim hats. You go to court to make money for us—well and good. We have enough now, don't we?" Her voice bristled with splinters and pain. "But still you go, wearing yourself out with magic. What if I lost you, what then? You're as bad as Alain, gambling and having fun while I sit here alone."

"But don't you like designing hats?" Had she been wrong, all this time? Camille stumbled on, grasping at what she thought she knew. "We've signed a lease on the shop."

"I like it now. I'm good at it. But hats were what I did to pass the time," she said, scornfully. "So I didn't lose my mind, sitting and waiting for you! You never even thought of that, did you, when you were drunk on la magie."

Sophie's words stung. Camille had left her alone, so many times. Too many. She had become caught up in the game, no different from card-obsessed Lord Willsingham.

"Lazare will never send me anything again," Camille said bitterly. "I think he's found someone new."

"Don't try to change the conversation. Of course he hasn't found someone new. And if you'd never used magic and pretended to be someone else—if you'd been honest and told him who you were, you wouldn't be worrying about this now."

Camille's throat burned as she willed her tears not to fall. She ached for Sophie to comfort her, to say that she didn't believe what she'd just said—even as Camille herself was starting to believe it—but Sophie remained standing on the other side of the room, immoveable.

"I'm sorry, Camille." There was no sympathy in her voice. "I'm going to take a promenade with Madame de Théron. As for the Vicomte de Séguin, I'm not going to marry him tomorrow, if that's what you are worried about. But if you love me, you will not try to stop me from having a little fun."

47

Downstairs, someone was knocking as if to break the door down.

It was an unfamiliar sound at the Hôtel Théron, to say the least. Camille laid her book on the table beside her as, in the hall below, the footman's shoes clicked unhurriedly to the door.

The huff of the door opening, a rumble of noises from the street. Male voices, insisting.

She shifted to the edge of her armchair.

Then the footman's clear voice, asking for a card.

Two minutes later, he was knocking at the little salon's half-open door. "There are some *boys* below who wish to speak to you. They say it is urgent." He added witheringly, "They have no card."

"From Versailles?"

"I doubt it," sniffed the footman.

In the mirror, her reflection wavered. She smiled, rubbed roses into her cheeks. It had to be Lazare.

Finally, a chance to see him as herself.

The white-blond girl, the talk of kisses: two days had passed since the masquerade and she'd put the girl out of her mind. Mostly. But she couldn't forget what Sophie had said about magic. If Camille hadn't used the glamoire to begin with, she wouldn't be worrying about Lazare now. Maybe it *was* time to stop. Maybe it was time to tell him the truth.

He might wish to never see her again. But wasn't there enough between them to overcome it? There had to be.

Smoothing her skirts, she followed the footman down the curving stairs.

There, on the patterned marble of the foyer, stood Rosier and Lazare. Rosier, restless, his hat clamped under his arm, and Lazare, leaning lazily against the wall in a serious breach of etiquette. The contrast between them—Rosier ill at ease in the richly decorated mansion, Lazare at home—could not have been clearer.

She nearly laughed. He didn't have to tell her he was an aristocrat. It was obvious.

When he saw her, his face lit with joy.

And suddenly she could think of nothing except that she hoped Madame Théron was out visiting friends and that the boys would linger a while.

"Mademoiselle!" Rosier said. "This is your *home?*"

"We are only renting rooms here," she said, remembering how worried she'd once been that they would see the dirt under her fingernails. Now she knew neither of them would have cared. How much had changed since she'd been ashamed to let Lazare come to the leaning house on the rue Charlot. Looking at them standing there, she felt almost dizzy at how far she'd come. "How lovely to see you both! Won't you come in?"

Rosier shifted uneasily. "No time to sit, I'm afraid," he said. "To be blunt, please help us."

She had never seen Rosier like this. Worried.

"What's the matter?" she said, quickly. "Help you with what?"

"There is still a difference of opinion about what that is, exactly," Rosier said, with a glance at Lazare. "To be brief, we need money to fund a public launch for the balloon." He nodded at Lazare. "Go ahead. Tell her."

She glanced from Rosier's expectant face to Lazare's. He looked up for a moment, caught sight of the garish putti painted on the ceiling. "Those are hideous."

"Truly," she said, laughing, and Lazare did, too—the warmth of it was like sunshine. "Tell me, what's happening?" she asked again.

Lazare took a deep breath, his dark eyebrows drawing together, and then the words tumbled out in a rush. "We need your help to secure funding for the balloon. We've run out of money."

"No surprise," Rosier said. "That said, there are many ways of raising funds."

"I have some money—" Camille began.

Before she could finish, the boys were holding up their hands, horrified. "Never," they said together.

"We're going to try *one last thing* before the public launch," Rosier said, exasperation creeping into his voice. "It's the only scheme that's been approved of by him. Just barely."

Begrudgingly, Lazare said, "I agreed to it, non?"

Outside, in the courtyard, someone shouted. Lazare swore under his breath. "Already? I told your driver we would be a few minutes." Opening the door, he strode down the low flight of steps and into the courtyard where a small, open carriage waited. When he saw Lazare, the driver began to gesticulate at the gate.

Camille lowered her voice. "Is something wrong between you two?"

"Between us?" Rosier ran his hand through his hair. "Nothing. But this business with the balloon has unsettled him, mademoiselle."

Through the doorway, she could see Lazare making soothing gestures at the driver.

"I've tried to convince Lazare of the public launch many, many times. You've heard me! He says it is not in the interest of natural philosophy." Rosier pulled at his cravat as if it were choking him. "I tell him, then, that the salon is the only answer, and he replies that he does not wish to debase himself by asking for charity!"

Camille began to suspect what was coming, but she couldn't fathom why they'd ask her.

"You're going to a salon? To raise money with a subscription?"

Rosier nodded. "Madame de Staël's, on the other side of the river."

Papa had told her of salons where the wealthy gathered to speak of ideas, literature and philosophy, the events of the day. He'd avoided them, certain that they would never invite a printer, whatever provocative and brilliant pamphlets he might write. Madame de Staël's was one of the most famous. It was said at court that she and her husband, and their guests, were a particularly revolutionary crowd.

Camille hesitated. However revolutionary they were, would they not dismiss her, a printer's daughter? "I want to help, of course, but I'm not certain—"

"But it's just the kind of thing you would like! Enlightened conversation! Interesting ideas! Debate!"

"Why not take someone like Armand," she proposed, "who knows so much about the balloon?"

Rosier groaned. "He should calculate things, not form words and speak them. We need your pretty face. We need you to tell your story." He frowned at his watch. "In less than one hour."

In the courtyard, Lazare was clapping the driver on the shoulder, turning back to the house. She needed to know. "Why *my* story?"

"I believe something happened to you on that flight. Didn't something change?"

Everything changed.

"Perhaps you can't see it," Rosier went on, "but your *wonder* will get them to open up their purses. A girl, describing what it is like to fly—

no one in a salon has ever heard that before. It will be a first, and they will want to fund an adventure like ours." Rosier held out his hand, a hardworking hand with only one plain ring on it, his thumb and forefinger ink-stained. "Remember your flight. Us, your friends. Save us again, Mademoiselle Camille."

Lazare was approaching the stairs. His beautiful face was expectant but also somehow protected against the possibility of defeat. It hurt to see it.

Even if she did not fully understand her feelings about Lazare, she did love the balloon. The roar of the brazier's fire, that moment of supreme lightness when the balloon lifted free of the earth, how she could see everything, the city below as pretty and as painless as a painting, the bright air, the closeness of *him*—

"I'll fetch my hat, Rosier."

48

When Rosier's carriage clattered into the rue du Bac, its passage was thwarted by a long line of others waiting ahead of them. "Promising," he said. "Lots of pockets to pick." He winked and let himself out, waiting at the tiny iron steps to help Camille down. Rosier led the way to the entrance of the grand house; Lazare walked next to her, thoughtful.

As they came to the stairs, Lazare took her hand. "Are you nervous?" he asked, low enough that Rosier couldn't hear.

"Yes," she admitted. On the way, in the carriage, she'd remembered how terrified she'd been to go up in the balloon for the first time. It felt a bit like that. "Are you?"

"Ridiculously nervous." He smiled warily. "I'd rather fly across the English Channel without a cork vest than do this."

She hadn't known he could be nervous. "I don't know if I'd go *quite* so far," she replied. "It's just asking for money—and if we don't get it, there will be the public launch."

Lazare nodded. "Though for that we'll have to sell several hundred tickets."

Hundreds? "Will there be many people here?" she asked Rosier.

"Probably closer to seventy-five. We would do well to persuade forty subscribers to fund us."

So many people, there to listen to her. She wished suddenly, desperately, that she'd thought to change into her dress. Its enchantments would have been a comfort.

At the door, footmen stood at attention. Camille, Lazare, and Rosier brushed past the fronds of potted palms and came into a crowded entry hall. Men and women mingled there, greeting one another. Camille noticed men in uniform, noblemen in gaudy suits. But there were men in plainer dress, too, wealthy merchants and other members of the bourgeoisie. And, by the window, three black-skinned men, bewigged and dressed in sorbet-colored silk of mint and lemon, heavy gold necklaces about their necks. Most of the women in attendance had affected the deceptively simple cotton gowns the queen wore, though there were some still in silk. All their conversations and laughter came together in a buzz of anticipation.

"And my role is what, exactly?" Camille asked Rosier and Lazare.

"Simply to speak about the balloon, if the opportunity presents itself," Rosier said.

"And if it doesn't?"

"How funny you are. It will—trust me. Let's see if we can gauge the mood of the room."

As she waited awkwardly just inside the door, Camille spotted Aurélie standing next to a man in military uniform. Thrilled to see her familiar face, Camille waved. To her dismay, Aurélie only responded with a formal bow. She had no idea who Camille was—she didn't recognize her as Camille and turned away.

"Come in, come in," said a stout man with frizzed gray hair. He clapped his hands together briskly. "Voilà les aeronauts! Entrez, entrez! Mesdames, messieurs," he called out to those assembled in the room, "certainly these daring young men of the air might weigh in on the question at hand?"

"And a daring young woman," added Rosier.

"What question is that, Monsieur Clermont?" Lazare said.

"The most pressing questions of natural history, bien sûr," a woman said. She was older than Camille; her height and intelligent eyes made Camille think of a kind of queen. Her jewelry was simple, her brown hair unpowdered. She held out her hands to Lazare.

"Madame de Staël," Lazare said, "let me introduce to you my friends and flying companions. Mademoiselle Durbonne and Monsieur Rosier, both of Paris."

"How wonderful that you have included a woman in your ranks." Madame de Staël nodded approvingly at Camille. "Are you an aeronaut as well, mademoiselle?"

"I am."

"And?" Behind Madame de Staël, a group of people moved closer. "I think I speak for all my friends when I say that I am so eager to know what it is like to fly."

Camille cleared her throat. She remembered the wind rushing through her hair, the sleek chill of the air, the clarifying perspective she'd had over everything. She tried *not* to think of how Lazare had stood so distractingly close, his mouth by her ear. "It's everything you might imagine. More, even."

"Go on," said a man with an enormous lily in his buttonhole. He flapped his arms in the air. "Take us with you!"

Rosier raised his eyebrows encouragingly.

Camille took a deep breath, steadied herself. All she needed to do was to tell them how it was. Show her wonder at the experience, wasn't that it?

"I was afraid, at first," she admitted. "I'd never dreamed of going up in a balloon."

The man nodded, encouragingly.

"One goes up so fast, n'est-ce pas? One moment one is on the ground, and the next moment, the faces of your friends become tiny white stones. Trees shrink down to handfuls of herbs, ponds and fountains to puddles—even the Seine becomes a trickle of water. The higher one goes, the flatter things become. I'd never experienced anything like it."

Camille had said everything in a rush, and when she stopped she noticed how still the salon had become. Expectant faces turned toward her. Did they wish to hear more?

"And you don't smell the streets," she added, and several people laughed. "The air is fresh; you pass through mists and vapor. In the distance I saw rain fall from a cloud."

"Oh, how lovely!" the man with the lily said.

"There is a lesson in being so high up, isn't there?" Rosier prompted.

She nodded. "I saw the neighborhoods of our city are not as separate as they might seem. From the air, there's not much distinction between a grand hôtel particulier and a common house divided into many apartments. I saw the edge of the world—I saw possibility."

A few people applauded. The sea of faces waited. It was so quiet she could hear the candles in the chandelier burning.

"And, mademoiselle?" asked the man with the lily.

And?

And what?

Instead of a shuttered printer's shop, instead of a knife at her throat, instead of having to mine sorrow to make coins or a dress, instead of everything that hurt or took away from her, the balloon had given her something. She hadn't known it then. But she did now.

"It gave me hope," she said. "Because what seems fixed—as if it will always be one particular way—if seen differently, may in fact be something that can be changed. A new world, don't you see?"

In the back of the room, someone coughed. The faces of the salon goers, pale as petals, fixed on her. They were, she realized, waiting. Waiting for something more, something shocking. Something surprising.

But she *had* nothing more.

She'd opened her heart and confessed that before she went up into the balloon, her view of Paris had been small, provincial. A mouse's view. These people, whose money could bring them anything—food, shelter, libraries of books, travel, education—took it all for granted. They found nothing in her story to celebrate because—she saw it in the furrowed brows and pleated mouths and folded hands—they could already imagine it.

Or thought they could, which was just as bad.

"It seems a noble venture, monsieur," said the man standing by the mantel, next to Aurélie. He wore a blue uniform with gold fringe on his epaulets. Camille recognized his face from the newspapers—he was the popular commander from the American wars, the Marquis de Lafayette. "But before we empty our pockets, tell me, what is the purpose of a balloon? Could it perhaps function as a kind of spy machine? Say, on the battlefield?"

"A brilliant idea, Monsieur le Marquis!" Rosier interjected. "Imagine, hundreds of sneaky balloons spying on the English—"

"Exactly what I was thinking," Lafayette said, approvingly.

Lazare stepped forward, his arms rigid by his side. His voice was clipped as he said, "A war machine?"

"Why not?" Rosier said, encouragingly. Camille saw he was frustrated and was trying to make the balloon seem useful, but this was all wrong. A balloon was not intended to be a machine of war.

Lafayette nodded. "We are of one mind, then."

Lazare's jaw clenched. Camille remembered when they'd been in the balloon and he'd spoken of his tutor, the one who'd been mistreated, the one who'd taught him to ask *why*. There had been happiness in his face then, but also something infinitely sad. A loss. Lazare, too, had taken a path other than the one he wanted to take, just as she had. The balloon was his salvation, his way out.

But what she saw now was that it wasn't only Lazare's hope, Rosier's, or Armand's. It had also become her own. Being with Lazare today—she as herself, he as himself—she saw it so clearly. This was *their* hope, all of them together. And she refused to let their balloon become a war machine, something to help generals with their killing.

"Monsieur," she began again, "we aeronauts believe that a balloon can be anything. Not simply a war machine, or a spyglass. Or," she added with a warning look at Rosier, "an amusement for the people."

Lafayette responded so politely he sounded bored, "And what should it be, mademoiselle?"

She felt Lazare's gaze on the side of her face, intense as summer's light. Like possibility. She knew what the balloon could be. "It can be a way out. A hope."

"Monsieur le Marquis," Lazare said brusquely, "you have commanded armies. An army needs shoes and muskets, bayonets and cannon. But is not hope just as important?"

Lafayette crossed his arms. "France's armies are already stretched thin. There's unrest in the countryside over the lack of bread, and these troubles will multiply in Paris. How can I ask for money for hope?"

Lazare shook his head, as if he could not find the right words. As if the salon had turned out to be what he'd thought it would be: a way to make money, no better than selling tickets to the public.

Anger thrummed through Camille. Hadn't she lived on hope when there was nothing in the pantry? It was all she had when her parents died, her brother became a monster, when there was nothing but the pain of turning coins and swindling shopkeepers in order to survive. Hope was the thing she'd made from her sorrow, and she would not let it be tossed aside.

She blazed out at the commander and the room of placid, watching faces. "What else is there but hope?"

Again, someone coughed. No one agreed, no one applauded. No one fetched his purse and opened it, counting out the coins.

Only silence.

"Come, come, monsieur," Lafayette said then, making his way to Lazare and throwing an arm over his shoulder. "I'm certain there is some angle we can take on this." As Lazare followed Lafayette to a corner of the room, he glanced once at her, his river-brown eyes regretful.

Rosier appeared at her elbow with lemonade in a crystal glass. "Now it's up to Lazare to rope them in. It's one thing to say you don't care about money; it's another not to take it when someone dangles it in your face."

"And if we don't get the money?"

Rosier snatched a tiny sandwich off a passing tray and tossed it into his mouth. "We recalibrate," he said between chews. "Pardon, I see an open pocket."

Rosier strode to the doorway to greet a lavishly dressed man and a woman who had just arrived. His clever black eyes laughing, persuading, cajoling, he made his way from that couple to others in the room. Selling the balloon as best as he could.

On the other side of the room, Lazare stood in a group of salon go-ers that included Aurélie, laughing at something she had said. The light from the open window fell on him, illuminating his lively face. Perhaps he would accomplish what she could not.

There was no point in her staying.

She left the crowded room that had already forgotten her, out through the grand foyer, pushing wide the heavy front door before the footman could open it for her. Into the bustling street and then north to the river, where she crossed the dark water clotted with boats, and then finally to the pale stone courtyard that now was home.

These many weeks at Versailles, she thought she'd become something. *Someone.* A person of abilities, a person with her own power.

But she hadn't. Alain had been right all along.

It was nothing more than illusion.

49

In the mirror, Camille tucked an oak sprig into her hat.

Her hands trembled from too much magic, and she wanted nothing more than to go out and lose herself in the maze of streets that was Paris. To not have to think. Question. Decide.

But before she could slip past the doorman and out onto the street, Madame de Théron called from her sitting room, where she was fanning herself against the creeping heat. "You're wearing leaves in your hat."

For Madame, the leaves were the sign that she was a traitor. Disloyal to the king. "It's not safe without them," Camille said, keeping back a smile. "Not since Desmoulins said green was the color of freedom and the people's cause. If you were to go out, madame, people would demand it of you."

"Never! Desmoulins wants the people to take arms against our king." Madame de Théron's lower lip quivered with indignation. "Because of him, the rabble have been threatening to burn our noble houses!"

She was not wrong. Desmoulins had said just that when he climbed onto a table outside the Palais-Royal and in front of an enormous crowd, raised his pistols in the air. People listening had torn off the leaves of nearby chestnut trees to wear green in their hats like their new hero. And then they had broken into sword-cutlers' and gunsmiths' shops. On the streets of Paris the mood was that of a dangerous dance: one false step and it would slide into chaos.

"What of the damned duc d'Orléans?" Madame de Théron asked.

"The king's cousin? He and some other nobles have joined the people's side. The duc does whatever he thinks will profit him."

"The duc is a scoundrel!" Madame de Théron snapped her fan on the arm of her chair. "We must obey the king, not argue with him."

"Even if he is wrong? What about the American War?" Papa had written a pamphlet about it; she remembered how the sums had astonished her. "More than one billion livres to help the colonists push England out when we could have used the money here? The price of bread just goes up and up."

Madame considered. "Peut-être. But the king is the father of France, don't forget."

"A father can be a tyrant. And if he is"—Alain's forbidding face swam before her—"then we must find another way."

"Hmph." Madame fanned herself. "The young think they know everything. They should be docile and obedient, but they never are."

Her mind on the news in the street, the anticipation of change, Camille turned to go and nearly collided with one of the maids holding a silver platter. On it lay three letters no bigger than her hand.

As Camille took them, she asked, "Has my sister returned home?"
She had not.

Where *had* Sophie gone? She'd left before Camille had set out, and had not yet returned. It wasn't like her. Or, Camille corrected herself, it wasn't like the old Sophie. The new Sophie was much—*sharper*. More to herself, working longer hours at Madame Bénard's before going to the new place to "measure" it, as she said. Always returning late, her cheeks pinked, a secret in her face. But there was no saying anything about it to her. When Camille tried to broach the subject, Sophie covered her ears or left the room.

She put two of the letters in her purse and opened the other.

> *Dear Mademoiselle—*
> *I hesitate to call again at the Hôtel Théron for Fear of*
> *Offending your Landlady, but I have something I must*
> *ask you. Will you come to the Workshop? This matter*
> *is—regrettably!—Unfortunate.*
>
> > *Your servant,*
> > *Charles Rosier*

Unfortunate?

She recalled Rosier's unease when he had last been here. It must have something to do with the balloon, but what exactly, she could not tell. She had been wondering if they had raised enough money at the salon—perhaps it had to do with that?

And perhaps Lazare would be there.

Perhaps she might have the courage to tell him the truth.

50

When she banged on the bright blue door, it was Rosier, not Lazare, who came to open it. He blinked at her as if he hadn't seen sunshine in days. Pale, worried, his hair frizzed.

"Mademoiselle Camille," he said. "Come in."

She stepped into the hall that led back to the riding ring. "Rosier, what's wrong?"

"Do you know where he is?"

"Lazare?" she asked. "I have no idea."

"Merde!" Rosier tugged at his hair. "Pardon! My mouth is not connected to my brain. Lazare is missing."

"What do you mean?"

"He is not here. Tickets have been sold for the public launch—"

"Already? What about the salon?"

"They didn't give enough, those stingy bastards. And that Lafayette!" He gripped his pipe so hard she thought he might break it. "So I prepared for the public launch. Bien. It was the best idea all along, non? I printed the posters. I printed the tickets and started to sell them. Très bien! Everyone wants to see the girl balloonist!" A wan smile brightened his face, but only for a moment. "And now Armand says there is a problem with the release valve again and a new one must be constructed. But tickets have been sold for the twenty-eighth of July! And Lazare vanished three days ago."

"Vanished? But that's not surprising. Isn't he always going from place to place?" It certainly seemed that way to her.

"Not this time." Rosier took a drag on his unlit pipe. "Something happened."

"What?"

"He came to the workshop—three days ago—upset. Distressed. He told me he had an idea of how to get what he hadn't been able to raise from subscriptions at the salon."

"But that wasn't his fault!"

"So I told him. Then he said he'd refused to take any more money from his parents. As if I'd asked him to!"

"Was that where the money came from before, do you think?" Camille asked.

"Apparently."

This. This was the thing that he had been hiding—she was certain of it. "What changed?"

Slowly, Rosier shook his head. "Who knows? Something they did? Some condition they placed on him? Whatever it was, it made him furious. Desperate. Distraught. And then—gone."

"He must be somewhere," Camille said, fretfully. "I suppose he's not at his parents' house?"

"No reply." Rosier stared blankly out at the quiet street. "Where could he possibly be?"

Slowly, it came to her. He could be anywhere—it was true. But there was at least one other place where he was likely to be.

"I think I know."

Rosier reached for his coat, hanging on a peg near the door. "Show me the way."

She hesitated. Rosier might not be shocked about her use of magic, or what she did at Versailles—he'd probably applaud it—but if Lazare was there for some hidden purpose, if he had told no one, it was not her secret to reveal. "I cannot, Rosier. But I will do my best to find him."

Heading home toward Hôtel Théron, Camille was soon back in the streets of their quarter. In their wealthy neighborhood, where the king's soldiers marched their patrols, no shop windows had been broken or their shelves emptied. Here hung rosy hams and robust sausages. Costly bread lay piled in baskets, carved with the baker's initials. And everywhere, it seemed, candies and chocolate and sweets were arranged like jewels.

Stepping into a bakery, she paid for a sticky bun. She took it out to the street to eat it, as she and Sophie used to do when they had a few extra sous. People had stared at them, eating on the street, but she and Sophie hadn't cared. How could they when they were so hungry and eating a bun was like devouring sunshine?

Camille took a bite. The bun was buttery, sweet with apricot and honey—but it didn't taste the same without Sophie, the two of them against the world.

"M'selle?"

A barefoot street urchin, his gaunt face sepia with dirt, appeared out of the crowds. He held out an empty hand; with the other, he mimed putting food in his mouth. His fingernails were black, his eyes filmed dull. Hopeless, even as he begged.

Her throat constricted.

What if she told him her fingernails used to be like his? Her belly, nearly as empty? Would he believe her, in her silk dress and cartwheel hat, her new shoes and her clean hands? She thought again of the red-haired running girl, her tiny stolen roll of bread, and where she might be now. It seemed another life. Despite everything she and Sophie had, she could not shake the feeling that something was still slipping through her fingers.

"M'selle? S'il vous plaît?"

The hair prickled on the back of her neck. She had to go back and talk to Sophie. She had to tell her she missed her, that she'd said and done the wrong things. Somehow their paths had diverged. Camille wanted to go back and start again.

"Take this," Camille said, handing the boy the bun. He turned to run away but she caught his arm. From her purse she took all the livres she had with her—ten, fifteen, twenty-two—and pressed them carefully into his hand, folding his fingers over the bright coins. "Keep them *safe*, d'accord?" she told him. "Only show someone you trust. Be careful!"

He nodded, once, then vanished into the crowds.

When Camille burst into the Hôtel Théron, there was still no sign of her sister, but Madame de Théron reassured her Sophie had merely gone for a ride in the park with her friends from the shop.

Upstairs, Camille dropped her purse on the writing desk by the window. Fantôme emerged and twined insistently around her ankles.

The purse had a strange shape to it, stretched out. The other letters! She'd completely forgotten.

She tore the violet one open.

Inside lay a tiny card. An invitation.

In honor of Aurélie de Valledoré on her birthday
Jean-Baptiste de Vaux, Vicomte de Séguin, invites you
to an evening of games and gaiety
The fourteenth of July 1789

Tonight.

Across the bottom, in a beautiful hand, Séguin had written:

All our friends will be there.

All our friends.

She hadn't seen Chandon since the opera, when he'd looked so desperately ill. She'd sent letters to him at the palace but had heard nothing in return. Nothing from Aurélie, either, nor Foudriard.

And if they were there, then perhaps—as she'd told Rosier—Lazare would be, too.

Her mind jumped from one idea about him to another, but it was always the same: what did he know? What did he think? But like the spotted dogs in Astley's circus, leaping from chair to chair, she never got anywhere. She just went around and around and around.

She could blame Lazare for being in disguise, for not telling her anything, but she wasn't any better. She could have set aside her disguise weeks ago. She could have been honest.

Sweetly, the clock chimed six times.

The other letter was dirty, stained—a contrast to the sweeping loops of her name across the front. She knew the handwriting immediately: it was from Alain. But how had he known her address? A prickle of unease crawled up her neck.

She did not open the letter yet, but held it in her hand. Weighing it. Remembering who he was.

She unfolded the paper. In the letter, he demanded that they meet to discuss something of great importance. "Why?" she wondered aloud. "What good would it do?"

There was a small fire in the grate; she dropped the letter into it. As she watched, it curled upon itself, first its edges blue with flame, then scorching to black. Gone.

To go to the party for Aurélie, hear her friends' banter as they sat at the tables and bet higher and higher until there was nothing she could think of but the next card that would be turned, the next number called, and to do it over and over—it would be a relief.

She laid the invitation on top of the writing desk, above the row of pigeonholes, where Papa's paper bagatelles stood. There was the haughty queen with her towering wig of printed words, the dragon roaring *Liberté*, the schooner with its sails that proclaimed, *It Is Time We Act*.

She picked it up, and from old habit, blew at it so that its sails billowed.

What had Papa intended when he'd fashioned the schooner so that these words were emblazoned on its sails? Writing—printing—was a kind of action. But she didn't think that was what he'd meant. She ran her finger gently along the bowsprit, touched the holes Papa had made for the cannons. She thought of him, how he must have looked when he was caught in the square, hanging the posters that had ended his career. Defiant. Secure in his truth, if nothing else.

He had meant for her to *do* something.

Lazare might not want to have anything to do with her, if she told him what she'd done with her magic. It wouldn't be fair, not when she still didn't know his reason for hiding his noble birth or the reason he went to Versailles.

Bien sûr, Papa's ghost might have whispered in her ear, there would be consequences, some of them not fair. How else would you know you had done something, if there was no change? No shift in the world?

She set the schooner down, gently.

She'd go to Versailles and find Lazare. *Distressed*, Rosier had said. *Distraught*.

And she'd find a way to do something—to tell Lazare the truth about herself.

She wished she'd seen Sophie before she'd left. There were things she wanted to admit to her, things that she'd been wrong about.

As the gravel crunched in the courtyard below, the horses stamping their feet, Camille worked the glamoire, the blood on the gown nothing to her. Inhaling, she felt the rich rush of magic as the dress embraced her, steadying her, drawing her to court.

51

When Camille arrived, it was evening, the moon a low sliver of silver in the sky, the party only recently begun.

Yet she could not shake the feeling that she was too late.

Untying the ribbons of her cloak, she paused at the open doors of the room. From inside, a thrum of voices and music. Servants were moving throughout the large, high-ceilinged space, lighting silver candelabras on the marquetry tables; two footmen had lit the many-armed chandelier and were hoisting it back up to the ceiling. Beneath it stood four gaming tables covered in green baize—all packed with aristocrats—but around one large table in particular, all the way back against the tall windows, observers stood three-deep. Camille felt the frisson of excitement in the room, a crackle of electricity. High stakes tonight.

As she handed her cloak to a footman, she saw the Vicomte de Séguin make his way toward her around the gaming tables. She thought about how taken with him Sophie had been at the fête galante. He was handsome, it was true: his strange bronze eyes, the long, fine nose, his square jaw, the knowing, arrogant mouth. As always, he was expensively dressed, all the way down to his red-heeled shoes. And rich. But there was something else about him that unnerved her, something that was there but not there. Like a cobweb. Or a smoky blur, like a breath on a windowpane.

He bowed. "Baroness de la Fontaine."

"Good evening, Monsieur le Vicomte."

"It was kind of you to come, when I'm sure you have so many things that keep you in Paris."

"I wouldn't miss a fête for Aurélie's birthday." Camille kept her voice light. "Nor cards."

"You are known for winning, madame." He glanced at his ornate pocket watch. "I so enjoyed meeting your sister—such a lovely girl. She is well, I trust?"

Another twinge of disquiet, like the scratch of a needle. "Of course. Is Aurélie already here? Chandon? Is he feeling better?"

Séguin made an impatient gesture. "They are at the tables."

"I'll join them, then." She was about to curtsey to Séguin, when a roar erupted from the large table at the back of the room. Someone shouted, "Bravo, Sablebois!"

Lazare.

She rose on her toes to see over the heads of the people in the room, but Séguin stood in her way.

"The game calls you, I see." His voice was strained. "I'd hoped to speak to you, but I won't keep you any longer, Baroness."

"Perhaps later?" she said, her eyes searching the room. *Where is he?*

"Certainly. What I have to say can wait. If you'd like to try your luck at the tables, the Marquis de Chandon's stepped in as dealer for me tonight." With a small bow, he backed away, letting her pass.

As Camille made her way through the raucous crowd, greeting courtiers she knew, she searched the tables for the dark gloss of Lazare's hair and the washed-out brown of Chandon's. He must not be so very sick anymore, if he were acting as dealer tonight. At the edge of the crowd surrounding the last table, she looked back over her shoulder. In contrast to the swirl and flash of the movement all around him, Séguin stood very still.

The tiny hairs on her arms rose.

The Vicomte de Séguin's face was impassive, held tightly in place by an inner discipline, more a sculpture of a face than a living one. Except for his golden eyes, which blazed with an emotion very much like fury.

52

Camille blanched when she saw they were playing faro.

It was not for nothing that the game had been outlawed for a hundred years. Friendships lost, fortunes, too; duels, murder, and suicide followed behind it like a ravening shadow. When Madame Lamotte had warned Camille not to gamble, faro was what she meant. But dire consequences and rumors never stopped anyone from playing. People lost great sums of money, but they also won big, more than at any other game.

And if one had debts, it was easy to believe faro's promises.

The card game was played at a long and narrow table. Several players sat on one side, as if at supper, with the dealer at the center of the table on the opposite side. Laid down the middle was a cloth on which had been printed one of every card in the suit of spades. Those who wished to bet placed their chips on the card they thought would come up when the dealer drew. Each round, two cards were drawn by the dealer from a small, wooden dealing box. The first was the dealer's card, called the "loser," and if a player had placed his money on that card, he would lose it to the bank. The second card was the players' card, the "winner," and if a player bet on that, he would win. A kind of abacus with pictures of every card in the suit was used to keep track of which cards had been played.

Each round allowed for a fresh bet, a chance to win back what one had lost. This was faro's delectable poison: the belief one might win again. To be made new, if only one dared to risk it. When nearly all the cards had been played, the stakes soared and the betting grew fierce. Dangerous.

Standing in the crowd around the table, Camille had been spotted by Aurélie, who nudged Lord Willsingham. He leaped from his chair and waved her over. "Take my seat, madame! We could use your luck!"

"Merci, Lord Willsingham," she called out.

"La Fontaine!" Willsingham shouted. "Make way! Make way!" People around him began to applaud and the crowd stood aside to let her through. "Sit next to the Marquise de Valledoré, won't you?" Willsingham said, pulling out the chair. "I'll just stand behind. Watch from a safe distance, what?"

As banker, Chandon sat at the center of the table, a leopard-spotted deck of cards in his hands. His skin was the gray of smoke. Harsh lines ran from his nose and pinched his mouth. She'd been hopelessly wrong to assume he was feeling better. He should have been at home, under a physician's care. But still he smiled when he saw her.

"How wonderful to have you here, madame."

"You know I love nothing more than a good game of cards," she said, making the observers laugh. She had often wondered how Chandon kept up his façade despite his illness, but now she knew. They both had their court roles to play.

Settling into her seat, she quickly kissed Aurélie on the cheek. "Happy birthday, mon amie."

"We'll see how happy it is," Aurélie said, archly.

On her left side sat Lazare.

His forehead rested in his hand, his elbow on the table among a cluster of empty wineglasses. With the thumb of his other hand, he drummed on the table. His fine, pistachio-green suit was wrinkled, his cravat hastily tied. His hair was covered by a powdered wig, which she'd never seen him wear before. Its stark whiteness cast into relief the shadows under his eyes. He looked bone-tired, as if he hadn't slept since she'd seen him at the salon.

Distraught, Rosier had said.

"Baroness," he said, his voice formal, flat. His dark brown eyes were nearly black. Lost.

Something was terribly wrong. In all her time at Versailles, she had never seen him at the gambling tables. "I didn't know you gambled, marquis."

"When I must." He glanced dully at Chandon, who was shuffling the deck. "Though I can't say I like it."

"Then why do it?" she asked. "How long have you been playing today?"

In reply, he turned his right hand over, palm up, on the table. His fingers were chalky white from playing carambole. There were some at court who bet on carambole or other billiards games, but she had never done it. They had a bad reputation.

She clasped his hand. It was hot, fevered, as if it could burn.

"You're not well," she said, her voice low. "Come, I'll find you a lemonade. We will—" She didn't know what they would do. She knew only she had to get him away from the table.

"There are cool drinks here. You have only to snap your fingers," he said, slowly, as he lifted her hand. She wondered if he meant to kiss it, but instead he drew it close and held it against the patterned silk of his waistcoat, over his heart. Beneath her palm, it was racing.

"Feel how fast it runs, Baroness?"

She nodded, apprehensive.

"As fast as when I took a gamble and kissed you at the opera?"

This was the kind of opening she'd hoped for as she'd sat in the carriage, spinning toward Versailles. But now she could not imagine saying anything. Lazare was so strange, himself and not-himself. "I don't know," she managed to say.

A muscle in his jaw twitched. "For the stakes are just as high now."

"Lazare," she said, keeping her voice down. "What are you doing? There's nothing that's worth this."

He dropped her hand and she curled her fingers into her palm. "Nothing?" he asked. "What about my life? My freedom? The balloon? I have no choice but to try my luck here."

"This is a terrible game, and a terrible idea." She added, quietly, "I could help with whatever costs you have—"

"Absolutely not." He rubbed his face roughly. "Chandon, credit me another thousand, will you?"

A buzz ran around the table as Chandon noted Lazare's name on an accounting sheet and counted out stacks of chips, stiffly pushing them to Lazare with a rake.

"Please listen," she tried again.

He only stared at his cards.

Taking out a handful of chips from her purse, Camille tossed them angrily on the table in front of her.

"Everyone ready?"

The betting was wild. Willsingham was a loud and eager gambler, making quips in his awful French, and his antics got the other players to loosen up and place their chips on the table. Lazare played grimly, as if spurred by some inner demon. Why would he not listen? Or at least let her help?

Opposite them, Chandon smiled wanly when the players laid down big bets. He comforted them when their cards were revealed to be losers, and called for champagne when their cards were winners. But for all his patter, something was wrong. Though the room was so hot that Camille was constantly fanning herself, Chandon wore his cravat tied high around his neck as if it were winter.

Séguin stalked the room, passing through the pockets of light and dark, bending to speak to the guests at the other tables, waving at a footman to bring someone more wine or the gambler's standby, a sandwich. Camille felt him watching her.

"Last three cards!" Chandon called out. "Place your bets for the turn. Odds are four to one if you bet wisely."

Camille checked the abacus. Strange—so many beads had never been moved. Whoever was keeping track of which cards had been played was doing a terrible job.

"Madame de la Fontaine?" Chandon raised an eyebrow. "Care to get rich?"

"Not this time. You'll sit out, too, won't you, marquis?" she said to Lazare.

"I'm in," Lazare said. He dropped a third of his chips on the three of spades, a third on the jack, and a third on number four. "Because that is the number of the aeronauts," he added with a bleak laugh.

Any other time, she would have rejoiced to be included in this number. But now? Not if the balloon was driving him toward ruin. He was drunk after days of playing, hollowed-out. And reckless: he'd placed all his chips on the board. He'd asked for a thousand earlier, but how much debt had he racked up before she'd arrived? She sensed it was a lot. Too much.

"I'm sure I saw a jack come up just now. Jacks are probably dead," she warned. "Why not bet on nine?"

"What does it matter, as long as I win?" Lazare rubbed his temple. "Les jeux sont faits, non?"

"The bets may have been placed, but that doesn't mean it's over." She couldn't let him destroy himself, even for the chance of saving the balloon, not when she might stop him. "Chandon hasn't called it yet," she said, urgently. "There's still time—why not pull out now? Keep your winnings."

"I aim to win this one."

Desperate, she tried once more. "Faro's a poisonous game, you know that. You start with a little, get used to the taste, and ask for more, forgetting how much you've taken."

Lazare stared straight ahead to where Chandon fidgeted with the dealing box that held the cards. Had he even heard her? He kept drumming on the table with his thumb. She wanted to shake him. Why wouldn't he stop? She tried to make Chandon see what was happening, but he fixed his eyes on the three cards left in the dealer's box.

When Chandon spoke, his voice cracked. "If everyone's placed their bets?"

All the noise and chatter stopped as Chandon's nimble fingers hovered over the first of the last three cards. He slid it, facedown, from the box and then, with a flourish, revealed it.

"Three!" someone shouted.

Chandon's face was grave as he raked a third of Lazare's chips toward himself. All around them, people muttered disapprovingly.

Lazare gave a short laugh. "I'll win the next two."

Chandon's hands rested on the spotted back of the next card. "Ready?"

He flipped it: the queen of spades.

Lazare groaned. He was now drumming on the table with both hands, agitated. Beneath his wig, the hair at his temples glistened with sweat. He had one more chance with the last card, the one they called the hock.

Please.

Under the table, Aurélie grasped Camille's hand.

Chandon's face was completely bleached of color. "Last one," he said, exhaling shakily. Someone in the crowd shouted "Vive Sablebois!" but was quickly hushed. The only sounds were the ticking of a mantelpiece clock and Lazare's nervous tapping.

Chandon placed his fingertips on the card and released it from the box. As he slid it out, it bent ever so slightly, and Camille caught a glimpse of the jack's pointed beard. A jack—Lazare had won!

She watched his grim expression, waiting for it to change to joy.

Chandon flipped the card.

It was a five of hearts.

53

Camille pushed her way through dresses and plumes and the haze of perfume and candles. Lazare had staked so much money—everything he had—and lost it.

All of it, utterly gone.

He had demanded to see the final card and Chandon had handed it to him while all the other players watched, some gossiping behind their fans about Lazare's unrefined behavior. He'd given the card back to Chandon and staggered away from the table, as if wounded.

She could not comprehend what had happened. No one had kept count on the abacus, so anyone's guess as to the last three cards would have been based on what he remembered being played. But Camille had *seen* the last card. And then—for she didn't doubt what she had seen—Chandon must have turned it. And probably many other cards as well, leading to that final play. That was why no one had kept track of the played cards on the abacus. Chandon had planned to cheat. And to cheat Lazare.

But why?

No matter how she puzzled, it made no sense. Lazare loved Chandon well, as far as Camille could tell. Had they quarreled? But whatever Lazare might have done to Chandon, this was going too far.

She found Chandon by the library's marble fireplace, warming his hands over the fire in the grate. Which wouldn't have been strange if it hadn't been the middle of July.

"Why did you do that? Cheat him?" Camille challenged.

"Camille." Chandon stared at the fire. "You shouldn't have seen that."

"But I did. Explain yourself! Why would you do such a thing? He's drunk, lost—I thought you and he were friends. Since you were little, taking fencing lessons together!"

"We are, as much as anyone can be in this nest of vipers." Chandon seemed even more exhausted than he had at the faro table. His once lively, handsome face was ghastly white. "I would have thought that you, of all people, would understand."

"Tell me how I should understand this, Chandon. You betrayed him." Camille felt that betrayal as if it were her own.

He inclined his head a fraction of an inch. "I did. But Séguin forced me to do it."

A finger of ice ran down her back. "How? What did he do?"

The cords in Chandon's neck were taut as wires. "Blackmail. Magic."

"Over what?" But then, with a sickening lurch, she knew. "Foudriard?"

Chandon's mouth worked, his lips struggling to shape the words. He could only nod.

Her heart ached to see him like this. "What he's done to you—has it made you ill?" All those times she'd seen Chandon sick, exhausted, coughing as if he would retch up blood. Growing weaker and weaker. Aurélie had offered her physician—and Chandon had refused. *Too much magic*, he'd told her, but only now did she see that whatever the

magic was, it hadn't been his to control. It was not something a physician could cure.

"And worse."

She clasped his hands. They were fever-hot. "What can I do?"

The tears that had been welling in Chandon's eyes spilled over. "As
a magician, you are in grave danger—you must flee Versailles. Now that
I am so—broken—Séguin has grown desperate. Promise me you'll go
now," he said.

Impulsively, she threw her arms around his neck. His chest convulsed
with sobs.

"We will put an end to this," she said into his ear. All magic eventually wore off. Didn't it? "Can we not get you away from Versailles? What
if we took you over water—to England?"

"I don't know that it would help," he faltered. "I suspect Séguin has
set a plan in motion in which I am only a bit player. If it succeeds, he
will no longer need me. And in any case, I am almost finished—another
week or two of this and I'll be neither pretty to look at nor fun to talk to."

"Don't say those things!" She remembered how Maman, exhausted
from working la magie, had succumbed so quickly to the smallpox.
And now her friend, too? "I won't watch you die. There has to be something we can do."

"There is." He brought her hands to his lips. "Promise me. Stay far
from this monstrous place. And get Sablebois away before he discovers
Séguin's cheated him. It will not end well."

Chandon nodded toward the room beyond the library, where the re-
freshments had been laid out. "You'll find him there. Hurry."

54

Lazare stood in the center of the room, drinking wine, alone. All the others had edged away from him, as if bad luck were catching. Under the costly silk of his rumpled coat, his shoulders slumped. Some of the powder from his wig had drifted, like snow, onto his jaw. All the light seemed to have gone out of him.

Camille's fingers ached with sadness.

Séguin had laid out an extravagant spread of food for his guests but Lazare did not seem to see it. He picked up a miniature sandwich and, as he stared into the distance, put it in his mouth. He chewed it as if it were dust.

She didn't know what to say, how to convince him to leave the palace with her. Would it make a difference for her to tell him who she was? Would he even listen?

He looked over as she approached. "You were clever not to play." Taking a glass off the footman's tray, he raised it. "To your good fortune."

"I won't drink to that. Not when the game ended as it did. And now that it's over—"

"I was a fool to play on. I have been very unlucky of late, in every way." He drained the wine, wiped his mouth with the back of his hand.

"Why don't you go home, then? It's never a good idea to stay when your luck is bad. It never changes as fast as one would like."

He focused on her for the first time. In his eyes was desperate longing, a wish for her to understand. "I'm short on cash, for the balloon." He made a choked sound that might have been a laugh.

She wanted to press him, ask what that laugh meant, but just then Lazare swayed on his feet. She reached out to steady him. "I'll send for someone to call your carriage."

"Not yet, Baroness. I'm going hunting."

"Now?" she asked, uneasily. It had to be nearly midnight. No one would venture into the woods at this hour. "I don't understand—what can you possibly hunt in the dark?"

"Foxes." He lowered his voice. "I've set a trap and I'm sure I'll catch one."

He was making no sense. "Here?"

"Of course," he said. "The palace is full of traps, did you not know?" Grabbing another glass of wine off the table, Lazare passed through the crowds and was gone.

She needed to go after him. She slipped behind a group of older bewigged and rouged men, their portly bellies straining the silk of their waistcoats. They were so involved in their conversation they hardly noticed her. The aristocrats were talking politics and discussing whether the nobles and the church could ever side with the commoners against the king. A heated debate broke out but Camille did not hear it.

For something had happened in the gaming room. Women were exclaiming in high voices, men booing loudly. She stood on her toes to see.

Lazare was leaving the faro table. Men clapped him on the back as he staggered away. Hadn't he lost everything? Where had he gotten the money to keep playing? And then, Séguin was leading him to an alcove by a window, very close to where she was standing.

"What's wrong, messieurs?" she said, coming forward.

Séguin gave her a small, resentful bow. "Nothing for you to worry about," he said. "Now, Sablebois, don't make a mountain out of a mole-hill. This is nothing. A minor setback."

"Perhaps to you it's nothing."

"You lost all you had, you're saying?" Was there a note of glee in Séguin's voice? "What about your father?" he went on. "Couldn't you appeal to him? Surely it's no sum for such a man."

Lazare seemed to grow bigger, taller. There was something ferocious in him Camille had never seen before. "You don't know me at all if you think I'd ever go to my father with my debts."

"Forget I said it." Séguin extended a hand but Lazare shrugged it off. "I'll write up an agreement so you can pay the debt off over time."

"Don't speak to me of debts. I'll agree to nothing, Séguin, and you know it. You cheated."

"Careful, Sablebois."

"You are the one who should be careful, *fox*." Lazare was breathing hard now, as if he'd been running. "At the end of the first game, I called the turn. No one had kept track of the cards, as is usually done to assure the players that the banker isn't cheating. I wonder why. But it didn't matter, because I have a very good memory for details."

Séguin stood very still. Waiting. Lazare's arms were straight at his sides, his hands hardened into fists.

"And I lost. Strange, non? Before I played in the next round, I examined the cards in the deck we'd played with. And do you know what I discovered? The card I'd bet on wasn't even in the deck." He jabbed his finger at Séguin. "I played one more time, to see what would happen. And you know what I discovered? You're a cheat."

"How dare you accuse me," Séguin said coldly. "It's obvious you're only doing it to get out of your debts. And I understand why. Certainly your father the marquis would hate to hear of them."

Lazare glanced behind him as if his father were there. "He will never hear of it because you will return my money to me. Chandon was the dealer, but it was your game."

Séguin shrugged. "I'll give you a letter to sign. You can pay me back with interest."

"Shut your mouth, Séguin." Lazare's voice was low, dangerous.

For a split second, Séguin's eyes went to where Camille stood by the curtains. "You can't have everything you want, Sablebois."

Then she knew.

It had gone so wrong. Always watching, Séguin had discovered she cared for Lazare. It couldn't have been difficult. He had seen them first together so long ago—at the Place des Vosges. With a deepening sense of dread, she remembered he'd seen them kiss at the opera. He had watched her at the masquerade. Always watching, always tallying the score.

Waiting.

She had to stop this, do what Chandon had said, and get Lazare away before something worse happened.

"Please, stop your argument," she begged. "Surely there's another way—"

"No one can have everything he wants," Lazare said. "I know that full well. But you've cheated me out of my money—twice in one night—and I refuse to sign a *contract* with a cheat, even if he pretends at being a nobleman."

"Pretends?" hissed Séguin. "How would you know what a nobleman is? *Sauvage*."

In an instant, Lazare's hand was on the pommel of his sword.

"Lazare!" Camille threw herself at him, grabbing hold of his sword-arm. An argument like this, a challenge to a duel, went against all the rules. The king had forbidden it. It was one thing to draw swords in the gardens as Chandon and Séguin had, when there was no one to see. But now the whole court was watching—Lazare would be banished.

Or worse.

"Step out of the way, madame," Séguin snarled. "This is an affair d'honneur, and I will not be prevented from getting satisfaction."

Camille turned to the crowded room, the white staring faces. "Cannot someone stop this? Won't you people do anything?" Was it because of who Lazare was, that no one did anything? Because he was somehow not a true aristocrat?

"Come away, madame," the Comte d'Astignac called. "This is between them."

"Heathen," Séguin spat into the expectant room.

In one fluid motion, Lazare drew his sword free.

The room broke into chaos. Men shouted for the queen's guards. Women were screaming; someone fainted. A tray was overturned; glasses splintered across the floor.

"Once more, I'm telling you to step away, madame," said Séguin, his voice pointed as daggers. "This is not your quarrel."

But it was. If she had not come tonight, what would have happened? Had Séguin been intending to cheat Lazare all along, or did he decide on that path when she'd gone to see Lazare? A sickening feeling came over her.

She had wandered into a trap.

"Don't do this!" She pulled at Lazare's arm. "Please!"

"No." Lazare tried to shake Camille off. "You've insulted me, Séguin, and I will be satisfied—"

The room hushed.

Baffled, Camille watched as all the guests crowded close. Their faces were blanks. Stunned. Aurélie was there at the front, her arm outstretched, her finger pointing at Camille's skirt.

It was changing.

55

Lazare's arm around her was a wing, or a sword.

With his open coat, he shielded her from the nobles' shocked stares and muffled their cries of alarm. As her disguise and her defenses fell away, there was only this: the shelter of his arm, the solid comfort of his chest against her cheek. She wished desperately she might close her eyes and lose herself in this moment. This safety.

He knew.

He knew, and he had not abandoned her.

Diving forward, shoulder first, he seemed not to care whose slippers he stepped on as the astonished crowd parted ahead of him. He half-carried her across a cool marble entryway and then out through glass doors banging closed behind them, over a gravel parterre, and down into the twilight shadows of the gardens.

In the darkness of the orangerie, they stopped. He still held her pressed to him, his hand cradling her head. Her ear against his chest, his heart drumming.

He took a ragged breath. "Are you well enough to stand?"

Camille struggled to make sense of what was happening. Without warning, the glamoire had faded. Everyone at the party had seen the dress change. Even Séguin. But they hadn't seen her face change—she was sure of it. A dress could be explained away, but not her face. That was happening now, her skin crawling as the magic left it.

Lazare had saved her.

Tears burned behind her eyes. All this time, she'd been so afraid to tell him. And now he'd guessed what was happening and hadn't cared about her magic. He had kept her safe.

Séguin must have arranged for fireworks, for suddenly, a flower of light burst high over the palace. Up above them, past Lazare's head, the windows of Versailles flamed with candlelight and, Camille knew, watchers hiding at the edges of the curtains. But here in the gloom, they were alone.

"Thank you," she said quietly. "For rescuing me."

Gently, he let go of her. Her dress was dissolving to tatters, her red hair flaming through the powder, the hollows and the fatigue once more excavating her cheeks, her neck, her eyes. She knew how ugly it was, the falling away of the magic. She blinked back tears.

"It *is* you, then," he marveled. His expression was uncertain. "Camille."

"It is." She exhaled. However awful she looked, she was relieved to finally be done with the hiding. "How long have you known?"

He took her hand, brought it to his lips. She felt his smile against her fingers. "Almost immediately, at the game of cache-cache. I suspected, anyway."

"And your flirting with the baroness?"

"I thought I was flirting with you."

He'd known her, under the magic, all this time. It was a strange joy: he'd not been fooled by her masquerade. He had *seen* her. "Why did you not ask?"

A melancholy expression tugged at his mouth. "I didn't understand how you did it. Nor why. Would you have told me?"

Behind Lazare, two silhouettes descended the stairs and crunched along the gravel walk. Camille and Lazare stepped off the path to let them pass; they were an older couple, the woman walking with her hand tucked confidentially around her husband's elbow. They all smiled as they greeted one another. It was like seeing two rare creatures, unicorns or giraffes—a court marriage that lasted.

When they had passed, Camille said, "I couldn't. The things you said about magic. I thought"—she steeled herself—"you would despise me for it."

"I don't like it because of how people have used it. But that's not important. I was worried about you." Cautiously, he said, "If I figured it out, don't you think that others will?"

"But no one else has." Except the other magicians.

"Are you sure? This is a dangerous game, Camille. Louis XIV, the Sun King, burned magicians at the stake! The National Assembly has promised us a constitution, there's rebellion in Paris—each day the people's attacks against the nobles grow. If an aristocrat magician were discovered at court, what do you think our Louis XVI would be forced to do?"

"He wouldn't kill us." But she wasn't sure. A king trying to stay in power might do anything.

"What if killing magicians—the symbol of all that's wrong with the aristocracy—would make the people of France love him?"

Why couldn't he understand why she'd done it?

"Lazare, you knew me, in my Paris life." The glamoire was fading; the trembling was coming on.

His grip tightened on her hand. "But why? Why risk death?"

"Don't you know?" It was like explaining why she'd saved the balloon from crashing. "I had no choice. My parents died of the pox, my brother took everything we had and gambled or drank it away. He might have killed me, with a knife or his fists. His debts were huge and his creditor wanted recompense. With my father's press gone, I lost my only skill. Magic was the one other thing I knew to do."

Once more, a flare of light cascaded over the palace roof.

"But surely, someone could have helped—some other way than this—"

Camille exhaled, exasperated. "Only someone like you would say that."

"Someone like what?" He let go of her hand, suddenly sober.

"Someone with choices."

Lazare turned his head to the midnight sky, as if searching for answers there. "You think I have choices?"

"You're an aristocrat. I saw your parents at the opera—they have money. An estate. Rooms at Versailles. They gave you a tutor!" she said, unable to stop bitter envy seeping out.

"And that means I have choices?" Lazare swallowed hard. "Look at my skin and tell me I have choices. Look at my clothes."

He pulled off his wig, grabbed hold of his own hair. Its beautiful inky darkness absorbed all the light. "Vous voyez? No French nobleman has hair like this. This is my *mother's* hair. My Indian hair. Didn't you hear what Séguin called me? *Sauvage*. And the rest of them?" he asked, angrily. "The courtiers ask me if I am the son of Tipu Sultan. They ask me if, when I'm 'at home,' I ride on elephants, and if a person can make his fortune simply by collecting huge pearls from the sand in Pondichéry. They think me exotic, like a tiger in the king's menagerie. The ladies covet my father's fortune, but only as long I wear a nobleman's disguise."

Lazare's chest rose and fell. White powder drifted on the air between them.

"You feel you have no choices." She'd believed changing her appearance would free her from the cage she beat her wings against. But somehow, even though she had money and every material thing she needed, she only felt more and more trapped.

"Do I?" His voice was wandering, lost. "I was thirteen when I was brought to Versailles. On the day my father and I arrived, we walked in these gardens. I had a little sailboat with me, its motor one I'd made myself. We passed a fountain, I put it in, but it stalled. So I did what I would have done at home, with Élouard: threw off my hat and coat and jumped in to fetch it. When I climbed out, my father was furious. Like an idiot, I asked he if was displeased the boat had failed. He told me he was displeased because a nobleman does not jump into a fountain to fetch a plaything. He didn't understand when I said it was an experiment, not a toy."

She felt his pain like a physical thing. "He wanted you to be someone else, an aristocrat."

"He must have loved my mother. But then," he said, despair etching his words, "why has he done this to me? He says I'm a Frenchman. The court at Versailles says I'm Indian. Why is it either/or? Can I not be *both*?"

"You *are* both. If we aren't free to be who we wish to be, what else is there?"

"And yet, here we are."

"You say it as if we're both trapped, that we will never break free." Trapped, free—what did it matter if there were still secrets between them? "Tell me," she said, "what did your parents wish you to do when they sent you to court, these past weeks? Was it connected to the money for the balloon?"

Lazare flinched, as if she'd hit him. "Rosier told you?"

"He told me only that you were distraught, and that you'd refused your parents' money. That was why I came."

"They intended to be generous, but they had so many conditions." His voice was hollow. "They wished me first to meet a girl, here at Versailles. If I liked her, they told me, they would arrange a marriage. But I never intended—"

"The daughter of the Comte de Chîmes?" It hurt more than she thought it would to speak of the pretty girl with the white-blond hair. "She was in your box at the opera, surely you considered it—"

"Is that what you think of me?" Lazare asked, bewildered. "Have I not done everything in my power to show you how I feel about you—all the while keeping your secret, for as long as you wished it? Yes, I sat with her in my parents' box, danced with her at the masquerade, but only to satisfy them. To buy myself time before I lied to my parents and told them I'd tried, but I could never marry her. Because I loved someone else."

Camille's breathing was shallow, too fast. She reached out, grasped the trunk of one of the orange trees. Pinpricks of darkness flickered at the edges of her sight. She felt close to fainting. She had been so utterly wrong.

"Who did you think I was, Camille? I refused my parents' money because I didn't want to be beholden to them in any way. You're just like these courtiers—believing in gossip and appearances when you might have asked me. You might have told me the truth."

"I wanted to, tonight. I wish I had done it before."

His fierce gaze roamed her face, caressing her cheeks, her chin, and dropping dangerously to her lips. In the darkness, his eyes were deep pools. More than anything, she wanted to kiss him. To put all of this confusion and hurt away, into a box they would never open again. To start anew.

She took a step closer, so close she heard the intake of his breath, felt the heat rise off his skin.

He drew her nearer, dwindling the space between them. "This is what we should have been doing all the while, don't you agree?"

"I do." She tilted her face up to his. *That mouth.*

"Camille," he said, tenderly tracing the line of her jaw. "After all this time, all this wondering, it is really you, isn't it?"

She saw herself reflected in his eyes, the gleam of starlight in them. He bent his head to her. Reaching up to touch him, her fingers grazed his hip—and the wide sash from which his sword's scabbard hung.

The duel.

"Lazare?"

Taking her hand, he turned it over and kissed her palm.

His touch sent shivers along her skin. "Please, listen—do not fight the Vicomte de Séguin."

Lazare let go of her hand. His face was suddenly, frighteningly *closed.* "Do not ask that of me."

"He's a dangerous magician. He's been blackmailing Chandon, threatening him—that's why Chandon cheated you at faro." She rushed on, trying to help him see. "This duel is part of some terrible plan. Chandon told me to take you away from here."

Lazare exhaled, running fingers roughly through his hair. "Magician or not, he dishonored me. He cheated. He threatened to speak to my father. He called me a savage."

There had been so many times since the game of cache-cache that she'd tried to explain away his birth. Fine clothes, fine manners—probably fine houses and horses and who knows what else. The true Lazare, she'd convinced herself, was the one that wanted to fly a balloon over the Alps. Who believed in the power of science to liberate people, to open their minds to new truths. To see things differently. To hope.

"If not for me, then for your old tutor," she pleaded. "Didn't you say he showed you a different kind of honor? A different way to be?"

"I'm trapped, Camille."

Nothing was worth this ancient aristocratic idea of honor. "Please, Lazare. I don't want you to die!"

"I must go through with this," he said, bitterly, "otherwise I cannot live with myself."

"But it's foolish, and wrongheaded, can you not see that?" she pleaded. "It's not who you are!"

He looked at her hard, his face taut with sorrow. "Then you do not know me."

Without another word, he left her, his sword swinging at his side as he disappeared into the dark.

56

Camille blundered through the trees. She found herself not near the stables at all, but lost in a small grove that seemed to have sprung up out of nowhere. The trees had hands to grab at her, roots to trip her. Branches snapped in her face and the path diminished into a track fit only for rats. Dawn was coming, but it was pitch-dark under the trees.

She had been so wrong. She had been an idiot, a fool. But there was still time, if she could find him. Time to persuade him.

"Lazare!" she called out. "Where are you?"

Her legs wobbled from working the glamoire. She stumbled against a tree, its bark rough under her hand, and stopped to catch her breath.

If she could not find Lazare, she needed to find the stables and Madame Théron's carriage. And go home.

There—through the trees, along the run of iron fence leading to the stables. Something was moving. Surely it was a man? In a pistachio-green coat?

"Lazare? Wait!" She stooped under a branch and ran toward the fence. "Lazare?"

"If only I knew where that bastard was."

Camille froze.

"But I suppose you don't, either," the Vicomte de Séguin said, stepping from behind a hedge. In the darkness, the silver embroidery on his waistcoat and cuffs glimmered. It felt as if years had passed since he and Lazare had shouted at one another, but here he stood, unnaturally fresh, as if he had just stepped out of his dressing room. He bowed. "I was sure it was you, Madame de la Fontaine. Or should I call you by your real name?"

"I hardly know what you mean," she said, as coldly as she could.

Séguin smiled silkily. "I've just been down to the stables and, deplorable as it may be to both of us, the Marquis de Sablebois is already on his way back to Paris."

"Quel dommage," she said with a nonchalance she did not feel. It was not safe here, in the shrubbery, with him. She'd no idea what he was capable of. Or what he might decide he wanted from her. Keeping her back straight, she picked up her skirts and willed her shaking legs to move faster. "I must return home myself."

"Shall we walk to the stables together, then? I have something to convey."

There was nothing she would like less, but no matter how fast she walked, in her big skirts and her stays, she could not outpace him.

"You come from a tête-à-tête with Sablebois, I'm guessing? I cannot imagine that he was happy to learn of your use of magic. I remember he has a particular dislike of it."

"Don't speak of him."

Cool as ever, Séguin kept pace with her. "Remember when I read your palm and gave you some advice? Not everyone at court is a lover of magic—or magicians. Hélas, those golden days are long gone. You wouldn't wish your secret to get out?"

Camille started. Would he expose her? Was this how he threatened Chandon?

"Whatever scheme it is you have going—winning lots of money, entrancing young noblemen, or just having a magnificent time—it is finished if the king learns what you really are. He hates magicians. I was just remarking on this to the Marquis de Chandon."

"And what if I told the queen about *you*?" Camille countered. "What if I told them all that you are a magician?"

"Be my guest. Tell them. See how they respond to flimsy charges brought by a *so-called* baroness from the provinces," he said with a sneer, "against the last remaining member of my ancient family. Expose yourself to their questioning and eventual ridicule when they discover who you are. I dare you."

A gauntlet, tossed to the ground.

She had nothing to match Séguin's reputation.

She was not as far as she'd hoped from that girl running in the street, tiny roll clutched in her hand, bare feet filthy under her petticoats. But Camille was not going back there, no matter what. She steadied her anger and her fear, channeling them as she would have channeled her sorrow to turn a card or a coin to something she could use. Séguin had nearly proposed to her; he wanted something from her. She didn't yet know what it was, but surely it was valuable, and if she played carefully, she might discover it. "I thought you were my friend," she said smoothly. "Or has that changed?"

In the half-light, it was hard to see his face. "Of course, mademoiselle," he said, kissing her hand. Camille fought the revulsion that clawed at her throat.

At the stables, she watched him step into his phaeton and drive back to the courtiers' wing of the palace. When she called for her own carriage, a groom appeared from one of the stalls, a wine bottle dangling from his hand. "Everyone's left, mademoiselle. Haven't you heard?"

She shook her head dumbly.

"We've destroyed the Bastille! Set the prisoners free! Taken its arsenal of weapons! Paris is on fire!" He punched a fist into the air. "Now all of you will have to answer for what you've done."

"What do you mean?" she asked, stupidly.

"You haven't heard? We attacked it—all the people of Paris. Liberated the prisoners! Several men," he said, "lost their heads."

It had come, then. The riots that Papa had predicted, the rising bread prices, the merciless taxation—the changes Papa had foreseen were galloping toward them.

The groom's face swam before her as she tried to think. Sophie was in Paris. She needed to return immediately. "But the carriage? It can't have driven back to Paris on its own!"

"Anything can happen on a night such as this," the groom crowed. "Anything!"

Camille wanted to slap him sober. "Is there no one who can drive me?"

"Everyone's asleep, except me."

"Wake my coachman, please," she said.

"How much have you got?"

She'd left her purse somewhere, dropped it when she'd fled the party. She patted her skirts where the hidden pockets were: empty. "I've nothing with me, but once we get to my house I can—"

"Promises, promises! And underneath, all lies, I'll warrant. What care have you people ever had for the likes of us?"

In the distance, beyond the palace gardens, thunder rumbled. In its roar, Camille heard the growl of cannon and muskets. If no one could be found to take her, what would she do? Walk? She was so desperate to go that she was ready to drop to her knees and beg when, for the first time, the groom seemed to see her tattered cloth-of-gold dress. She saw him realize the gown she wore looked like a castoff.

"Wait." He squinted. "You're a servant? Why do you want a carriage at this time of night?"

Camille didn't hesitate. "I have to get home to my mistress. You know how they are, not caring one jot for us, only their greedy selves." At least her despair was real. "If I don't, she'll sack me for certain. Then what will I do?"

"You should have said that to begin with," the groom said, more kindly. "We must stick together, non? I'll fetch the coachman and you'll be on your way."

He ran off, shouting.

A wave of nausea rose into Camille's throat. She had become just like the aristocrats she'd once loathed: heedless, careless, distracted. People were being beheaded in Paris and she had left Sophie there.

Alone.

57

Somewhere in Paris, the Théron carriage shuddered to a halt. Outside, a man was shouting; the carriage tilted as one of the horses shied, its hooves clattering on the cobbles.

Camille peered between the curtains. A thickset man holding a torch stood by the lead horse, his fingers threaded through the bridle's cheek strap, close to the bit. In the torchlight, the horse's neck shone black with sweat. The man shouted questions at the coachman.

What if they wouldn't be let through? She wanted to scream in frustration. How could she have left for Versailles without knowing Sophie's whereabouts?

Somewhere a drum was beating, quick and tight, its tempo like her heart's.

She had to get back to the Hôtel Théron.

It was so dark it was impossible to make out any buildings. Only around the torchlights' halos could she see anything. Outside, the voices rose, louder, angrier.

She sat like that—small, nervous sweat trickling down her back—for what felt like hours. She did not know how many prisoners had escaped or how dangerous they were, or who had done the beheading. The city exulted, hungry. The walls of the carriage felt thin as paper. She was both hidden and exposed, a mouse holding still under a cloth.

Then the carriage jounced as the coachman stepped down from the box. A moment later he opened the door.

"Mademoiselle," he said, carefully. "The people have attacked the Bastille, searching for weapons. Some prisoners were freed—not many—but in defending the fortress, the governor of the Bastille was killed. I am sorry to say they cut off his head with a knife and paraded it on a spike around the city. Soldiers have been mobilized to keep the peace. It will take some time before we will be allowed to pass. Others ahead of us are waiting, too."

But Camille could not stay. "Where are we now?"

"Not far from the Hôtel Théron. Four streets distant."

"Thank you for being honest." She gathered her skirts. "I must go."

"Mademoiselle, it's not safe!"

"My sister—" Camille's voice cracked. "I'm worried for her. I didn't see her before I left for Versailles and now—"

The coachman nodded. "Slip out quick. Keep your wits about you and stop for no one." Locking one door, Camille unlatched the one opposite. Not far away, an explosion.

If she hesitated, if she delayed—

She closed the door behind her and ran.

Paris was a scene from hell.

Rioters ran along suddenly unfamiliar lanes, shouting, "Down with the nobles!" The weaving light of the torches they carried distorted their faces. "Down with the king and the queen, his Austrian whore!"

Fleeing down the center of the streets, Camille stumbled into a group of young men in leather aprons—*Butchers' apprentices,* she thought wildly, *or ironsmiths?* Their faces blazed. One of them gleefully beat a drum as he shouted for the others to march in time. Two of the biggest shoved someone ahead of them. A nobleman. Not much older than her friends. His wig hung askew, and he was bleeding from a cut on his temple. His costly lace cravat had been ripped from his throat; he'd also lost his coat and one of his red-heeled court shoes. Crimson choke-rings marked his neck.

He stumbled as they pushed him on. In that instant, as his captor yanked him to his feet, he saw Camille. He took in her gold dress, the glittering brooch she'd forgotten to unpin from her shoulder.

Run, he mouthed.

She ran.

She fled down alleyways and through the ragged streets of her old neighborhood, always heading toward the safety of the Hotel Théron. In the rue de Perle, there were broken windows, doors wrenched off their frames. A load of bricks lay scattered on the floor of a bakery, dusted with flour. Baskets lay upturned, the bread gone; a strongbox yawned open, empty. She crept along the walls, keeping to the darkest darks of the shadows, until she came to the gate of the Théron mansion.

"Monsieur Tounis!" she hissed into the deathly stillness. "Monsieur! It's I, Baroness de la Fontaine!"

Far away, in the depths of the house, a lock clicked over.

Was it opening or closing? "S'il vous plaît, Tounis, dépêchez-vous!" She rattled the gates and instantly regretted the noise it made.

Somewhere, maybe two streets away, glass shattered. Raucous laughter echoed over the rooftops. A cart stacked with wood ambled by, the carter encouraging his horse to go faster—such an ordinary, everyday thing, but tonight the carter's haste made her cower.

"Monsieur Tounis!" She had nowhere to go if the gatekeeper was too afraid to open the gate. Each moment that she stayed in the street was a moment too long. Sophie must be wild with worry, waiting in their rooms. She and Madame de Théron would have worked themselves into a state—

There! A light bobbing in the shadowy courtyard.

Someone was coming with a lantern. It flared up and she recognized the gatekeeper's slight form. Camille pressed her forehead against the gates, nearly weeping with relief.

"Is that you, Baroness?" he said, his voice low.

"Yes! Please, let me in—it's not safe out here."

He lifted his lantern and his face loomed up at her out of the dark. "Mon Dieu!" His hands fumbled with the lock. "You are covered in dust! And the state of your dress!"

"Please be quick!"

He unbarred the gate and she slipped in. Now that she was safe, her legs threatened to fold. "My sister?"

"It's been a terrible night," he said. "Lean on me, Baroness. Madame de Théron will cry tears of relief when she sees you."

Before Camille was past the entrance hall, Madame de Théron threw her arms around her, not caring about Camille's dirty dress.

"How we waited for you!" she wept. "We thought you were dead! You look terrible, not at all yourself! We feared—at Versailles—what would the crowd do there? Monstres!" She covered her face with her ringed fingers.

"I'm sorry you were so frightened, madame! At Versailles we knew nothing of what had happened." In the salon behind Madame de Théron, a fire danced in the grate, but there was no sign of Sophie. "Is my sister asleep?"

Madame de Théron blinked. "Mademoiselle Sophie?"

Yes, my sister! Remember her? Camille wanted to shout. "I must tell her I've returned," she said to Madame and the gatekeeper, who continued to stare at her as if she were a ghost.

She ran up the steps, taking them two at a time.

Upstairs, their pretty sitting room was silent.

No candles lit, the curtains still open, as if no one had closed them that evening. Fantôme hopped down from a chair and meowed plaintively.

The skin on the back of her neck crawled. "Where is she?" Camille asked the cat.

In Sophie's room, the bed had not been slept in. One of the doors to her wardrobe yawned open. All of Sophie's best dresses were missing from their hooks, her embroidered shoes vanished from their racks. Her summer coat, dove-gray with yellow peonies embroidered on the cuffs, was gone. So was the petal-pink cloak Camille had worn at Notre-Dame. Even Sophie's wool cloak, the one with the collar of dyed mink, was no longer there.

It was July and Sophie had taken her winter cloak.

"She's not coming back," Camille said to the empty room. "Where has she gone?"

The floor tilted and she steadied herself on Sophie's dressing table. Fantôme watched unblinking from the center of the room. There had to be a simple explanation. Sophie would never run away. Even if she were angry with Camille. She wasn't the kind of person who would simply set out somewhere.

At least, she hadn't been. Who knew anymore what Sophie might do?

She would go back down and ask Madame. Perhaps Sophie had said something to her.

As she turned to go, she saw it.

Tucked between the glass and the frame of the mirror above Sophie's dressing table was a letter.

58

Chère Camille,

I am so very sorry I left without speaking with you.
But perhaps it is for the best. I fear you would not have
understood.

I'm certain you will be worried, but don't be. I have
gone to meet him. He has promised me a wonderful life.

No one has forced me—this is what I want. Even
fairy-tale princesses sometimes get to bring about their
own happiness.

Please forgive me that I kept this a secret from
you. Alain has given his blessing and I hope you will,

*too, when you see how happy I am with my future
husband.*

*You know him already—Jean-Baptiste de Vaux,
the Vicomte de Séguin.*

Je t'embrasse—
Sophie

Camille read the letter twice.

Sophie had eloped. *Sophie had eloped with the Vicomte de Séguin.*

Her sister was in terrible danger.

Stumbling from the room, she raced downstairs. Madame de Théron and Tounis the gatekeeper still stood aimlessly in the entry, waiting for her.

"Sophie is gone!" Camille nearly screamed. "Why did you say nothing?"

"I tried, but you ran upstairs. Mademoiselle never came home this night. Gallivanting about and now she's—dead, I presume!" Madame de Théron covered her face with her handkerchief and sobbed.

"Tell me, please, who fetched her?" Camille asked Tounis.

"Your sister left before the madness started in the streets. I told Madame not to worry," he said, pleased with himself.

"But where did she go?"

He shrugged. "She didn't say."

"Did she go by foot? Or did someone come for her?" Camille has been with Séguin nearly the entire night. He must have had an accomplice, or sent a servant.

"A nice carriage came for her," he recalled. "That young man was there, too. He stepped out and helped her in."

They were cursed-slow, these people, as if they had all the time in the world. "Who? What did he look like?"

"Well-dressed?" Tounis examined the painted ceiling, as if the answer might be discovered there.

"His hair, monsieur," Camille hissed. She felt as if she would suffocate in this pretty room with its cherub ceiling and dainty chairs and its nonsensical people. "What color was it?"

"Fair, I think. No, no, I know! Reddish like yours."

His words rang tinny in her ears. *Reddish like yours.*

"I didn't recognize him," he went on. "But your sister seemed to know him quite well. When he arrived, she kissed him." He nodded sternly at Camille.

"You fool, Tounis!" Madame snapped to attention. "Mademoiselle Sophie's a good girl and she's not kissing and going off with just any young man in a carriage! That was her *brother*! Don't you remember? She introduced us several weeks ago."

"Not my brother," stammered Camille. Had Alain given more than his *blessing*? Had he arranged this?

"Oh yes." Madame de Théron nodded. "I'm sure he heard what was happening in Paris and he came to take both of you girls to safety. Of course the Hôtel Théron is a fortress, so really, it was unnecessary," Madame said. "But *you* are a mess, Baroness, and you look like a corpse."

"Please, sit," the gatekeeper said, patting the chair cushion as if he suddenly were the host. "I will bring you a cognac."

Camille was made to sit by the fire, to tip the fiery liquid down her throat. Its heat steadied her. She needed to think what to do next. Where would Alain have taken Sophie? Surely not to wherever he lived. They must have gone to a house the Vicomte de Séguin had in Paris. And she had no idea where it might be. How would she find them if they wanted to remain hidden? Sophie was headstrong and Alain was right there at her elbow, guiding her to her doom.

For certainly it was doom to marry a magician such as Séguin.

Camille rubbed her aching neck. What would she do? What *could* she do? Sophie had run off with a powerful aristocrat who had no scruples to prevent him from doing whatever he liked. Maybe he would never marry Sophie, only seduce her. And then abandon her. The strangest thing was that he had nearly proposed to Camille, too. Perhaps he wanted one of them—and either Camille or Sophie would do. But why?

What was it Séguin had wanted to talk to Camille about? And Alain, in his letter? She feared she now knew.

"Baroness de la Fontaine," the gatekeeper said, "you look ill. I will bring you another cognac."

As soon as he left, Camille reached out to touch Madame de Théron's hand. "Can you be discreet, madame? My sister is in grave danger. May I have your advice?"

Madame de Théron blinked. "Of course. There is not one person in Paris or Versailles who will not come to my aid," she said, any uncertainty gone from her voice. "Whatever has happened to our darling Mademoiselle, whatever needs to be done, I will help you."

"I fear my sister may have gone away with a nobleman. Eloped."

She gasped. "You mean he seduced her? Here, in my house?"

"I don't think he came here, madame. The man asked my brother to fetch her, but I don't know where they've gone." Camille exhaled shakily. "I don't know what to do!"

Madame de Théron exhaled. "You must go to the queen."

Marie Antoinette? "What can she do?"

"Ban the rake from court! Send him away, before he can defile your sister. To be banished would be a kiss of death for a man like that!"

Yes. For someone like Séguin, it would be. She could not imagine him anywhere else but the gilded rooms of Versailles. "But I'm nothing to the queen. Why would she help me?"

"For my sake, bien sûr!" snorted Madame de Théron. "You will go with a letter from my own hand. And then watch how the queen brings him to heel." She swallowed the rest of her brandy. "In this lawless new world, there are still a few rules."

59

At Madame de Théron's urging, and with her letter to the queen heavy in her purse, Camille turned back on the dusty road to Versailles. As they made their way out of Paris, they passed the Bastille with its tumbled towers. The drawbridge was down and alongside its moat, a group of men and women were shouting songs and shooting off muskets.

Camille gritted her teeth. She would do what needed to be done.

If she hadn't brought Sophie to the masked ball, she would never have encountered Séguin again. Unless—they had somehow met before that? On those *walks* Sophie took? But it didn't matter. If Camille had kept a closer watch on Sophie, she would never have had the chance to elope with him.

What had happened with Sophie was her fault—she saw that clearly now.

She remembered how she'd trusted the high wall surrounding the Hôtel Théron to keep danger out. If she hadn't been blinded by Versailles' glitter, she might have moved them somewhere farther away— Lyon? Nantes?—where distance would have been the wall and Alain would never have found them.

But she hadn't.

She had lost sight of the most important thing.

Once at the palace, Camille wove her way through the clusters of gossiping aristocrats in the Hall of Mirrors, all of them exclaiming about the frightful storming of the Bastille as they planned all tomorrow's parties. By the windows that opened onto the balustrade, she spotted Aurélie, the Baron de Guilleux, and Lord Willsingham together, deep in hushed conversation. When Camille drew close, their faces brightened with relief.

Aurélie threw her arms around Camille. "Ma belle! We were so worried when we heard the news from Paris! But you seem fine, non? Whatever happened to the dress you were wearing last night?"

"I'm not certain," Camille said carefully. "The dye had been poorly fixed—I spilled wine on it and the color started to run. It was too ruined even to give to my maid."

"Sadly, there are much more important issues than ruined dresses, mesdames," Guilleux said. His sunburned cheeks were stubbled with a day's-worth of beard. "Baroness de la Fontaine, Lord Willsingham has offered his carriage to take Aurélie back to her estate. I will accompany her."

"Come with us, Cécile," Aurélie said hurriedly. "There's not much to do in the country and pardieu, my husband adds nothing to dinner conversation but lectures on the best kind of rabbit hutch or some such idiocy. But it's lovely there and I would be overjoyed to have you with me." Aurélie's smile faltered at the edges. "Please. I will fear for you if you stay here."

"Damn me, this trouble is going to stir up you nobility," Willsingham said in his terrible French. "Once people break in one place, they break in every place."

"He means," Guilleux said, patting Willsingham on the shoulder, "that things are going to get worse for us from now on. And I don't doubt it. It's only a matter of time and then we'll all find ourselves with our heads on pikes."

"Julien! It won't come to that," Aurélie exclaimed.

"It will if you stay here," Willsingham said. "Go to your estates in the country. And if you don't feel safe there, come to England. My roof has holes but the house is large."

"But how will you get to your estate? There are bread riots in the provinces!" Camille said, thinking of her friends in their lavish carriages. "My brother, who was to be sent to guard the grain wagons, told me. Anyone, but especially nobles, suspected of hoarding grain has been threatened—some even killed. How can you know it will be safer there?"

Aurélie's pretty face grew somber. "I don't. But at Versailles I have only a room on a hallway with a tiny lock on the door. Anyone who comes to the palace can find me, eventually. At our estate, at least we have a moat." She smiled. "A deep one. And many guards. We could hold a siege there. Imagine, Cécile!" she said, warming to her subject. "We would be utterly safe."

A castle with a moat would be heaven, if she had Sophie with her. "Soon, perhaps—but my sister is in Paris. I can't leave yet." She hesitated. "Chandon? Have you seen him?"

Aurélie shook her head. "I've searched everywhere. He looked terrible last night. Tell him, when you see him, that he should go home, too. Don't let him wait too long, d'accord?"

Camille nodded. She couldn't speak.

"Then this is good-bye for now," Aurélie said, kissing Camille. "Our first stop is Tours; we leave immediately. You have my card. Come anytime—no need to send word, just come."

Camille embraced Aurélie and then watched as the three of them hurried down the glittering hall. Maybe she would go, once she got Sophie to see that eloping with Séguin was disastrous. They both would be better off away from Paris.

As she made her way to the queen's rooms, Camille rehearsed Madame Théron's instructions. She would give the letter to one of her ladies-in-waiting. She would be polite, but not afraid. Determined. The queen must take pity on her, see the danger of the situation—help her. At the doors to the queen's antechamber, Camille paused, set her shoulders back, and pressed the flat of her hand to her bodice, over her stomach. The dress shifted to meet her palm, reassuring her with its sangfroid. Camille brought a smile to her lips and went in.

There was no queue of courtiers waiting to speak to the queen at her morning toilette. Instead, Marie Antoinette sat almost alone at her dressing table, her morning robe loose around her shoulders. Behind her stood her long-nosed hairdresser, deftly coiling a lock of the queen's hair into place. In front of her, pots of rouge, tubs of creams, and several hairbrushes spread out across the table. Mixed among them were a hand of cards, facedown, and a tiny, half-empty cup of chocolate.

"Majesté," said one of the ladies-in-waiting, as she folded a Kashmiri shawl. "Madame la Baroness de la Fontaine is here."

Camille made a deep reverence, relieved that she hadn't forgotten Sophie's lessons.

The queen's blue eyes met Camille's gray ones in the mirror. "Venez, venez," she said.

Her hairdresser, the famed Léonard, raised a charcoaled eyebrow as Camille came forward, but then bent assiduously over the queen's hair.

Marie Antoinette gestured to an embroidered stool that Camille knew was usually occupied by the Duchess de Polignac. "Madame la Duchess is going on a visit to Switzerland," the queen said brightly, "so it does not matter where you sit. There are no more rules, madame. N'est-ce pas, Léonard? It's all falling down like a child's tower made of sticks." She made a wry face in the mirror.

Camille sat down slightly behind the queen, so that she could see Marie Antoinette's reflection in her looking glass, and hazarded a small smile. Under the queen's eyes purple shadows lingered, and her forehead was creased with deep lines. "These are frightening days, Majesté."

The queen nodded. "Léonard, can't you add something to make it fuller?"

"Fullness is overrated, Majesté," he said. In the past, he'd favored towering wigs but today his own hair was tinted a subdued brown and tied back with a black ribbon. "My friends in Paris tell me it is about to become démodé. Sleek, simple—that's what I imagine for these times." He waved his jeweled fingers at his own hair. "Comme ça. Slowly, slowly we will change your hair, and then, pouf! No one will remember how it was. But today, Majesté, only a subtle shift."

In her fist, Camille clenched the fabric of her dress. How could they speak of hair at a time like this?

"Slaves to fashion, aren't we all? The queen of France, cowed by her hairdresser. People might say this is something new, but it's always been like this, hasn't it, Léonard?"

Léonard bowed. "Majesté."

Why would the queen not get to the point? Camille had no time to endure the whole of Marie Antoinette's toilette.

One of the ladies-in-waiting pulled dresses from a tall wardrobe and sorted them into two piles. Another stood at the queen's enormous jewelry chest, slipping glittering handfuls of necklaces and bracelets into a plain leather case. They might have been preparing to go to one of the other palaces, like Saint-Cloud, to hunt, but the hush that hung over the packing, the quiet speed: it felt to Camille as it had when she and Sophie left their old apartment on the rue Charlot. The queen was preparing to escape. While Camille was pushing her way deeper into the webs of Versailles.

Marie Antoinette checked a tiny white-and-gold clock on the dressing table. "What is it you wished to talk with me about, madame?"

"It's a matter concerning my sister."

"A younger sister?"

"Yes. Unmarried." Camille willed herself to continue. "I have reason to believe she has eloped with the Vicomte de Séguin."

"That would indeed be horrible," the queen said, her voice measured. "I assume your father hasn't given his consent? Why is he not here to speak to me?"

"I'm an orphan, Majesté, and my husband is dead."

The queen made a soft, clucking sound. "What a pity. No brothers?"

"Only one. He's a drunkard and of no help to me."

In the glass, Léonard gave the queen a knowing look.

"I know little of what the vicomte does when he is not with us," she said. "He is a very private man, n'est-ce pas?"

"But what am I to do?" Camille said, frustrated. "Sophie is only fifteen. I thought you might—"

"Might what?"

What *had* she thought the queen would do? Order Séguin to divulge his secrets by threatening to cast him from court? To hand over Sophie?

"I beg you, help me, Majesté! You are my last hope. Perhaps you might order him to return her to me? To her family?"

"Ah." The queen adjusted her necklace. "Myself, I obeyed my mother, and my brother, in all things. But—just consider, madame—is it possible your sister wished to go with him?"

From what Sophie had written in the letter she'd left at their rooms, she did believe herself in love with the vicomte. "Yes, Majesté, it is possible. But I don't think she understands how he might—use her."

Sighing, the queen touched the glass stopper of a perfume bottle to her throat. The scent of crushed roses hung in the air. "My dear madame, then there is not much that can be done. I will ask Monsieur le Vicomte what his intentions are, but if he means to wed her—"

From the back of the room, one of the ladies-in-waiting glided forward with a porcelain plate edged in gold. On it lay a folded note, which the queen snatched from the dish and read. "Hurry, Léonard. His Majesté is returning from Paris after speaking with the mob. I must be ready to greet him, as beautiful as I can be. Understood?"

Léonard nodded. "Will you put on your earrings, madame, or—"

"You do it. My hands shake." The queen stared at her reflection as Léonard scooped up the earrings from their satin-lined box. Her pale chest rose and fell quickly.

Camille was about to address the queen again when Léonard gestured toward the door. The message was clear.

Willing herself not to scream with frustration, Camille stood. "Thank you, Majesté. I appreciate anything that you can do for my sister," she said as she bowed deeply. She rose, expecting the queen to have returned to her toilette, but found instead that Marie Antoinette was looking at her in the mirror.

"Madame, if you do find the Vicomte de Séguin, remember one thing."

"Yes, Majesté?"

Her voice dropped to the lowest of whispers, pitched so it wouldn't carry.

"He cheats."

Chandon had said the same thing, the first time Camille came to court. It felt as though he had said that to her a year ago, a hundred years ago, in the reign of another king, another queen.

Séguin cheats. This was the queen's best advice? Her royal help?

Walking backward out of the room, Camille made three deep reverences and, turning, blundered through the doorway into the antechamber, where she paused to settle her swaying skirts. The little room was only big enough for two chairs and a small table, on which stood an enameled music box.

Camille seethed. She didn't know what she had expected from the queen; she had no illusions that a queen was anything like a god. But Marie Antoinette did control things at court. Why ever had she listened to Madame de Théron? Camille might be back in Paris, scouring the streets, talking to Madame Bénard at the shop, searching for Alain—anything but standing here with empty hands.

She picked up the music box, weighing it. Imagined hurling it into the oval mirror on the far wall and watching the mirror shatter, the shards crash to the floor.

"Why ever would you do a thing like that?" a rich voice said from the doorway.

Camille turned.

Séguin reclined against the doorjamb, his ringed fingers resting lightly on the jeweled pommel of his sword. His close-fitting cream-colored suit was, as always, richly embroidered, uncreased, and immaculately clean. She could see what Sophie found irresistible: he was handsome, powerful, and very rich. He took a step forward and his cologne slipped into the room ahead of him: incense like in church, the bitter bite of cloves.

"Madame la Baroness," he said, bowing. "Quelle surprise."

Camille suspected there were no surprises where Séguin was concerned. "I'm trying to find my sister," she said, speaking as lightly as she could. "Perhaps you know where she is?"

Séguin stepped further into the room. "I might."

"You must tell me, monsieur."

"Must I?" he said, teasingly. "Has anyone told you how charming you are when you're angry? In the tumult of last night, I may have forgotten to do it myself."

The past days and weeks were a blur, something Camille couldn't see clearly, a view through a rain-streaked windowpane. But she knew that Séguin had been ready to propose marriage, once—even if she'd stopped him from saying the words. He might still care for her, and that would be something to use. A coin to turn.

"I'm anxious to see her, Vicomte. She's been gone two days. Do tell me, where is she?" She kept her voice pleasant. *Pretending.*

"If you wish to know more about your sister, come to my apartments in the courtiers' wing in a half-hour's time. I'll be happy to tell you everything I know. Any footman may direct you. You must excuse me, mademoiselle—I have business with the queen that cannot wait."

He strolled into the queen's chamber and called out a greeting.

Camille set the music box down on the table. Her palm was slick with sweat.

In the anteroom's gilt-edged mirror, she saw the queen embrace the Vicomte de Séguin.

60

Hurrying through seldom-used passages, Camille managed to avoid the Hall of Mirrors with its gossiping crowds, the courtiers grumbling outside the king's chambers. She slipped unseen through what had once been an unknowable labyrinth of hallways, but was now as familiar to her as the lines on her palm. The problem of Sophie was a puzzle without a solution. How would she get her back?

Perhaps Sophie didn't even wish to return. Camille would have to prepare herself for the possibility. If Sophie said no, Camille could tell her that Séguin had almost proposed to her first. She could reveal that he was a dangerous magician, blackmailing Chandon and weaving a web that Lazare was also caught in—but even then Sophie could laugh and say it was nothing to her.

Another problem was Séguin himself. As Camille took a back staircase, she thought of his still, watchful face, his knowing smile. How he'd blackmailed Chandon by using his love for Foudriard. The vile things he'd said about Lazare and the poor. The way he caught her off-guard, made her afraid to meet him when she was alone. *What he knew about her.* In those moments, he seemed to be her mortal enemy. But then she remembered how his fingers had gently traced the lines of her palm while he'd offered to help her avoid the traps at court, his almost-proposal in the king's garden, his fury when he'd caught her looking for Lazare at the party.

She paused at the top of the steps, hand on the banister. It seemed very much like the behavior of someone in love.

With half an hour to waste, Camille forced herself to take her time. She might never again return to Versailles. Wandering down lesser halls, she passed dozens of rooms, listening to the lonely echo of her heels on the floors. These last two months, she'd used these hidden passages and servants' stairs when she felt the glamoire waning; they were usually empty. She rarely saw anyone else, and if she did, they were using the passages for the same reason she was: to avoid being seen. They would nod at one another, and keep going. These corridors had been safe places. But today they were eerily quiet.

At a window, she heard raised voices coming from outside. In the courtyard below, a farm horse had been hitched to a wagon. It was piled high with bureaux, thin-limbed side tables, great trunks wound around with ropes, a long mirror. In front of the wagon waited a dull black carriage, nothing fancy, two mismatched horses in its traces. A man in a drab suit, a white wig in his hand, stood arguing with the wagon driver.

The door of the carriage snapped open and a woman descended, so plainly dressed that Camille's first incongruous thought was that she was a servant. Then she recognized the woman's elegant way of walking, the way she held her head: she was the queen's favorite, the Duchess de Polignac. Snatching the wig from her husband's hand, she thrust it at the driver and pointed for him to get down. Once the driver was on the ground and wearing the wig, her husband climbed up onto the box and took the reins. She returned to the carriage with the driver and closed the door once both of them were inside. With a crack of the whip, the horses lunged into a canter; the wagon lumbered after them and soon was gone.

Dread crept along her skin, cold as ink. The queen had said the powerful Polignacs were going to Switzerland. And perhaps they were. But disguised as servants? Their wagon was loaded with the most expensive things they had. They were fleeing Versailles, just like Aurélie.

As Camille watched, another carriage pulled into the courtyard, and a second couple, older, slower, made their way to it. This woman wept into her handkerchief. They were all leaving, escaping the coming storm. Camille walked faster.

The empty corridors showed another side now. Instead of clandestine, they seemed abandoned. Haunted. Under the ceiling, black mold bloomed where rain had come in. A painting had been cut from its frame, which now hung blindly on its nail. Outside a closed door, a reeking chamber pot waited. No servant had come to empty it. Chandon had said the glamoire the magicians had worked for the Sun King was crumbling like old cake. Now it was decomposing.

When she found the vicomte's door, it was no different than any other.

She knocked and a valet admitted her, stiff and as proud as his master. He showed her into a high-ceilinged sitting room. A fine old tapestry hung on the far wall. In it, a curly-haired unicorn knelt by a fountain, stirring the water with his horn. Among the books and piles of paper, she hoped she might find some evidence that Sophie had been there: a glove or a glossy green feather from her hat.

But there was nothing.

When the Vicomte de Séguin entered the room, he bowed, elegant as always. "Bonsoir, Baroness—or should I say, Mademoiselle Durbonne? I hope you've been comfortable."

Of course he would make certain to use her real name, to remind her of her powerlessness. Where was she supposed to start? She took a deep breath and plunged in: "I wish to know the whereabouts of my sister, monsieur."

Séguin waved his hand at his valet, who stood silently by a bookcase. "You may go."

It didn't mean anything that he'd dismissed his servant, Camille tried to tell herself. It's commonplace. Still, the sound of the door clicking closed made her uneasy.

"Your sister is safe, mademoiselle. And happy. She would never want to worry you."

"I'm certain she is," Camille said, though she wasn't at all sure. "Is she here? I'd like to see her as soon as possible."

He smiled, as if with regret.

"Why not?" Camille insisted. "She's my sister."

"What do you think I am? A monster? She's at my home in Paris, which is in fact where she wished to go. She'll be quite safe there. Until you decide." Séguin opened the lid of his snuffbox and offered it to her.

Camille stared. "Decide what?"

"What you will do." He took a pinch of snuff. "I don't wish to marry her. Wasn't that obvious when I tried to ask for your hand?"

Obvious? Who could possibly know what he meant to do? "Sophie believes she is in love with you."

"Your sister is in love with my title, my money—" He gestured at the things in the room. "Everything I have."

"Why take her, then?"

"Come, you must have anticipated it. You're so clever at cards," he said. "It's one of the things I admire about you."

Séguin has set a plan in motion. But what was it? "How long have you been planning this?"

Séguin shrugged. "Since you ignored my overtures, in the king's garden. Perhaps I was too subtle?" he added, more to himself than to her.

"Why should you want anything to do with me? I'm a pretend baroness, a printer's daughter." It made no sense. "Besides," she said, grasping onto the one particular he'd mentioned, "it was an accident that I ran into you there."

"There aren't many true accidents, mademoiselle. And if it hadn't been there, it would have been somewhere else. Eventually." He shook out the lace under his cuffs. "And no, it wasn't your upbringing as a printer's daughter that drew me to you. In fact, that is something I've had to overcome."

He held out his ringed hands to her. She shoved hers deep into the folds of her skirt.

Séguin laughed. "I like the way you consistently resist me—how's that for an answer?" He took another step closer; Camille tried not to shrink from him. "I have wanted you since I first sat with you at the gaming table and watched you turn cards with la magie. How innocently you did it, as if there were not two magicians observing you! Do you remember that night? You had that snuffbox? I wanted you as soon as I saw how much you *cared*."

A cold hand crept up her spine. It was such a strange thing to say. "I don't feel the same way."

"In time, you might." He shrugged. "Regardless, if you wish to see your sister, you will do as I say."

"What is that?"

"Marry me, of course."

No.

"You would secure the well-being of your sister. And your own status at court. You do not perhaps understand how very rich and well connected I am."

"Haven't you heard what happened at the Bastille?" Camille flashed. "It's the end for people like—you." She'd nearly said *people like us*. The old Camille would never have made that mistake.

"You think a mob will pass through the gates of Versailles and tear the palace down?"

"Why not, when they've got nothing to lose?" Something hard and angry in her rejoiced as she imagined the rotting palace collapsing on itself, crushing Séguin and the rest of the court beneath it.

"That's how a gambler thinks," Séguin said, disparagingly.

Camille seethed. This conversation was pointless. She didn't need to be here, listening to his proposals. Now that she knew where Sophie was, she had to return to Paris. Madame de Théron would help her find Séguin's house. She would bring the police. They would free Sophie.

"I'm going to see my sister."

He sighed, as if exasperated at the behavior of a child. "Your *sister* wishes to be with me."

"She's fifteen years old, monsieur. She knows nothing of the world!"

"She knows more than you think. She came willingly; it was easy to arrange through my man in Paris. Whatever friends you have will not be able to take her from me, not when she is my wife. She is my ace, mademoiselle—wouldn't *you* play a card like that if you wanted very, very much to win?"

"I would not," she said, shakily.

"Then we'll trade cards. Marry me and your sister goes free."

A clock chimed the hour. There had to be another way.

"Say yes, mon trésor." He held out his ringed hand to her. "For that is what you will be: my treasure."

Over his shoulder, the tapestry unicorn dipped its horn in the water. A maiden held the unicorn's golden leash in her small, white hands. Her face was sad, downcast, as if to say, *We are all in chains.*

A sob caught in her throat. She and Lazare had parted angry, maybe never to be reconciled. Chandon was dying because of the Vicomte de Séguin; her own brother was a hopeless drunk whose body would turn up on the banks of the Seine one day, the pockets of his coat flipped inside out. And Sophie had followed a path the vicomte had laid out for her, stone by stone. Camille had believed she'd changed their path, but now she was standing on one built by someone else—one that led to a trap.

Her life was fraying. What had once felt like a rich, damask fabric was now threadbare, just the net of warp and weft sagging in her hands.

Séguin waited, still as one of the statues in the gardens outside. It didn't matter if he wanted her—whatever that meant to someone like him. Beneath that golden façade he *was* a monster. The thought of spending all the days of her life with him—sharing his bed, his marble-white hands on her, his poison words dripping in her ear—made her insides heave with revulsion.

But she could not stop there. As when she gambled, she thought of what might happen if she played a certain card, how its effect would ripple through the coming rounds.

She imagined saying no.

Séguin would marry Sophie. Or not, if he could force her to do as he wanted without marrying her. If Sophie ever defied him, he would not shy away from hurting her. He could punish Camille by never letting her see her sister. And then Camille would end up doing whatever he wanted. He could keep her and Sophie apart, as long as he liked.

Forever.

The realization hit her like a blow. If Camille turned on her heel and left this room, she might never see Sophie again. And if Sophie became unhappy with Séguin, Camille would not be able to help her.

She'd had a chance to prevent this from happening. She should have told Sophie after the masquerade that Séguin was a magician. But she had been selfish, hurt. Foolish.

The room was so quiet she could hear him breathing.

He seemed capable of anything.

There had never been a choice, not really. She had to save Sophie. She did not know how, yet. Not exactly. But she had something Sophie did not. The thing both of them had so often wished to be free of. The thing Camille could not give up, even as it threatened to destroy her.

Magic.

In her mind, she fanned out all her cards. None were lucky, but this one seemed better than the rest.

She played it. She said yes.

61

Séguin took Camille's hands, both of them, and pressed them to his lips. "Mademoiselle. You have made me happy beyond imagining." There was a sudden openness to his face, like a mask had dropped away.

Perhaps he did care for her. All those glances, the palm-reading, what he'd said in the king's garden—she'd thrown them all away like cards she didn't want. But perhaps she could use them now. What was it Chandon had told her? *You must be the Baroness of Pretend.*

She smiled a courtier's unbreakable smile.

"We'll dine here tonight?" he suggested. "I'll send my valet to the kitchens. And we can discuss the wedding. We'll marry quickly, *non?*"

She nodded, slowly. The dress was unhappy, its fabric suddenly rough against her skin. But until she had a better idea than the one idea circling in her mind, she had to play along.

"We'll see Sophie before the wedding, n'est-ce pas?" she asked. "I need to speak with her about everything that's happened. I'm afraid she won't be pleased." If Sophie truly did care for Séguin, she would be furious with Camille. But if that were the price of getting Sophie away from him, she would gladly pay it.

"Bien. We'll visit her in the morning. But, until then, a glass of wine." He unstoppered a crystal carafe that glowed garnet from a side table.

She was suddenly very thirsty. "Of course, monsieur."

He held out two glasses. "You must call me Jean-Baptiste."

Camille took one and drank. The wine was deliciously rich, somehow alive. She took another sip. And another. It would help steady her.

"Jean-Baptiste." Her tongue stumbled over the unfamiliar syllables. "When will we see my sister tomorrow? What time?"

"How eager you are! By midday? I can do many things, but I cannot shorten the distance between Versailles and Paris."

Camille rubbed her forehead. Séguin's voice seemed suddenly strange, as if it were coming from a far distance. And the carpet seemed to shift under her feet. On the wall, the tapestry's sad unicorn turned its head to her. The tapestry's flowering plants twined and twisted. She blinked.

"To think I was once foolish enough to believe you cared for the Marquis de Sablebois," he mused as he set his wine down. The glass was full.

"Very foolish." Her words echoed strangely in her head. *Séguin cheats.* "There is something in the wine," Camille mumbled. Her head swam, and as if in a dream, she slowly opened her hand and let the empty glass tumble onto the carpet. "What is it?"

"Just something to help you rest, my darling," he said, catching her elbow. "A bride must sleep well before her wedding."

She thought she heard the tapestry's chained unicorn laugh. "I don't wish to sleep now! I wish to see Sophie," Camille said, tears in her eyes. "I've been so worried about her."

"Tomorrow."

She knew what she wanted to say but the right words did not come. "Why did you drug me?" she managed to say. Suddenly, her knees gave way, but Séguin held her up, his hand like iron around her waist.

"Just to be safe," he said in her ear. "Time is running out, mon trésor, and I've waited so long."

A thousand years ago she'd wondered if what he wanted was to push her up against a wall in an empty room, thrust her skirts above her knees. Now he might do anything. If she shouted for help, no one would come. She tried to blink back the tears, but they streamed heedless down her face.

And then Séguin kissed her, on her wet cheek—she felt his teeth and his tongue scrape against her skin. She recoiled, but he had her by the arm.

"What are you doing?" she hissed.

He touched her face. It was almost a caress. "The tears of a magician are too valuable to waste." Slowly, Séguin licked his fingertips, one by one. "They are the most powerful magic, shed in pain, full of sorrow and lost wishes."

Camille drew a ragged breath. Underneath his cologne, she smelled cold magic. Cinders. Dead fires. Ash. "Don't touch me."

Séguin gently smoothed Camille's hair back from her face. "Ah, ma chèrie, give it time. It could be your magic, too. This is the way we aristocrats did it before. The queen once showed me a magician's library, hidden behind a wall in an unused room. In it were grimoires from the time when magicians vied with the kings of France for power. They did not always use their own sorrow. Sablebois was right, that night in the gardens: we used to take the blood of the poor. It was by studying the grimoires that I made Chandon my well."

"You took his blood?"

"Or his tears. It didn't matter—I needed his sorrow."

"With this magic you have nearly killed him, you *monster*."

Séguin chuckled. "Chandon is so openhearted that it was too easy. But if he refused, I would have asked the queen to have Foudriard sent elsewhere. Somewhere Chandon could not follow. Say, on a tour of duty in Sénégal? Or in Indochine? It takes months to reach those places. If the boat doesn't sink first."

Imagine if he were sent elsewhere and I not allowed to go, Chandon had said.

"I hate you."

"Come, that's a little severe, isn't it? We magicians do what we need to do, and I needed more magic. Alas, I went a bit too far. There were so many things for which I needed the magic that I took too much from him. I won't make that mistake with you." He licked another tear off his finger as if sucking at the remains of a caramel. "This time, I'll be careful."

"Why do you need more? To avoid the pain?" Camille wobbled backward, her heels catching in the carpet. She groped for words. "You'll hurt me and take my tears? My blood?"

"*Hurt* is a strong word. You can be cleverer than Chandon and give me your sorrow willingly. If not, I can always encourage the sorrow to come forth. Your sister might help."

"You cannot mean to hurt Sophie to give me more sorrow!" Her voice was small, plaintive as a child's. "I won't let you."

Séguin pointed a ringed finger at her. "Now, now! You promised. What is yours is mine, and what is mine is mine. N'est-ce pas? Come, it won't all be bad. We'll mix sorrow and happiness." He put his arm around her and murmured, "Chandon was a nothing. You and I— together we will rise. Victorious. We will be the court's second monarchs, the King and Queen of Magic."

He had conjured for her a nightmare of pain and sadness. And he believed it a beautiful thing.

What was it she'd thought to do, to escape this trap? She could not remember. Her mind was numb as stone. Her limbs too heavy. She tried to resist, but the drug had filled her with suffocating oblivion. It was useless. She sank onto the thick carpet.

Somewhere above her, Séguin snapped his fingers. A door opened.

"Monsieur?" the valet asked.

"The next apartment," Séguin said. "Now."

62

Séguin and his valet carried Camille to another apartment farther down the long hall. The valet pressed his hand over her mouth. His hand was so large it covered her nose. She was in danger of fainting.

Suddenly, at the end of the hall, a light bobbed: a candle. Someone was coming. Someone would save her.

Camille writhed and kicked to get loose.

"Remember your place, mademoiselle," the valet said, cuffing her with the back of his hand.

"Attention—not like that, you fool," Séguin said. "*You* don't hurt her."

"Unless she acts up," the valet said.

"Unless she acts up," Séguin agreed.

Woozily, the dress showed her a memory: the deep silence of the charred box. Camille knew what the dress was trying to tell her. She must bluff and pretend. Be silent.

And wait. She let her head loll against Séguin's silk-clad shoulder. He reached up and patted her cheek. "We're almost there."

When Camille woke, the moon was a high white coin in the dark sky.

Her head throbbed. She sat up and rubbed her temples, taking in her surroundings. She had slept, apparently, on a sofa in an unfamiliar room. In the dim light, she saw it had been hastily vacated. Dark rectangles on the walls showed where paintings had hung, bureau drawers yawned open, and abandoned clothes lay crumpled on the floor and flung over the backs of chairs. Pieces of broken mirror glinted on the dressing table. It was as if the levelers of the Bastille had stormed in and ransacked this room.

The events of the evening came back to her, memories and conversations like swaths of smoke. She had been so naive. She'd believed Séguin would simply turn Sophie over to her. But he had prepared. The poisoned wine was waiting. He'd found an empty room in which to imprison her.

Camille rose unsteadily and went to the door. She pressed her ear against it and listened. It was quiet. Slowly she turned the door handle. Locked, of course. How many hours were left before she could see Sophie? At the edge of the horizon, the black sky blurred to deep blue. It was past midnight, then, maybe two or three o'clock. The windows opened, but there was nothing outside—no drainpipe, no ivy—that she could climb down to escape. She could call for help, but who would hear her?

And if she somehow escaped, what would happen to Sophie?

Now that she knew what Séguin wanted from her, she must shuffle the deck, rearranging the cards she'd been dealt and how she might play them.

There had to be another way.

Since Maman and Papa died, there had been no one to help her. There had been no one to take over and say, *Sit back. I will take care of you.* She'd had to do it herself. La magie had been her tool and in some grim way, an outstretched hand. It pulled her up and out of the despair that followed her parents' deaths, Sophie's illness, Alain's descent into drink and debt. She'd hoped to give it up. But without it, what did she have?

If only she could understand why Séguin needed her. She'd thought it might be love. But not any longer. What he did felt nothing like love. It was instead a desperate need for more magic. But what great expenditure of magic was he making, such that he drained the life from Chandon and was ready to do the same to her? She could not fathom why he needed so *much*.

She didn't think she could muster the energy to work the glamoire once more to change her dress. Someone—she hated to think which one of them it had been—had undressed her down to her chemise. Her stays, her hoops, and the court dress lay on the floor. It looked sad and shapeless, abandoned, and she had to turn her back to it to keep from crying. Her mother had worn it, and it hadn't helped her. Camille had worn it and this was where she had ended up.

In the bluish half-light, though, the dress seemed to shimmer with magic, calling to her. Camille lifted it up, pressed it close, and felt the dress pleading with her, desperate to be worn.

One last time.

As she stepped into the gown, the bodice laced itself. She pricked her finger with the brooch and let three drops of blood fall onto the dress, imagined it pale as morning, silver-gray, almost without color. A mourning gown? A wedding gown? She didn't know. Listening to her, the dress took her sorrow and transformed, changing its shape, its color bleeding away until it had become the one Camille imagined. It stiffened around her ribs, curving to fit her.

She had no magic brushes to change her face. On the dressing table, among the shards of broken glass, lay a few nearly empty pots of paint, but she didn't see how being prettier could matter today. Carefully, she reached out to touch one of the pieces of glass. It was long and sharp, an icicle or a dagger.

Dimly, she began to see what she might use her magic to do. Séguin did not want her dead. That knowledge she tucked away, like a weapon. Slipping the shard of glass into her pocket, she went to the window, pulled back the curtains. The trees in the gardens were still only a shadowy suggestion of something yet to come.

She had treated Sophie terribly. Like a child who couldn't be trusted to make her own decisions. She'd hidden so much from her, worried it would hurt her.

In protecting her, she had rendered her defenseless.

Tomorrow she would tell Sophie everything. She would beg her forgiveness. Camille bit the edge of her fingernail. Sophie might never forgive her. What Camille had done was so terrible Sophie might not want her for a sister.

Camille turned her hands over and held them to the window's faint light. Up the middle of the palm of her right hand ran the twinned life lines, one of them crossed with a star.

Here are two lines: you and your shadow life. One path is thin, but whole. The other is broken.

When Séguin had read her palm, she'd wondered about his warning. If someone had asked her then which path is the path that is thin but whole, she would have known the answer: her old life, the life in Paris.

But now she wasn't so sure. It seemed to her that a thin and narrow life was just as unwanted as a broken one.

They came for her hours before dawn.

63

The priest intoned the words of the marriage ceremony, stumbling nervously over the Latin words. His voice echoed around the chapel's stone walls, slowly at first, and then faster as Séguin tapped his foot on the marble floor. Camille's toes were like ice in her thin, beribboned shoes. She focused on the cold, allowing it to keep her awake. Alert. When Séguin and his valet had come for her, she'd greeted them from her dressing table as if she were a great lady taking a social call. In his cobalt suit embroidered with white roses, Séguin had bowed to her, and she'd bitten back her shame and revulsion. Everything hinged on the least amount of resistance.

Séguin had been pleased with the dress she'd conjured. He'd waited, drumming his fingers on the inlaid dressing table, as she put up her hair with another woman's pins. Her face in the shattered mirror was a ghost's, smudged with sleeplessness.

"If you won't work the glamoire for your face," he said, smoothly, "at least put on whatever powder you can find, mademoiselle."

Obediently, she lifted pot lids until she found some, then dabbed it on as well as she could with her fingers. She followed with circles of rouge, pushing the paint hard into her cheeks.

"That's better," he said, coming closer.

She stiffened. He held something in his hands, and in the strange half-light of the abandoned apartment, it seemed—for a heart-clenching moment—like a garrote to strangle her with. She exhaled when the cracked mirror showed not a wire but a string of gems, which he clasped around her throat: a necklace of pearls studded with tiny diamonds. And then, from a pocket, he produced matching earrings, swaying on their clips. She slipped them onto her ears.

"Beautiful." He kissed her neck, above the necklace's clasp, letting his lips linger. Camille tried not to pull away. The dress rustled against her skin, showing her churches and cold rings and years of marriages that had required the strength of every magician who had worn this dress. *Wait*, it whispered. *Be ready.*

It speaks? Camille thought with horror.

And then the dress showed her Camille herself, weeping in the locked room, and she understood: it was this last sorrow that had brought the dress fully to life.

"Come, mademoiselle," Séguin said. "Your sister waits, but now, to church."

She had protested, begged to see Sophie first, but to no avail.

In the church's vestibule, Séguin had wrapped her fingers around a quill and, as if she were a child, guided her name at the bottom of a densely written paper. Above her blotted name, he scrawled his own, trailed by a series of titles and houses and estates. Both the sweating priest and Séguin's valet signed as witnesses and a copy was given to an altar boy who disappeared into the shadows, the white paper winking in his hand. The marriage would be recorded somewhere, copies of that paper made. Even if she ever managed to escape him, that contract would be there, unyielding as a manacle.

The priest reached the end of his recitation and from his pocket Séguin produced two rings, handed one to Camille, and slipped the other onto her fourth finger. An emerald as big as her thumbnail, encircled by tiny pearls.

This is only the form of it, she told herself. *You already signed the contract, and your reasons were good ones. The best ones.* And now, his ring. She remembered to sway a little on her feet, so that Séguin had to support her by the elbow as he slipped the ring on.

"You have made me happy, Vicomtesse de Séguin," he said, over the priest's Latin litany, and pulled her close. As his body pressed against hers, she felt, against her hip, the pommel of his sword.

Everything in Camille wanted to wrench away, to flee down the echoing nave of the king's chapel, but she told herself to be loose and easy, a doll made of rags and no thoughts.

Then he kissed her, full on the mouth. He tasted of ash and power and death.

64

Séguin was silent as the carriage sped away from Versailles. Instead of speaking, he half pulled and resheathed his sword over and over, the biting whine of it making Camille's stomach churn. She'd asked, again, to see Sophie and he'd waved his hand as if swatting a fly. *Soon* was his answer to everything. He told her to pull back her cloak so that he might see how the necklace he'd given her lay around her throat and reminded her: now that she was the Vicomtesse de Séguin, she should cast off her other jewels. Camille curved her hand around the teardrop brooch pinned on her shoulder, the one she used to draw blood for the glamoire. "This? It's been in my family for a long time."

"A sentimental attachment, then."

Camille nodded.

"I see." Séguin straightened the cuffs of his coat, adjusting the lace underneath, and drew the curtains.

In the carriage's suffocating closeness, Camille sought to prepare herself. She knew what she would say to Sophie. She would beg for forgiveness for all the misguided things she had done. And in case anything went wrong—Séguin did something to stop her, though she could not think what he could do that he hadn't already done—she had the brooch, the dress, a shard of mirror-glass in her pocket. It was not much, but it was not nothing. She remembered how reassuring the snuffbox's weight in her pocket had been on her first visit to Versailles, and how easily it had slipped away.

Not this time. She refused to give away what she had. As Séguin's horses raced toward Paris, in their thudding hoofbeats she heard, *Sophie, Sophie, Sophie*.

Eventually the carriage slowed, the horses blowing, the traces of their harness jingling. Camille sat up as the carriage rolled to a stop. Outside, a bird warbled its liquid call. She leaned forward, listening intently. She should have heard the rumble of dray wagons and the thump of their horses' heavy hooves, the cries of vegetable sellers and fishmongers advertising their wares, beggars and street-sweepers and knife-sharpeners and women going to market: all the cacophony of Paris stretching itself and coming awake.

"Why is it so quiet?" she asked. "What's happened?"

Again the bird sang out, its call echoing as if over open ground.

"Where are we? Where have you taken me?" Camille reached for the curtain but Séguin caught her hand.

"In such a hurry to see your sister? I understand, ma chère, I truly do." He brought her hand to his mouth and kissed the inside of her wrist. "There's just one bit of business I need to attend to before we can go see her. It shouldn't take long." Séguin knocked on the ceiling of the carriage and the coachman opened the door. Camille tried to see past him, but he filled the doorway as he got out.

Camille dug her fingers into the pile of the seat cushion, steadying herself. Carefully, she reached into her pocket and took out the shard of mirror. It glinted in her hand as she closed her fingers around it. As she stepped down, she gave her other hand to Séguin, who stood waiting by the door.

They were not in Paris.

Instead they stood at the edge of a cow pasture. Mist rose, wraithlike, off the damp ground. At the field's far edge, a grove of trees made a screen against the sky. Close by, under a spreading oak, several horses were hobbled, rhythmically cropping grass. A few people stood near them, their silhouettes vague against the flat grays of dawn. One of them wore the bright blue of a cavalry officer's uniform. As the fog wavered and thinned, he looked her way.

Foudriard.

Her breath came in short, shallow gasps. She could not think why he would be here.

Close by in the long grass, a divan chair, and in it a reclining figure. Chandon.

No.

There was no other word in her mind, no other sound, as a lanky boy rose smoothly from a crouch to stand next to Foudriard. She knew him, too. His back was toward her, and in his hand he held a sword, a silver slash in the mist. His hair was midnight, and as Foudriard put his hand on the boy's black coat and said something to him, he turned around.

Lazare.

Helplessly, she watched as he took in the carriage, Séguin, her hand in his—all of it. In his deep brown eyes flashed pain and bewilderment. He tried to take a step forward, but Foudriard held him back.

"Camille?" he faltered.

"What is this?" she said to Séguin. "What are you doing?"

"Come, madame, you are cleverer than that. This is the duel Sablebois demanded, don't you remember?"

It was as if he'd hit her. She stepped back, trying to understand. "You cannot—"

"I can. And I will."

Above Séguin's cravat, a strip of bare skin showed. A tender, vulnerable place. She closed her hand more tightly around the shard. "I forbid it. I won't—"

His clipped laughter rang across the field. "You have no choice. You will sit and watch. Do you know how a duel plays out? It is nothing like two boys drawing swords by a shrubbery in the gardens at Versailles. We will choose our weapons and face off. One of our seconds—the Baron de Foudriard for him or the Chevalier Lasalle for me—will call for us to start. Then we will fight, and one of us will win."

The warning came back to her once more, unbidden: *Séguin cheats.*

"There are rules, of course," he went on, "because what is a nobleman without rules and honor? He who draws first blood is the winner. He may stop the fight then, if he chooses. Or if he allows, the duel goes on, until one of us yields." Séguin closed his hand around Camille's, the one that held the shard.

"And if he does not yield?"

He squeezed Camille's hand. Tight, tighter, until the shard bit into her palm. Pain raced from her hand through her arm to her shoulder. With an effort, she forced her hand open. The shard fell to the ground. Blood limned its edges.

Camille's hand oozed scarlet, and underneath the smear of blood ran a deeper, wine-dark gash where the glass had cut her. She pressed it to her skirts to stop the bleeding. In response, the dress rippled against her palm.

Séguin leaned closer, his voice slippery as silk. "And if he does not yield? I will kill him. Just think of all the sorrow I will take from you then. It could last years. A lifetime."

Over Séguin's shoulder, she saw Foudriard throw his arm around Lazare's shoulders and walk him away. He glanced back at her, his face anguished.

"Go stand with the others," Séguin told her. "I need to choose my weapon." With a smile of satisfaction, he stepped on the mirror shard and ground it underfoot. He then strode through the grass ten or fifteen paces to where his second, the Chevalier Lasalle, stood waiting beside a stack of black sword cases.

Her hand had stopped bleeding, but it ached. Worse was the damage to the shard of glass. She stooped and tentatively parted the grass. Most of it was gone, smashed into pebble-sized fragments, but one or two longer pieces remained. As she picked the largest one up, it flickered in her hand, like silver.

Something from nothing.

Slowly, she made her way to where the other people stood. They took in every detail—readying it for court gossip, Camille guessed, and she could just hear, among the whispered words: *magician.*

Chandon could not rise from his chair when she approached. Less than two days had passed since Séguin's party, but Chandon was already much, much worse. Whatever Séguin had done to him—was doing to him—had blanched his skin and carved the flesh from under his cheekbones. Once impeccably fitted, his pearl-gray suit hung painfully loose, though he still wore his sword on a flamingo-orange sash. His hair was streaky with stale powder and greasy pomade. And his smile, when he saw Camille, was sad, the stretched smile of an old man.

"How quickly things have changed, madame, in just a handful of hours," he said without his usual spark. "I fear congratulations are in order?"

Camille fell to her knees by his chair. "I have married him," she choked. "To save my sister. I fear it was the wrong thing to do."

"Oh, ma petite. We do our best, don't we? You his wife, and I his sorrow-well, one dance-step from the grave, and all to protect—as best we can—those we love. How low the mighty are fallen. Both of us pawns, and—apparently—neither of us very good at chess."

Camille threw her arms around him and pressed her face against his shoulder. "I don't know what to do."

"We're gamblers, aren't we?" He coughed. "We'll find something to turn to our advantage." He did not sound certain.

"But Lazare is the finer swordsman, isn't he?" Camille said, hoping that by saying it she made it true.

"Everyone knows it but Séguin. He's too blinded by the color of Lazare's skin to recognize how much his superior our boy is." Chandon gestured across the field to the trees. "Here he comes now."

There was not much time.

Lazare stood so close that their bodies almost touched, the air between them charged, like a living thing. His beautiful face was utterly razed. "You came here with him?"

"Yes," she managed.

"Was it our fight at Versailles? You could not forgive me?" He clenched his hands into fists. "I cannot forgive myself."

"Hush," she said, softly. She glanced to where Séguin and Lasalle were examining the sword-cases. "Séguin convinced Sophie to agree to marry him. She believed it was love, but it was his way to control me. I've only made things worse. He will be able to torture us both, to get what he wants." She wanted to embrace him, feel the safety of his arms around her, but instead, she squared her shoulders.

"And what does he want?"

"Me." Her voice was flat. "I told you. He's a magician."

"But not like you?"

Camille heard the hope in his voice. "A magician—even I—needs sorrow to work magic, either the magician's sorrow or someone else's. To save himself the pain, Séguin used Chandon. By threatening to have Foudriard sent away, he inflicted misery on Chandon so he could use his sorrow. That's what they fought over, that time when we played cache-cache. Chandon is nearly dead from it. He'll use me next, until I become a husk." A sob gripped her throat. "Until I am gone."

Lazare took her face in his hands. "Look at me, Camille. You are not next. I swear it. Do you hear me? *I swear it.*"

Lazare's honor was fierce and righteous, but how could it mean anything against someone like Séguin?

"You must go," Camille said. "He will see—it will be worse for both of us—"

Lazare's eyes were nearly black with emotion. "I will not let this happen."

She thought of Sophie, hidden somewhere, waiting to be married; Séguin's lips and teeth on her own cheek as he drank her tears; the altar boy with the marriage contract in his hand vanishing into the shadows. "But how, Lazare? He is a magician. He cheats at everything. He wants to kill you."

"Not if I kill him first." That easy smile.

Oh, Lazare. "You'll do this for me? Even though I am a magician? If the king finds out, you will be outlawed, punished, your reputation ruined—"

Slowly, lovingly, he traced the line of her cheekbone with his thumb. "Since that night—when we fought—I've learned I never cared for those things. I only thought I did."

He was about to say something more when Foudriard called him. They were waiting.

65

For a moment, all was stillness.

Not even a bird sang.

Lazare and the Vicomte de Séguin faced one another, one fair, one dark. Ten brief paces between them. An impossible distance.

Yet nothing at all.

The seconds—the Baron de Foudriard and the Chevalier Lasalle—waited apart, each at one end of the field. A soft dawn wind tugged at their raven cloaks. Next to them on the ground, sword cases lay open, gleaming blades nestled against red cloth. In each one, an empty space.

Séguin's face was statue-still, a mask of poise. With the slightest of gestures, he indicated Camille should cross the field to stand on his side.

She gave a fierce shake of her head: no. He would have to come over and drag her if he wanted her to leave her friends. When he saw her refuse, he set his shoulders back, nothing more.

Unlike Séguin, Lazare had stripped off his coat. Dressed in his waistcoat and white chemise, he seemed young and somehow small. Camille always thought of him as so grown-up, but beneath the wide sky, he looked his seventeen years. Vulnerable. The breeze played in his hair; his face was alive with intent as he raised his sword. With a terrible pang, Camille realized that this was not simply an act demanded by aristocratic rules of behavior. For centuries aristocrats fought duels to settle conflicts. It had been their way of being above the courts, above the law. But this was something else. This was a fight to the death.

Didn't you hear what Séguin called me?

Sauvage.

Behind the two still figures, fog lifted off the lake in loose gray skeins. Drops of water pattered from the leaves. Séguin raised his sword. Camille clenched her fingers around Chandon's arm.

"Allez!" shouted the Chevalier Lasalle.

The world was sliced open.

Lazare ran, swinging his sword. Séguin leaped forward to meet him.

The blades rang out as they parried, each boy cutting and blocking, stabbing at the soft places that opened up: a rib cage under a coat, an arm. Lunging forward, Lazare caught Séguin's blade with his and wrested it to the ground. For a moment, the blades were almost still, grinding against one another. With a grunt, Séguin threw off Lazare's sword and paced away, unconcerned about turning his back to Lazare. As always, there was no discomfort in his face—only an absolute and terrifying certainty.

He pivoted on his heel and they charged again, each of them slashing, striking. Séguin swung at Lazare's head—Foudriard shouted—and Lazare ducked. The blows kept coming, steel on steel.

But there was something wrong with Lazare's sword. Deep notches appeared in its edge, as if it were made of some lesser metal. Worried, Camille said, "Chandon, what's happening to his blade?"

"I don't know." He sounded bewildered. "A cheat of Séguin's, some magic I have never seen."

As Séguin ran at him, Lazare feinted and sliced through Séguin's coat, but drew no blood. Over and over again, Lazare slashed at his opponent. Each time, Séguin slipped away like fog. Then he moved in, methodically cutting at the places that Lazare, in his fury, left exposed.

Throat.

Heart.

Flank.

But his blade did not meet flesh or bone and Séguin got no closer to Lazare. The next time Séguin raised his sword, Lazare jumped to the side, and struck, his blade hissing through Séguin's sleeve and slicing the palm of his hand. Séguin put it to his mouth to stop the bleeding.

"Arrêtez!" the Chevalier Lasalle shouted. "First blood!"

Breathing hard, poised on his toes, Lazare waited to see Séguin's reaction. But Séguin did not listen to Lasalle calling for him to stop. He did not even hesitate. Taking advantage of the pause in the action, he lunged forward again, cutting Lazare across the chest. Lazare pressed his hand against his torn chemise; his fingers came away sticky, crimson.

"Stop!" shouted Foudriard as he ran toward them, pulling his own sword.

But Lazare rushed at Séguin as if the world and its rules were nothing now. Wielding his sword like a whip, Lazare struck Séguin's weapon so violently it fell from his hand. Séguin stumbled backward and slipped in the wet grass, his hands out behind him.

His face went white with rage.

Ten paces away, Lazare paused, sword in hand, smoldering.

They stared at one another, tense as wires. Lazare—bright, fearless, bloody—had bested Séguin.

It was over. Lazare was alive, safe.

On the other side of the lake, in front of the green wall of trees, the mist brightened.

The Chevalier Lasalle stepped between the duelists. "Marquis de

Sablebois, you drew first blood. The duel is finished. Still, I must ask: do you consider your grievance settled?"

Lazare ignored Lasalle. Instead, he pointed his notched sword at Séguin's upturned face. "Get up, cheater," he growled. "Stand up so I can kill you."

As he climbed to his feet, Séguin's face twitched in a horrible smile.

"Wait, Monsieur de Sablebois." The chevalier's face creased with confusion. "The rules say you must put down your sword and declare yourself: are you satisfied?"

Somewhere, a blackbird sang out. Lazare held his sword upright, his left arm curved up behind him for balance. Ready.

In Lazare—proud, determined, brave—she saw worlds of shadow and pain and heartbreak. His father, his divided self. And Séguin, who had cheated them both. He had denied them the happiness they wanted. He had denied them one another.

Sensing her sorrow, the dress embraced her. Its memories streamed through Camille: other duels, other men, young and old, handsome and rich, grievances and hate and love and warm blood pooling around still bodies—all the dress had witnessed. And the shiver of its voice in her mind: *I am armor. It is not over.*

Camille met Lazare's eyes, trying to say silently everything she was thinking. He nodded and lowered his sword. "I am satisfied, Monsieur Lasalle."

A sigh rippled through the observers; someone clapped.

"As far as my *own* honor is concerned," he continued. "But I cannot leave Camille Durbonne and her sister Sophie in the Vicomte de Séguin's keeping. If I'm to be satisfied, he must free them. Before all these people."

Against Camille's skin, the dress stirred. Agitated. Camille tensed, waiting.

Lazare cleared his throat. "Release them and this is finished."

Séguin looked pityingly at Lazare. "Madame gave herself willingly to me. Is that not so?"

Lazare's face filled with confusion, disbelief. Camille moved her head a fraction: no.

"She did," Séguin purred. "She is my wife and there is no law in France that will let her leave me. She is bound to me utterly, in body if not yet in soul. Imagine that, Sablebois. My hands on her. She always by my side, in my bed. You thought she loved you? You have lost her forever."

Séguin's dangerous smile was a weapon. But it was something else, too. With a sharp stab of understanding, she suddenly knew: Séguin needed her.

Lazare swayed, as if uncertain about where he might go next, and then sank to one knee in the slick, crumpled grass. He dropped his head into his hand.

Behind his back, Séguin's bronze stare brightened, the way a knife does when it is honed.

She saw it and understood: there was no world in which Séguin would let her go.

From inside his waistcoat Séguin pulled a dagger, its hilt heavy with jewels, the blade's tip forked like a serpent's tongue. The acrid scent of magic poured off it like smoke.

Camille reached in her pocket for the piece of glass.

She remembered Alain putting his knife to her throat, how she held still to save herself and Sophie, and all the things that came after that, sorrows unspooling like thread into endless night. She refused to go back to that place where she had nothing.

Magic was not something apart from her, something she could give up. It was the power of her deepest feeling. The power of who she was. And from nothing, she would make something.

She uncurled her fingers. In her palm lay a glass knife, nearly invisible, its edges already bright with her own blood.

Séguin sprang at Lazare.

Everything slowed.

Camille wrenched forward, racing for the closing space between them. Her shoes slid on the wet grass. To the left, blurry, she sensed Lazare stand up. Foudriard running, both of them shouting.

As she flung herself between Lazare and Séguin, her glass knife outstretched, she hazarded one last bet, based only on the look on Séguin's face: he would not kill her.

Lazare howled her name.

The dress steeled itself against what was coming.

Séguin slowed, his golden eyes wide with surprise, and tried to stop. But the grass was slick.

She stabbed at him with her glass knife, felt the blow of his body against hers wrench it from her hand.

His dagger struck her under the ribs. The dress screamed as the blade sliced through its silk and into the quilting of Camille's stays.

She slipped and lost her balance, fell to the ground.

Séguin loomed over her. "Stay back," he warned the others, "or I will kill her!"

Desperate, she felt in the grass for her knife, but she could not find it anywhere. It had vanished. She pressed her hand to her dress— pleading, hoping—but it was silent as death.

She had one more card to play. "You will not kill me, Vicomte," she said. "I am too dear a thing to you." As she lay there, she had the strangest feeling of wanting to laugh. "Everyone here knows you for a magician. Kill me and you have no standing at court. No sorrow-well. Nothing."

Séguin started to speak but instead grunted, as if in pain. Wonderingly, he touched his throat. He stared at his fingers when they came away red. Above his cravat, under his jaw, she saw it: a violent, crimson line. The glass knife.

He looked at her with disbelief. "You have a magic weapon?"

And then Lazare was there, grabbing the back of Séguin's coat, hauling him away. When Lazare released him, he sank to his knees. Blood poured from his wound as Lazare shouted for the surgeon.

While Foudriard kept his sword pointed at Séguin, Lazare knelt by Camille and pulled her into his arms. Camille let go. All the effort, all the pain, she let it fall away as she sank her head against his shoulder, tucking her face into the warm hollow of his throat. His pulse beat against her mouth as she inhaled: sweat, the iron bite of his blood, the sweet scents of crushed grass, horses, and skin. There was absolutely nothing about him that smelled of ash or cinder or magic.

"I thought I'd lost you . . . a second time," Lazare choked. Even with dirt and grime glazing his skin and blood caked along his jaw, he was heart-stopping. "Will you forgive me?"

"For what?"

"For walking away from you, that night in the gardens. I was lost. I could see how proud and stubborn I was being, but I couldn't escape myself."

"Our shadows are tied to us, like it or not." Camille brushed back a strand of hair from his face. "All we can do is run faster."

He kissed her gently above her eyebrow. "Whatever shadow I might have, you have utterly vanquished it."

"Vicomtess!"

She and Lazare stumbled to their feet. Across the grass, Chandon was making his way toward them. On his tired face was a wicked grin. In his hand he swung his cane—not like a crutch, but a weapon.

"See there?" he said, stabbing his stick at Séguin. "Is that a poisoned blade you just happened to have with you?" He snatched the dagger from Séguin's hand. "You were always terrible at duels."

On the ground, Séguin contracted in pain. The blood running from his throat had darkened to a deep, reddish black. In his face, furrows grew like cracks in ice, racing along the sides of his mouth, stretching across his forehead. He no longer looked nineteen or twenty. Magic had made him an old man. His hair grayed, age spots speckled his cheeks. Shadows swam under his eyes.

All the while, Séguin chanted to himself.

"What strange magic is this?" Chandon scoffed. "Something you read about in one of those grimoires?" As Séguin's glamoire had fallen away, Chandon had stood up straighter, as if a great weight had been lifted from him. His face had gained back some of its high color, its gaunt hollows smoothed. Scornfully, he said, "Why don't you use your own sorrow, Séguin? Or are you too dead inside to feel anything?"

Séguin stopped muttering his spell. It was clear that he expected something to have changed.

But it had not.

He stared at Camille. "You cheated."

"You've never had to make the best of the cards you were dealt, have you? You've always gotten exactly what you wanted." Determined tears stood in Camille's eyes. "You assumed you had the winning card, but you hedged your bet. I did not cheat. I played my ace, and won."

66

Lie still, Séguin," Foudriard said. "The surgeon's coming."

White wig askew, the surgeon shouted as he hobbled toward them. "All this noble blood spilled!" He sank to his knees next to the vicomte's still form. "Are you still with us, monsieur?"

"After everything he has done to all of us," Chandon said, pain crackling in his voice, "he deserves to die."

Séguin's lips moved. The surgeon bent close, listening. "Monsieur wishes to speak with his wife. Where is she?"

Camille stepped backward and bumped into Foudriard. He steadied her, his arm around her shoulders. "He will die, there is no doubt," he said kindly. "You're under no obligation to speak with him. It's your choice."

Her skin crawled when she thought of everything he'd done to those she loved. What he'd planned to do to her and Sophie. He would have made their lives a living hell such that they would beg for death to release them. What should she do? She listened for the dress to advise her.

But it was silent, more silent than it had been even in the burned box.

Clouds drifted across the pale blue sky; a scatter of swallows flew over the long grass. In the wind that hushed across the field, she heard Maman's voice.

There are others more unfortunate than you, mon trésor.

She had hazarded it all, and she had won. There was only one more thing she needed.

"Shall I go with you?" Lazare asked.

Camille shook her head. "I'll speak to him alone. I need to know for certain where Sophie is."

"Hurry, madame," urged the surgeon. "He fails fast."

In the trampled, rust-red grass, Camille knelt by Séguin's shoulder. Wrinkles and age spots continued to bloom across his face. *Too much magic.* The back of his hand, his enormous blue ring, the lace of his sleeve—all were gaudy with blood.

"I want your help, but I won't apologize," he said. A bright rivulet trickled from the corner of his mouth as acrid fumes of magic leaked from him. "You are stronger than I thought, Camille."

"Where is my sister?"

"At my house in Paris." He coughed. His throat was filling with blood. "Chandon knows where."

She sat back on her heels, studying him. "Why did you do this? To me? To Chandon?"

With a grim smile, Séguin said, "For the old ways, so they would not be brushed aside by revolution. For things to be as they were. For the queen."

Marie Antoinette had refused to help Camille, and yet, had warned her that Séguin was a cheat. Had she meant this, that he had used magic for her sake? "Tell me."

"I helped her. Who else do you think tucked up that sagging chin? Who was it that polished her skin from crepe to satin? When she discovered what I could do, there was no end to her requests. 'Monsieur le Vicomte, give me parties like those in fairy tales. Give me clothes no seamstress could make. Give me a face and body more beautiful than any woman's. Versailles' magic is fading—renew it! The people of France hate me, they talk of rebellion. Make them love me. Bring back my son.'"

Resurrection? "But that's not possible—"

"No. Not even for me." Séguin thumbed away a bubble of blood at the corner of his mouth. "The more threatened she felt, the more she feared the people would tear her from the throne, the more desperate she became. She called it cheating, when I spilled my blood to work her glamoire. She felt none of the cost. Her insatiable hunger for la magie would have killed me. What was I to do?"

"Not enslave another person—not force me to marry you—"

"Caught like I was, what would you have done, magician? How irreproachable would your decisions have been?"

The sun had risen above the trees. Its light filtered through their uppermost leaves, tracing them in gold. Camille didn't know what she would have done, had it been she and the queen. But she knew what she'd done when her sister's life—her life—had been at stake. She'd given herself over to the aching sorrow of turning coins, then to the black singing rush of the glamoire, and finally, when all paths in the labyrinth came to dead ends and there were no cards left to play, she'd given herself up. Séguin had never intended to give up anything.

"I would have done what I had to," she said, bowing her head.

"Madame," the surgeon called. "I must see my patient."

Séguin's eyes had left her face and were pitched to the sky. In their yawning pupils, Camille saw clouds race overhead. "I'm sorry I couldn't be what you wanted," she said, quietly.

"You were, in my dreams, if nowhere else." He coughed again. "Do something for me, will you?"

Camille took in his ravaged face, his broken shell of a body. He had been just as trapped as she. But she'd had something he didn't: someone to love and care for, and that had saved her. She would grant him this last wish.

"Don't let them bind me, stuff me with poultices." His voice was barely audible. "I have lost my magic and what is a magician without that? I wish to die, Camille. To be free of this." He gestured vaguely at something she could not see. "This *world*."

Standing at the window of an abandoned apartment at Versailles, poison spooling in her blood, her empty hands on the windowsill: hadn't she also wanted to be free of the world she'd found herself in? Hadn't she also wanted liberty, a choice?

Camille nodded.

"Then go tell the surgeon," he said, his once-beautiful voice a harsh croak. "Be gone."

Camille stood. She was dizzy. Her clothes, her skin, everything reeked of blood and burned magic. The surgeon tried to shoulder past her but she put her hand out. "Leave him, monsieur," she said. "He does not wish to stay."

She waited, hands knotted in her skirt. The boy who lay crumpled in the grass had only brought her suffering. She had wished him dead and herself free of him, and now it had come to pass. And yet, tears burned in her eyes. For a reason she could not understand—for had it not nearly destroyed everything she loved?—she grieved the unraveling of magic.

Would the winds of change sweep all magic away? And if they did, who would she then be?

Séguin's breathing grew more labored, strident. Then his face, which had already fallen into ruin, grew still. The surgeon held a mirror to his mouth. "He is dead."

"I cannot recognize him," Foudriard said as the surgeon's men came with a litter to carry Séguin's body away.

"I would always know him by his rings," Chandon replied, slowly. "I saw that sapphire cabochon every time he hurt me. I hope I live long enough to forget it completely."

Where Camille stood, the leaves of grass were crushed and smeared with blood, even the tiny white heads of clover. Over the lake, the mist had vanished. Instead the sun glittered on the water, turning it to diamonds.

Lazare still held his sword. When he reached Camille, he wrapped his left arm around her shoulders and pulled her close. She pressed her cheek against his chest. Under his coat, she heard the regular beat of his heart. She wanted to climb inside, to take refuge there.

His lips brushed her forehead. "Camille Durbonne," he whispered, "we have been released."

67

In Lazare's carriage, Camille dropped her head against his shoulder, her eyelids flickering with fatigue. The glamoire she'd worked in the abandoned room was leaving the dress, and now her body shook with fatigue.

"I can't remember when last I slept," Camille mumbled. "Days ago? Weeks?"

"Nearly there," Lazare said. The wound across his collarbone had stopped bleeding.

Trembling, she took his bloodied hand in hers. It steadied her.

As the carriage raced from the Bois de Boulogne to the city center, the open spaces gave way to farms and vineyards, then buildings and cobbled streets. To the east, she knew, lay the ruined fortress of the Bastille. It would never again be a prison.

It was hard to comprehend what had happened in the last few days. Everything was changing. The constitution Papa had wished for would soon come to pass. No longer would the French people be shackled by the greed of the nobles or the church; they would rise up and take what had been stolen from them.

A new France.

The carriage came to a halt in the courtyard of Séguin's mansion. Walls of warm limestone rose up on three sides; somewhere a hidden fountain burbled. Camille had hoped she might see Sophie's face in one of the many windows, but all were blank.

What if Séguin had lied? What if she wasn't here? Or if she was in some danger?

Her fatigue forgotten, Camille flung herself out of the carriage and raced up the low stairs to a set of glass doors. "Open the door!" She banged so hard the glass shivered in its frame.

No one came.

Camille rattled the door handle but the door remained stubbornly closed. What if Sophie were tied up, locked in? "What if she can't come because she's hurt?"

Lazare unwrapped her hands from the door handle. "Wait, Camille. We've had enough injuries." He took the pommel of his sword and smashed one of the glass panes, then reached in to unlock the door.

They burst into a large entry hall tiled in marble and hung with tapestries. Lilies like stars in a silver vase. Ahead of them lay the house's receiving rooms; to the right, the broad steps of a marble staircase curved up and out of sight. It smelled of magic and ash.

A maid emerged from one of the rooms. When she saw them, she blanched. "Monsieur Durbonne, come quickly!"

Dazed, Camille could not think who the maid meant. Papa? Then a boy stepped into the hall.

Alain.

It was the first time Camille had seen him since he'd threatened her in front of their old apartment on the rue Charlot. He didn't seem to be drunk. He was no longer wearing his filthy uniform. Instead he was dressed in an expensive chestnut-brown suit, his cravat white, his face clean-shaven.

"Bring Sophie here, Alain," she said through clenched teeth. "Now."

"You cannot order me." Splotches of angry color rose in his face. "Neither of you have any business here. Get out."

Lazare loosened his sword in its sheath. "We know she's here, monsieur."

"What will you do, slay me?"

Camille had no time for this. She grabbed her skirts and ran. She dodged Alain and raced toward the stairs. Behind her, she felt his hand catch at her dress—but then Lazare's sword sang out and Alain fell back.

In the hall, she stopped. A door swung open and Sophie's slender figure emerged. For a moment she stood there, silhouetted, hesitating.

"I'm sorry, Sophie," Camille said into the silence. "I made so many mistakes."

At the sound of Camille's voice, Sophie ran toward her. "Camille!" she cried, as she embraced her.

Camille held Sophie tight. "I was so worried about you," she whispered, the words rushing out. "I thought I would lose you—I was wrong not to tell you about him. I knew what he was, but I hid it from you. I thought I was protecting you! I'm so sorry, mon ange. I will never forgive myself. But Séguin's dead now," she said into Sophie's ear. "His magic is gone."

"I thought *I* was saving us!" Sophie said, with something like a sob— or laughter. "I thought I would marry him, we would be rich, and you could stop working your magic. We would finally be free. We'd have a new life." She caught her breath. "But I was wrong, too. He was so kind, before I agreed to come here. I had no idea how terrible he truly was. The things he promised he would do to me—to you. They were awful."

"He trapped us both."

Sophie touched Camille's cheek, wiping at the blood. Softly, she asked, "Did you marry him?"

Camille nodded. "I didn't know what else to do. I thought to use my magic—and I did—but I had to marry him first."

"But you did it for me," Sophie said in a small voice.

Camille held her close as Sophie's ribs heaved under her stays. Finally. Finally.

Wiping away her tears, Sophie pointed to Alain where he stood by the door. "Our *dear brother* was the one who convinced me to write the letter to you and to come here." Her voice shook with fury. "*He* was the one who furthered my connection with the vicomte; did you know that? He brought the vicomte to Madame Bénard's so he might flirt with me and take me for walks. Alain convinced me that Séguin would marry me, and I was fool enough to believe him. Séguin kept me here as bait in the trap for you. I was nothing—nothing to him! He said the cruelest things to torture me! As if he knew what I feared the most. And Alain was just as bad—worse," she spat. "You were absolutely right about him."

"You'll sing a different tune when the vicomte returns," Alain said. "All of you. I did what was best for me, and for Sophie. Did you even consider us," he said to Camille, "while you were gallivanting about Versailles and sailing around in balloons and doing God-knows-what with *him*—"

"Tais-toi, Alain," she warned. "I may have done wrong, but I tried to do right. You forgot that distinction long ago. You forgot what right was when you stole from us, when you cut me and hit me."

"You deserved it all."

Lazare brought the point of his sword to a spot above Alain's cravat. "Careful, monsieur."

"I took care of you both." Camille ached with regret. All those nights of playing cards until she could barely stand, working the glamoire over and over until the inside of her arm was a constellation of crimson wounds and her soul felt hollowed out. She had grown thin and so sick, while Sophie grew sleek on good food and rest. And then when they had money, and Alain had asked for it, hadn't she given it to him?

"I never wanted your help." His face flushed. "When I asked you for money outside the courtyard door, in the letter—that was because Séguin forced me to. He wanted to weaken you. I only played my part."

As if playing a part meant he shouldered no blame. "He was the one who held your debts?"

"That was how it started," he admitted. "We had *nothing*, if you remember, when our parents died. So, like all of Paris, I went to gamble at the Palais-Royal. I was careful and played small at first, low bets, but when I kept winning, I moved to the big tables and the high stakes. And why not?" he said, scowling at Camille. "I was good, and I was lucky.

"Then, my luck changed. I lost. Many times. Still, there were many who were happy to lend me livres or louis to tide me over, so I might play again and win it all back. But something was wrong. I could never win as much as I needed to," he said, as if it still mystified him. "There was a nobleman who often played, and offered to help. Séguin was rich, and in the beginning he never asked to be repaid. Sometimes he'd beg something small from me in return for the money he gave me. Like that miniature of you and Sophie."

"You gave him that? When?" Camille demanded. If Séguin had been given the miniature, he would have recognized her and Sophie. From the very beginning.

"What does it matter?"

Lazare was unable to contain himself. "Don't you understand? Séguin nearly ran over—or pretended to run over—Mademoiselle Sophie in the Place des Vosges!" he exclaimed. "Did Séguin know of her then?"

"Who knows?" Alain said. "Sophie was fine, wasn't she?"

That was the day she'd run into Lazare outside the apothecary's. And she'd been to the apothecary because Alain had hit her. And when he'd hit her, and she'd sprawled bleeding on the floor, she'd seen that his watch chain was empty. Séguin had recognized Camille the first time she'd seen him.

"You had betrayed us, even then," Camille said, her rage icy cold. "Séguin knew what he was doing—if not when he nearly knocked her down, but certainly when he saw her face. Our faces." Pacing to the door with its broken pane, she tried to gain control of herself. Through the shattered glass, she watched the coachman wiping the carriage wheels carefully, lovingly, clean of mud.

"And then, Alain, let me guess? When your debts were sufficiently large so that you could not deny him his request, he told you he wished to meet your little sister? That he might make her a nice offer of marriage? And then, he'd call it even."

"It wasn't like that!" Alain stormed. "Sophie wanted to! She was *pleased!*"

"I didn't know what he was, Alain," Sophie said. "Didn't you always tell me I'd marry high? I wanted so to believe you. I trusted you. But the vicomte was horrible."

"That's enough." Alain's chest heaved. "Now that you got your little story, get out, both of you. You don't belong here."

Except—Camille suddenly realized—she did.

Standing there in her tattered cloth-of-gold dress, under thirty burning candles, the scent of Séguin's magic mingling with the lilies' fragrance, and his cipher woven in gold into a tapestry that hung on the wall, Camille did, in fact, belong.

She spoke to the maid. "When Monsieur leaves the house, lock the door behind him."

"What the hell?"

Camille blazed at him, defiant. "As it happens, I married the vicomte early this morning. Didn't you realize that was part of his plan? I'm the new Vicomtesse de Séguin." The title felt strange in her mouth, but powerful. "The vicomte, however, is dead. This house belongs to me."

Alain stared, bewildered. "Dead? But I was to have what I wanted! He promised. For what I'd done—helping him get to Sophie, delivering his letters, softening her up—he was to give me the management of his country estate, while he remained in Paris."

"It's no longer his estate, Alain. It's mine."

"She's right," Lazare said. "Your part is finished."

Alain grabbed the great silver vase, chased with gold, by far the richest object in the hall. "I'll take this, then. As payment for services rendered."

Camille shook her head. "You know what I'll give you in payment, brother? Your freedom."

"I already had that," Alain sneered.

"Did you?" Camille said, rounding on him. "The Vicomte de Séguin was a *magician*. Unlike mine, his promises were cinders that crumbled to ash as soon as you picked them up. How did you not realize this? If I'd refused to marry him, and he'd married Sophie—or kept her as his mistress, his slave—he would have made your lives a nightmare. And he'd never have given you anything. Whatever he might have been once, the Vicomte de Séguin loved power and power alone. He would never have relinquished one atom of it."

This was the end, then. It was over.

But she might still say what she needed to with love instead of hate. She cleared her throat. "I cannot know what you shall think of me, nor if you ever will wish to see me again. That's your choice." Then she gestured out to the streets of Paris. "*This* is what I am giving you, Alain. It is the finest, and rarest, of gifts. Now go and do something good with it."

68

On the second floor of the mansion she was still learning to call home, Camille tapped on Sophie's bedroom door. Her sister slept late these days, recovering from the ordeal that Séguin and Alain had put her through. She didn't share the details with Camille, and in turn, Camille did not pry. They were Sophie's wounds, her hurts. Camille only did her best to let them heal.

From inside the room, she heard a bird warbling—a canary Lazare had sent to Sophie to hasten her recovery.

"Come, but don't let in Fantôme!"

For the first time in many days, Sophie sat up in bed, her hair hanging in a smooth braid over her shoulder, the bird clutching her index finger. "Careful not to startle him!" she exclaimed as Camille came in.

Smiling to herself, Camille took her usual seat by the head of the bed and clasped Sophie's other hand where it lay on the embroidered coverlet. The bird fixed a suspicious black eye on Camille.

"Don't worry, little . . . ?" Camille didn't know if it had a name.

"Louis. The sixteenth." Sophie's lips quirked.

"Majesté," she said to the bird, "I'm not here for an audience with you. It's Sophie I've come to see. I'm so happy to see you better, my darling sister."

Sophie ducked her head. "I may look fragile, but I'm stronger than I appear."

Camille kissed her on the cheek. Everything she wanted to say jostled in her mind. If she hadn't left Sophie alone so much, if she hadn't focused on life at court and had really listened to her sister, couldn't all of this have been avoided? "I'm so sorry, Sophie. For leaving you, for not trusting you, for getting so caught up in everything that I lost my way—"

"Enough, Camille!" Sophie burst out. "Yes, you should have dealt better. You should have trusted me. When Maman and Papa died, I did grow up. You just didn't see it."

"I am so sorry."

"You've already apologized. Some of it was my fault, too, n'est-ce pas? I wanted to believe I could save us by marrying Séguin. That was wrong." The bird trilled. "See?" Sophie said, mock-serious. "The king agrees."

"It wasn't just you. Alain was in debt to him, completely ensnared."

"The vicomte enchanted our brother."

Surprised, Camille asked, "With magic?"

Sophie shook her head. "Séguin was everything Alain and I had been striving for, everything we thought we wanted—don't you see? Séguin was our fairy-tale ending."

It wasn't just Sophie and Alain. Maman, Grandmère, and back before her, people telling and retelling these dangerous stories. *Believing* in them, and by believing remaking the world in the stories' image. Until they felt true. Despite the wash of sunlight flooding the room, a chill crept along Camille's neck. "He would have used you horribly, to increase my sorrow. That was what he intended, in the end. We were to be his way out of suffering."

With her little finger, Sophie stroked the top of the bird's head. "We escaped, though."

Camille shivered. All that blood, the trampled grass. The magic, and the sorrow. "We escaped with our lives, but just barely."

"I think we escaped with quite a bit more than that," Sophie teased. Louis flapped off her finger onto the arm of a candelabra. "We have this beautiful house! We have an enormous estate, which Séguin bragged about endlessly while he held me captive. You should have heard him, telling me how many heads of cattle he had and all the taxes he got from his poor farmers. And somewhere in the attics there's probably trunk after trunk loaded up with gold louis!" She peeked sidelong at Camille, suddenly serious. "And you have the Marquis de Sablebois."

"He isn't a prize!"

"*I* think he is."

Camille gave her sister a gentle shove. "You know what I mean."

"In any case, we are now rich *and* we escaped a very dangerous magician. Camille," Sophie said, hesitantly, "you won't keep working the glamoire, will you? Or turning coins? Now that we have everything we need?"

Camille hesitated. It was true: they had all they needed.

But perhaps magic was more than survival? The queen might have had Séguin banished, or stripped of his estates and money, if he did not cheat for her, as she'd called it. He'd worked magic to survive, just as she had, in the beginning. But why had Chandon used it to win at cards? He had money and he was the best player at court, even without magic. Why endure the sorrow if he didn't have to? She remembered again the itch of magic on her skin, the way it nearly compelled her to transform herself. Perhaps that was the beauty and the terror of la magie: taking things that no one wanted—bad cards, scraps of metal, sorrow itself—and then making something of them.

Camille said, "We no longer need the money, do we? And the dress was damaged in the duel."

The bird hopped across the coverlet, pecking at a row of silk tassels.

"I could mend it if you like," Sophie said. "I've done it before."

This time, though, the dress felt *dead*. "If I'm not going to work magic anymore, does it matter?"

"I was so envious, you know," Sophie said then, quietly, "that you could work magic."

"But why?" When Sophie was silent, Camille pressed on. "I didn't like having to be the one to do it, but—I'm glad you were spared."

"Don't you see what it means, that you could work magic? You *missed* our parents. I did too, bien sûr, but I also thought everything would come right, in the end. But you understood what we'd lost," said Sophie. "And from that sadness, you worked magic."

Magicians needed sorrow. And deep sorrow existed only because of love. That was why Séguin had wanted her, hadn't he said so? Because she felt deeply. And, she wondered, was it also because there had been something about her that made *him* feel deeply? Even if it were only his fear at losing her.

"You always wanted to change things, Camille. Our situation, our lives. You even wanted to help Papa change the world." A proud smile crept across Sophie's face, as if she were playing her best card. "Et voilà! Now you don't have to work la magie any longer. You needn't worry about me, at least for a little while. I have plans."

"Already?"

"I gave my notice to Madame Bénard. Before Alain brought me here, we stopped at the shop and I told her I was leaving." Sophie smiled wickedly. "She was not pleased. She knows everyone came for my hats, not hers."

"Well done! But, Sophie—what if we have to leave Paris?"

"Because of the Bastille?"

Camille was haunted by the wild, righteous jubilation in the faces of the window-breakers that night the Bastille was stormed. And the boys shoving that aristocrat into a dark future of—more beatings? A grisly death? After the Bastille fell, life in Paris had continued on, but the shadow remained. In the way that one can see in a lake the reflection of what's around it and what's *underneath*, Camille sensed the violence of that night was still there. How did everything return to normal, after something like that?

"You're not worried?"

"Even before the Bastille was destroyed, people were setting fire to aristocrats' houses," Sophie said. "Will it really get worse? Is Paris no longer safe?"

Once upon a time, Camille knew what it was to be safe. Or thought she knew: food, shelter, freedom from hurt. All those things were still necessary—there were so many people who had none of them—but this was something else. She didn't know exactly what it was, but she could feel it, like sun on her face after a long winter. A chance to rise up and catch the light: to be something more than she'd believed she could be.

"I don't know, but something is *happening*, Sophie. Perhaps something great—I hope so—but perhaps something terrible. If we stay in Paris, and I start a press, I can do my part in telling the truth about it."

"You must," Sophie said brightly. "And things will settle, I know it. I have too much I want to do. The confectioner's hat shop will be fantastic, non? I'm already imagining a revolutionary hat—it'll be a lovely one, not one that sticks a brick from the Bastille on top and calls it macaroni."

Camille laughed. "What's a macaroni?"

"Someone very fashionable." She waved Camille toward the door. "Now go! And buy a printing press with all the money you have in the bank, d'accord? And thank Lazare for Louis?"

Camille nodded, blinking back sudden tears. "I will."

As she opened the door, the canary—in a flash of yellow—settled on top of its bronze cage and began to sing.

69

There was a quick rap on the door and a maid came in. "He's here, madame. Waiting downstairs."

Camille stood at the long mirror, wearing a pale yellow dress and pinning her hat onto her elaborately coiffed hair. Working magic had taken its toll on her, but today the shadows were gone from her face. She couldn't help smiling. "Tell him I'm coming."

Two weeks had passed since Séguin's death.

His la magie–ravaged body had been buried, quietly, with no family present. It seemed he had none, or none who came to claim him. Camille had let her maid dye one dress black, for the funeral, but had refused to wear mourning any longer than that. No one had reprimanded her;

everywhere there was a feeling as if something had shaken loose, as if slowly the old ways were cracking, if not yet crumbling. Without much fuss, the marriage document was produced and Camille Durbonne, no longer a faux baroness but a true vicomtesse, took possession of a large estate west of Paris and an elegant mansion in town. At first she'd thought to sell it and put everything that had to do with Séguin behind her, but slowly it grew on her, the aristocrat's house. She decided she'd keep it as her prize.

This morning Camille had been up at sunrise, pouring cream in a dish for Fantôme, checking the weather. The sky was the faint blue of washed silk. No clouds, only a gentle wind.

It would be very fine.

In the corner of her dressing room stood a japanned wardrobe, lacquered black and red. The door hung slightly open. In darkness shone the cloth-of-gold dress. Yesterday Sophie had neatly mended the tear Séguin's dagger had made and now it was nearly invisible. Camille gently brought a handful of its fabric to her lips. She kissed it, but felt only the weakest trembling of emotion along the woven roses enmeshed in its silk.

"Thank you," she said.

In response, the silk rustled, a sigh of longing traveling through the cloth in her hand, faint memories of the blazing candles' heat in the Hall of Mirrors, a dewed velvet lawn, Lazare's face when he saw that Camille lived. She waited for more, but the dress had once again fallen silent.

The clock on the mantelpiece struck eight. "Madame!" the maid called from the hall.

Downstairs, she found Lazare waiting under the archway leading to the dining room. He had on the same suit he'd worn when she'd first seen him, his hair tied back with a black ribbon. After everything they had been through, he was even more beautiful to her than he had been that day.

He bowed deeply, taking her hand. He laughed when he saw her fingers. "You're covered in ink."

"You think I do everything by magic?"

Gently, Lazare straightened them out and kissed them.

My heart.

He nodded toward the dining room. "Is this it?"

"It is! Voilà—my printing shop," she said. "Do you like it?"

Under a magnificent chandelier and between pairs of crystal sconces on the walls stood a small printing press. Containers of ink, type, and cases covered the long dining table that ran the length of the room. Piles of paper teetered at angles. She'd spent long hours printing the pamphlets for today.

"I do," he said. "Tremendously." He rubbed his jaw. "You must be the first noblewoman to have a press in her dining room."

"Suitable for these strange times, don't you think?" she said as she hefted two twine-tied bundles of pamphlets off the floor. She handed one to Lazare.

"Rosier's translation is good?" he asked, reading the top sheet.

"I'm sure it is. He limited himself to the second paragraph."

"Let's hope there are some readers in the crowd," he said, tucking the bundle under his arm. "Shall we go?"

Camille felt she might rise on the wings of her own happiness. "I don't think I can wait any longer."

70

An enormous crowd had gathered, from apprentices and milliners to university students from the Sorbonne—even nobles and wealthy merchants. Children waved tiny flags with balloons on them. Friends had promised to come from Versailles to celebrate the occasion, and Camille was eager to be together again. At the front of the crowd played a marching band, their horns tipped to the sky, the snare drum quick and merry.

Behind the band, the balloon was tethered to a small platform, its gondola draped in tricolor bunting. Its silk shifted slowly in the wind, revealing new letters that spelled out its name: *Heart's Desire.*

It was happening.

Despite everything, it was happening.

As Camille and Lazare descended from the carriage, Rosier came running. "The hero and heroine!" he exclaimed. "Since last I saw you together, you two fought a magnificent duel! And won!"

She smiled. "Lazare was magnificent, at least. I merely did what I could."

"That's an understatement," Lazare said.

"And who did you vanquish?"

Camille saw Lazare look toward the balloon as if he wanted to climb aboard and disappear.

"Only an evil magician," Camille said, laughing. "A story for another time."

"*Aeronauts Defeat Magician?*" Rosier suggested. "Sounds very promising. Come—I've got your costumes here." Leading them through the edge of the crowd, he took Camille and Lazare to a makeshift screen, behind which Rosier had laid out on chairs a costume for the king, and another for the queen. Lazare picked up the light blue sash. "I can't wear this. Only the king wears the cordon bleu."

"Don't be an aristocratic stickler, Lazare. Those people"—Rosier gestured emphatically toward the crowd—"want to see something impressive. You wish to fly over the Alps—they have paid handsomely for their tickets and wish to feel joy! Be elevated by wonder! The spectacle! Et cetera, et cetera. You can't deny them that, after everything that's happened in Paris. They need it. And you're the one who must deliver it."

While they argued, Camille lifted up the gown Rosier had laid out for her. It was very much like something the queen would have worn—a gown à la Polonaise in dusky pink with a narrow yellow stripe. Next to it, on a pole, hung a white wig, trimmed with ribbons and plumes. Camille shuddered. It looked like a head on a spike.

She took a deep breath. In all this madness, with the fear that had spread across the countryside, the attacks on noblemen believed to be hoarding grain, the king's mercenaries in the streets of Paris, what was the purpose of a balloon? What good could it possibly do?

"It suits you, mademoiselle," Rosier said.

Camille pressed the dress close: it would be a perfect fit. "Where did you find this? It's beautiful."

"At the Foire du Saint-Esprit, of course. Might even have been the queen's, for all we know."

Near the balloon, Armand was shouting for Rosier.

"Duty calls," Rosier said, pulling out his watch. His eyebrows elevated practically to his hairline. "The launch is in seven minutes, mes amis! Please hurry, or I'll have to start screaming." He raced away, jostling a path through the crowd, leaving Lazare and Camille standing together behind the screen.

From the other side, they heard a low and steady roar. How many were there in the crowd? A hundred? A thousand?

"I can't do this," Camille and Lazare both said at once—and then burst out laughing.

"It's ridiculous to pretend to be the king," Lazare said, exasperated. "His Majesté would never, ever go up in a balloon. And the people don't want to see the king in a balloon—not now. Not after the Bastille."

"Perhaps they'd want him to sail away somewhere." Camille smirked. "But we can't do that. Sail away, I mean."

"Can't we?" Lazare asked hopefully. "Are you certain?"

"What about the pamphlets?" she said, though she was secretly pleased with his idea of sailing away together.

All around them, the people of Paris were congregating. On their way to their seats, tickets in hand, talking and laughing, they passed to one side or the other of the screen, like a river around a little island. They were here to see the balloon. Rosier was right about the power of the spectacle. But this spectacle couldn't be two people dressed as the king and queen. It had to be the balloon and two ordinary citizens. The hope of it. The possibility.

Camille took a deep breath. "Let's go."

Halfway to the platform, by the ticket-taker's tent, Sophie, Chandon, and Foudriard were waiting for them. Chandon and Foudriard embraced Lazare and then Camille, Chandon especially pulling her close. "When I dragged you into that card game, never did I expect you would save my life," he said. "I am so grateful to you. More than I can say." He kissed her on the cheek. "If there is anything you need, you will always tell me, non?"

"I will, dear friend," Camille said. When she pulled back and saw how his handsome face was more like his own, less haggard, and how the lively color had returned to it, she thought she might cry with happiness.

"And you, madame? Will you return to court?" Foudriard asked.

"I'm not certain. Suddenly I have an estate to oversee and a house in town to put in order. I suppose it will depend on what happens next." As she said this, she became acutely aware of Lazare next to her.

Foudriard bowed. "Whatever you do, it will be admirable, madame. The courage you showed at the duel is exactly what I hope for from my officers."

Camille blushed. "You're too kind, as always. And you two? Will you stay at court?"

"Lazare!" Rosier called.

"Excuse me," Lazare said and took off through the crowd to where Rosier stood waving.

"The only thing that kept me there was my chevalier, and Séguin's threat to take him from me." Chandon exhaled. "Now we'll go to my parents' place in the country to rest and drink cider."

"Not for long, though," Foudriard cautioned. "The Marquis de Lafayette has just been appointed the commander-in-chief of the new National Guard. Officers will be much in demand in Paris and elsewhere."

"What's happening, Foudriard?" Camille asked.

"Unrest in the countryside, I'm afraid."

"And Aurélie? Has anyone heard from her?"

"Guilleux sent a letter," Chandon said soothingly. "They arrived safely."

"I don't know how long this peace will last." Foudriard sounded worried. "The discontent began last year, as grain prices went up, and now that the reforms the peasants hoped for haven't happened, they're marching against the nobles and refusing to pay their taxes. I don't blame them."

"Again, wishing me bankrupt!" Chandon exclaimed. "Perhaps I will have to join the revolutionaries."

"And why not?" Camille teased.

"If they could protect me from blood-sucking magicians, I might consider it."

The Vicomte de Séguin was gone, but there were thousands of aristocrats like him. Possibly they were magicians, but more than that, they were people who believed in the old ways, the hierarchies and the taxes, the muzzled press and the class system and the *rules*. If there was any hope for France, the system would have to be taken down, piece by piece.

And magic would be gone with it.

On the night the Bastille fell, Camille had sensed it: the river of history had bent its course. That life at court carried on, for the most part oblivious, meant that the change would be that much more abrupt. Perhaps even a kind of war if the people were not listened to.

Change was coming, rising on the wind.

Tears pooled in Camille's eyes. "Adieu, Chandon."

"How could you say such a dreadful thing?" Chandon squeezed her hand tight. "You must say instead, 'À bientôt.' For we will see each other very soon again."

"Of course you're right," she said, kissing him on the cheek. "See you soon."

Knuckling away tears, he gave Camille a little push toward the platform where Lazare stood, next to the balloon. It tugged at its tethers, its silken shell shimmering in the wind. "That gorgeous boy is waiting for you."

As she made her way along the edge of the rope that cordoned off the crowd from the platform, Rosier and Lazare came running up alongside.

"Mademoiselle!" Rosier exclaimed. "What are you wearing? This is not the plan!"

"Rosier," Camille said, "remember at the salon, when Lafayette asked, 'What good is a balloon?'"

"Yes." He gave an impatient sigh. "And? I imagine you're going to say the purpose of a balloon is not to make money. Which we just did, by the way, lots and lots of it. You'll get your balloon adventure over the Alps, Lazare."

Lazare shook his head in disbelief and embraced Rosier. "I don't know how you do it, you madman, but you're incredible." He turned to Camille. "What is the purpose, then?"

"The purpose is to fly. That's it! Don't you see? It's about hope. If we go up, dressed like ourselves, bedraggled and human, then we give people hope. Everyone longs for freedom. To fly and to *rise*. We can show them it's possible."

"She's right," said Lazare. "We go as ourselves. No more pretending, n'est-ce pas, Camille?" His eyes were very serious.

"Never again."

Together they entered the balloon's chariot and—after doing a final check of the fire, the ballast, and the newly repaired release valve—Armand closed the wicker door behind them. "Bonne chance, mademoiselle," he said without a trace of irony. "The sky stands open."

"Let us go that way," she responded and was rewarded with a quick grin, which made her happier than she'd imagined a grin from Armand ever could. Rosier shot up a flare—the crowd gasped—and his helpers unwound the lines from the long stakes plunged into the earth.

Standing by the brazier, Camille held Lazare's hand. She didn't ever want to let it go. The events of the last weeks dimmed in the face of the vast crowd, some standing, some sitting, all of them cheering. "How strong they are, all of them here, gathered to see this. I can't believe it! All for your balloon."

"*Our* balloon."

Camille watched him watching them. As emotions played across his face, tears pooled in his eyes. He didn't try to brush them away.

"Have you become sentimental, Lazare?"

"Not at all, ma belle," he said, pulling her close. "Imagine how I'll be when we sail over the Alps."

Rosier released another flare, and Camille startled, ducking her head against Lazare's shoulder.

"Here we go!"

Slowly, serenely, the balloon rose, higher and higher until the lines flapped loose and she was no longer tethered to the earth. The crowd gasped, waving their flags. Tearing at the twine around the pamphlets, Camille grabbed a handful and tossed them overboard. As they fluttered and swooped to earth, hundreds of hands shot up to catch them.

"Which is your favorite part?" she asked Lazare as the balloon steadily rose.

"From the Americans' Declaration of Independence? You don't already know?" Lazare teased.

She wanted to hear the words from his lips. "Tell me."

"'The pursuit of happiness.'" He drew Camille toward him. "Which I intend to pursue."

"Oh? How?"

"Our world is changing. I don't know what's going to happen today, or tomorrow, or the day after that, but whatever it is, Camille, I want to go through it with you."

Everything inside her rose up to meet him—everything, everything, everything. She reached up to gently trace the scar from the duel, then let her fingers linger in the tender place under his jaw where his pulse beat.

"Mon Dieu," he said, low in her ear, "in all my dreams, I never imagined this." And then, with the wind spinning around them, they kissed.

Slowly, she eased her hands around the back of his neck. His arms slid down her back to her waist, bringing her closer. And then, his mouth against hers, she gave herself up to the kiss.

The heat and desire and wanting of the kiss at the opera was still there. But that had been a changeling kiss, a turned coin that could at any time twist back to what it was, a bent nail or dented button. But this? This was true gold, a solid gleaming certainty.

Below, the crowd roared.

When they broke apart, laughing, their arms around each other's waists, Camille caught sight of Chandon and Foudriard, Sophie and Rosier, standing together. The wind caught Sophie's hair and shook it out as if it were a banner made of cloth-of-gold. She waved, blowing kisses. There were roses in her cheeks.

Her friends' faces soon became indistinguishable, the crowd no bigger than her palm. Hands clasped, Camille and Lazare watched as the city of Paris, its cobbled streets and tiled roofs, its squares and vineyards and mansions, drifted beneath them. At the ruined fortress of the Bastille, people carted off bricks for souvenirs. At the Tuileries, swarming members of the staff prepared for the king's visit. And through all this chaos and glory snaked the Seine, the sun glittering silver and gold on her waters as she wound her way into the future.

Glossary of French Terms

Aidez-moi—Help me

Absolument parfait—Absolutely perfect

Adieu/Adieux (pl)—Farewell, goodbye

Affair d'honneur—Affair of honor

Allez/Allons-y—Let's go

Alors—Well, then

Ancien régime—Ancient regime, the time before the French Revolution

Après vous—After you

Arrétez—Stop

Attendez—Wait

Bien—Good

Bonne chance—Good luck

Bonjour—Hello

Bravo/brava—Good; word of praise, often for performers (Italian; masculine/feminine)

Ça, alors—My goodness!

Cache-cache—Literally, "hide-hide"; the game of hide and seek

Calme-toi—Calm down

Ça depend—It depends

Ça suffit—That's enough

Ça va—Literally, "It goes"; used to ask how things are going

C'est parfait—It's perfect

C'est rien—It's nothing

C'est vrai—That's true

Chapeau/chapeaux (pl)—Hat

Château—Palace

Chat méchant!—Naughty cat!

Comme ça—Like this/that

Comprenez?—Do you understand?

Désolé/Désolée—Sorry (masculine/feminine)

D'accord—Okay

Dépechez-vous—Hurry up

Dis-moi—Tell me

Dieu/Mon Dieu—God/My God

Écoute-moi—Listen to me

Enchanté/Enchantée—Enchanted, often used when meeting others for the first time (masculine/feminine)

Encore/Encore une fois—One more time

Entrez—Enter

Fantastique—Fantastic

Formidable—Wonderful

Galerie des Glaces—Hall of Mirrors

Grâce à Dieu—Thanks be to God

Hélas—Alas

Immédiatement—Immediately

Incroyable—Unbelievable, incredible

Je t'embrasse—I embrace you

La belle veuve—The beautiful widow

La chimère—Chimera; monster

Le dernier cri—Literally, "the last shout"; the latest thing

Le loup—The wolf

Le Roi Soleil—The Sun King

Les jeux sonts faits—The bets are placed

Ma belle—My beauty

Madame/Mesdames (pl)—Madam

Mademoiselle/Mesdemoiselles (pl)—Miss, misses

Ma fille/mes filles (pl)—My girl or my daughter/my girls or daughters

Mais c'est merveilleux—But that's marvelous

Maître—Master

Ma soeur—My sister

Merci—Thank you

Merde—Shit

Mon ami/mon amie/mes amis (pl)—My friend (masculine/feminine)

Mon ange—My angel

Mon chere/ma chère—My dear (masculine/feminine)

Mon coeur—My heart, my beloved

Mon Dieu—My God

Mon étoile—My star

Monsieur/Messieurs (pl)—Mister or Sir

Monstres—Monsters

Mon trèsor—My treasure

Nécessaire—Literally, "a necessary"; a makeup box

Ne t'inquiète pas—Don't worry

Non—No

Oh là là—Oh no! (what your friend might say if you dropped your phone in a Parisian puddle)

Oui—Yes

Paille maille—Pell mell (also known as pall mall), a forerunner to croquet

Pardieu—By God

Pas de tout—Not at all

Pas encore—Not yet

Peut-être—Perhaps

Pardonnez-moi—Excuse me

Quel dommage—What a pity

Quelle surprise—What a surprise

Sangfroid—Literally "cold blood"; composure in the face of difficulty

Sérieusement—Seriously

S'il vous plaît/ S'il te plait—Please; literally, if it pleases you (formal/ informal)

Tais-toi—Shut up

Tant pis—Too bad

Tempus Fugit—Time Flies (Latin)

Une très petite—A very small

Venez—Come

Vingt-et-un—Twenty-one

Viens ici—Come here

Voilà/Et voilà—Here it is

Vous comprenez—You understand

Vous voyez—You see

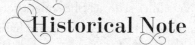Historical Note

This book began as a flickering daydream: a girl sitting at an old desk, writing a love letter with a quill pen. The ink she was using was made from her tears. When I zoomed out, I saw she was wearing an eighteenth-century dress, and when I zoomed out even further, I realized she was sitting in a room with walls filigreed in gold. Was she at the palace of Versailles? It certainly seemed that way. That girl eventually became Camille, and when I wrote this book, I wanted to make sure that the world of 1789 Paris and Versailles was as alive in it as it was to me that day.

Though *All That Glitters* is a work of fantasy, it includes historical events and people. Sometimes the historical record tells us exactly what happened: Jean-Sylvain Bailly *did* climb up on a door that had been pulled off its hinges to speak to the National Assembly in an indoor tennis court. The Marquis de Lafayette *did* attend salons, but I've found no record of him ever talking about hot-air balloons, though other people, such as Benjamin Franklin, had a lot to say about them. Whenever I've invented lines for historical figures like Lafayette, I've tried to stay true to what we do know of them from the historical record, but in the end, it's fiction.

Here's a bit more about the real people, places, and events that figure in this book.

Louis XVI: Born in 1754, Louis was the last king to rule France before the French Revolution. Governing France wasn't his favorite occupation, though; he preferred hunting or assembling and reassembling locks. On July 14, 1789, the day the Bastille fortress fell, Louis wrote one word in his diary to describe the day's events: *Nothing.*

Marie Antoinette: Born in 1755, she became Queen of France when she was fourteen. Coming from the more relaxed Austrian court, she found the rules at Versailles stifling. She sought refuge in fashion, gardening, and interior design, but her extravagant habits made her an object of ridicule and hatred for the French people. If you want to read more about her, I'd recommend Antonia Fraser's biography, *Marie Antoinette: The Journey.*

Louis-Phillipe II, Duc d'Orléans: Born in 1747, Philippe was the king's cousin and in line to the throne of France. To help pay off his debts, he turned his magnificent Parisian palace, the Palais-Royal, into an entertainment free-for-all with restaurants, cafés, gambling halls, and gathering places for political radicals. Just after the events depicted in *All That Glitters,* Orléans became a revolutionary, adopting the name "Philippe-Egalité"—Equality Philippe—and siding with the Third Estate (the commoners) in their grievances against his cousin the king. In an interesting twist, his personal secretary was Pierre Choderlos de Laclos, the author of the scandalous book *Les Liasons Dangereuses,* which Camille keeps trying to finish reading.

Fashion: Though the French court had long been seen as refined and elegant, it was Marie Antoinette who became France's Queen of Fashion. During her reign, fashions changed so quickly that dresses needed to be restyled for every event and new hats were created overnight to celebrate current events, such as a French naval victory. The queen's hairdresser, Léonard Autié (so famous he went by his first name), designed Marie Antoinette's much-imitated extravagant pouf hairstyles. He sometimes collaborated with celebrity stylist Rose Bertin, who dressed Marie Antoinette and those who wished to look like her. I was inspired by Bertin when thinking about Sophie Durbonne's career; like Bertin, many young women found new careers in the growing fashion industry, which gave them increased social status and mobility.

Money: In 1789, French currency was still primarily in coins, though that would change later in the year with the production of paper money called assignats. The basic unit of account was the livre. A gold louis was worth 24 livres; the double louis d'or, 48: the demi-louis d'or, 12. The little copper sol (or sou) was valued at 1/20 of a livre.

Balloons: In the early 1780s, hot-air balloons were all the rage. Commemorative handkerchiefs, earrings, toys, and hairstyles all celebrated these new objects of wonder and scientific achievement. In August 1783, the Montgolfier brothers, Charles and Étienne, sent a balloon up from Versailles as the royal family watched. It was the first to carry passengers: a rooster, a duck, and a sheep. The first manned flight in a montgolfière (as the new balloons were called) took place a few months later; the pilot was Jean-François Pilâtre de Rozier, known to be both charming and fearless, and his copilot was the noblemen François Laurent, Marquis d'Arlandes. Soon the craze spread to England, where the dashing Italian aeronaut, Vincent Lunardi—about to crash his balloon in a field—doffed his hat to a pretty milkmaid, who took hold of the balloon's basket and saved him. That moment was one of the inspirations for this book.

The Storming of the Bastille: Along with the Tennis Court Oath, the fall of the Bastille is considered one of the first events of the French Revolution. On July 14, 1789, crowds of people, worried that mercenary armies stationed in Paris were about to attack, descended on the old Bastille fortress in search of guns and ammunition. The fortress was also a jail, housing seven prisoners. After the armed crowd stormed the fortress, they decapitated its military governor with a knife and released the prisoners. A few days later, enterprising Parisians were selling pieces of the rubble from the fortress as souvenirs and giving tours of the interior, where a broken printing press was passed off as an instrument of torture.

People of Color in Eighteenth-Century France: Though they don't often appear in movies or novels set in this time period, there *were* people of color in France in 1789. Diaspora from the French colonial empire had arrived in France from places like North America and India; slaves were often brought to France by their masters from plantations in the Caribbean. Most of their stories have gone untold, though we know a little about some of them. One such person was Joseph Boulogne, Chevalier de Saint-Georges, whose father married one of his slaves and brought her and their infant son to Paris; the Chevalier grew up to be a famous swordsman and composer. Another was Julien Raimond, born to a French father and biracial mother in the French colony of Saint-Domingue (now Haiti). Raimond moved to Paris and successfully petitioned the National Assembly to grant free-born men of color the right to vote. Last, there was the Senegalese orphan girl, raised as an aristocrat during the French Revolution, who inspired Claire de Duras's best-selling 1820s novel, *Ourika*. Did a person like Lazare live in Paris in 1789? I don't know, but he certainly could have. In *All That Glitters*, I've tried, based on historical research and my own experience, to imagine such a life as Lazare's into being.

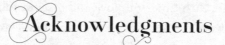

Acknowledgments

First, to Molly Ker Hawn, the best agent an author could wish for: thank you for championing this story, always being in my corner, answering all my questions, and guiding me on this journey—for everything, really. You are magic.

To my editor, Sarah Dotts Barley, who loved (and understood) this story from the beginning, saw what needed to be done, and helped me get there. Your enthusiasm and generosity made hard work feel light. Merci pour tout, Madame B. A big thank-you, too, to my publisher, Amy Einhorn, and all the fantastic people at Flatiron/Macmillan who have made this book a real thing, especially Patricia Cave, Adriana Coada, Anna Gorovoy, Keith Hayes, Lauren Hougen, Nancy Trypuc, and Emily Walters. Thanks, too, to Jenna Stempel-Lobell for the title lettering.

Thank you to Venetia Gosling and the truly wonderful team at Macmillan Children's Books, for bringing Camille's adventures to the UK and beyond, and to Albatros Media, for sharing this story in the Czech Republic.

In *All That Glitters*, the Marquis de Chandon tells Camille the history of French magic. As he describes it, Louis XIV employed a team of magicians to make Versailles the glittering palace of his dreams. I was lucky enough to have a posse of my own to help me create this story. Karin Lefranc and Rebecca Smith-Allen befriended me at my first writing conference and agreed to read for me (verdict: pretty words but no real plot). They have been with me through the highs and lows, brainstormed like geniuses, and read too many drafts of the story to count. Rebecca introduced me to an online writer's group, The Winged Pen, all of whose members have encouraged me and been cheerleaders for this book. I want especially to thank Julie Artz and Michelle Leonard, who offered important feedback, and to Gabrielle Byrne, who read the manuscript twice, each time with love and insight. Julie and Gabrielle also whispered words of wisdom in my ear while I was querying and many other times. Thank you *all* for your help and your friendship.

I was lucky enough to get involved with the mentoring program Author Mentor Match in its inaugural round. My mentor, Emily Bain Murphy, was the first person outside my critique group to read the manuscript; she believed in this story all along. Thank you, too, to Alexa Donne, who shared her wealth of behind-the-scenes knowledge with me.

Merci mille fois to Alwyn Hamilton, who so generously suggested ways to improve my French. Any errors are, of course, my own.

Thank you too to the authors who so generously blurbed this book and helped it take its first steps in the world.

I would also like to express my appreciation for my friends in academia, Dr. Tita Chico and Dr. Carolyn Dever, who helped me make contact with Dr. Gillian Dow, Dr. Scott M. Sanders, and Dr. Scott Manning Stevens. Their recommendations for reading in turn helped shape my construction of French views on race, as well as Lazare's imagined experience.

There is no ledge so precipitous that Jeff Giles cannot talk me down from it. Thank you for being just a phone call away. Thanks, too, to Bridget Hodder, who recommended I take the plunge on a change I'd long been considering.

A huge cheer to the dear and lovely friends who stuck with me— and celebrated with me—as I wrote this book. In particular, so much love to Karen Cullinane and Sonja O'Donnell, as well as Heather Liske, whose insights helped me fix a story problem at the eleventh hour.

Thank you, too, to my father, Manohar Panjabi, who supported me without needing to understand what I was doing, and to Kim Reid Panjabi and Mary Trelease. Brian Trelease was thrilled when I sold this book. Bri, I hope you are reading over my shoulder.

At the end of these acknowledgments, I come to the people who were there at the beginning: my two boys, without whom this book would not exist. Plot magician Lukas Trelease encouraged me to write this story, gave feedback, and when I was ready to throw it in the trash, helped me out of the hole. Tim Trelease believed from the beginning. He supported me day and night, through all the twists and turns that make up the writer's life, and I could not be more grateful. I love you both.

Finally, to all of you who dream, who want more from life, who are willing to use your magic to remake yourselves and *rise*: this book is for you.

Read a scene from Lazare's point of view

Hide-and-Seek

"Count again, will you?" The Baron de Guilleux's voice echoed down the shadowy grass. "We've got three more who want to play."

Lazare raised his arm in silent assent. From where he stood, far down the lawn by a towering yew hedge, Guilleux and the other players were only dim shapes. Ghosts, or shadows. Turning away, he walked beside the hedge until he came to the black water of the Apollo fountain, the "safety" the other players would have to reach before he tagged them out. It was as good a place to count as any.

Around him the greenery rustled in the late-night wind. In it the sweet scent of orange flower mingled with sharp cut grass. High above, the stars were small and bright, and in the trees near the palace, a peacock cried, eerie and haunting. Even he could admit the gardens of

Versailles were beautiful. Compared to the mayhem of Paris, it was another country.

He wished to be anywhere but here.

As he readied himself to count, Beatrice de Calonne stepped out from behind the fountain. In the almost-light, the pretty daughter of the Comte de Chîmes gleamed. There were diamonds in her white-blond hair and around her neck, wrists, and fingers, even sewn into the neckline of her dress. On her head she wore one of the flower crowns Guilleux had given them all, its bloodred poppies making her look like a princess of the fairies.

"I'm tired of this game, Lazare," she said, smiling beguilingly up at him. "Could we not find a place to be alone?"

"One!" he called out.

Delighted screams erupted from the other side of the hedge as the players rushed to conceal themselves. Twigs snapped. Someone swore.

"Two!" Lazare turned to Beatrice. "I promised Guilleux I'd be the wolf. You could join them?"

She came closer. Her smile was sweet, but behind her blue eyes was iron, determined as the teeth of a trap. For months he'd been trying to free himself, but the harder he struggled, the tighter it held.

If only he could pull himself loose, he knew where he would go.

Back to Paris. Back to Camille.

Behind *her* cloud-gray eyes were worlds coming into being. Oceans stretching to horizons, fathomless as the sky. And there were mysteries, ones he ached for them to share. More than anything, being with her was like flying: the risk, the delight, the fire of her. Uncertainty, and desire.

He forced himself to remember where he was. Whom he was with. "Three! Four!"

Slyly, Beatrice said, "I didn't come here to play cache-cache."

"Five!" he called out hoarsely, as if by shouting he could banish Camille from his thoughts, and keep his attention on the game. "I thought you'd enjoy it. I'm sorry if I misled you into thinking it would be something else."

Behind him, branches cracked; hidden deep in the hedges, someone giggled and was quickly shushed.

"Six!"

"You could not mislead me if you tried!" she laughed. "Why only yesterday I told my father that you were well settled at Versailles, having given up whatever you were doing in Paris—"

Resentment prickled at him. "Do you mean my balloons?"

Sweetly, she said, "They're only an amusement, n'est-ce pas, like this game of cache-cache?" She took his hand in her soft white one, tracing the scar on his knuckle. Despite himself, he shivered. "When we are engaged—"

"Seven, eight!" Lazare shouted hollowly into the treetops. Once Armand had told him to count as the balloon shot into the sky: How far to the peak of that roof? To the spire of that church? *Counting*, he'd said, *kept the worry at bay. Count, and observe.*

But for how long?

Four months ago he'd agreed to meet Beatrice. To make his father happy, he'd said yes to a few card games in the palace, walks along the Grand Canal, a dance. He'd never promised to court her. But she and her parents and his parents had prattled over his silence, as if it meant yes instead of no. Many times he'd tried to tell Beatrice how he felt, but everything he said and did was misinterpreted, transformed into what she wished it to be.

Then lightning had struck.

His balloon in the sky, a sudden storm rolling into Paris. The ballast had been too light, the anchor had failed . . . and like an answer Camille had appeared in the green field. Spattered with mud, her red hair streaming behind her, she'd chased down the balloon and pulled it safely to earth. Then he'd believed she'd saved him a crash. Now he saw it was more than that. She'd saved him from sleepwalking, from thinking that he could keep doing this.

"Nine!" He tried again, more bluntly this time. "We are not truly a match, Beatrice." *The things you want are things I will never want.* "You know that as well as I."

"You say that, but you could change." When he did not reply, she asked nonchalantly, "Are you in love with someone else? Is there a girl in Paris?"

He glanced at her sidelong. There was no way she could know. Could she?

"Ten!" he shouted through gritted teeth. He wished he could tell her: *Yes, there is a girl in Paris I care for.* But that would get back to his parents, and the consequences would be dire. They'd cut him off from his money. No more balloons. They'd force him to return to Sablebois. No more Camille. He couldn't risk it. "You deserve someone better than I."

"Perhaps I do!" She bit her lip. "Half the court is in love with me."

Then why not let me be? On their one walk beside the Grand Canal, she had talked brightly of all the things they would do when they were married. An apartment at Versailles, positions at court, a grand house in Paris, salons and carriage rides at Longchamps and masquerades. That was the future she wanted. And to do it, she needed a husband.

"You deserve someone who will rise with you at court." Carefully, he added, "You must see that I can never be that person, Beatrice." In the shadowy light, he tried to gauge her reaction, but she gave nothing away.

"I wish to rise," she insisted, "and I wish to do it with you. You are handsome and rich and clever—everything a courtier should be." She laid her hand on his shoulder. "You only have to change your mind."

Nearby leaves rattled as one of the players edged toward the fountain. He had nearly forgotten the game.

"Eleven!" he choked out. To Beatrice he said quickly, "When I reach twenty I must find the others. After that, we'll talk—"

She shook her head, the teasing smile firmly in place. "You cannot expect me to wait so long!"

"Another time, then." He hated that he couldn't bring himself to say: *This cannot be.*

"Tomorrow," she decided. "We will ride out with our parents. It'll be lovely, non?"

It would be a nightmare. They would talk of card games, discuss the queen's clothes and who held power at court, admire a ribbon Beatrice had bought for her pet lamb. He shouldn't have to go. But if he did, his parents might finally see how ill-matched he and Beatrice were. They might say, *Enough.*

"Twelve!"

"Bien!" she said, as if he'd agreed to something. "See you then, Lazare." And with that she walked away, skirts swaying as she cast a glance at him over her shoulder. He knew she meant for him to follow her to the palace. Instead he counted slowly from thirteen, studying the starlit lawn, the trees, the dark mirror of the fountain: nothing moved.

All was hushed. Anticipating.

"Twenty!" he sang out. "Here comes the wolf!" But instead of searching right away for the others, he hid in a gap between two white statues, half buried in the yew hedge. There, in the green dark, he leaned against the statue's base. He pressed his forehead to the cold stone, and thought: *I don't have join her in the palace. I don't have to do what everyone else wants.*

There had to be a way out.

Suddenly, he knew: he could tell Rosier. Rosier knew how Lazare felt, and he knew Camille. And besides, didn't Rosier always have a plan? All Lazare had to do was tag the others, finish this game, and return to Paris. Shakily, he exhaled. The idea of a strategy steadied him. Tomorrow he'd go to the workshop and ask Rosier for help. And then he'd leave this behind, once and for all.

He did not have to wait long before one of the players stepped out of the shrubbery. He didn't recognize the girl; with her pale blue gown, a crown of clover blossoms perched in her powdered hair, she could be anyone. She paused, listening hard.

He dared not move.

Slowly, her skirts in her hands, she tiptoed toward the fountain. When she was almost there, he leapt out from behind the statues. "Got you!" he cried as he tagged her.

"You sneak!" The girl shoved his hand away. "The wolf isn't supposed to hide!"

His throat constricted. There was something about her voice's sweet lilt, its passionate spark, that reminded him of Camille. Low, he said, "All's fair in love and cache-cache."

She spun to face him. The dress she wore was extravagant silk, and it fit her like another skin. Her storm-gray eyes blazed above the pout of her too-red lips. In the faint starlight, her smooth, white face was impossibly perfect, the scattering of freckles he expected to see there—reminders of sunlit days outdoors—somehow magically erased.

It was Camille, but not.

His mind churned, seeking something to hold on to, but there was nothing. He was tumbling, grasping only air. Why was she here, dressed like this? *Who was she?*

"You?" she gasped.

In her startled, almost angry eyes he saw himself reflected. No longer was he the aeronaut, the inventor, the boy who'd taken her up to the tower of Notre-Dame to show her the city at night. Instead, he was an aristocrat. And a liar. But hadn't she been lying too?

"Why not?" he blurted out.

"That's all you have to say?" Her words crackled with indignation.

Icy dread crept through him, as if they were about to crash.

Was she a courtier? Was this secret the mystery he'd sensed about her? It hurt to think it. Or perhaps she was here in disguise—but why? He wanted answers, but with the others hiding and listening all around them, he couldn't ask her. *Wait*, he told himself. *Observe.*

"Forgive me, have we met before?" He bowed low. "Lazare Mellais."

Camille stiffened, as behind him branches shuddered and Aurélie, a wreath of roses crowning her black hair, burst gleefully from her hiding place. "He's also the Marquis de Sablebois," she announced to Camille as she flung affectionate arms around his neck. "Unlike me, he never mentions his title unless his has to."

He turned to Camille, unfamiliar in her courtier's dress, and said, hoping she would understand, "My title is a suit that doesn't fit."

Camille—this terrifyingly beautiful version of Camille—just stared at him. Hurt and bewilderment radiated from her, like a bird stunned by the glass it had crashed into, thinking it was the sky.

He had done this.

How had he not dared tell her the truth when they were at Notre-Dame? Had he thought that, like a storm, the fact of his being a nobleman would somehow . . . blow away? Instead of kissing her, he should have been braver. He should have told her the whole truth of who he was: not just his name, but his title, who he was destined to become. But he'd been afraid of disappointing this girl who'd seemed, like him, to want nothing to do with Versailles and court life.

So then why was she here?

Statue-still, he waited to see what she would do. If she didn't acknowledge that she knew him, he'd have to pretend he didn't either. That every charged moment they'd spent together had never happened, as if she were nothing to him.

It felt like cutting out his heart.

And Aurélie, he knew, missed none of this. Since the summer when he, Aurélie, and Chandon had met at Versailles, he'd often seen her green eyes narrow as she puzzled out some court intrigue. Now her clever gaze glinted shrewdly from Camille to Lazare and back again. What did she see? What if she mentioned Beatrice?

Quickly, he asked her, "Will you introduce me to your friend?"

"Isn't she the loveliest?" Aurélie said, as if challenging him to say more. "This is Cécile, the Baroness de la Fontaine."

"Enchanté." He bowed again. She curtsied, her face blank.

"She's recently come to court," Aurélie added. "Her husband's dead."

His head spun, but he played along. "Aurélie, what are you saying?"

Aurélie tossed her head. "She doesn't care. Husbands aren't any good unless they're gone—which you would know, Lazare, if you were required to have one."

He knew all too well. To both of them he said, "My apologies."

"Not at all," Camille nonchalantly replied, as smoothly as any courtier.

Hers was the rich voice he loved, the lovely face he'd cradled in his hands as he'd kissed her at Notre-Dame—but suddenly made strange. Had it all been an illusion? Was this who she truly was, a courtier at Versailles? Or was the girl from Paris who'd rescued him the real Camille?

She yawned prettily. "But I wonder if it's not time for me to go. It's almost morning and I've a long ride back to Paris."

Wait, he wanted to say. *Wait for me.*

Perhaps there was still a way to speak to her away from the others, to explain what he was doing and who he was. And to ask her to tell him the same.

Aurélie begged Camille, "But you mustn't, not yet—"

Just then Chandon broke free of the shrubbery. He must have joined the game with Camille and Aurélie, but unlike them he looked disheveled, as if he'd been playing for hours. His jacket hung open, the top button dangling loose. Gone was his crown and his cravat was wrenched askew, stained with blood from a livid scratch on his cheek. His hazel eyes burned with uncharacteristic fury. Behind him skulked the Vicomte de Séguin, striking, immaculate, the smile on his face cruelly knowing.

"You're hurt!" Camille cried.

As Lazare stepped forward to help his friend, he saw real worry twist her features. So she knew both Aurélie and Chandon? They were friends? This was proof, then, that she'd been to Versailles before. She'd never told him. But then again, why would she have, when he'd never mentioned Versailles either?

"It was Séguin who did it," Chandon announced. "He forgets himself and behaves like the ruffian he is." Roughly, he tugged his jacket closed. What had Séguin tried to do—seduce him? Threaten him?

"Blame it on me, of course," Séguin sneered. "It was the way you were scrambling through the shrubbery."

"I was hurt trying to get away from you," Chandon spat.

Camille held out her hands to him, and Séguin's attention snapped to her. His gold eyes raked over her body in a way that made Lazare seethe. At court it was said that Séguin was a magician, someone who used magic to trade in pain and suffering. It was inhumane. Depraved. Magic was a relic of the ancien régime, and it disgusted him. Not for a moment did he doubt the rumors: ever since Lazare had known him, Séguin had been the kind of person who took whatever he wanted.

Camille.

Her attention on Chandon, she didn't seem to see what circled above her: a hawk, sighting its prey.

Lazare closed his hand around the pommel of his sword. Abruptly her gray gaze met his.

He was suddenly aware of his heart running hard.

There was still a universe of mystery behind her eyes. That was unchanged. It was just—he'd somehow forgotten that a cosmos also held darkness. Secrets.

When she'd raced across the field to save the balloon—to save him—he'd believed she was fearless. How else could she do what she'd done? Up close, holding her tight as the balloon rose, he'd seen he was wrong. She *was* afraid. But she'd refused to let the fear control her.

She wore the same fierce look as she faced them all here on the lawn, a gambler pushing her luck. Whatever terrible risk she was taking, he would not let her fall.

He would keep her secret.

For now.

All That Glitters
by Gita Trelease

PLEASE NOTE: In order to provide reading groups with
the most informed and thought-provoking questions possible,
it is necessary to reveal important aspects of the plot of this
novel—as well as the ending. If you have not finished reading
All That Glitters, we respectfully suggest that you may want
to wait before reviewing this guide.

1. At the beginning of the story, Camille, Sophie, and Alain are
   in danger of starving and becoming homeless. Camille uses
   her magic to bring them to safety and financial security. Yet
   the magic exacts a great cost. Does she do the right thing by
   using it? What else might she have done?

2. Camille goes to court despising the aristocrats, but over time
   her feelings change. What do you think of the portrayal of the
   aristocrats in the novel? Should Camille have been more careful? What leads her to misunderstand the dangers at court?

3. Sophie has a romantic—and conventional, for the time period—
   understanding of what her journey in life should be: marriage to a wealthy man. Camille doesn't agree that this is the
   path her sister should take. What do you make of this conflict
   between the sisters? Who is in the right?

4. In the Grimms' version of "Cinderella," Cinderella takes refuge
   from her awful family at her mother's grave. As she weeps,
   her tears water a little tree that grows there. Eventually the
   tree gives her dresses to wear to the prince's party. In *All That
   Glitters*, magic also comes from sorrow. What do you think
   about sorrow being fuel for magic? For you, does sorrow have
   a purpose? Or is it something you'd rather get rid of?

5. The transitory magic of the glamoire makes Camille perfectly
   beautiful and alluring. Is there a danger to a magic that "per-
   fects" people and objects?

6. Lazare, like Camille, keeps secrets for much of the story.
   Should he have told Camille earlier who he was? Why do you
   think he didn't? What holds Camille back from telling him
   the truth about herself?

7. The title of the book, *All That Glitters*, is adapted from a line in Shakespeare's *The Merchant of Venice*. In that play, a suitor must choose the casket that conceals Portia's portrait in order to win her hand. Unfortunately he selects the golden one. Inside is a portrait of Death, on which is written:

All that glisters is not gold;
Often have you heard that told.
Many a man his life hath sold
But my outside to behold.
Gilded tombs do worms enfold.

How do these lines and the title itself shed light on the story? What are the things in the story that "glitter" but turn out *not* to be gold? Are there people and things that don't glitter but *are* gold?

8. Séguin justifies his treatment of Chandon and Camille by blaming it on Marie Antoinette's desire for beauty and power. Do you think he is telling the truth, or does he have other motives for forcing Camille to marry him? Do you have any sympathy for him or his situation?

9. The death of Maman and Papa is like a bomb that sets all three Durbonne siblings scrambling to pursue different dangerous paths. Which of them has the hardest time with it? Are the siblings' reactions understandable? Forgivable?

10. The enchanted dress Camille wears to court is almost a character in itself. She feeds it blood to work the magic that disguises her as an aristocrat. Do you think the dress's power comes from her blood? Or from something else?

11. The hot-air balloon craze of the 1780s plays an important role in the story. Would it have made a difference if Lazare were not an aeronaut but instead someone who was developing, say, a new kind of microscope? How does the balloon matter to Lazare? To Camille? To the story? Paris in 1789 was a time when those who had everything were, for the most part, willfully ignorant of the vast majority of people who had nothing; the aristocrats' beautiful but decadent way of life paved the way for their eventual demise. Do you see parallels to our own time? What is the same? What is different?

Read on for a sneak peek at
Gita Trelease's next novel

Everything That Burns

1

Giselle had only two bouquets of yellow roses left.

It was late afternoon, and August's withering heat hung over the flower seller and her blooms. Like the other girls who'd stood there since early morning, selling bouquets in the shadow of the church of Sainte-Chapelle, Giselle had lined her wicker tray with evergreen branches. Not only did they show off the roses to advantage, they also kept the blooms fresh.

But on a steaming day like today, even cedar boughs were not enough.

While the other girls' flowers had drooped, the edges of their petals etched brown with decay, Giselle's had stayed perfect. As if newly picked.

Glancing at her posies, passersby couldn't help but think of a dewy garden in the early morning, its cool air alive with green perfume and the liquid trills of birds. A place where trouble and striving didn't exist. In that imaginary garden, there were no bakers strung up from lampposts for the crime of running out of bread, or children crushed beneath the wheels of an aristocrat's carriage. There were no grain shortages or rumors of aristocratic plots against the people. No vagrants or arsonists, no beggars or bloodthirsty magicians.

Amid the revolutionary chaos of Paris, this was no small illusion.

To conjure a garden from a tray of cut roses was to set people to dreaming, and if that dream cost several sous, what of it? It was worth it to hand over the coins, and to take the bouquet—its thorns snipped neatly away—and press it to your nose, inhaling all that was good and sweet while the hot reek of the river Seine, ferrying all manner of rotten things in its water, faded far away.

Giselle knew this, and priced her blooms accordingly.

"You." A man approached, a nobleman, Giselle guessed, by his fine suit and silver-capped cane. Lace spilled from his cuffs, unapologetically expensive, and above his spotless white cravat, his mouth was large, too eager.

"Oui, m'sieur?"

"I'll take the prettiest one." As he waited for her to give him a bouquet, he cocked his head and watched her.

Giselle smiled only vaguely in his direction and chose the finer of the remaining bunches. With some customers, it was best not to meet their gaze, for they took it as encouragement. She suspected he was one of those, and the sooner he was gone, the better. Curtseying, she handed over the flowers. The livre he gave her—without asking for change—she slipped into the hem of her apron. *Safe*. She waited for him to leave. Irritatingly, he did not.

"How fresh your flowers are!" He stared not at the bouquet, but at her. "What trick do you use to keep them that way?"

"I stand in the shadows, m'sieur," she replied. "Where it's cool."

Of course that wasn't the whole truth.

Her friend Margot got ice from a warehouse at the city's edge. Her lover was the night guard, and he let her in. In the gray morning, before she left, he'd brush away a heap of sawdust, chip off a shining sliver, and give it to her along with a kiss. Margot kept a chunk of that ice tucked under the oranges and strawberries she sold near the Louvre palace. And because Giselle shared with Margot the boughs she cut from trees at an old cemetery, Margot always asked her lover to cut a second shard of ice for Giselle.

The ice was a wonder. Trapped inside were thousands of tiny bubbles, like pearls. She wished she could keep the ice in the open and watch it change over the course of the day. Becoming something else. But flower sellers were poor, and a flower seller with the money to buy ice would be no flower seller at all, but a thief. So she kept it hidden under the green boughs on her tray. It wasn't magic, but it felt like it. A secret.

The nobleman had drawn close now.

Too close.

Behind him stood a girl her own age. Well dressed, freckled, auburn hair coiled under a straw hat, its swooping brim wider than any Giselle had seen. Tucked under her arm was a bundle of papers, tied with string. She seemed nervous, and Giselle gave her an encouraging smile. If the girl came forward to buy the last bouquet, the nobleman might move on and leave her be.

But the only smile she got was from the man, and it was a wicked one. "You are so lovely, mademoiselle—une très belle fleur."

"I'm not a flower." She shifted her wicker tray so it rested on her hip, keeping a distance between them. But he was tall enough to reach over it, and behind her was the high stone wall of Sainte-Chapelle.

Once more, Giselle glanced toward the girl in the hat standing behind him. It was too much to hope she might intervene. Wasn't she but a girl, just as Giselle was? Giselle knew there was beauty in her smile, the cocoa-brown gloss of her hair, her flowers' sweetness. But after that? She was only a poor girl trying to stay alive. If their places were reversed, she knew in her heart she would never do for a stranger what she was hoping the girl in the cartwheel hat would do for her.

"I'm naught but a flower seller, m'sieur."

"Come, come!" he cajoled. "Are you certain?" And then, as if it were the most natural thing in the world, he grasped her hand. In his palm, pressed hard against hers, was a louis d'or. She recognized its size, the shape it made against her flesh. A gold louis was more than she could earn in weeks. Enough to take her friends to a café in the Palais-Royal, where they'd dine like queens. It'd be late, the sky deepest midnight, but inside the candles would burn bright as stars. They'd order champagne and roasted chicken. There would be a rich sauce, slices of bread to mop it up. And after, stewed apples swimming in cream. She imagined what it'd be like to sit at a table with white linens and clean plates while someone waited on them, where they could laugh and talk and dream. For once, not to be striving to keep fear and hunger at arm's length. For once, to belong.

That was what a gold louis was.

But she wouldn't take it. She was afraid of what he wanted in return.

Tugging hard, she freed her hand and held the glinting coin out to him. Across her palm curved a red line where the louis had bitten into her flesh. "M'sieur, you've already paid for the flowers. This is too much."

Frowning, he asked, "Too much for what?"

"I'm sure I don't know," she said, obstinate. What made him think he had any rights over her? "Take it, m'sieur."

He came nearer, mouth twisted, face purpling. As he pushed against her tray, her last bouquet tumbled into the dirt. Gone. She didn't dare pick it up. Instead, she took a step backward, then another. "Please!"

"You are a *nothing*," he hissed. "You are a girl on the street, fresh one day and spoiled the next—how dare you? It's not for the likes of you to tell me what is too much." He spun, theatrically, to address the passersby. Sunlight danced on his silver-topped cane as he raised it high. "Is this what revolution has brought us? Flower sellers who think they're the equals of men?"

From behind him, someone scoffed. Was it the girl in the hat?

Giselle took another step back, and found the church wall unyielding against her back. "I don't think that!"

Though of course she *did*.

He must have seen the defiant spark in her eyes, because he thundered, "See what she has in her hand! She stole that gold louis out of my pocket!"

"That's not true!" Giselle threw the coin at him as if it scorched. Surprised, he caught it. "Now leave me be! I haven't done anything wrong."

"Can we let this impudence stand?" the man bellowed, and in the crowded street, several hatless men, their brick maker's aprons red with clay, stopped to stare. "Shouldn't she be punished?" the aristocrat asked as the crowd eddied around him.

No one asked a question of *him*. No one said: *What is the truth?*

She'd seen it before. People didn't care to know who was right and who was wrong before they joined in. No matter what was happening on the street—a circus or a hanging—it was as exciting as the theater. Better, even, because you never knew how it would end.

Then someone screamed: "À la lanterne!" *To the lamppost! String up the thief!* A dozen voices took up the blood-chilling cry. Giselle shrank back, as if she could somehow disappear. Where to go? If she slipped through the church's shadow, raced to the river and across the bridge, perhaps she could vanish in the tangle of crooked alleys and lanes she knew so well. But if by some miracle she escaped the mob, there was still the police. His word against hers. There was no question whom the court would believe.

Her breath came shallow and fast.

The terror of a prison cell at La Petite Force, the iron lock and bars. But worse, much worse was what would happen to the others: Margot, Claudine, Little Céline with her sweet smile and sticky hands. Without them, what or where would she be? Her legs trembled as the circle of people tightened around her.

There was no way out. She might die here today. Hanged from a lamppost or a tree. Her head stuck on a—

Then the girl in the hat stood in front of her, blocking the others from view. Her gray eyes burned. "You must disappear! If the crowd doesn't get you, the police will, and they won't believe a word you say." She grasped the leather strap of Giselle's wicker tray. "Leave this and run! People have been killed for less."

Giselle bent her head and the strap slid along her back as the tray came away in the other girl's hands. "But I need it—"

The expression on the other girl's face said, *Not as much as you need your life.* But somehow she understood, for she said, low, "Meet me in the little square at the end of the island, by the old oak, before six. Now go!"

Giselle choked out a "merci" and then shoved past the man, running faster than she'd ever run before. Past carriages and vegetable sellers and a juggler in a tattered costume, her breath in her throat, her heart a wild drum. Behind her came the mob, relentless as a cresting wave.

© Tim Trelease

Born in Sweden to Indian and Swedish parents, GITA TRELEASE has lived in many places, including New York, Paris, and a tiny town in central Italy. She attended Yale College and New York University, where she earned a Ph.D. in British literature. Before becoming a novelist, she taught classes on writing and fairy tales. Along with her husband and son, Gita divides her time between a village in Massachusetts and the coast of Maine. Gita is the author of *All That Glitters* and *Everything That Burns*.

www.gitatrelease.com.
🐦 📷 @gitatrelease